Learn to Read

With Classic Stories

Grade 2

Columbus, Ohio

Acknowledgments

McGraw-Hill Children's Publishing Editorial/Art & Design Team

Vincent F. Douglas, *President*
Tracey E. Dils, *Publisher*
Phyllis Armelie Sibbing, B.S. Ed., *Project Editor*
Andrea Pelleschi, *Story Editor*
Rose Audette, *Art Director*
Jennifer Bowers, *Interior Layout Design and Production*
Nancy Allton, *Interior Layout Production*

Also Thanks to:

Melissa Blackwell Burke, *Story Reteller*
Edith Reynolds, M.S. Ed., *Editor*
Nancy Holt Johnson, B.S. Ed., *Editor*
    Story Illustrations:
        Wendy Rasmussen, *The Three Wishes*
        Marion Eldridge, *Aesop's Fables*
        Lydia Taranovic, *Rumpelstiltskin*
        Clive Spong, *Rapunzel*
        Jeannie Winston, *The Little Mermaid*
        Steve Haefele, *Paul Bunyan*
    Activity Illustrations:
        Carlotta Tormey, *The Three Wishes*
        Ginna Magee, *Aesop's Fables*
        Bill Petersen, *Rumpelstiltskin*
        Carlotta Tormey, *Rapunzel*
        Mitch Heinze, *The Little Mermaid*
        Steve Haefele, *Paul Bunyan*

Published by American Education Publishing, an imprint of McGraw-Hill Children's Publishing.
Copyright © 2004 McGraw-Hill Children's Publishing.

All rights reserved. Except as permitted under the United States Copyright Act, no part of this publication may be reproduced or distributed in any form or by any means, or stored in a database or retrieval system, without prior written permission from the publisher, unless otherwise indicated.

Send all inquires to:
McGraw-Hill Children's Publishing
8720 Orion Place
Columbus, OH 43240-2111

ISBN 0-7696-3352-8

1 2 3 4 5 6 7 8 9 WAL 09 08 07 06 05 04

Table of Contents

Introduction for Parents and Teachers 4

Classic Stories
- The Three Wishes 6
- Aesop's Fables 40
  - The Ants and the Grasshopper 42
  - Belling the Cat 49
  - The Boy Who Cried Wolf 58
  - The Fox and the Grapes 68
- Rumpelstiltskin 74
- Rapunzel 108
- The Little Mermaid 142
- Paul Bunyan 176

Reading Activites
- The Three Wishes 211
- Aesop's Fables 225
- Rumpelstiltskin 239
- Rapunzel 253
- The Little Mermaid 267
- Paul Bunyan 281

Reading Skills Checklist 295

Answer Key 297

Everyday Learning Activities 316

Introduction for Parents and Teachers

The Importance of Reading Classic Tales

Storytelling is an art that started long before stories were recorded and published. Orally passed from storyteller to storyteller in front of a crackling fire, many stories changed form, yet maintained similar plots and themes. We may credit these tales to names such as Jacob and Wilhelm Grimm, Charles Perrault, Joseph Jacobs, and Jørgensen and Moe, but in fact, these storytellers collected century-old stories from oral sources, crafted them, and wrote them down in the form we now enjoy.

Classic fairy tales and folk tales around the world are similar in their themes of good versus evil and intelligence or cleverness versus force or might. The details of the stories may change, but the themes remain universal.

Many fairy tales contain elements or suggestions of violence, such as the threat of being eaten by giants, witches, or ferocious wolves. In part, this violent bent emerged because early fairy tales were intended primarily for an adult audience, not for children. Fairies were often cast as the rich and powerful, with the main human character representing the poor, oppressed common person. The tales served as beacons of hope for the underprivileged in ancient times when there was little chance for social mobility.

Many psychologists today believe that fairy tales are good for children, because these tales represent what all people fear and desire, and thus help children face their own fears and wishes. Other psychologists say that children benefit from hearing stories with some element of danger, and then being reassured with happy endings in which the small, apparently powerless hero or heroine triumphs after all. This is especially true when a supportive parent takes the time to discuss the stories with his or her child and provide specific, personal reassurance.

Knowing classic stories and their characters will help ensure that your child begins to have a rich background in cultural literacy. Classic stories also expand the world of children by enriching their lives and empowering their learning. The tales present characters who undergo struggles and emerge transformed, thereby helping readers discover more about themselves. When your child identifies with these characters, he or she might better understand his or her own feelings and the feelings of other people.

Classic stories present diverse cultures, new ideas, and clever problem-solving. They use language in creative and colorful ways and serve as a springboard for your child's writing. Most of all, classic stories delight and entertain readers of all ages by providing the youngest reader with a solid base for a lifelong love of literature and reading.

About This Book

Learn to Read With Classic Stories has two main parts—the classic stories and the reading activities. The **classic stories** are a collection of fairy tales, fables, folk tales, rhymes, and legends. This collection may be read and reread regularly. Kindergartners and first graders will probably need some help reading the stories. Second and third graders should be able to read the stories more independently. When the book is finished, it can be saved as an anthology to begin or add to your child's home library.

Follow-up **reading activities** are included for each story to build your child's vocabulary and comprehension skills. These activities focus on skills such as phonics, word meaning, sequencing, main idea, cause and effect, and comparing and contrasting. Additional language arts activities center on grammar, punctuation, and writing. A unique feature of this book is that the activities are closely linked to the stories and not presented in isolation. They are taught within the context of the story. The benefit of this feature is a more meaningful learning experience.

Kindergartners and first graders will probably need help reading the directions, but children of this age should be able to complete the activities with a minimum of assistance. Second and third graders should be able to complete the activities more independently.

The activity pages are perforated for easy removal. There is also an **answer key** at the end of each book for immediate feedback.

A one-page **bibliography** at the end of each story is provided to guide you and your child to further reading. This list contains other tellings of the same story, usually one traditional and one with a twist, so your child can compare different approaches to the same story. Several enjoyable, age-appropriate books that are related in other ways to the story are provided as well. This list of books will come in handy during visits to the library.

A **reading skills checklist** on pages 295–296 can help you monitor your child's progress in reading comprehension. Of course, no two children progress at the same rate, but the checklist suggests appropriate reading goals for your child. Sample questions are listed for each skill. You may ask these before, during, or after reading to assess your child's ability to apply the skills.

At the end of the book you will find several pages of **everyday learning activities** you can do with your child in the subject areas of reading, writing, math, science, social studies, and arts and crafts. These activities will extend your child's learning beyond this book.

About "The Three Wishes"

"The Three Wishes" is a story with a long history. It is told around the world in various ways. While the details differ, the retellings have much in common and usually follow a pattern. A man is granted three wishes because of a good deed he has done. The man and his wife waste the wishes through foolishness or greed.

The tale was most likely part of an oral tradition in many European countries. One early printing of the tale came from the famed French storyteller Charles Perrault. It appeared as part of a collection of three tales in verse. Years later, Madame de Beaumont translated it into English and published a version of the tale as part of the *Young Misses Magazine* in 1761. Even the Brothers Grimm include a version of the tale in their collections, but theirs differs considerably because it has a religious basis.

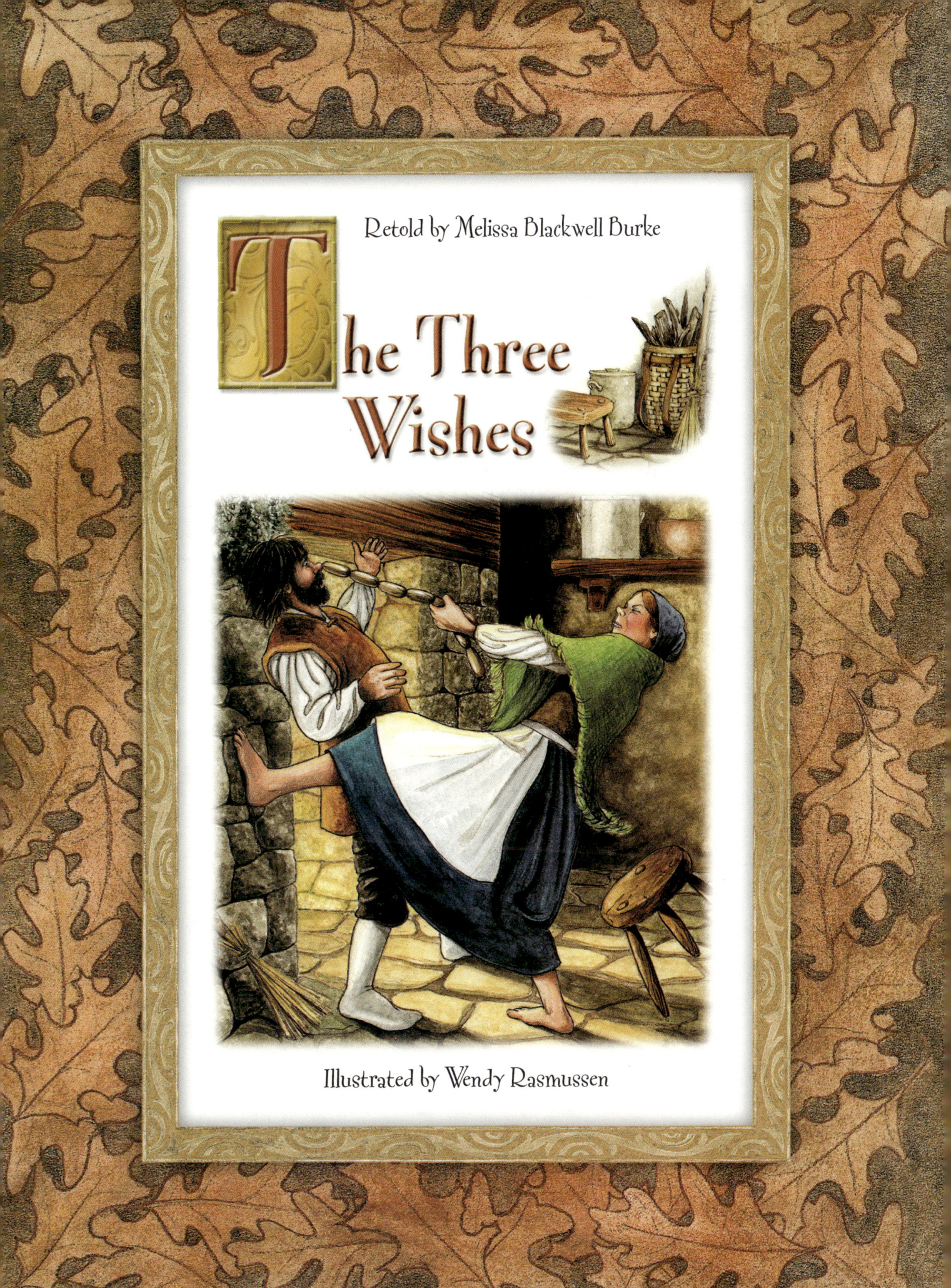

Long, long ago, a man and woman lived near a great forest. Every day, they went into the forest to cut wood.

The man and his wife worked as hard as they could. Still, they were poor and often went hungry.

One morning, they set off to work as always. But on this morning, they walked farther into the forest than ever before. Suddenly, they came upon a huge oak.

"We could cut many logs from this tree," said the man.

The woman agreed. "We could sell the logs. Then we would have enough money to buy food for many days."

Just as the man was about to swing his ax, a beautiful fairy appeared. "Please don't cut down my tree," she begged.

The man and his wife were so surprised, they could hardly speak.

"Very well," the husband finally said.

"We'll spare your tree," said his wife.

The fairy flew up into the air at once. She twirled around happily. "Thank you!" she cried. "For this, I will grant you three wishes, whatever they may be."

With that, the fairy flew to the treetops and disappeared.

The couple could hardly believe their good luck. All day long, they dreamed about the wishes they would make.

"We might wish for a fancy coach to ride in," said the husband.

"Or fine clothes of silk and satin," said the wife.

"Perhaps a grand house with a lovely garden," they said together.

They talked on and on. There seemed to be no end to what they could wish. They thought of great chests of jewels and piles of gold coins. It could all be theirs for the asking.

Finally, the man and wife tramped home. They were tired and hungry and cold.

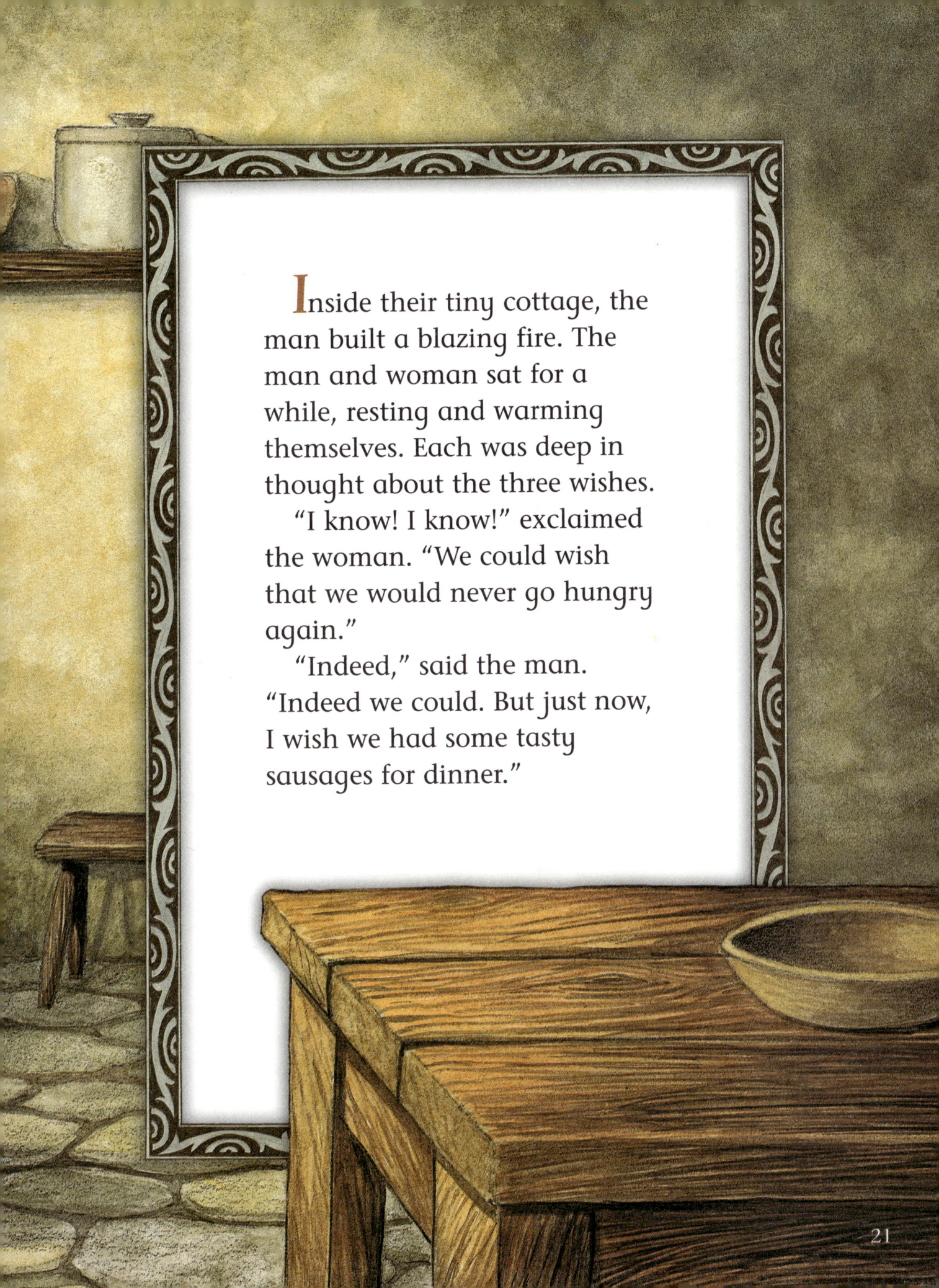

Inside their tiny cottage, the man built a blazing fire. The man and woman sat for a while, resting and warming themselves. Each was deep in thought about the three wishes.

"I know! I know!" exclaimed the woman. "We could wish that we would never go hungry again."

"Indeed," said the man. "Indeed we could. But just now, I wish we had some tasty sausages for dinner."

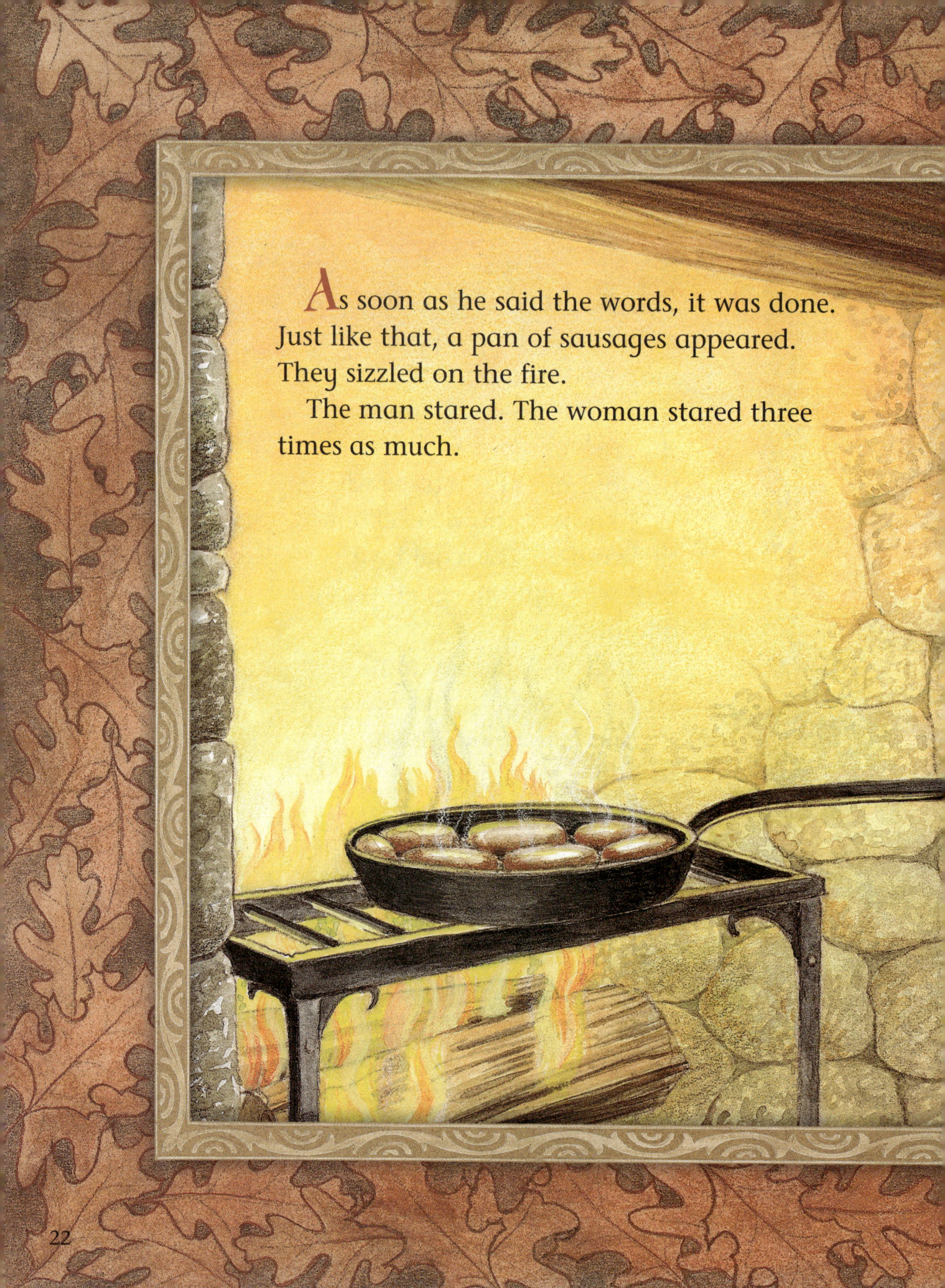

As soon as he said the words, it was done. Just like that, a pan of sausages appeared. They sizzled on the fire.

The man stared. The woman stared three times as much.

"That was a foolish thing to do!" the wife cried. "See what you've done! Why, I wish those sausages were hanging right from your nose!"

As soon as she said the words, it was done. Just like that, the sausages hung straight from her husband's nose.

"See what you've done!" cried the man. "Who's being foolish now?"

The man gave the sausages a pull, but they stuck. The wife gave the sausages a pull, but they stuck.

The two pulled and tugged together, but it was no use.

They plopped themselves down in front of the fire.

"What's to be done now?" asked the man.

The two thought about their very last wish.

They thought again of the fancy coach. They remembered the fine clothes. They longed for the grand house with the lovely garden. They pictured the chest of jewels and piles of coins.

"But what's the good of all that now?" asked the wife. "You'd have to live your whole life with sausages on your nose."

"Indeed," said the man sadly. "Indeed."

The two knew that there was but one thing they could do. They would have to wish the sausages off the man's nose.

The two wished their last wish.
As soon as they said the words, it was done. Just like that, the sausages were back in the pan. They sizzled on the fire.

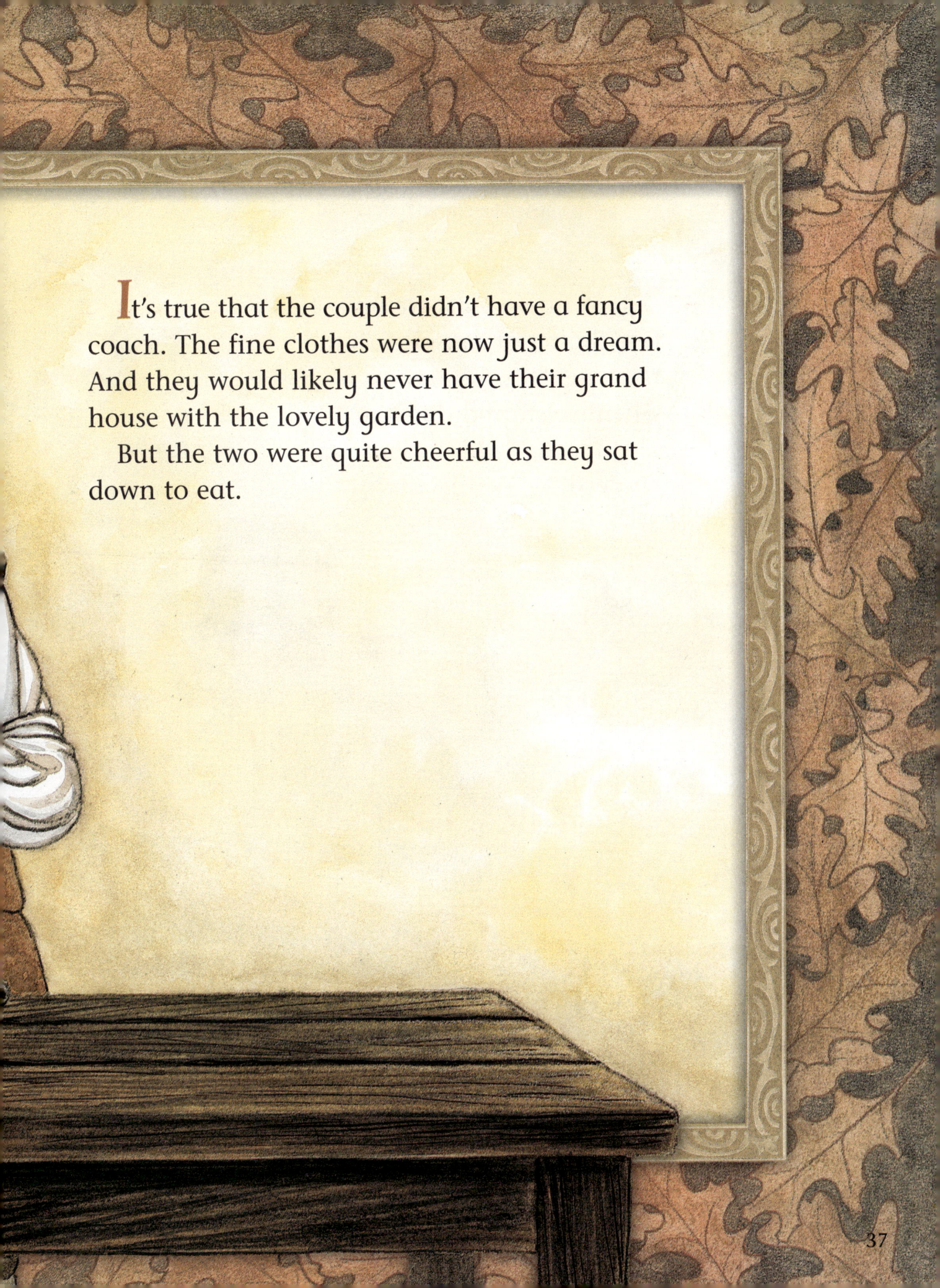

It's true that the couple didn't have a fancy coach. The fine clothes were now just a dream. And they would likely never have their grand house with the lovely garden.

But the two were quite cheerful as they sat down to eat.

"Why, at least we have this fine dinner of sausages," said the wife. "It's more than we had when we started this day."

"Indeed," said her husband. "Indeed!"

Bibliography
"The Three Wishes"

Zemach, Margot. *The Three Wishes: An Old Story*. New York: Farrar Straus & Giroux, 1986. In this warm-hearted retelling of the tale, an imp grants the poor woodsman and his wife their three wishes.

Silverstein, Shel. *The Giving Tree*. New York: HarperCollins, 1986. This is a touching story about the relationship between a boy and a tree. As the boy grows to manhood, the tree gives and gives, always providing what he needs at that time in his life.

Atkins, Jeannine. *Aani and the Tree Huggers*. New York: Lee & Low Books, 2000. This book was inspired by true events in northern India. A girl named Aani and members of her village take a brave stand against crews that come to cut down their forest.

Lionni, Leo. *The Alphabet Tree*. New York: Dragonfly Books, 1990. Letters grow on the Alphabet Tree, but when they are tossed about by the wind, they find out that there's strength in . . . letters? They first learn how to band together to make words and then become even stronger when they form sentences with an important message.

Cherry, Lynne. *The Great Kapok Tree: A Tale of the Amazon Rain Forest*. San Diego: Harcourt Brace Jovanovich, 1990. In the Brazilian rain forest, a woodcutter falls asleep. While he is sleeping, the creatures who live there plead with him not to destroy their home.

About Aesop's Fables

Aesop is thought to have been a Greek slave who lived in the mid-sixth century. Some stories say that he was a man with an odd appearance and a gift for storytelling. Others question whether he existed at all. Nonetheless, Aesop is credited with a collection of fables that aim to teach various lessons. There are several hundred fables in all. Most feature animal characters, such as a fox, a wolf, or a lion, that learn from the mistakes they make.

Retold by Melissa Blackwell Burke

Aesop's Fables

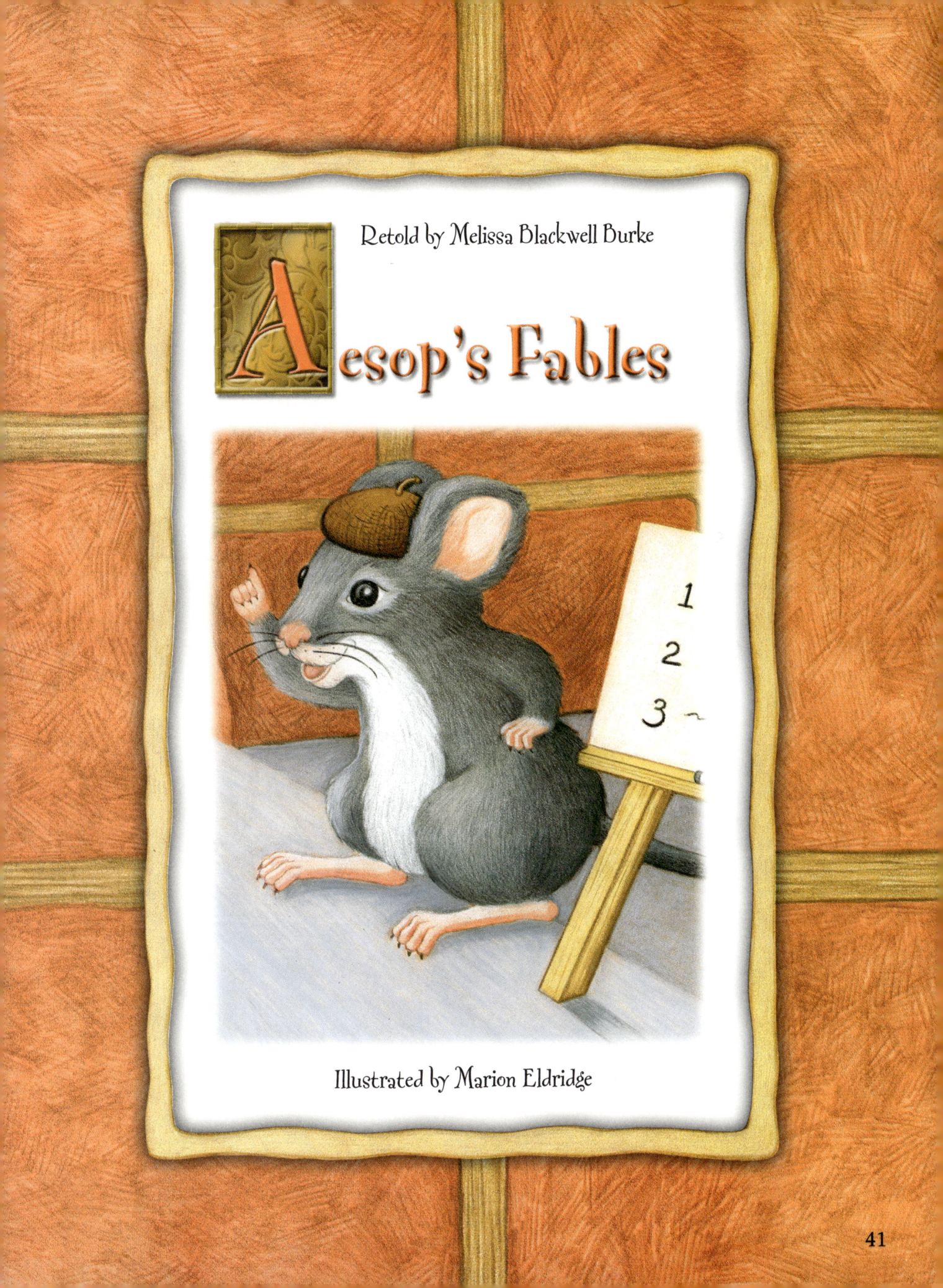

Illustrated by Marion Eldridge

The Ants and the Grasshopper

One summer's day, some ants were hard at work. They were carrying an ear of corn back to their nest.

Along came a grasshopper with a fiddle under his arm. "Hello, ants!" he called. "Come and dance to my song!"

"We can't stop now," said one of the ants. "We are storing up food for the winter. You should be doing the same thing."

"Why should I worry?" asked the grasshopper. "There is plenty to eat right now. It's a fine summer day. Why not have some fun?"

The ants shook their heads and kept working.

Each time the ants saw the grasshopper, he was laughing and singing. And each time, the ants reminded him that winter was on its way. But the grasshopper couldn't be bothered to think about work.

Soon enough, winter came. It was cold, and there was snow everywhere. The grasshopper could not find any food. As his hunger grew, he came upon the ants. There they were, taking corn and grain from their stores.

The grasshopper then wished he had spent less time making music. He wished he could turn back time and listen to the ants.

There is a time for work and a time for play.

Belling the Cat

A long time ago, some mice lived in the basement of a large house. The mice spent their days sleeping and their nights looking for food. They were very happy until the house's owner bought a huge cat. Now, they feared for their lives.

The mice were afraid to come out at night. When they did, they had to be on a constant lookout. They never knew when the cat might pounce upon them.

This went on for days and days. The mice wanted to find a way to solve their problem with the cat. They decided to have a meeting.

Plan after plan was discussed. Every time one mouse suggested an idea, another mouse found a problem with it. No one could come up with an idea that worked.

Just then, a very young mouse stood up. He said, "I have a plan that I think will work. It is a simple plan, really."

That got the other mice's attention. "Tell us more," one of them said.

53

The young mouse said, "The problem is that we never know when the cat is coming. If we knew when she was near, then we could run away."

"Yes, yes!" said the other mice. "We already know that. But what can we do?"

"We must hang a bell around the cat's neck," said the young mouse. "We will hear the bell when the cat is near. Then we will know when we need to run."

The mice agreed that this was a wonderful plan. They were surprised that no one had thought of it before.

Some of the mice began to pat the young mouse on the back. One did a dance of glee. Then an old mouse stood up and spoke.

"It's a grand idea, indeed," said the old mouse. "I have just one question about the plan. Which one of you will bell the cat?"

It is one thing to say what should be done. It is quite another matter to do it.

The Boy Who Cried Wolf

Every day, a shepherd boy went to the meadow to tend his sheep. He sat for hours with no one to talk to. As he watched the sheep, he would often gaze down at the village.

One quiet day, the boy played with his dog. Then he piped a tune. But after a little while, he had nothing else to do. He began to think about what he would do if he saw a wolf.

59

The boy knew he could shout for help. Then the villagers would think he had seen a wolf. They would come and help the boy drive the wolf away from the flock.

That's exactly what the boy did. "Wolf! Wolf!" he cried, even though he had seen nothing of the kind.

Just as he thought, the village people heard his cry. They dropped their work at once. They ran up the hill, ready to drive the wolf away.

But when the villagers got to the flock, they saw no wolf. Instead, they found the boy laughing. He thought he had played a funny trick. The villagers were not pleased, and they returned to their work.

A few days passed. The villagers continued working as usual.

Once again, the boy got bored. He remembered how funny the villagers had looked running up the hill. So once again, the boy dashed across the hill, yelling, "Wolf! Wolf!"

But there was still no wolf, as the villagers soon found out. Again, the boy laughed at his trick. Again, the villagers were not pleased.

A few more days passed, and the boy sat watching the flock. All of a sudden, a wolf came flying across the hill and sprang upon the sheep!

The boy yelled at the top of his lungs, "Wolf! Wolf!"

This time the villagers didn't even lift their eyes from their work. "He has fooled us two times before," they said. "He will not fool us again."

That day, the boy lost a great many sheep. And the wolf? Well, that tricky fellow slipped quietly back into the forest.

Those who often don't tell the truth are not believed when finally they do.

The Fox and the Grapes

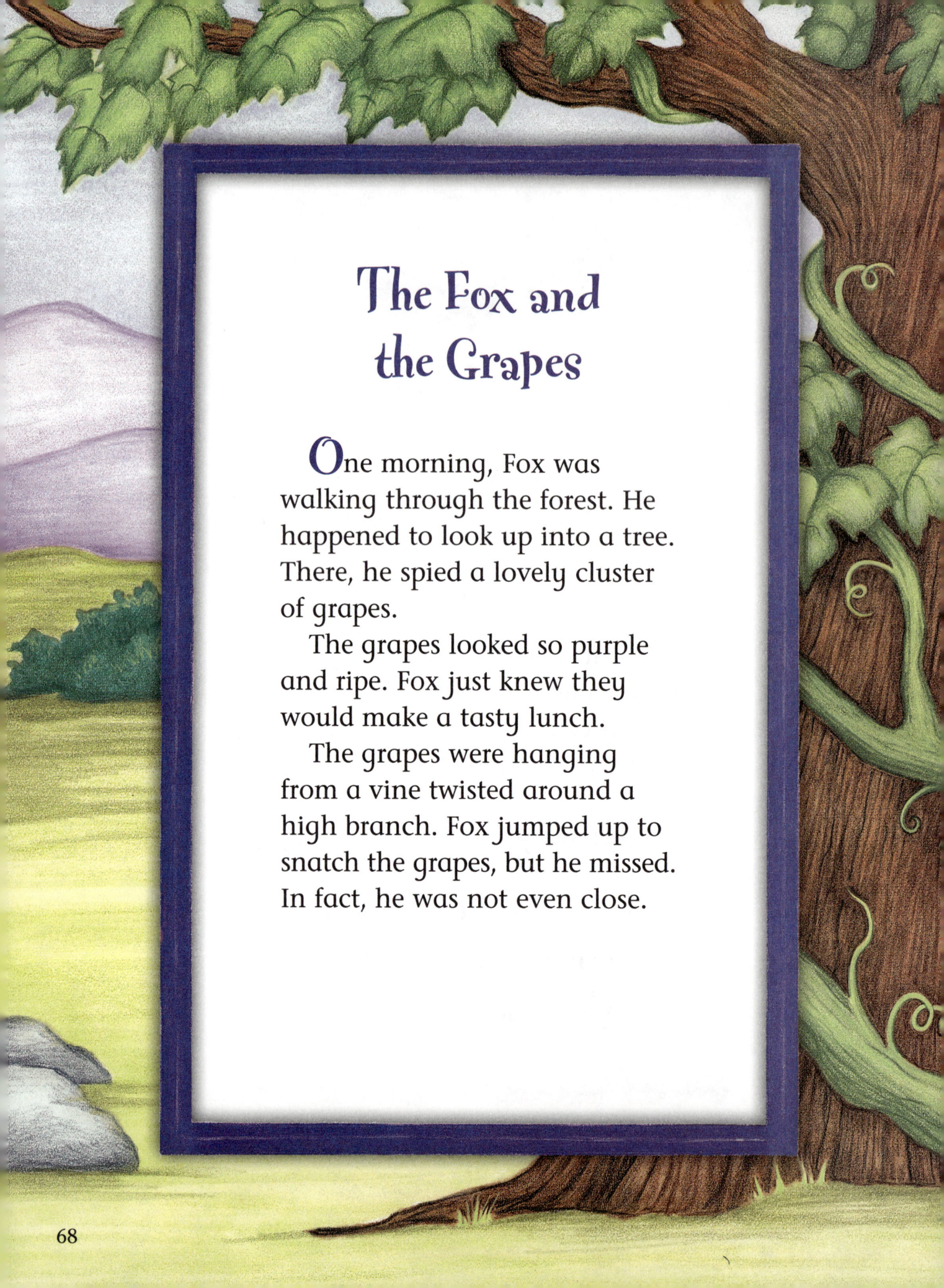

One morning, Fox was walking through the forest. He happened to look up into a tree. There, he spied a lovely cluster of grapes.

The grapes looked so purple and ripe. Fox just knew they would make a tasty lunch.

The grapes were hanging from a vine twisted around a high branch. Fox jumped up to snatch the grapes, but he missed. In fact, he was not even close.

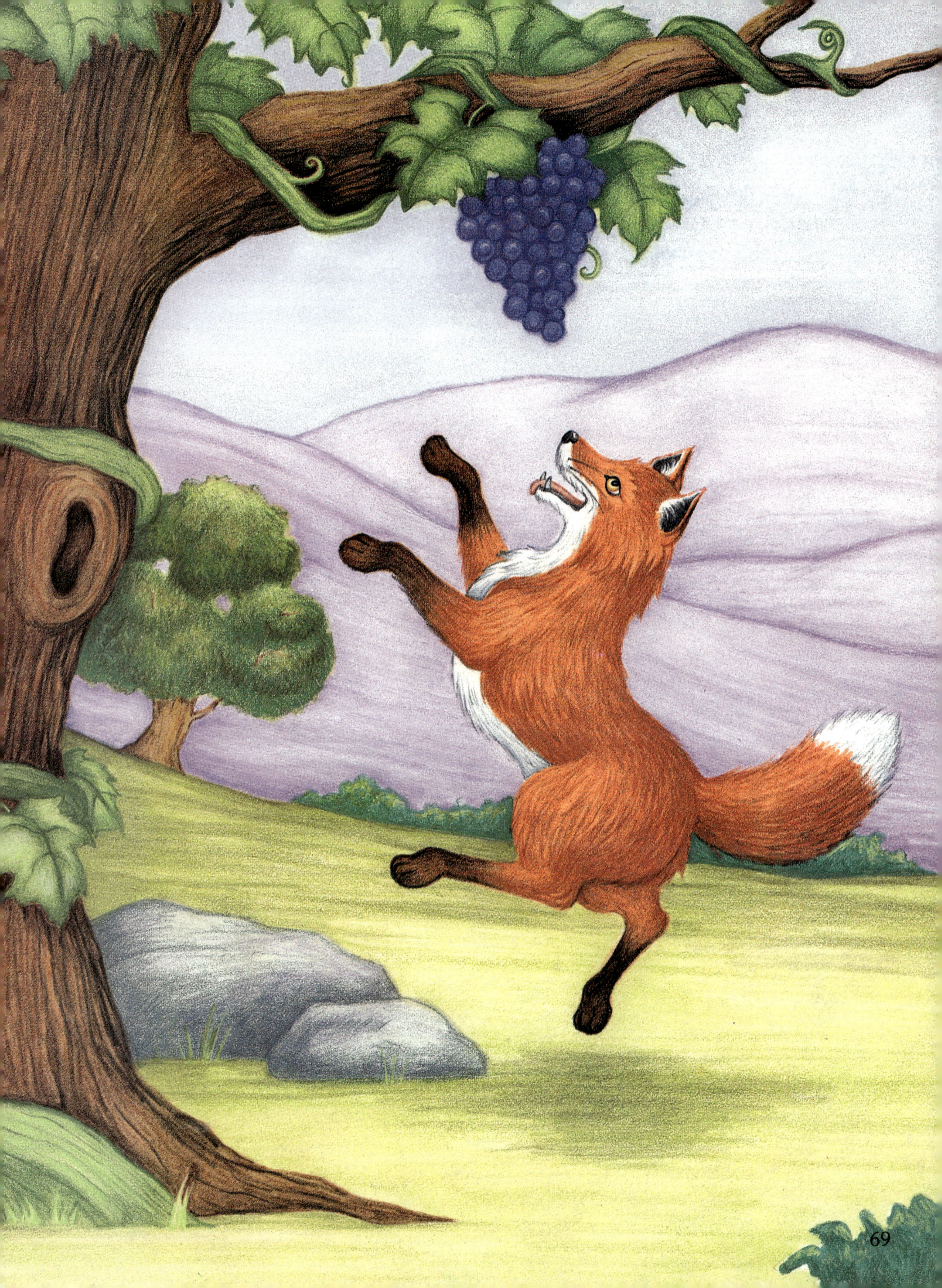

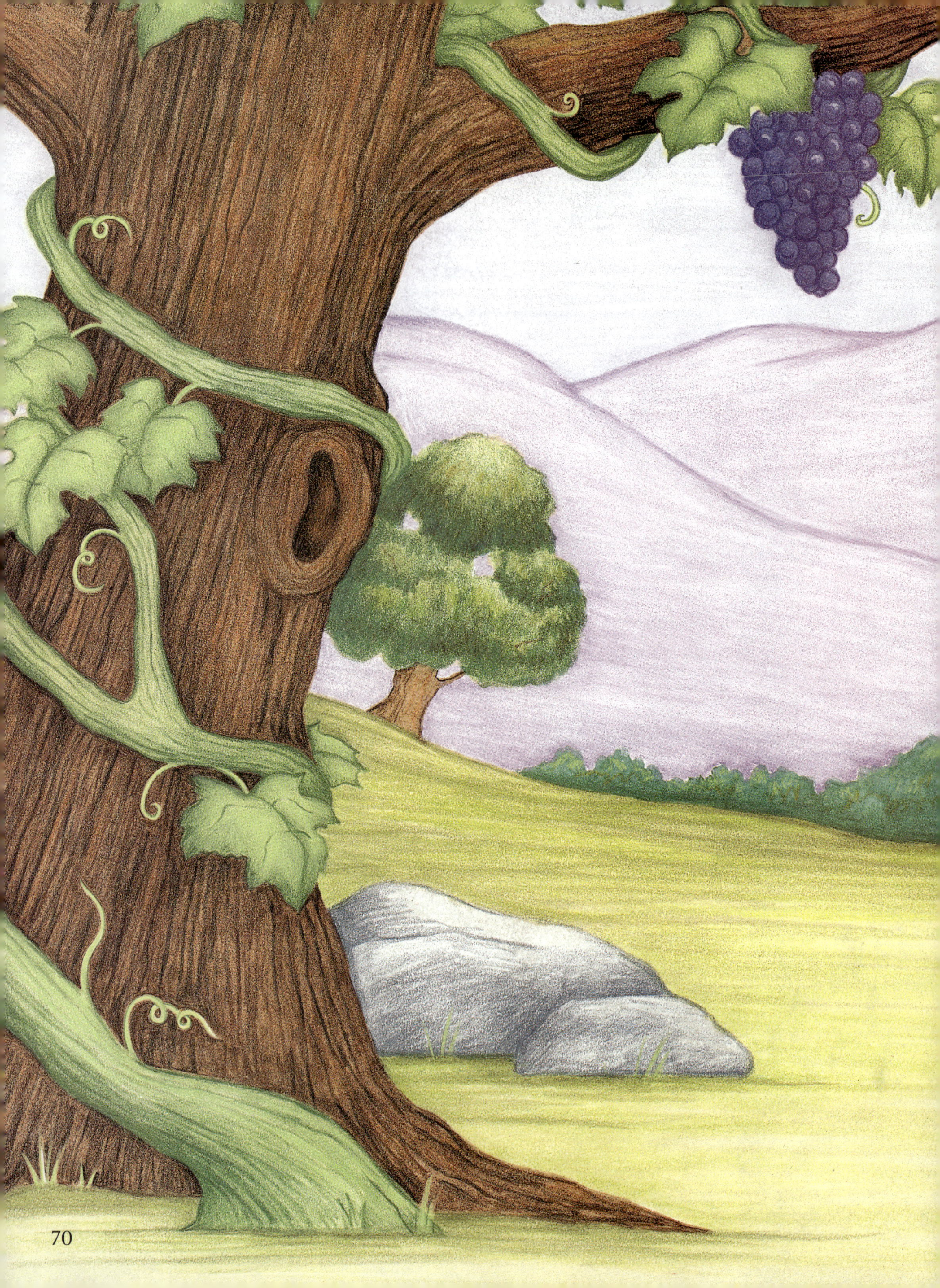

Fox really wanted the grapes now. This time, he decided to take a running leap. Still, the grapes were out of his reach.

Fox tried time and time again to reach the grapes. But he was not able to reach them. Finally, he sat down in disgust.

"How foolish of me!" Fox said to himself. "Why am I trying so hard to get a bunch of grapes? They are probably sour anyway!" And with that, Fox walked away.

Some people will talk badly about things they cannot have.

Bibliography
Aesop's Fables

Aesop. *Aesop's Fables: A Classic Illustrated Edition*. Compiled by Russell Ash and Bernard Higton. San Francisco: Chronicle Books, 1990. This collection of Aesop's fables includes many familiar fables as well as some that are not so well known. The illustrations, from a variety of older editions, were created by such esteemed artists as Randolph Caldecott, Arthur Rackham, and Alexander Calder.

Aesop. *The Aesop for Children*. Pictures by Milo Winter. New York: Scholastic, 1994. This is a classic and comprehensive collection of Aesop's fables.

Yolen, Jane. *A Sip of Aesop*. New York: Scholastic, 1995. Thirteen well-known fables are told in short, clever verses, with the moral clearly stated after each.

Lobel, Arnold. *Fables*. New York: Harper Trophy, 1983. These whimsical fables are rather different from Aesop's, but they still offer morals worth thinking about. This book won the 1981 Caldecott Medal.

Brown, Marcia. *Once a Mouse . . . : A Fable Cut in Wood*. New York: Atheneum Books, 1961. A hermit can change his little pet mouse into a cat, a dog, and then a tiger in this beautifully told Indian fable, but there's a lesson to be learned. This book won the 1962 Caldecott Medal.

About "Rumpelstiltskin"

"Rumpelstiltskin" is one of the fairy tales published by Wilhelm and Jacob Grimm in their famous collection of German tales. As with most stories that were told over and over, passing orally from one person to another, there were many versions by the time the story was written down. The tale appears in most European countries. In some British versions, the little man's name is not Rumpelstiltskin, but Terrytop, Whuppity Storrie, or Tom Tit Tot.

Retold by Melissa Blackwell Burke

Rumpelstiltskin

Illustrated by Lydia Taranovic

75

Once upon a time, there was a miller who had a beautiful daughter. He loved his daughter very much. He also loved to brag about her.

One day, the king rode by the miller's house.

"Your Highness," said the miller, "I would like you to meet my daughter. She is very beautiful."

"Indeed, many fair maidens live in this land," said the king.

The miller wanted the king to think his daughter was special. So he said the first thing he thought of.

"Well, my daughter can spin straw into gold!" the miller said.

"My good man!" the king said. "Let us see about that."

So the miller took his daughter to the palace.

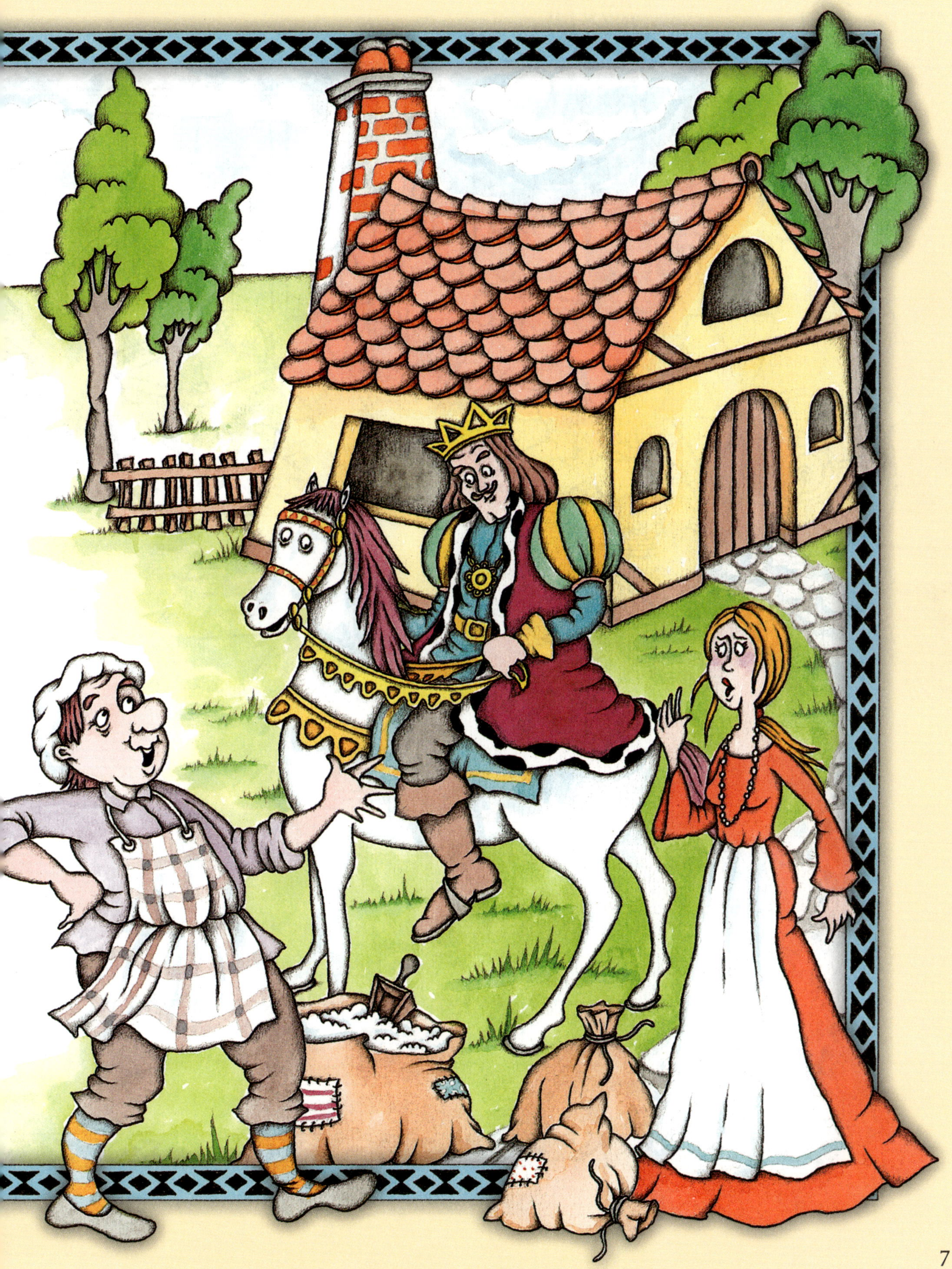

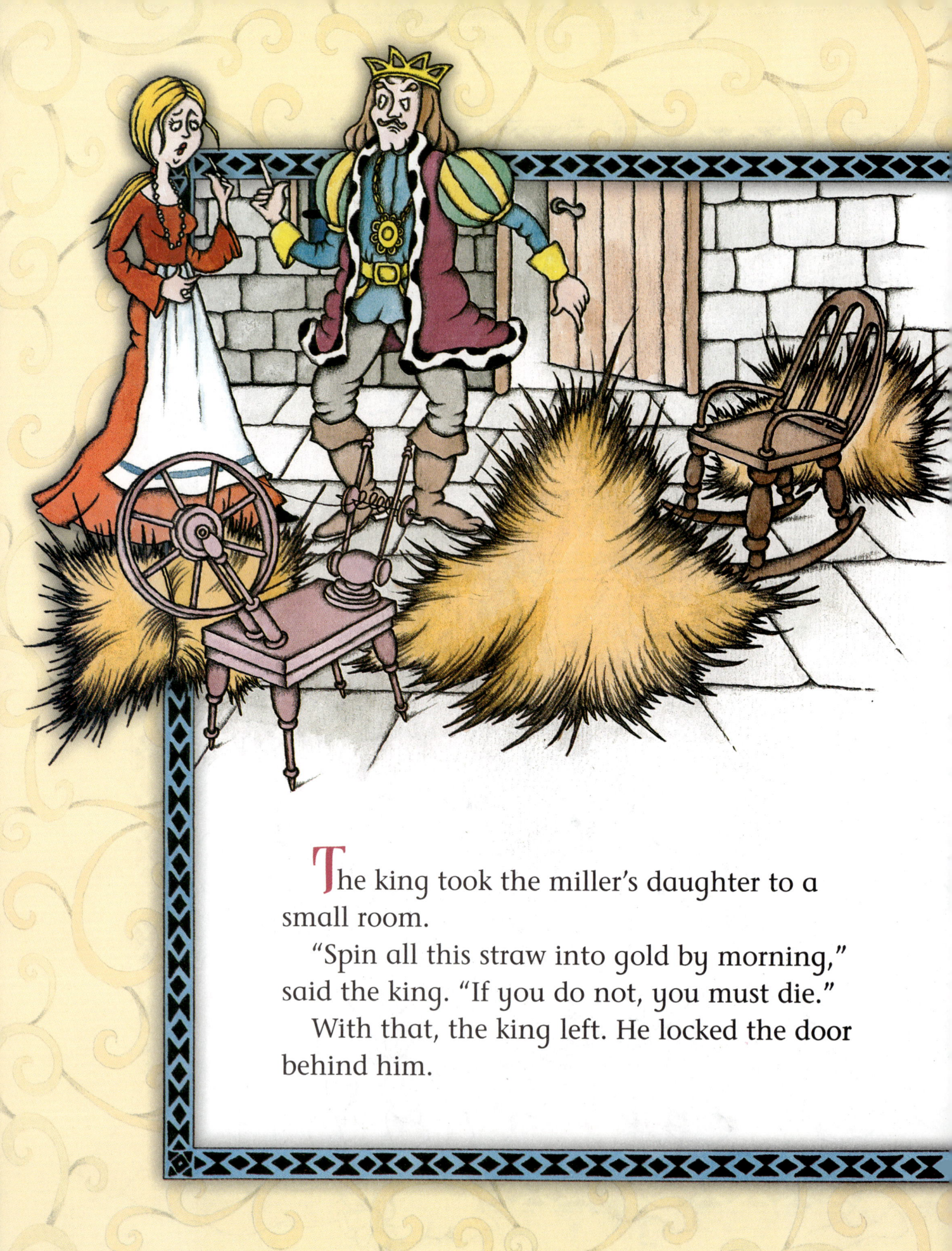

The king took the miller's daughter to a small room.

"Spin all this straw into gold by morning," said the king. "If you do not, you must die."

With that, the king left. He locked the door behind him.

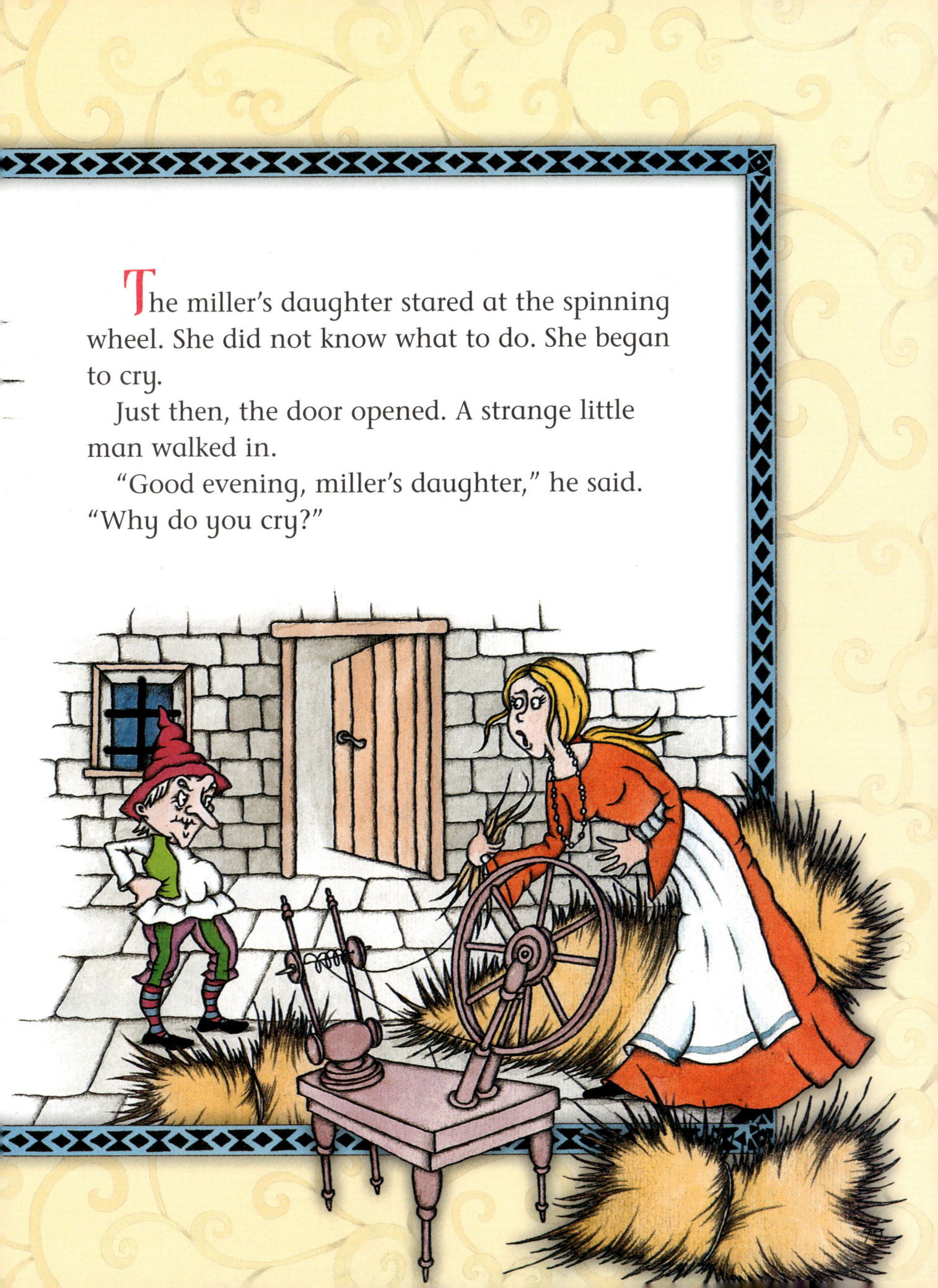

The miller's daughter stared at the spinning wheel. She did not know what to do. She began to cry.

Just then, the door opened. A strange little man walked in.

"Good evening, miller's daughter," he said. "Why do you cry?"

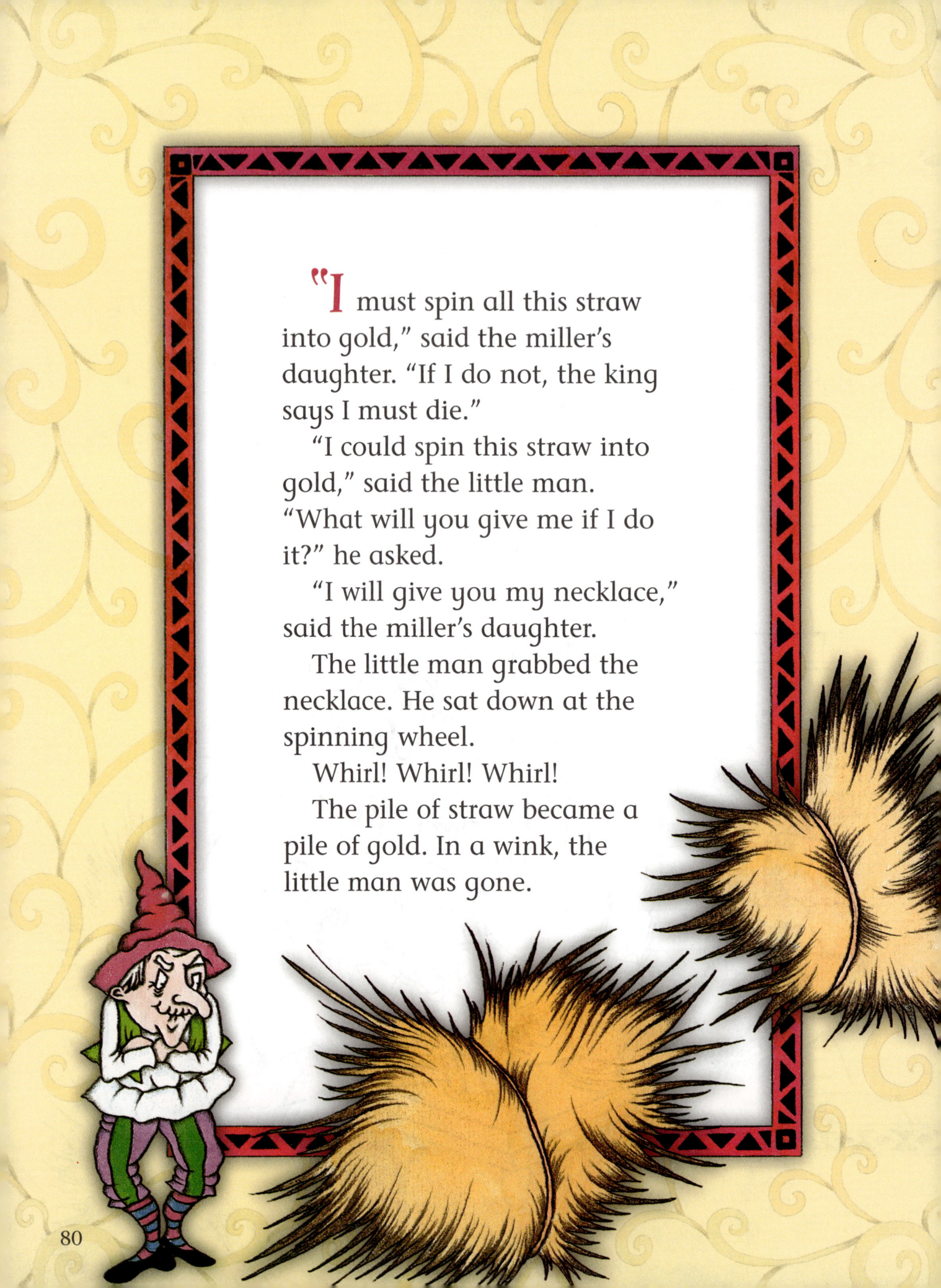

"I must spin all this straw into gold," said the miller's daughter. "If I do not, the king says I must die."

"I could spin this straw into gold," said the little man. "What will you give me if I do it?" he asked.

"I will give you my necklace," said the miller's daughter.

The little man grabbed the necklace. He sat down at the spinning wheel.

Whirl! Whirl! Whirl!

The pile of straw became a pile of gold. In a wink, the little man was gone.

81

When the sun came up, the king came into the room. He looked around and smiled.

"I am pleased," said the king, "but I want more gold."

He took the miller's daughter to a bigger room. It had more straw.

"Spin all this straw into gold by morning," said the king. "If you do not, you must die."

With that, the king left. Again, he locked the door behind him.

The miller's daughter began to cry.

Again, the door opened. As on the night before, the little man came in.

"Good evening, miller's daughter," he said. "I could spin this straw into gold, too. What will you give me if I do?"

"I will give you my ring," said the miller's daughter.

The little man grabbed the ring. He sat down at the spinning wheel.

Whirl! Whirl! Whirl!

The piles of straw became piles of gold. In a wink, the little man was gone.

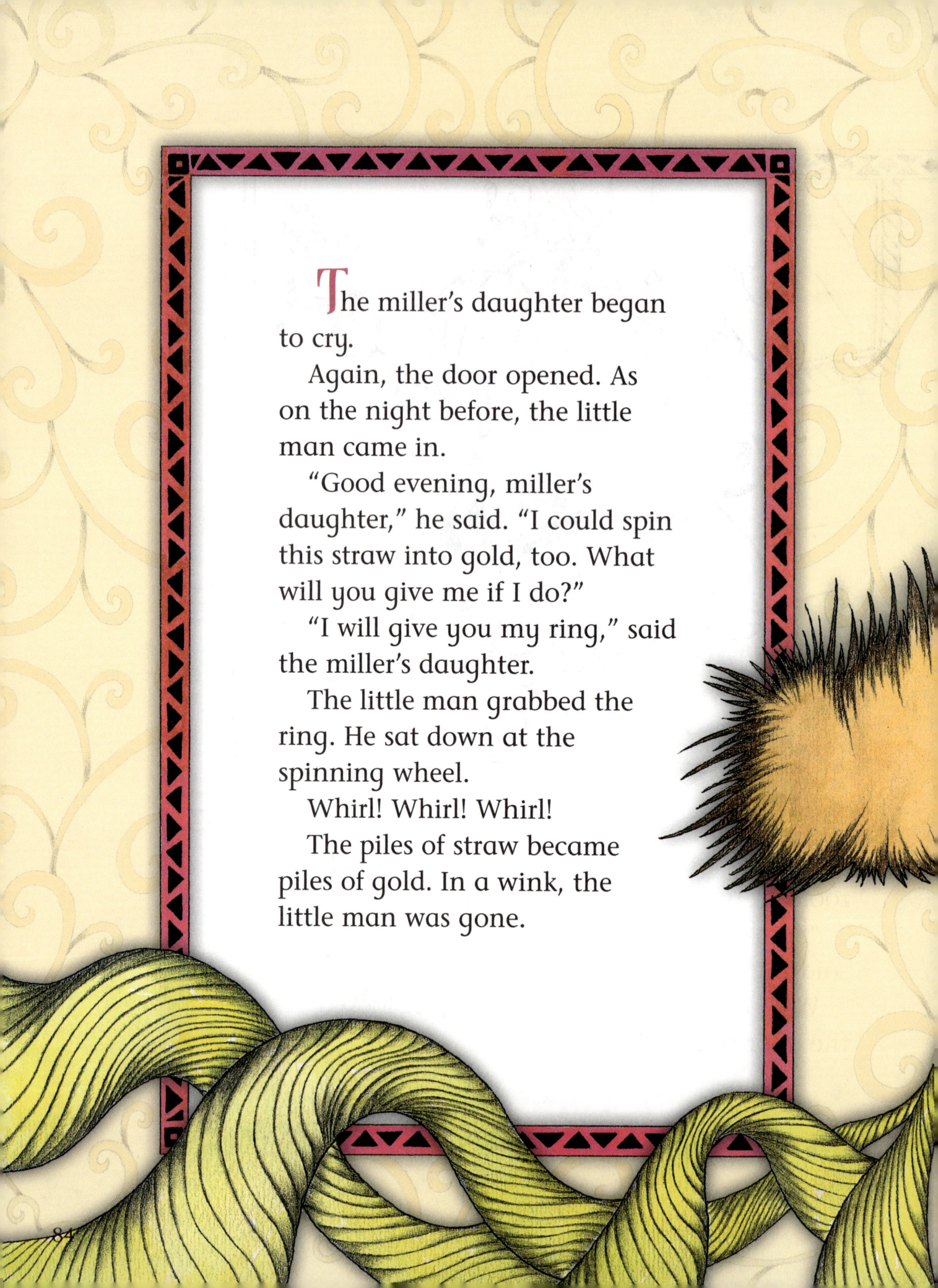

85

When the sun came up, the king came into the room. He looked around and smiled. "I am very pleased," said the king. "But I want more gold."

He took the miller's daughter to a huge room. There were many piles of straw.

"Spin all this straw into gold by morning," said the king. "If you do, we will marry. If you do not, you must die."

The king left and locked the door.

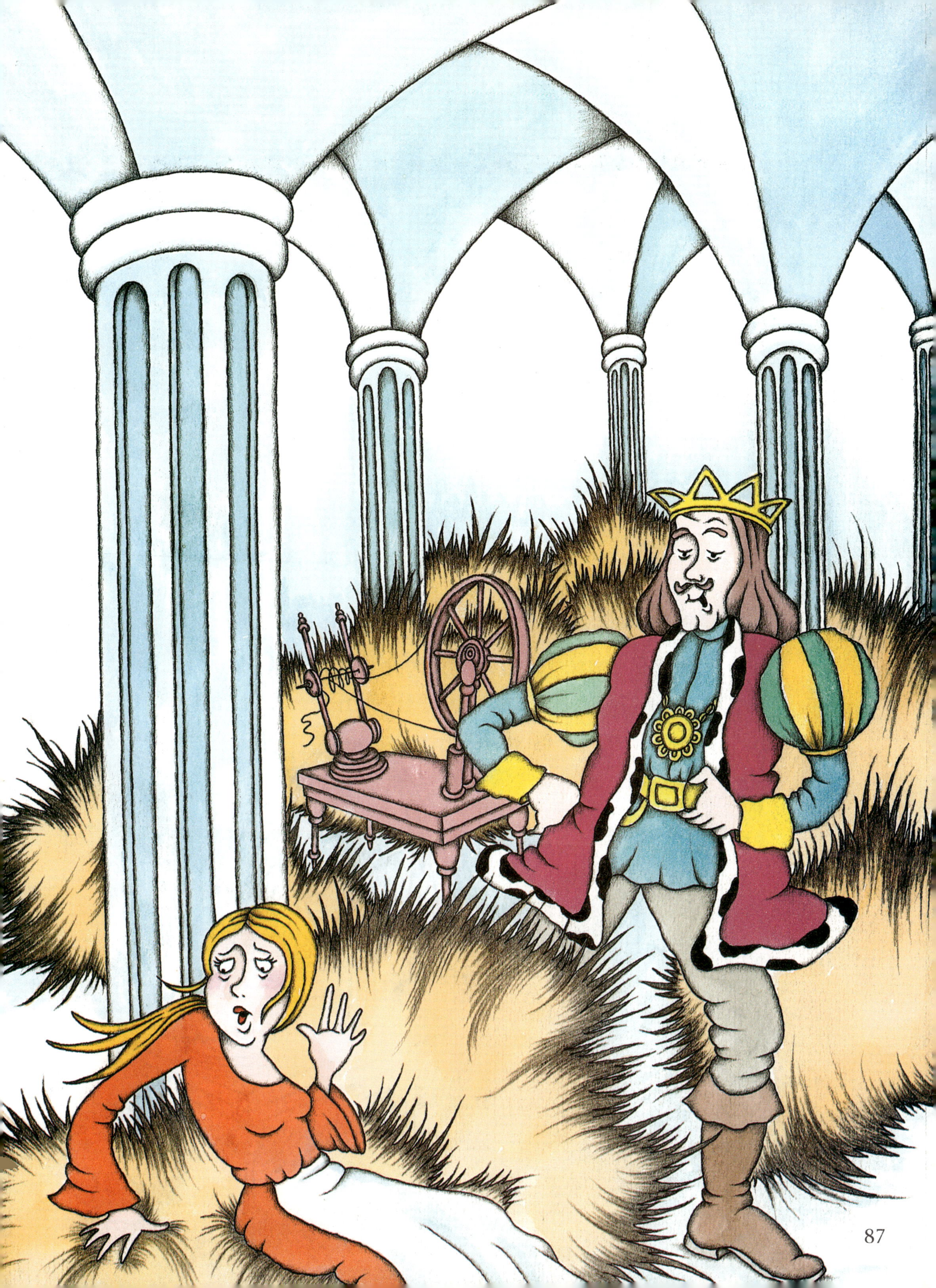

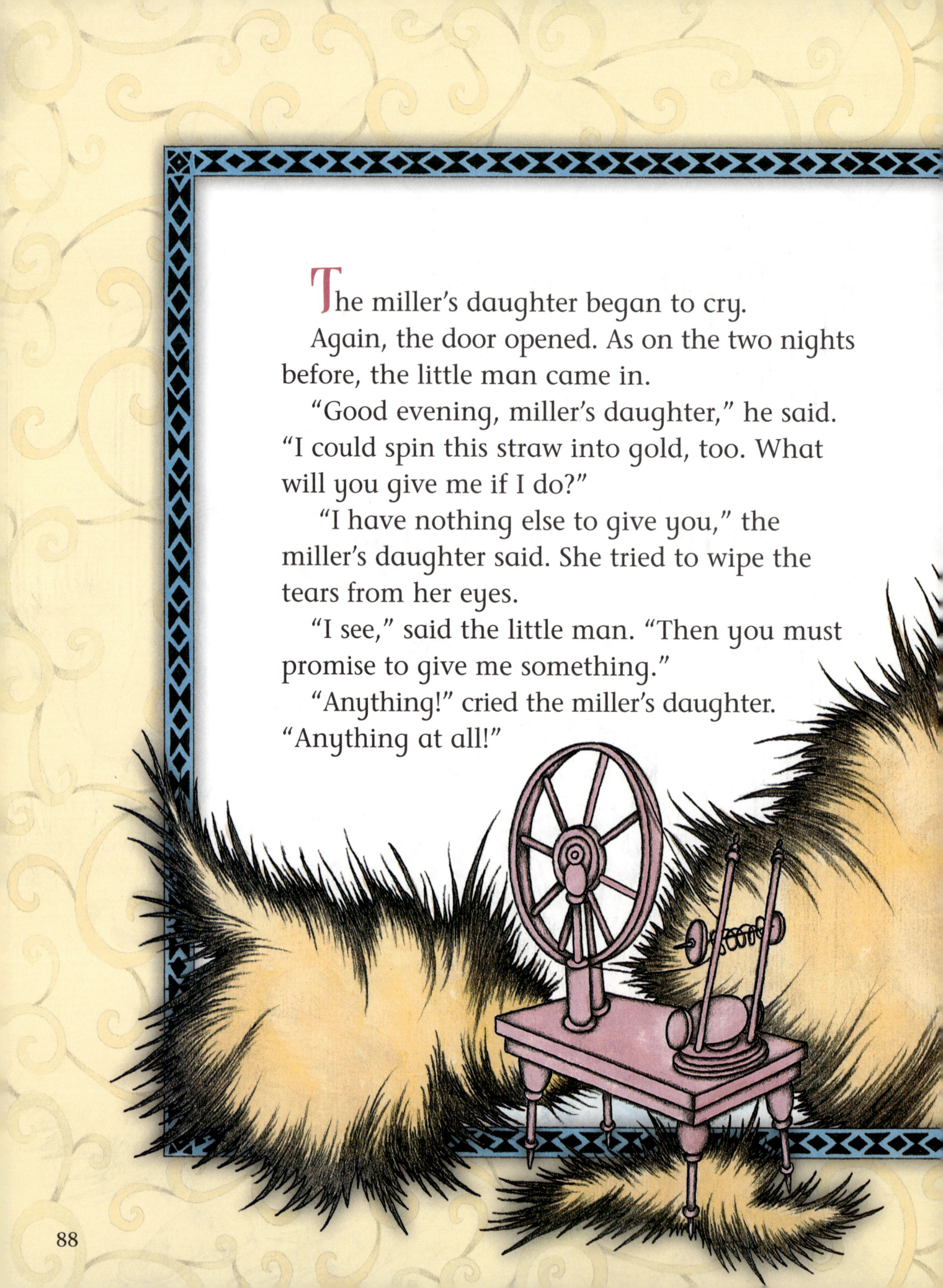

The miller's daughter began to cry.

Again, the door opened. As on the two nights before, the little man came in.

"Good evening, miller's daughter," he said. "I could spin this straw into gold, too. What will you give me if I do?"

"I have nothing else to give you," the miller's daughter said. She tried to wipe the tears from her eyes.

"I see," said the little man. "Then you must promise to give me something."

"Anything!" cried the miller's daughter. "Anything at all!"

89

"I want your first child," said the little man.

"Oh!" cried the miller's daughter.

"Promise!" said the little man.

"I promise!" said the miller's daughter.

The little man sat down at the spinning wheel.

Whirl! Whirl! Whirl!

The piles of straw became piles of gold. In a wink, the little man was gone.

When the sun came up, the king came into the room. "How grand!" said the king. "My dear, we shall be married today."

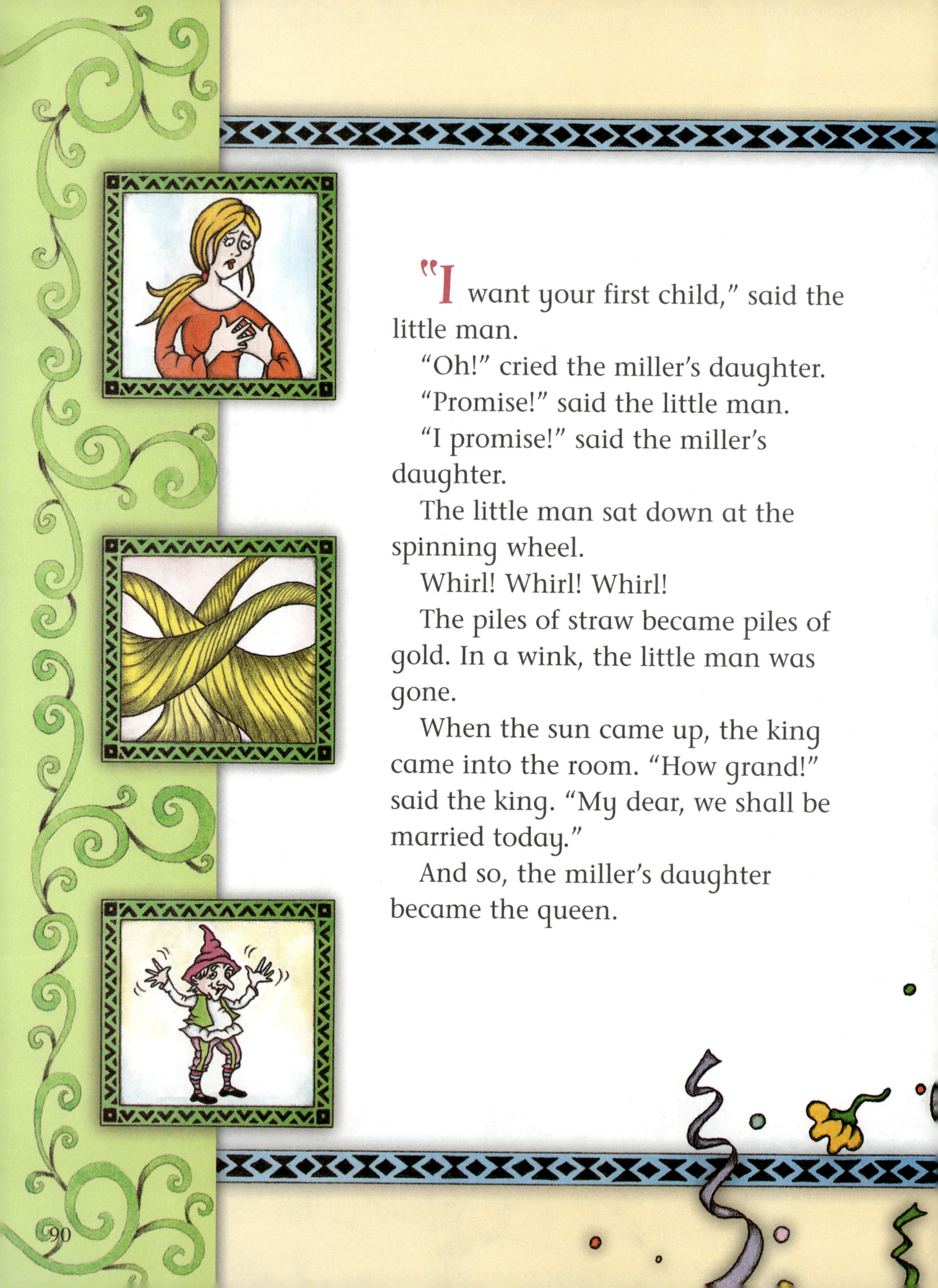

And so, the miller's daughter became the queen.

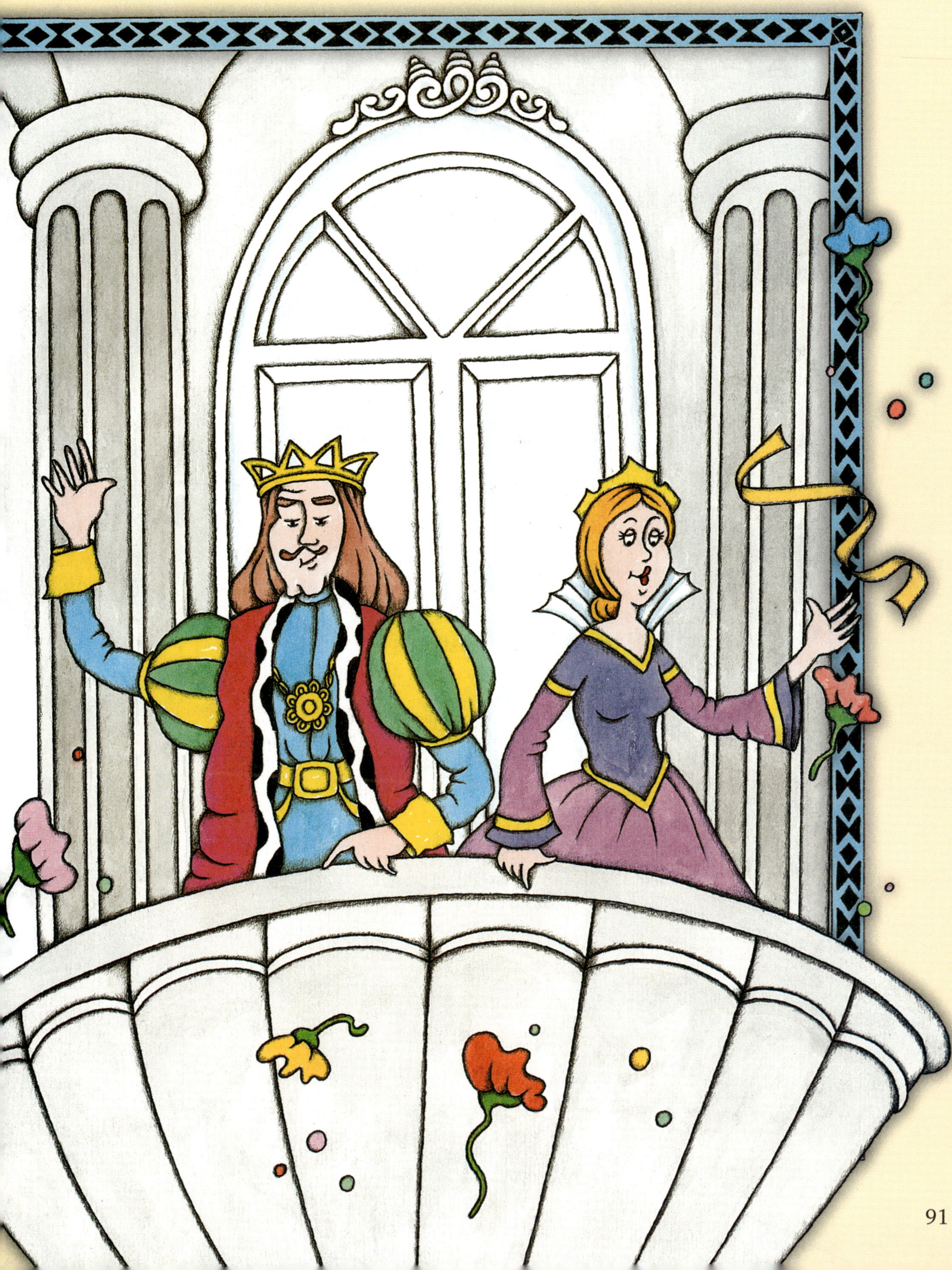

A year later, the queen became a mother.

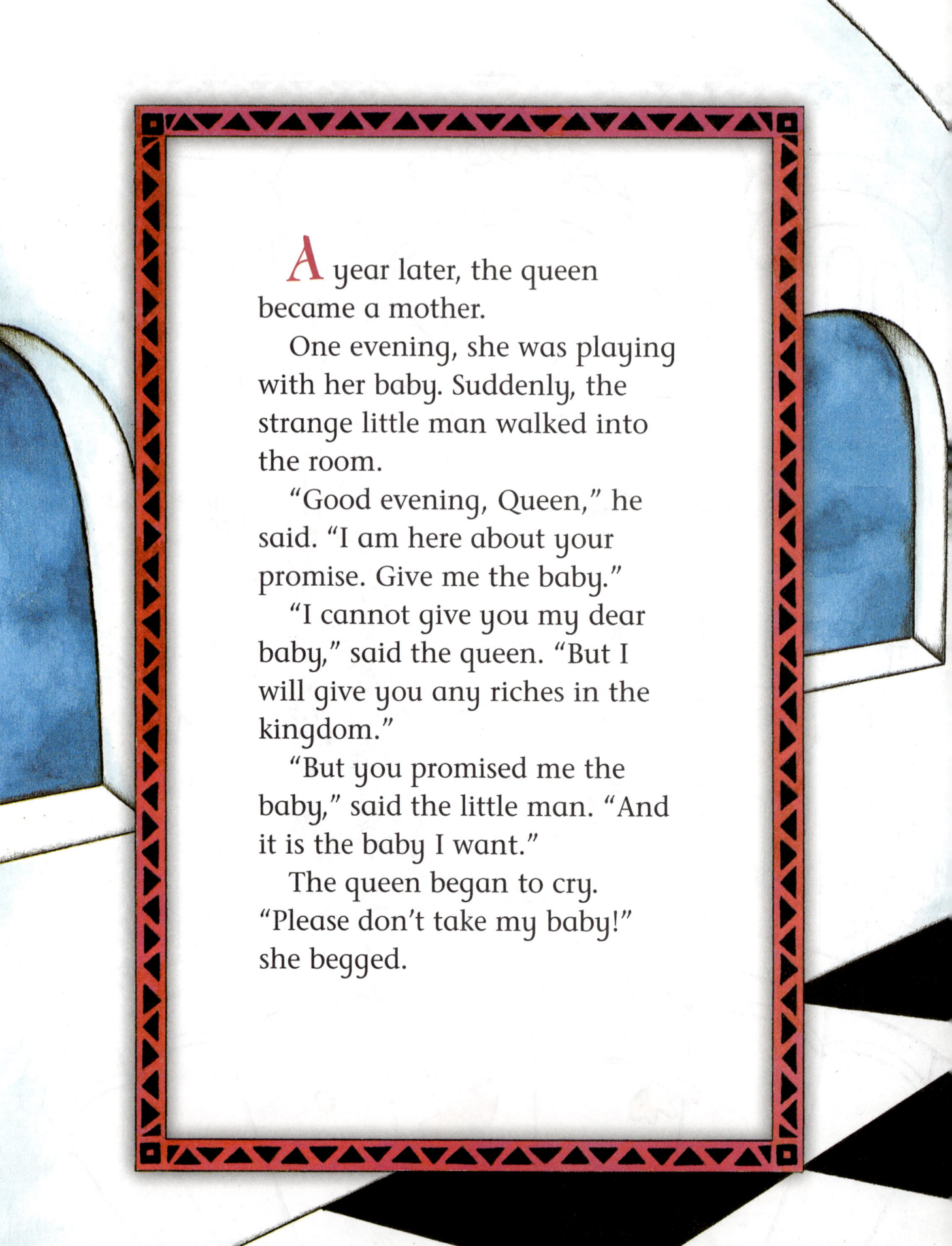

One evening, she was playing with her baby. Suddenly, the strange little man walked into the room.

"Good evening, Queen," he said. "I am here about your promise. Give me the baby."

"I cannot give you my dear baby," said the queen. "But I will give you any riches in the kingdom."

"But you promised me the baby," said the little man. "And it is the baby I want."

The queen began to cry. "Please don't take my baby!" she begged.

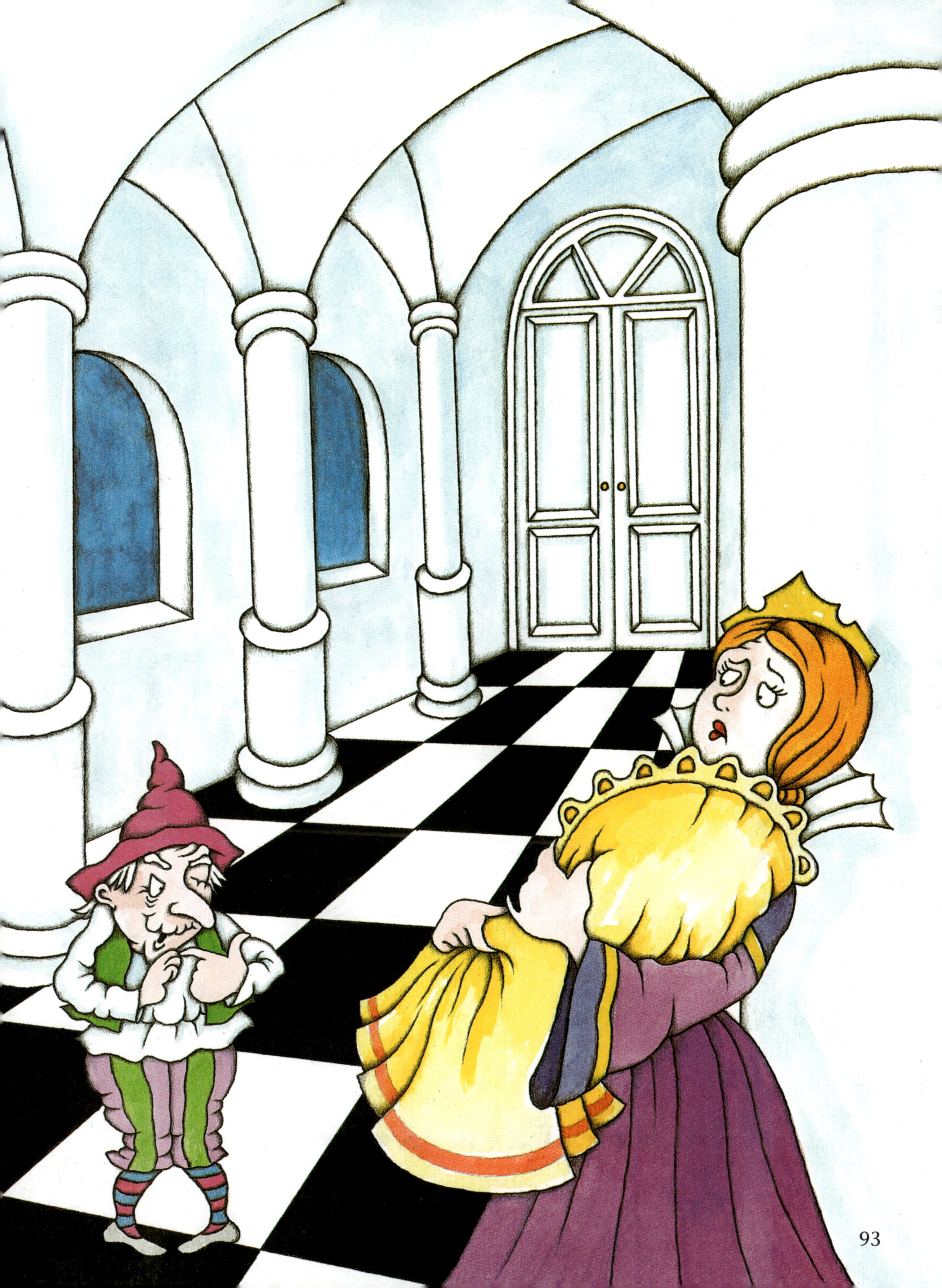

"Very well," said the little man. "If you can guess my name, you may keep the baby. I will give you three days." And with that, the little man was gone.

The next day, the queen sent servants to every corner of the land. "Find out the names of every person in the kingdom," she said. "Report back to me this evening."

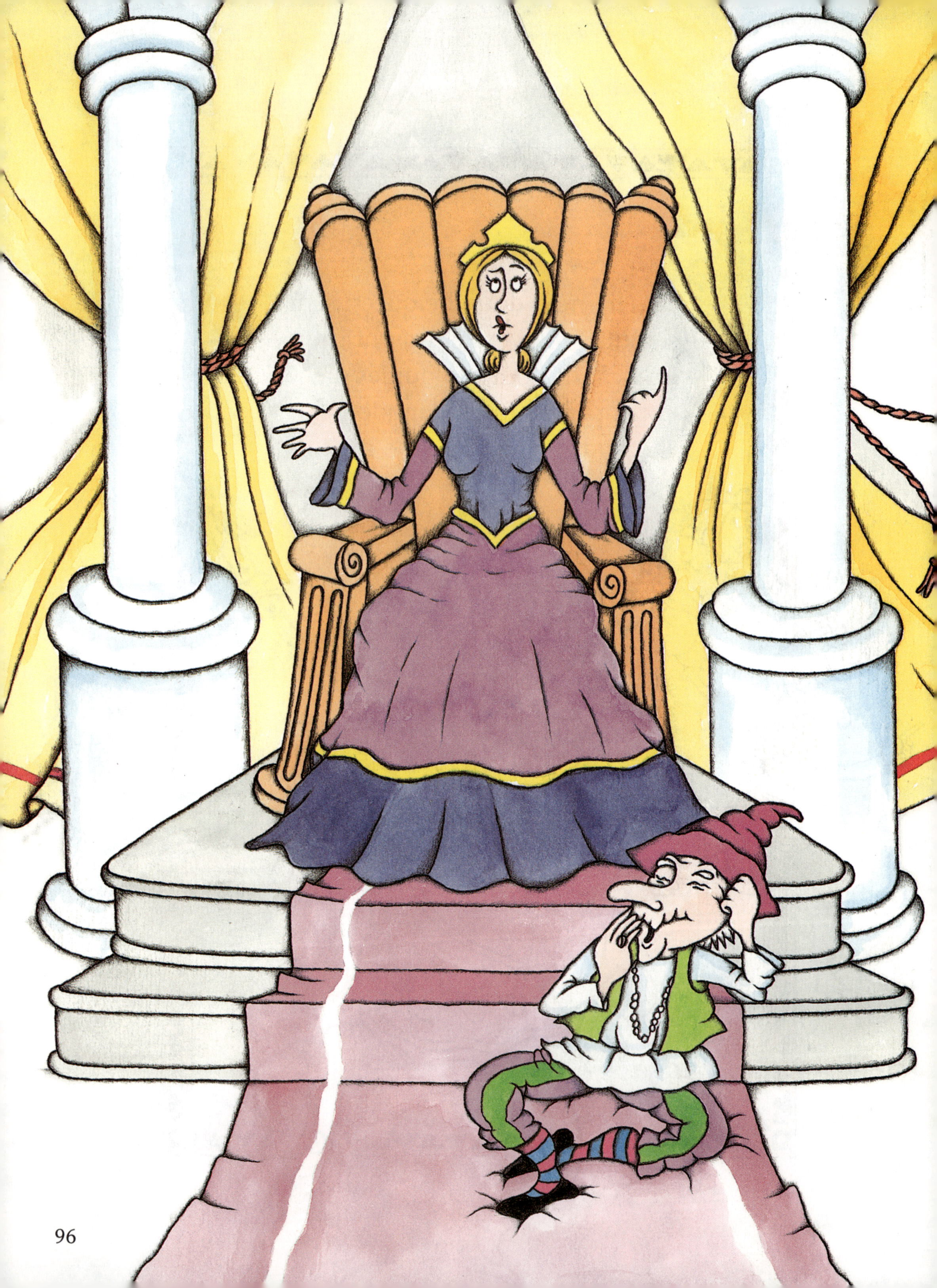

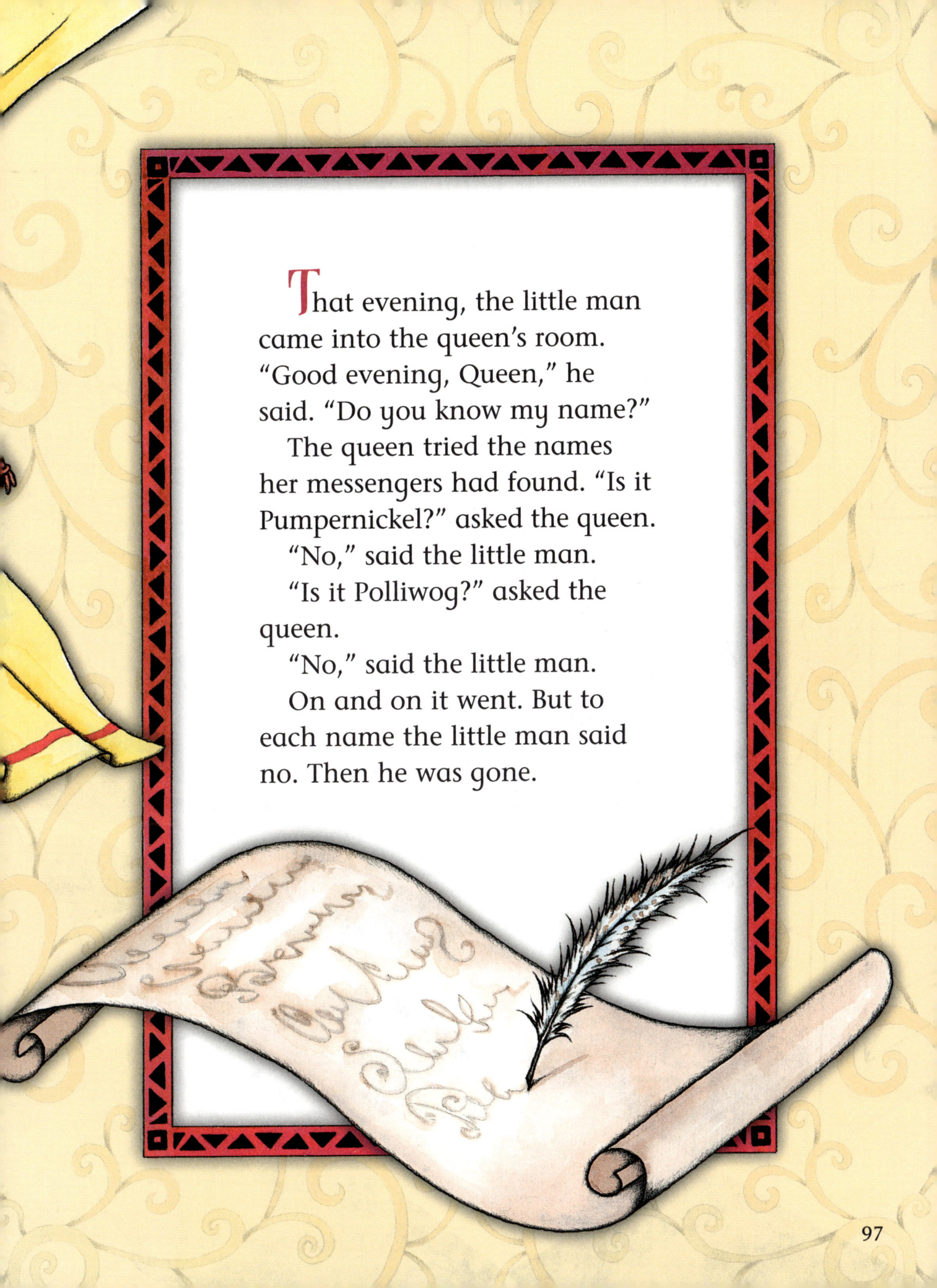

That evening, the little man came into the queen's room. "Good evening, Queen," he said. "Do you know my name?"

The queen tried the names her messengers had found. "Is it Pumpernickel?" asked the queen.

"No," said the little man.

"Is it Polliwog?" asked the queen.

"No," said the little man.

On and on it went. But to each name the little man said no. Then he was gone.

98

On the second evening, the little man came into the queen's room. "Good evening, Queen," he said. "Do you know my name?"

The queen tried more odd names her servants had found. "Is it Wilberforce?" she asked.

"No," said the little man.

"Is it Sheepshanks?" asked the queen.

"No," said the little man.

And on and on it went. But to each name the little man said no. Then the little man was gone.

The third day, the queen was desperate. She called her servants. "Are there no other names you can tell me?" she pleaded. "No other names at all?"

"Well," said one servant, "I did hear something very odd. I went deep into the forest. I saw a little house. In front of the little house was a fire. Around the fire, a little man was dancing."

101

The servant said, "While he danced, he sang:

'Tonight, tonight my little cakes I bake. Tomorrow, tomorrow the queen's baby I take. Lucky I'll go as lucky I came, for Rumpelstiltskin is my name!'

"Excellent work!" cried the queen.

On the third evening, the little man came. "Good evening, Queen," he said. "Do you know my name?"

"Is it George?" she asked.

"No," said the little man.

"What about Harry?" asked the queen.

"That is not my name," said the little man.

"Then, could it be, perhaps, Rumpelstiltskin?" asked the queen.

The little man became very angry indeed!

"Who told you?" he shouted, stamping his foot. "Who told you, I say?"

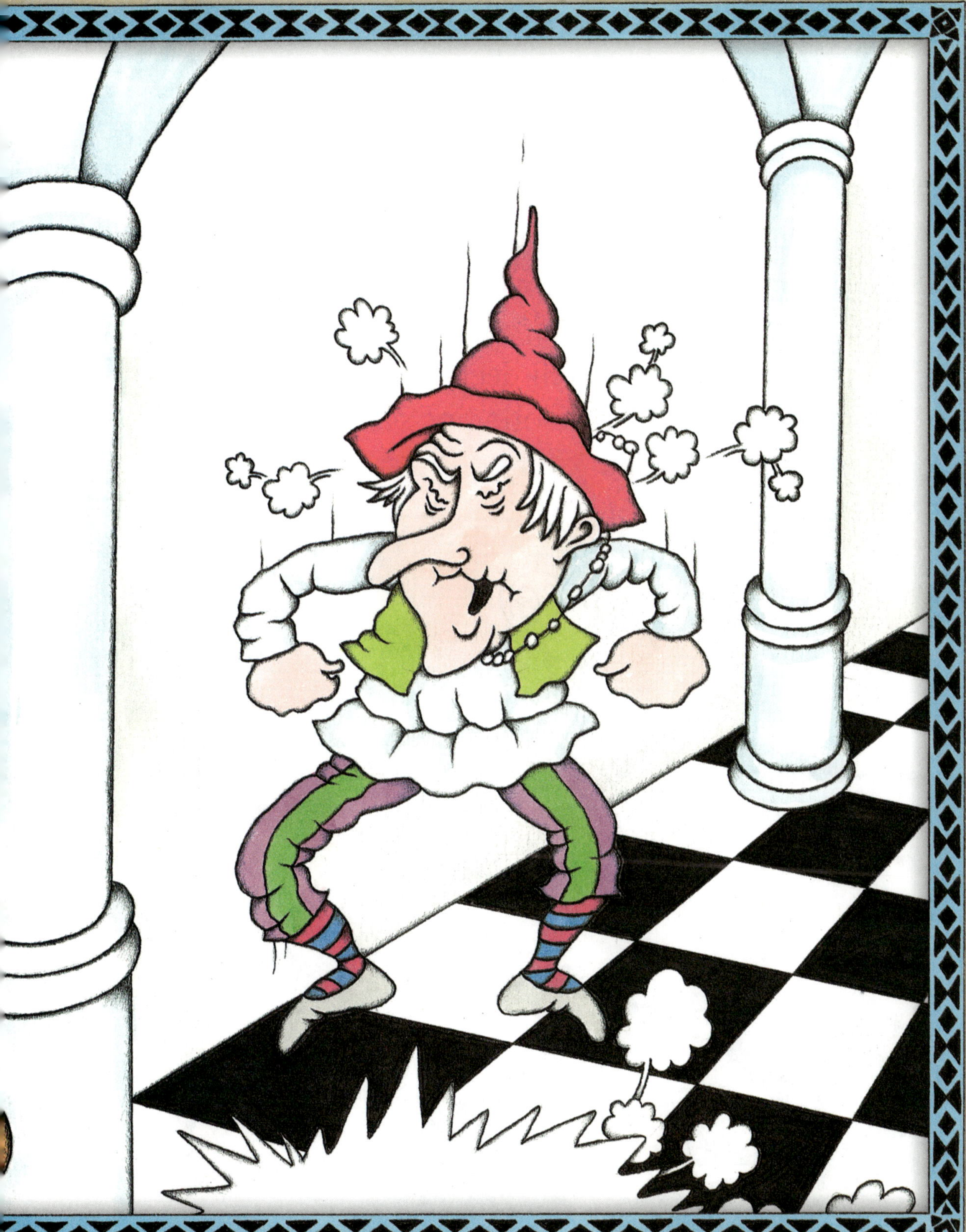

He stamped his right foot so hard that it went through the floor. Then he stamped his left foot as well. He stamped them so hard that he fell deep into the earth. And no one has seen Rumpelstiltskin ever again.

Bibliography "Rumpelstiltskin"

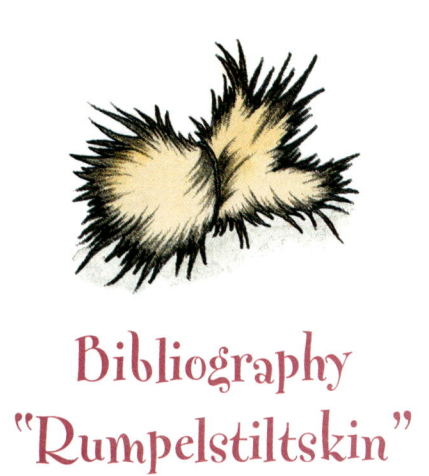

Galdone, Paul. *Rumpelstiltskin.* New York: Houghton Mifflin, 1990. This retelling of the classic tale of Rumplestiltskin is enhanced by Galdone's lively illustrations.

Stanley, Diane. *Rumpelstiltskin's Daughter.* New York: William Morrow, 1997. What if the miller's daughter hadn't married the king after all? In this thoroughly modern version of the tale, she runs off and marries Rumplestiltskin instead! Now, their 16-year-old daughter has been captured by the same greedy king and placed in a tower to spin gold, but she teaches him an important lesson. (Don't forget to check out the paintings on the castle wall for a few surprises.)

Yamate, Sandra S. *Ashok by Any Other Name.* Chicago: Polychrome Pub. Corp., 1992. Ashok looks like a simpler name than Rumpelstiltskin, but to an Indian-American boy who wishes he had a more "American" name it can present a complicated problem. Classmates' mispronunciation of Ashok's name is the least of his problems. What he really wants is to be a part of the group.

Sadu, Itah. *Christopher Changes His Name.* Buffalo, NY: Firefly Books, 1998. Tired of having an ordinary name, Christopher decides to change it, again and again. Christopher finally realizes that his name is a special one.

dePaola, Tommie. *Tom.* New York: Putnam, 1993. Tommy's grandfather wants Tommy to call him Tom and not Grandpa, because, he explains, they were "named after each other." This is an autobiographical tale of Tomie dePaola's relationship with his own grandfather.

About "Rapunzel"

"Rapunzel" is a popular part of the Brothers Grimm's collection of famous German folktales. However, before it appeared in the Grimm's collection, it underwent many retellings. The story first appeared as a fairy tale from Naples, Italy. Published in *The Tale of Tales* by Giambattista Basile, the story was called "Petrosinella." The story line is much the same, beginning with an expectant mother craving an herb grown by a witch. This time the herb is parsley, called *petrosine* in Neapolitan.

From that source the story was retold by a French noblewoman, Charlotte-Rose de Caumont La Force. It was called "Persinette," based on the French word for parsley, *persil*. This version has a fairy rather than a witch.

The story was later translated into German by Joachim Christoph Friedrich Schulz. He changed many details of the story. One of them was the parsley. He switched it to another herb, called *rapunzel* in German and *rampion* in English. The Brothers Grimm based their tale on details from Schulz's "Rapunzel."

Retold by Melissa Blackwell Burke

Rapunzel

Illustrated by Clive Spong

Once upon a time, there was a couple who longed to have a child. Years passed with only the two of them. At last, it seemed that their wish would come true. The wife would soon have a child.

Before the baby was born, the wife liked to sit by a window. It looked out on a grand garden filled with beautiful flowers and plants. The garden was a wonder, but no one dared to enter it. It belonged to a witch who surrounded it with a high wall.

One day, the wife caught sight of a bed of rapunzel. The herb looked so green and fresh. The wife knew at once that she must have some of it. Day after day, she could think of nothing else. She grew pale from wishing for the herb.

"Whatever is the matter?" the husband asked.

"I must eat some rapunzel from that garden," the wife answered. "If I do not, I will die."

The husband loved his wife very much. He felt he must find a way to get her some rapunzel.

The husband climbed over the wall and into the garden. Quickly, he grabbed as much rapunzel as he could carry. He scrambled back over the wall and into the house.

His wife was delighted with the rapunzel. She immediately made a salad of the herb and gobbled it up. The rapunzel tasted so delicious that she begged for more.

115

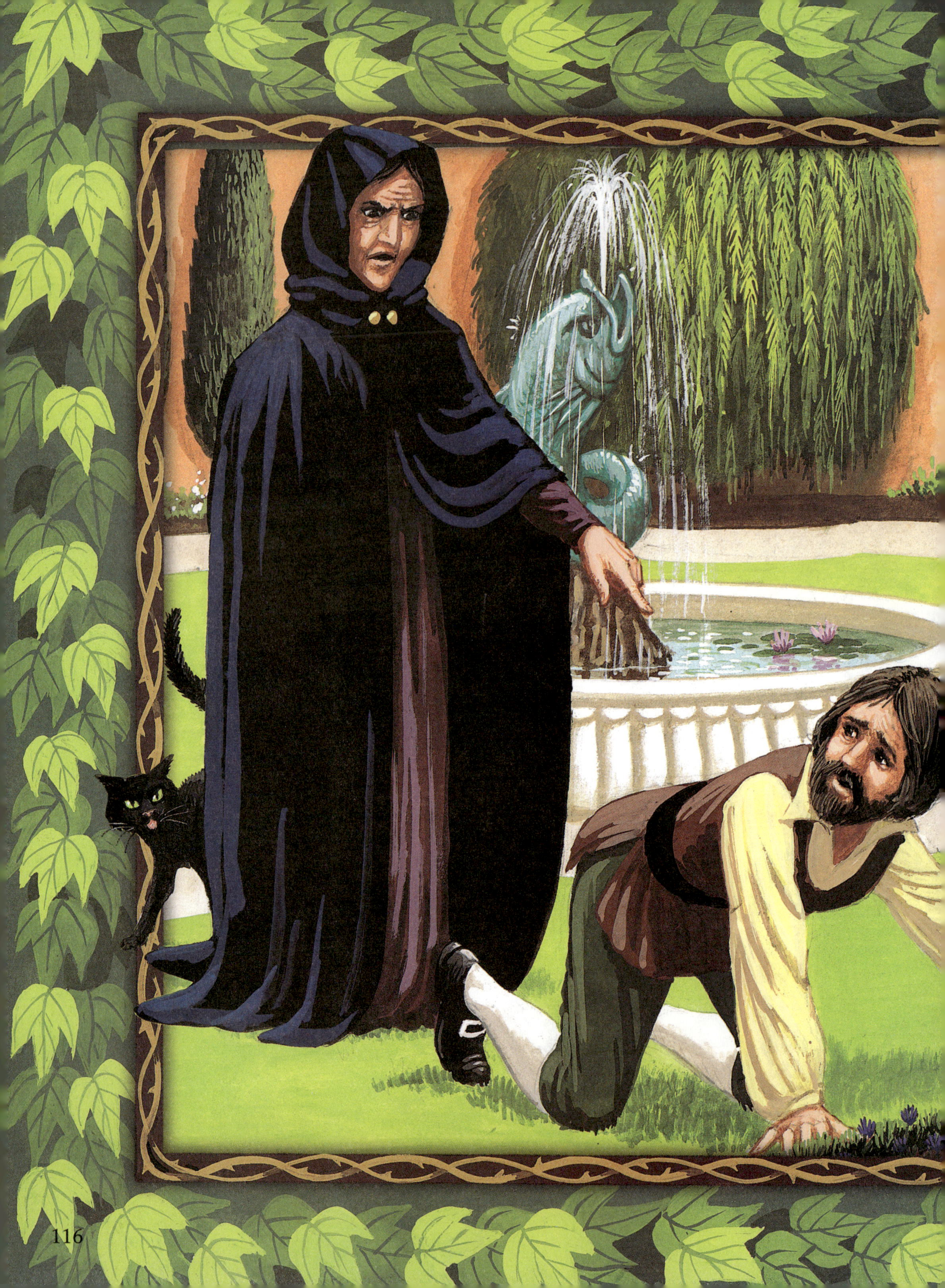

Once again, the husband made his way into the garden. He reached out his hand to gather up the herb.

Suddenly, the witch was upon him. "Thief!" she cried. "How dare you steal from my garden? You will pay dearly for this!"

The man was very frightened. "It is for my wife, who will soon have our child," he said. "She sees your rapunzel from our window. She has the greatest longing for it. I feared that without the rapunzel she would die."

At his words, the witch grew calm. "Very well," she said. "You may take all the rapunzel you need. But there is a price. You must give me your child."

The man did not know what to do. Finally, he decided that he had no choice but to agree.

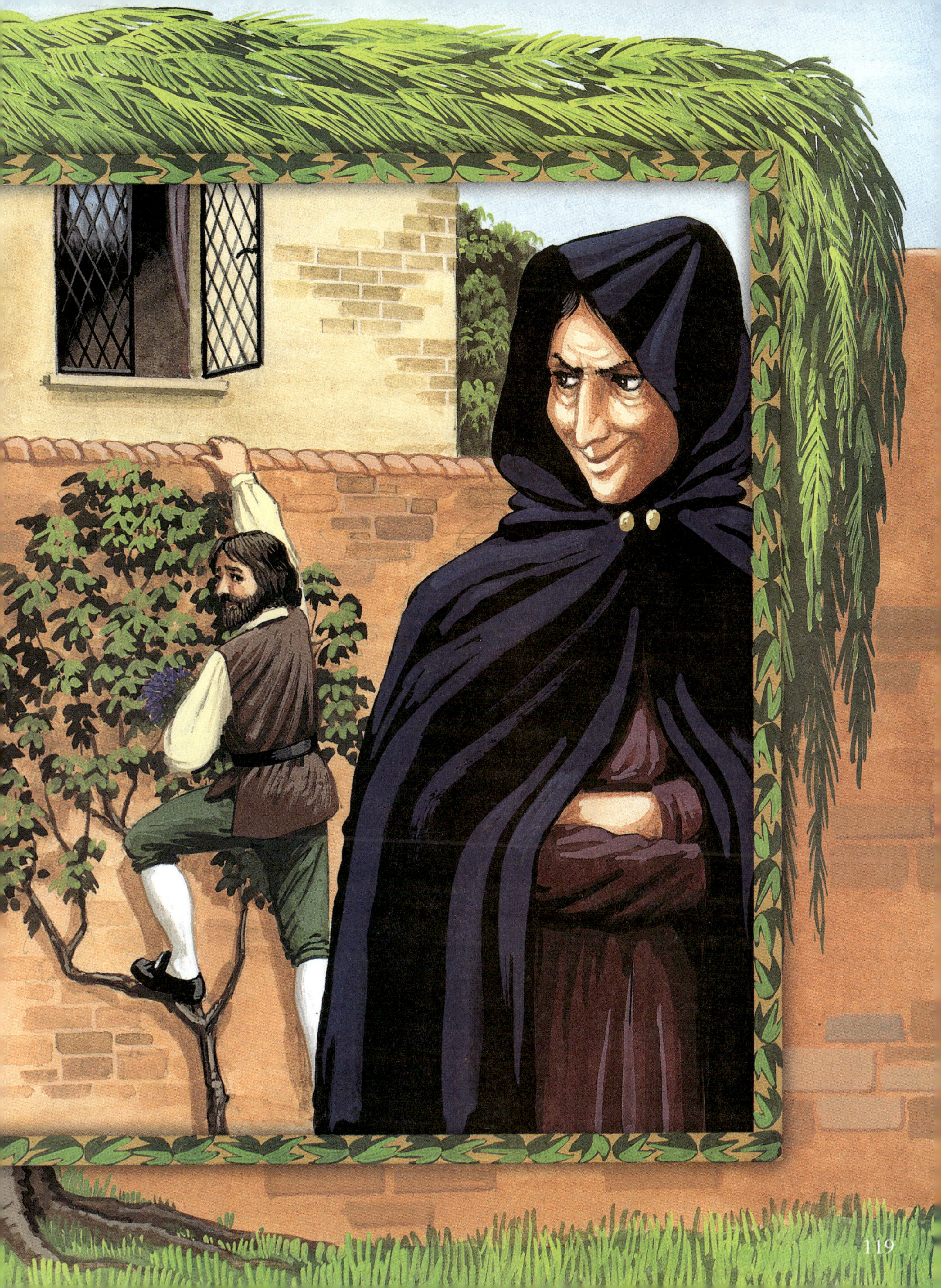

The minute the child was born, the witch appeared. She named the baby girl Rapunzel and took her away.

The witch had never before cared for anyone. But she loved Rapunzel deeply. Rapunzel grew into a beautiful child. Her eyes sparkled, and her cheeks glowed. Her long, golden hair fell in lovely waves.

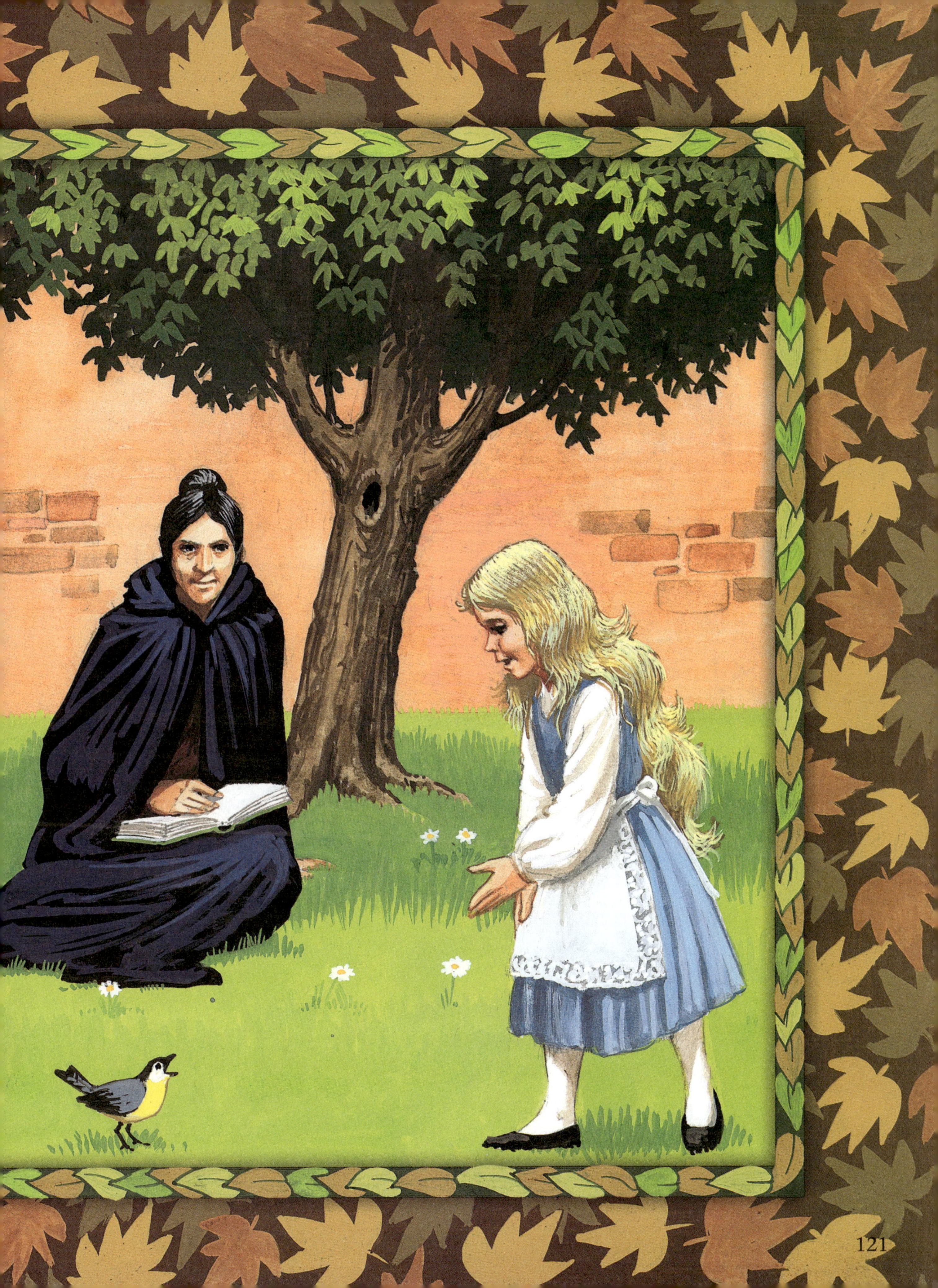

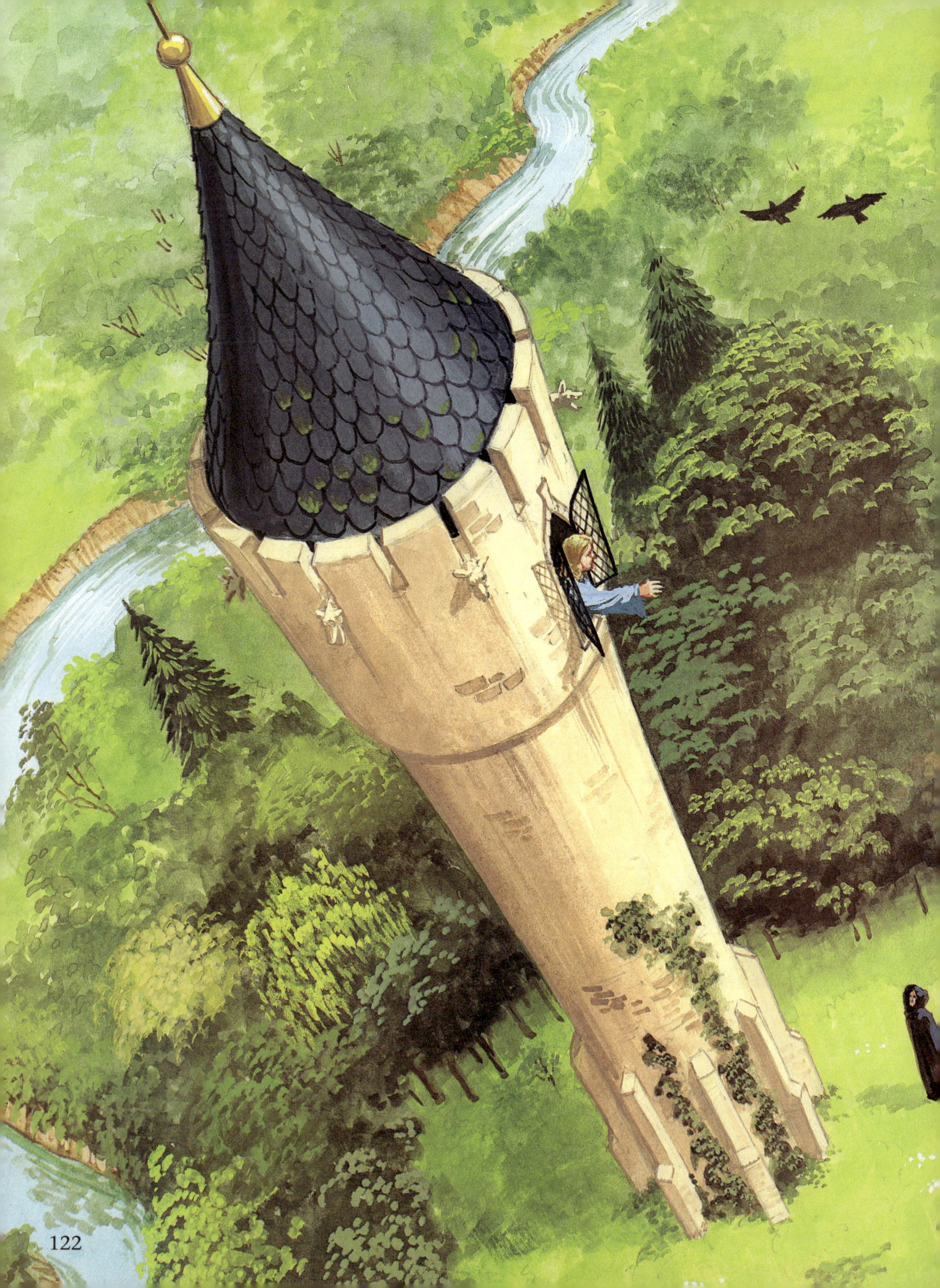

Years passed, and the witch feared Rapunzel would someday leave her. So she decided to lock Rapunzel away from the world. She took her to a tower deep in the forest. The tower had no door and only a single window at the very top.

For years, Rapunzel lived alone in the tower. The witch visited each day. She would stand below the window and call out, "Rapunzel! Rapunzel! Let down your hair!"

The girl would unpin her long, lovely braids and wind them around the window hook. Then she would let them tumble to the ground. The witch would then climb up the braids to the window.

For hours each day while she was alone, Rapunzel sang to the forest birds. One day, a prince rode through the forest. He stopped when he heard singing. It was the sweetest, yet saddest, voice he had ever heard.

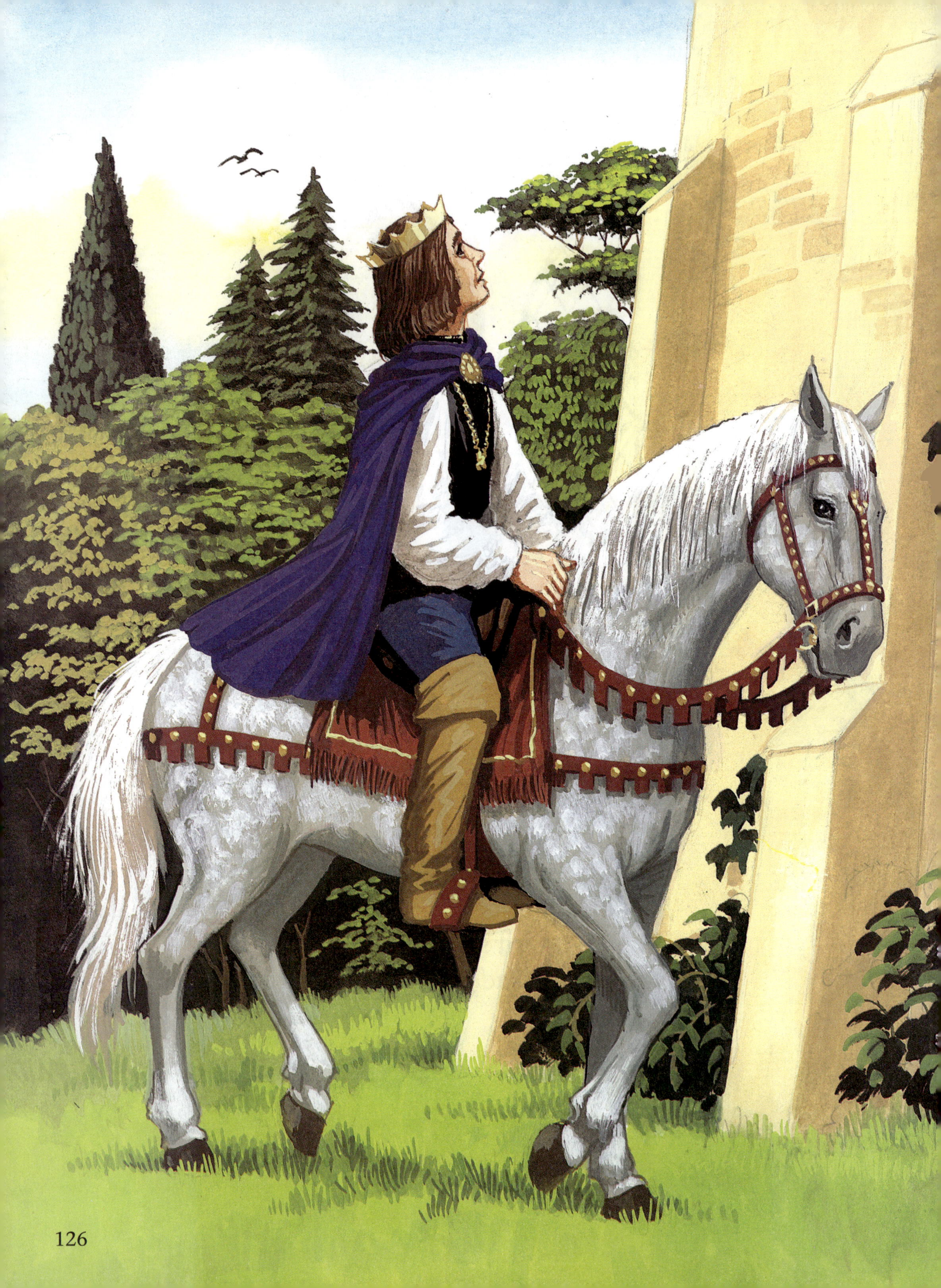

The prince wanted to see who was singing. He circled the tower but found no way in. At last, he gave up and rode back to his palace.

The prince kept thinking about the beautiful voice. He returned to the forest day after day to find out who was singing.

One day, the prince caught sight of the witch. He stayed behind a tree and listened.

"Rapunzel! Rapunzel! Let down your hair!" the witch called. Now, the prince knew what he needed to do.

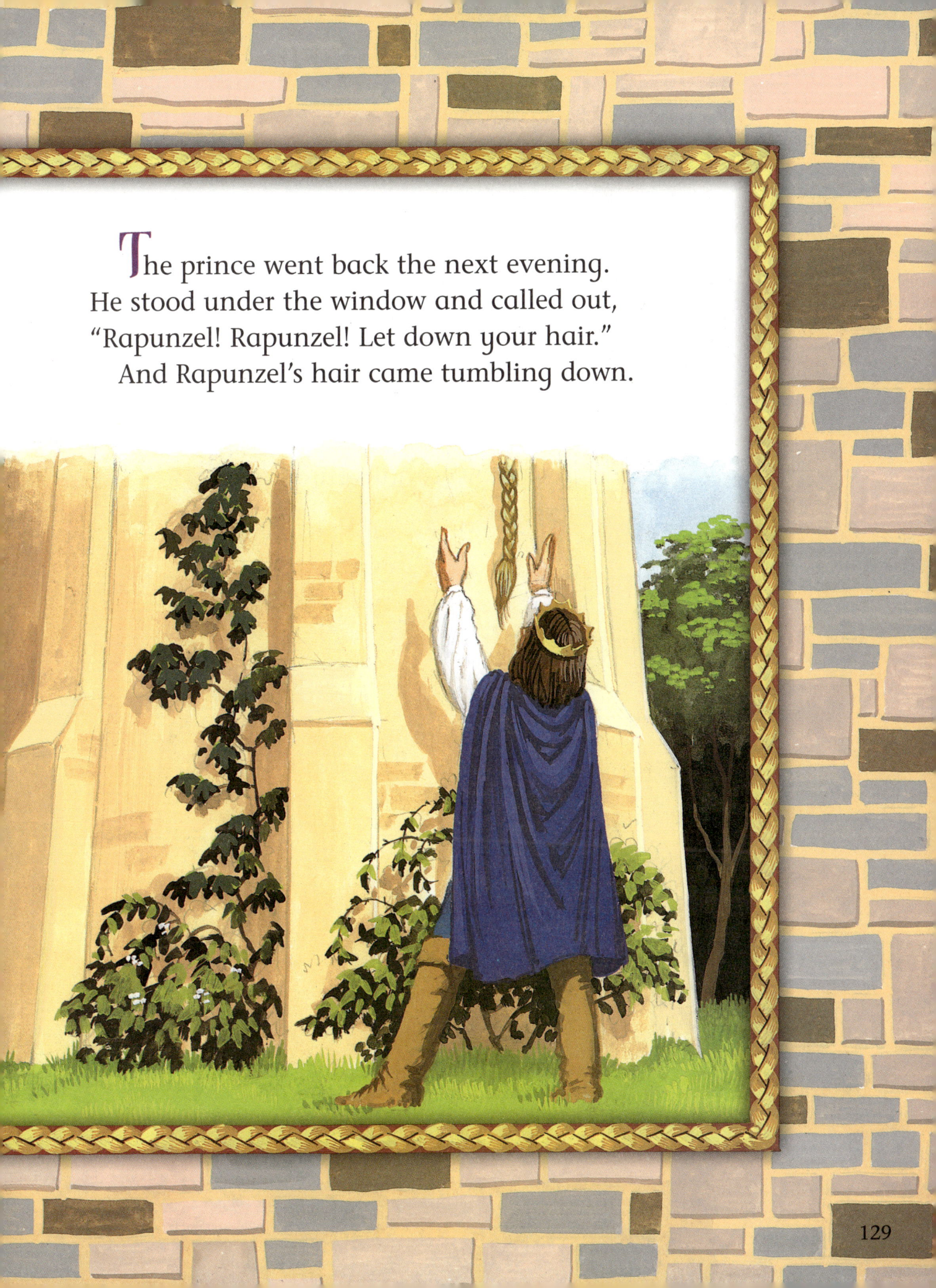

The prince went back the next evening. He stood under the window and called out, "Rapunzel! Rapunzel! Let down your hair."
And Rapunzel's hair came tumbling down.

The prince climbed up and stepped into the tower. At first, Rapunzel was quite afraid. She had never seen a man before.

But the prince was very kind. The two of them talked for hours and fell deeply in love. They were married in the tower that very night.

131

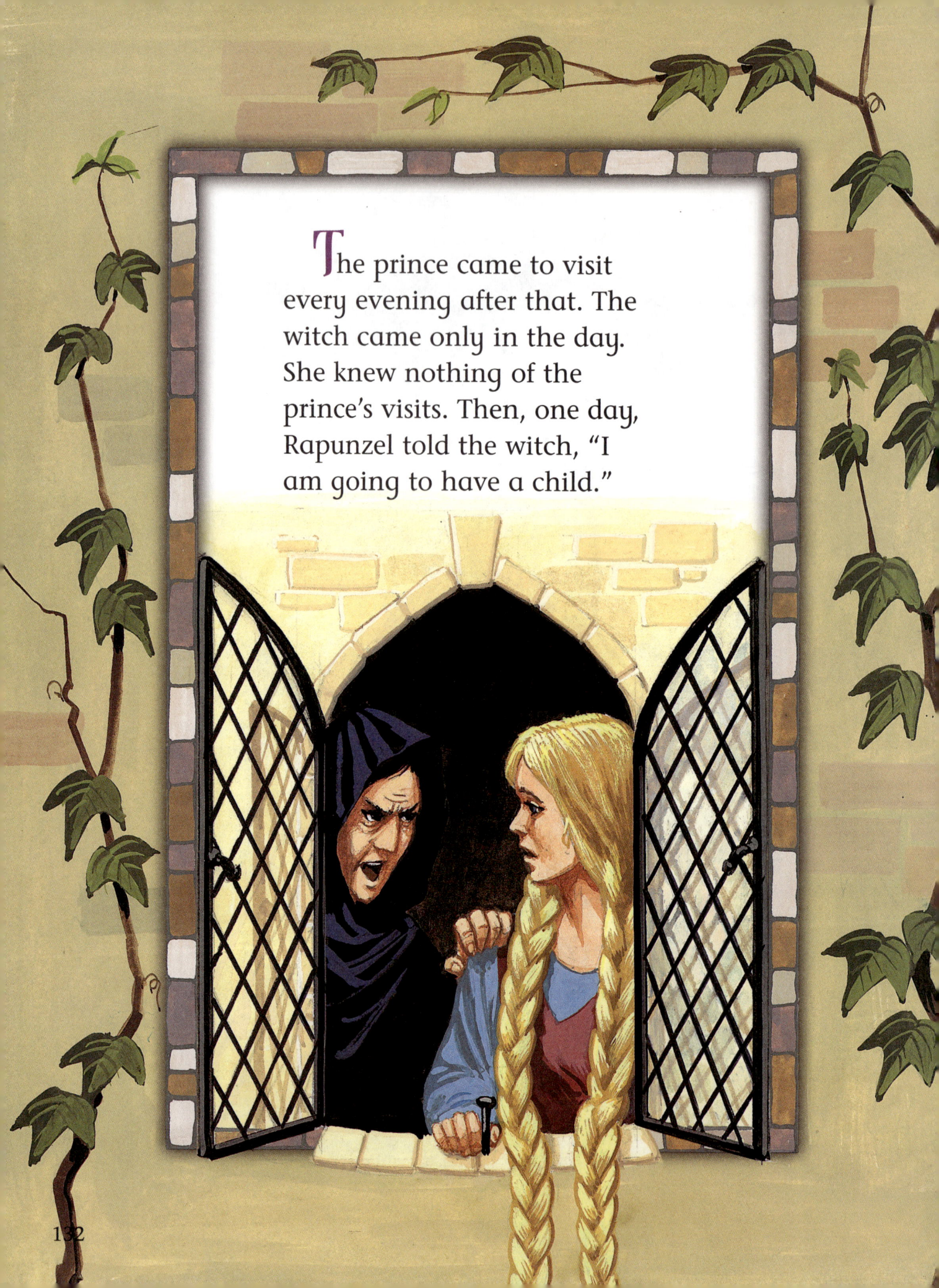

The prince came to visit every evening after that. The witch came only in the day. She knew nothing of the prince's visits. Then, one day, Rapunzel told the witch, "I am going to have a child."

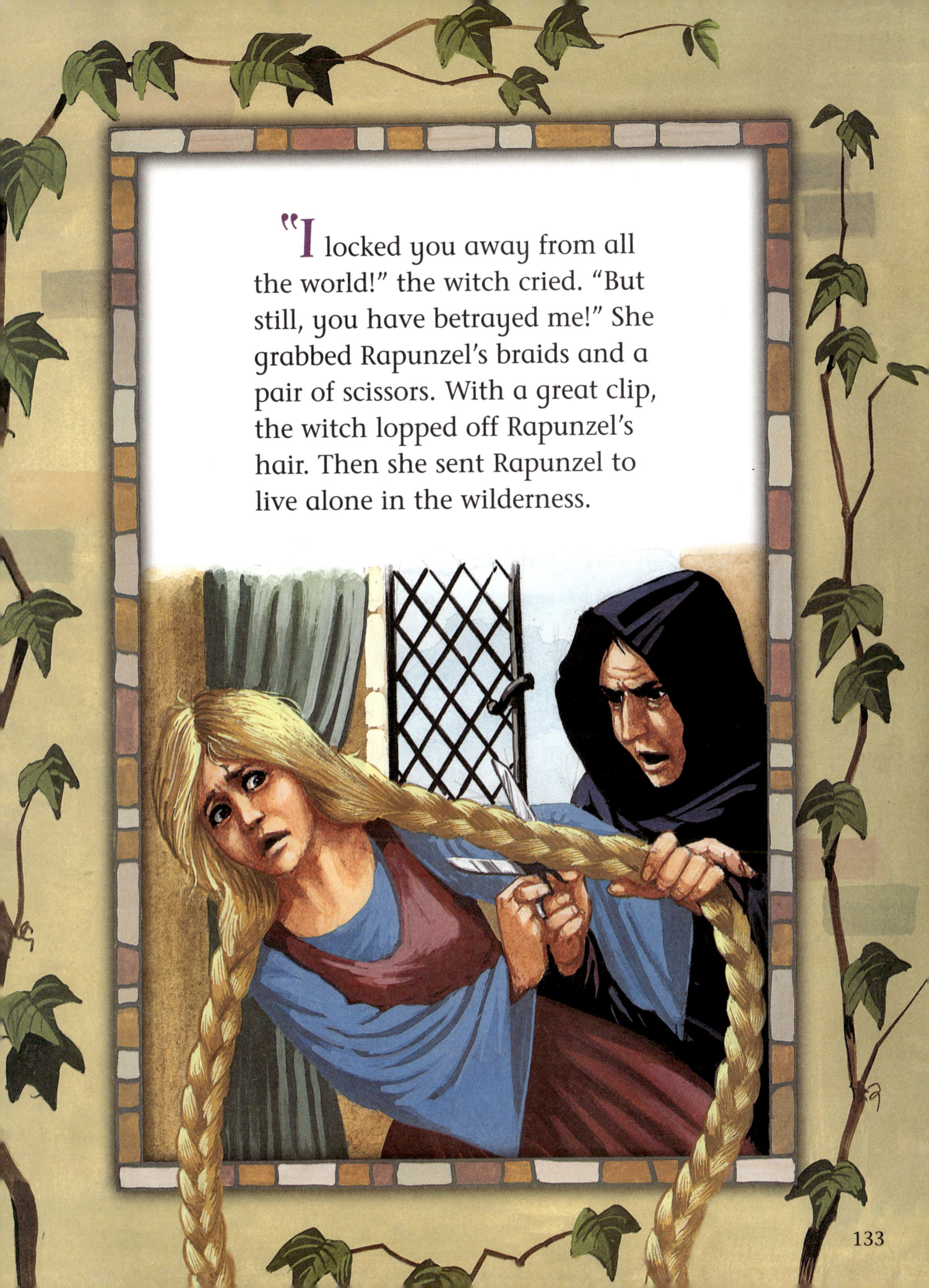

"I locked you away from all the world!" the witch cried. "But still, you have betrayed me!" She grabbed Rapunzel's braids and a pair of scissors. With a great clip, the witch lopped off Rapunzel's hair. Then she sent Rapunzel to live alone in the wilderness.

That night, the prince came to see Rapunzel as always. He called out, "Rapunzel! Rapunzel! Let down your hair." The braids fell down the side of the tower as always.

The prince climbed up, but when he got to the top, the witch was waiting.

"So, you have come to see your darling?" cackled the witch. "Well, she is lost to you forever! And now, you are lost, too!"

135

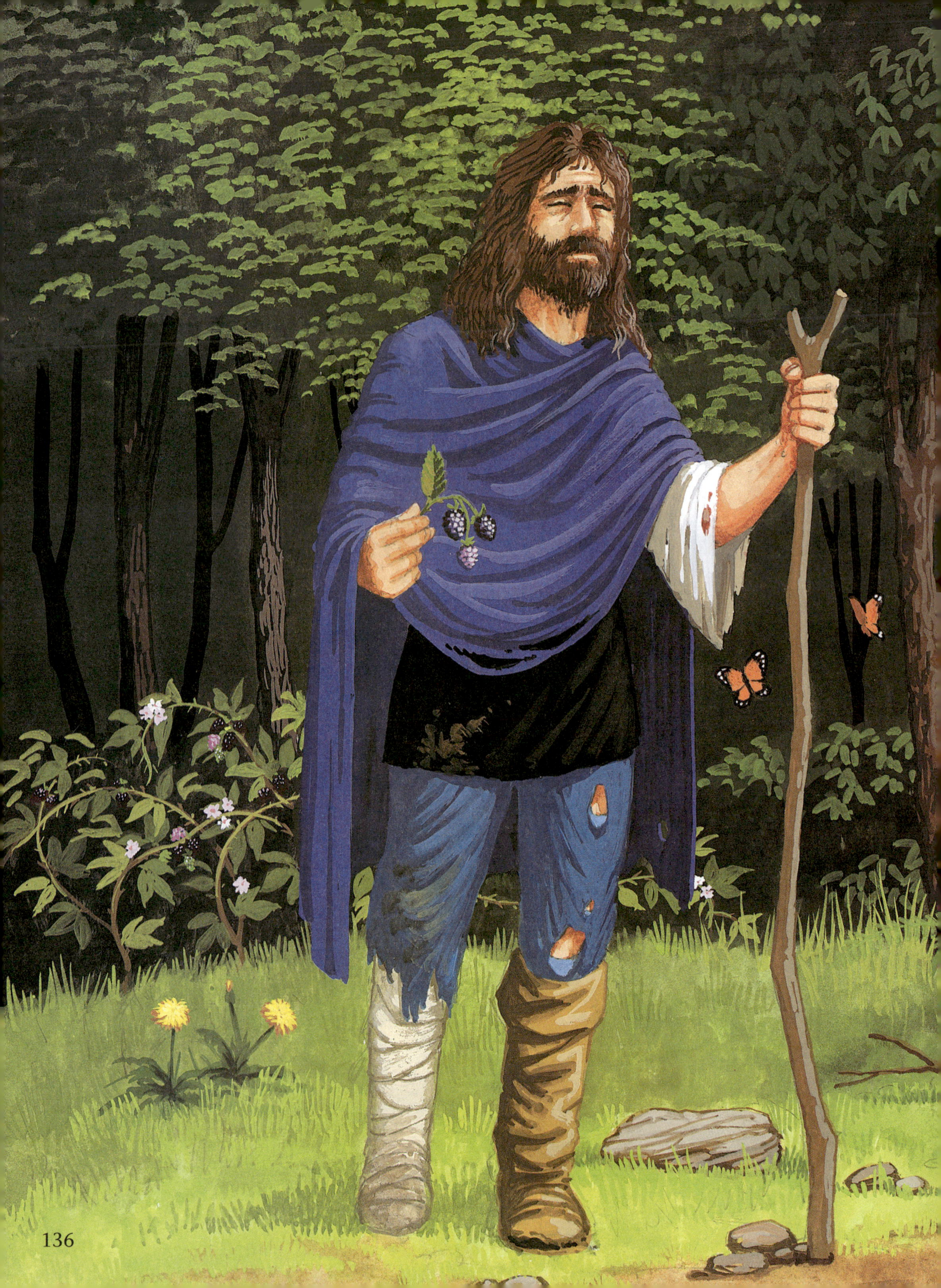

The witch let go of the braids, and the prince fell from the tower. He landed in a bed of thorny brambles which blinded him.

Blind and broken-hearted, the prince stumbled through the forest for a year. One day, by chance, he came upon the wild place where Rapunzel was living.

There, the prince heard a voice singing. It sounded to him both beautiful and dear, and he rushed toward it. When Rapunzel saw the prince, she swept him into her arms, weeping. Her tears fell into his eyes. At once, the prince's eyesight returned to him.

The prince gazed at Rapunzel. And just beyond her, he saw their two children. In the wilderness, Rapunzel had given birth to twins—a boy and a girl.

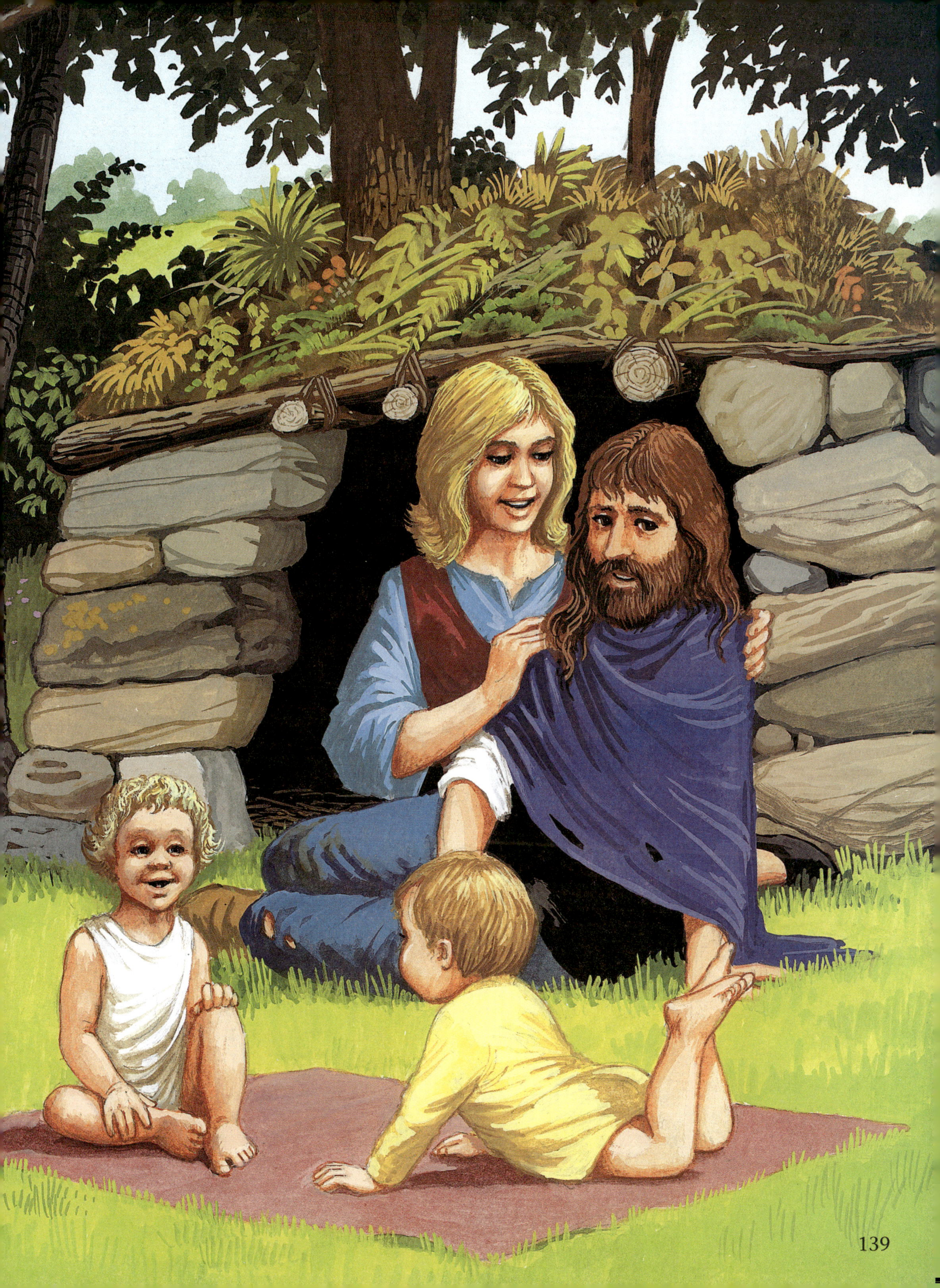

The prince hugged his children. Then he and Rapunzel joyfully carried them out of the wilderness and back to the prince's kingdom. And there they lived happily ever after.

Bibliography
"Rapunzel"

Grimm, Jacob and Wilhelm. *Rapunzel*. Retold and illustrated by Paul O. Zelinsky. New York: Dutton, 1997. The beautiful Renaissance-style art illustrating this well-researched classic tale won it the 1998 Caldecott Medal. This annual award is given to the illustrator of the year's most distinguished American picture book for children.

Vozar, David. *Rapunzel: A Happenin' Rap*. New York: Doubleday, 1998. This updated version of the classic tale is set in the big city and retold in a fresh rap beat. The wild, bright illustrations by Betsy Lewin match the tone perfectly.

Rogasky, Barbara. *The Water of Life: A Tale from the Brothers Grimm*. New York: Holiday, 1986. In this tale, illustrated by Trina Schart Hyman, a prince tries to save his dying father by finding the water of life. During his search, the prince encounters an enchanted castle and a beautiful princess.

Grimes, Nikki. *Wild, Wild Hair*. New York: Scholastic, 1996. Rapunzel is not the only character with hair problems! Tisa decides to hide one Monday when it's time to have her hard-to-manage hair combed. When eventually her hair is done, she loves it so much she can hardly stop looking at it!

Madrigal, Antonio Hernández. *Erandi's Braids*. New York: Putnam, 1999. Hair becomes very significant to the Mexican family in this tale illustrated by Tomie dePaola. Mamá needs money to buy a new fishing net, so she tries to sell her hair for making wigs. Her hair is too short, though, so Erandi unselfishly offers her own beautiful braids.

About "The Little Mermaid"

Hans Christian Andersen's 156 fairy tales are some of the most popular children's stories in the world. They have been translated into more than 100 languages.

Many elements of Andersen's own life show up in his writing. He was born and raised in Odense, off the coast of Denmark. Andersen's father was a poor cobbler and his mother a washerwoman. But Andersen's life was rich with literature. His father loved to tell folk tales and to read to his son from *The Arabian Nights*.

Andersen left home at the age of 14 and worked as an actor in the Royal Theater in Copenhagen. He sang songs and performed scenes from plays by Danish playwrights. What he saw there was very different from his own home, and the experience inspired some of his writing.

"The Little Mermaid," first published in 1837, is just one of Andersen's tales that featured the ocean and royalty. Two other themes in the story that may reflect Andersen's life are feeling like an outsider and being unlucky in love. Parts of the story can be connected to Danish folklore and Norse myth, but the characters, the setting, and specific events are Andersen's invention.

The story of "The Little Mermaid" is so popular that a statue of the Little Mermaid stands today on the waterfront in Copenhagen, the capital of Denmark.

Retold by Melissa Blackwell Burke

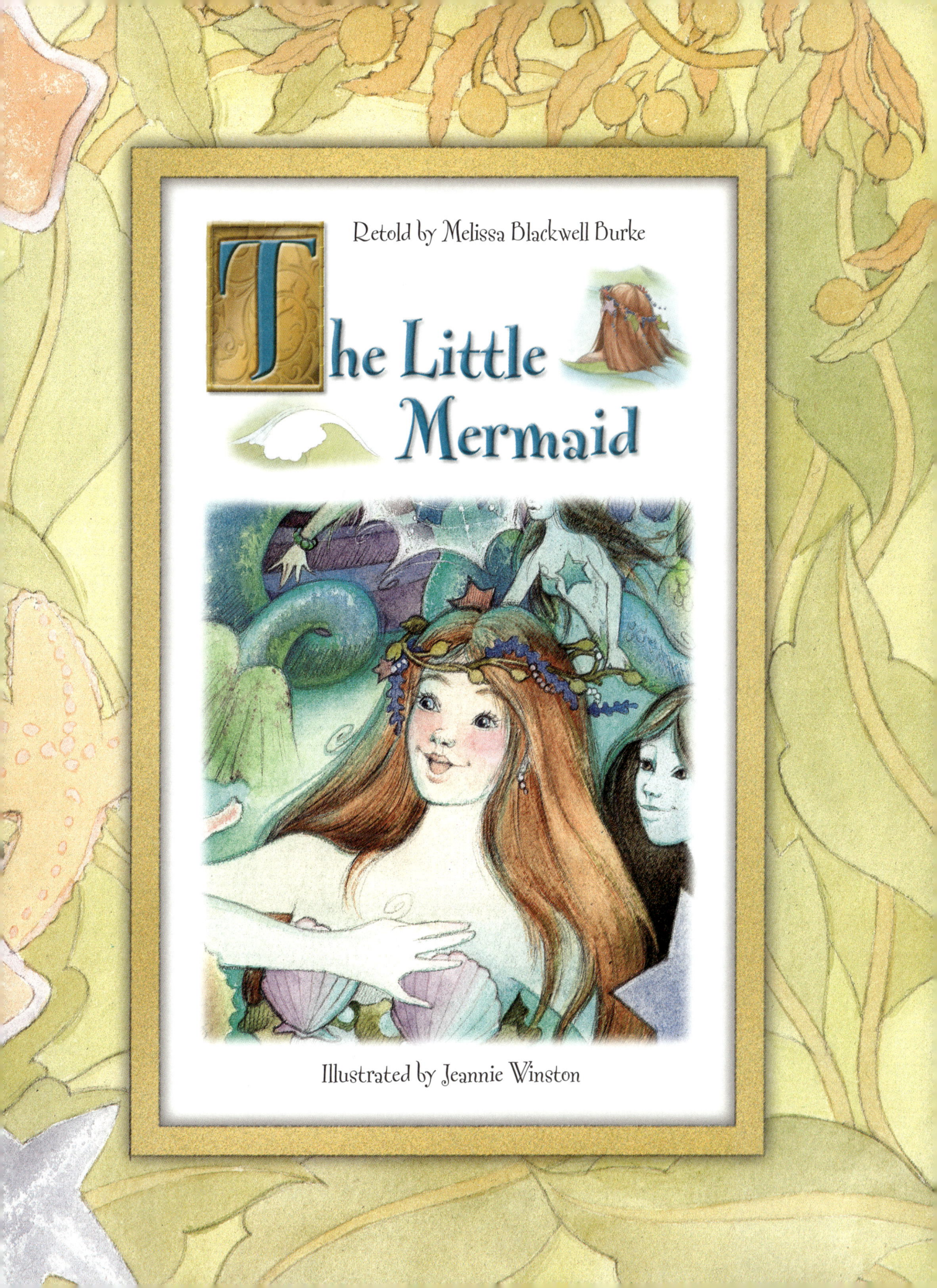

The Little Mermaid

Illustrated by Jeannie Winston

Out where the sea is deep and blue, the Sea King ruled. He lived there with his six beautiful mermaid daughters. The Sea King's wise mother lived with them, too. She helped with the young mermaids.

The youngest mermaid was the prettiest of all. Like all mermaids, she had no legs. Instead, her body ended in a fish's tail. Her skin was rosy and her eyes were the deepest of blues. Her voice was the most beautiful ever heard.

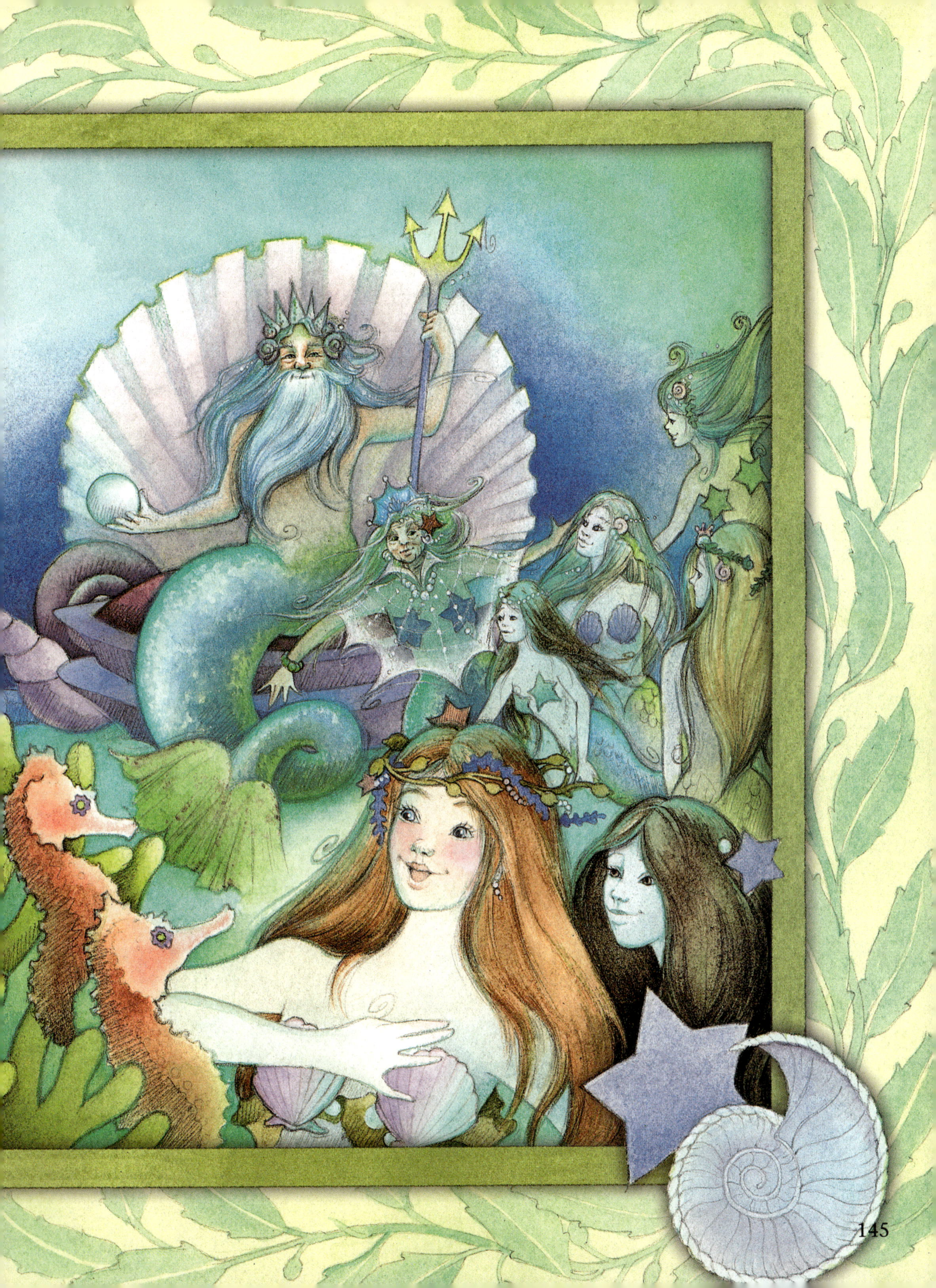

The Little Mermaid often sang with her sisters. All day long, they sang and played. In the evening, they listened to their grandmother tell stories. The Little Mermaid especially loved the tales of life above the sea, where there were stars and flowers and trees.

"When you are fifteen, you may swim to the top," her grandmother said. "You can sit in the moonlight and see for yourself."

The Little Mermaid could not wait to see land. She thought of little else except the wonderful sights to come.

Finally, the Little Mermaid's fifteenth birthday came. Her grandmother gave her a wreath of pearls. Then light as a bubble, the Little Mermaid rose to the surface.

The Little Mermaid raised her head above the waves. She swam near a big ship. She saw many people in fancy clothes. One handsome young man stood out from the crowd. He was a prince, celebrating his birthday.

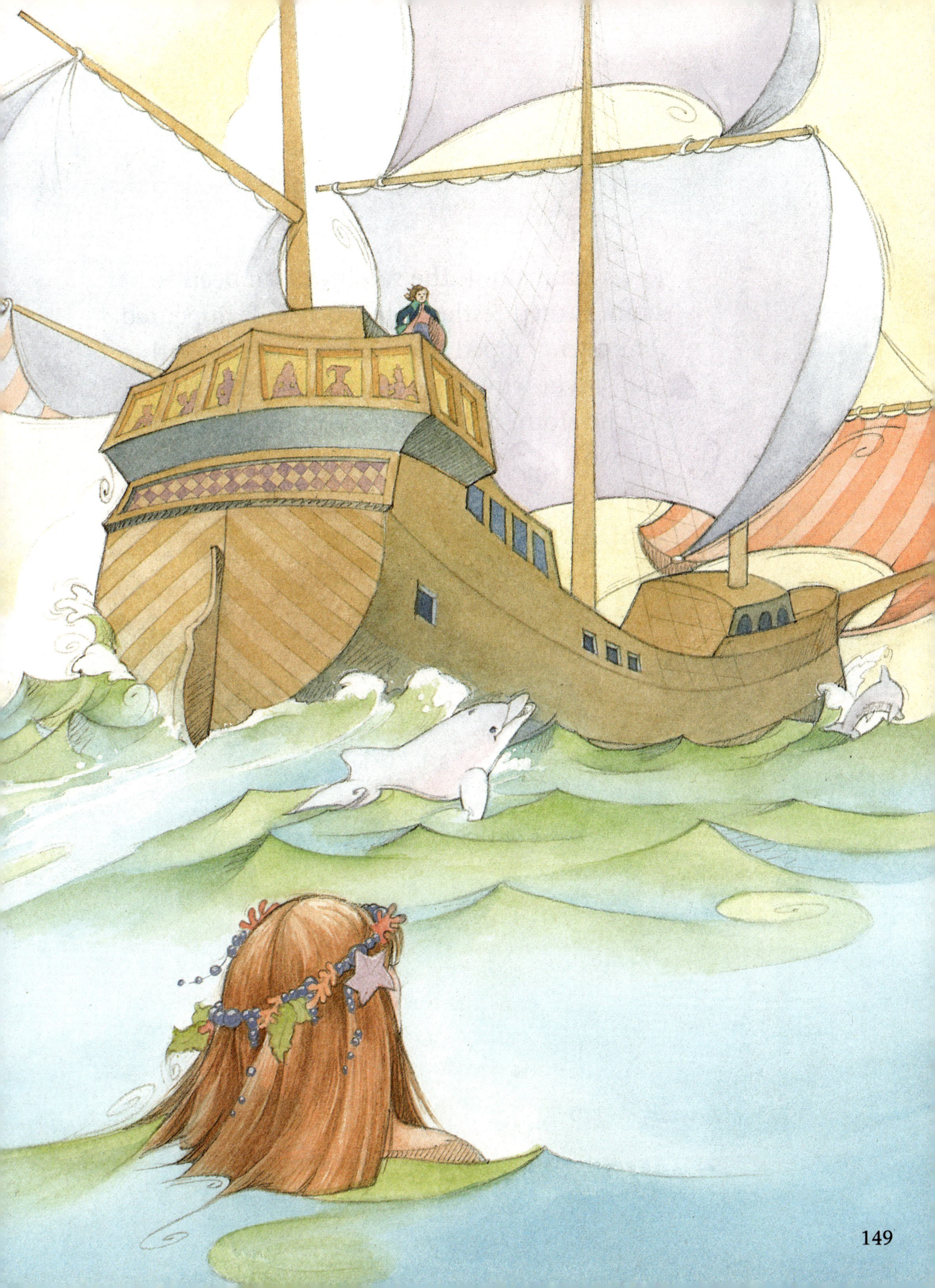

In an instant, the sea that had been so calm turned restless. Heavy clouds appeared. Thunder clapped. Lightning shot across the sky. Great waves began to pound the ship. As the storm raged, the ship's mast snapped in two.

The Little Mermaid saw the prince fall into the sea. She knew at once that she must save him. She dove deep into the water. At last, she found the prince and swam with him to the surface. She held his head above water.

The Little Mermaid let the waves carry them to the shore. She gently laid the prince on the sand. She kissed his forehead and dove back into the sea. The Little Mermaid waited behind some rocks. She wanted to make sure someone would come to help the prince.

Soon, a young woman hurried toward the prince. He sat up and smiled at the woman.

The Little Mermaid felt sad. The prince hadn't smiled at her. He didn't know that she had saved him. Full of sorrow, the Little Mermaid swam home.

Time passed, but the Little Mermaid was still sad when she thought about the prince. She found out that he lived in a palace by the sea. The Little Mermaid swam up each night to watch the prince. She grew even fonder of him.

The Little Mermaid longed to know more about the land above the sea. "Grandmother, do humans live forever?" she asked.

"People die, just as mermaids do," explained Grandmother. "But I've heard that a human soul lives on. Mermaids become foam on the water."

"How could I get a human soul?" asked the Little Mermaid.

"The only way is for a human to love you with all his heart," Grandmother said. "If you married, you would get a soul."

At that moment, the Little Mermaid knew what she wanted to do. She made her way to the Sea Witch's home where hundreds of sea snakes rolled around in the bubbling sand.

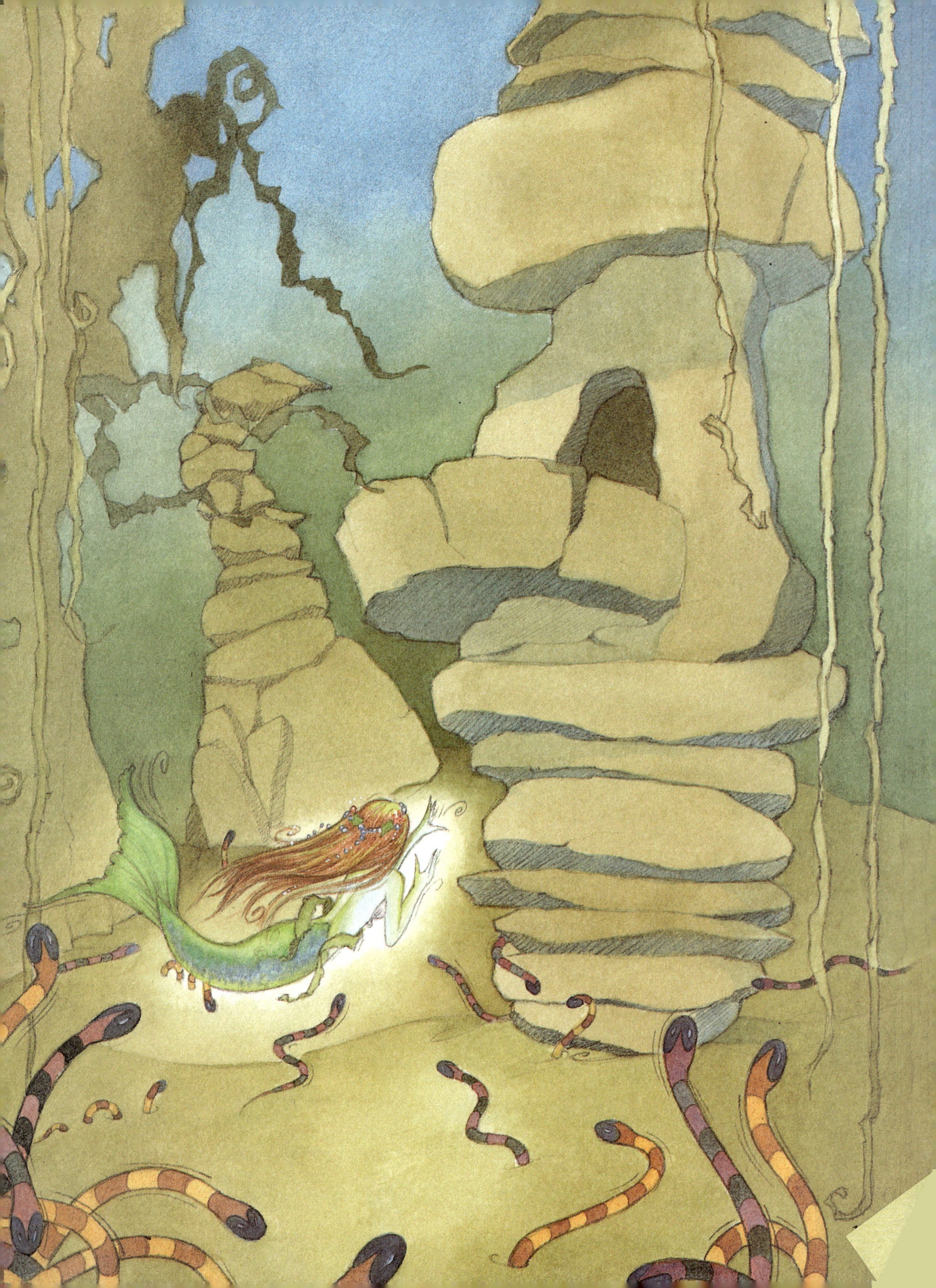

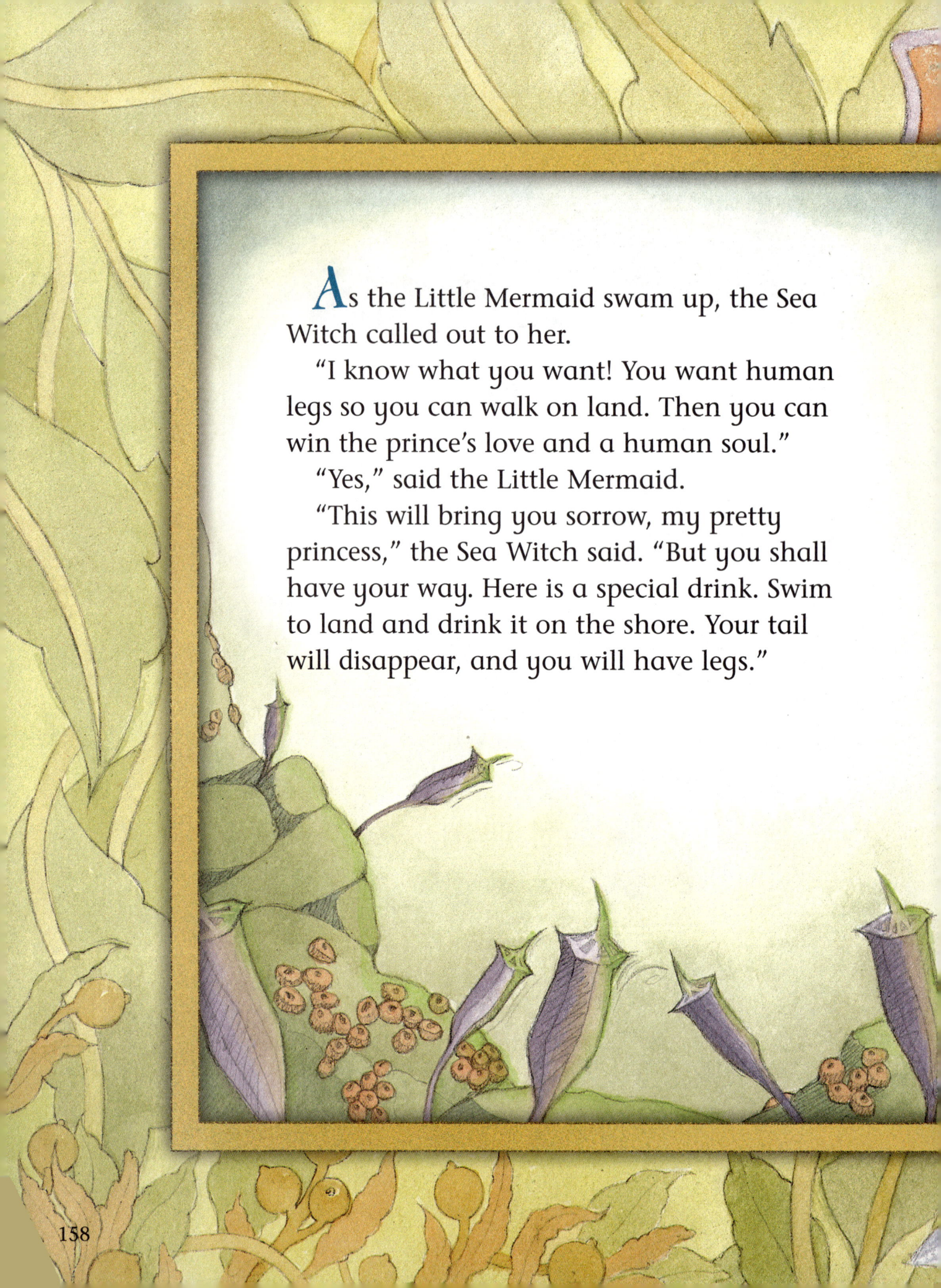

As the Little Mermaid swam up, the Sea Witch called out to her.

"I know what you want! You want human legs so you can walk on land. Then you can win the prince's love and a human soul."

"Yes," said the Little Mermaid.

"This will bring you sorrow, my pretty princess," the Sea Witch said. "But you shall have your way. Here is a special drink. Swim to land and drink it on the shore. Your tail will disappear, and you will have legs."

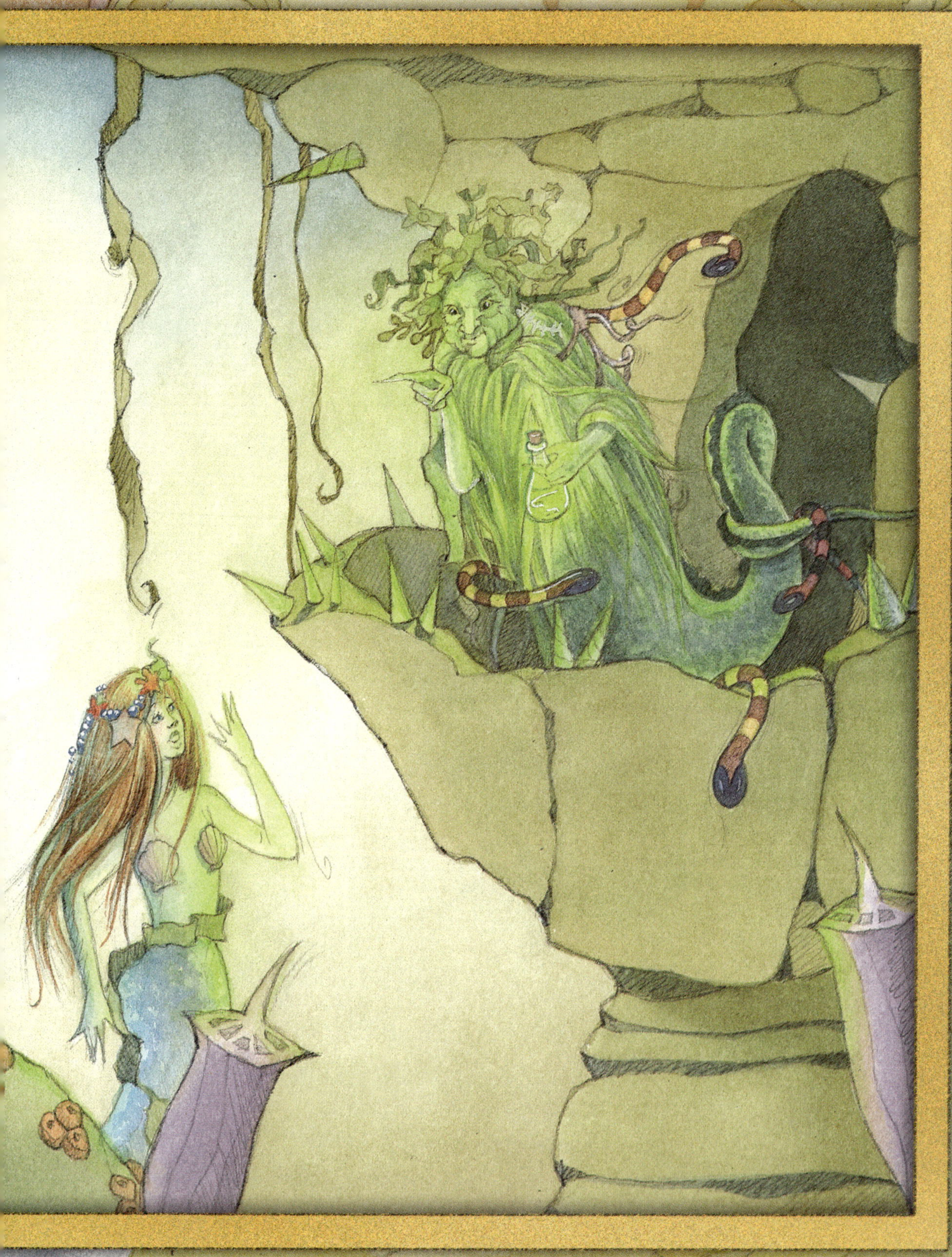

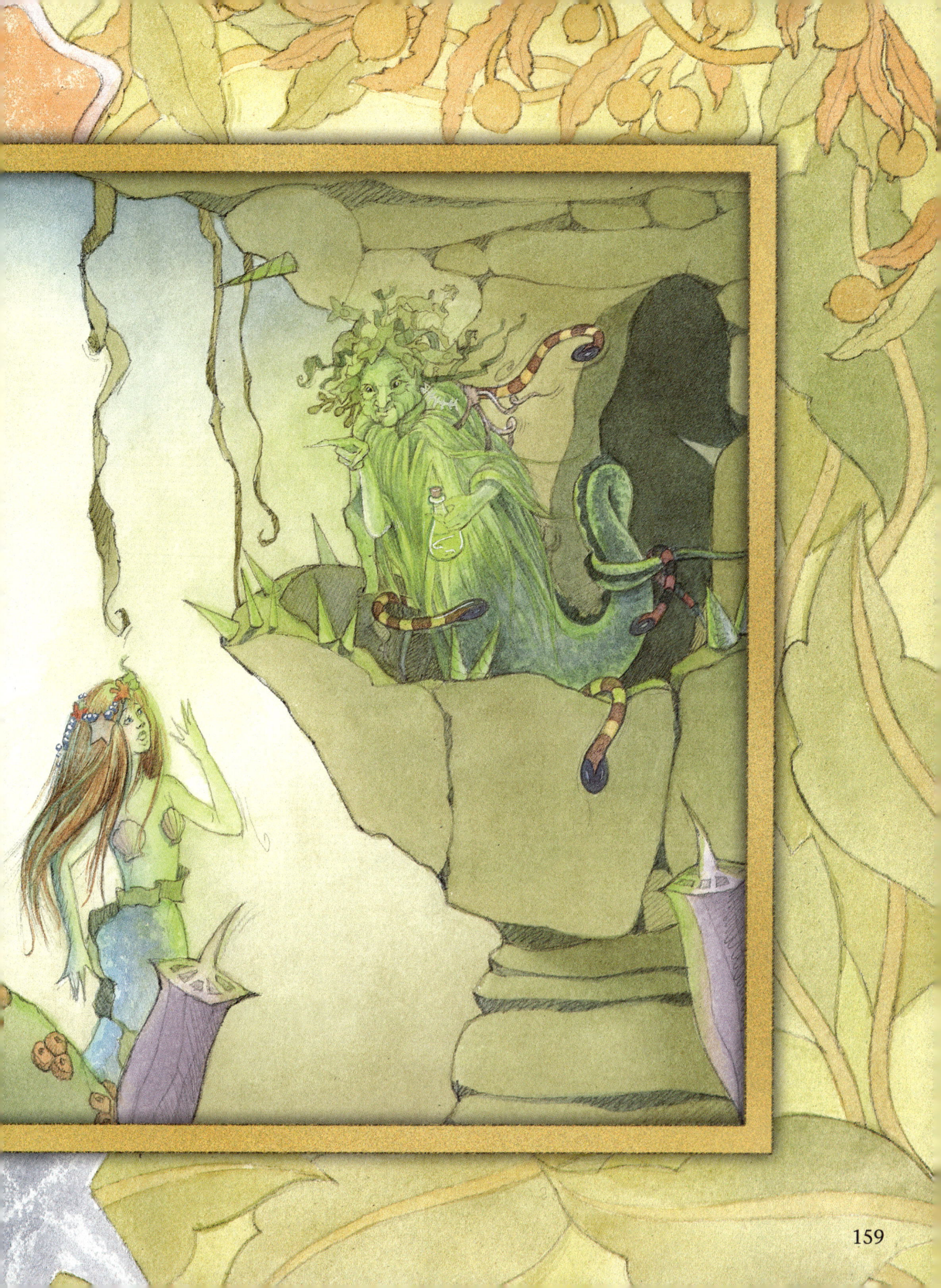

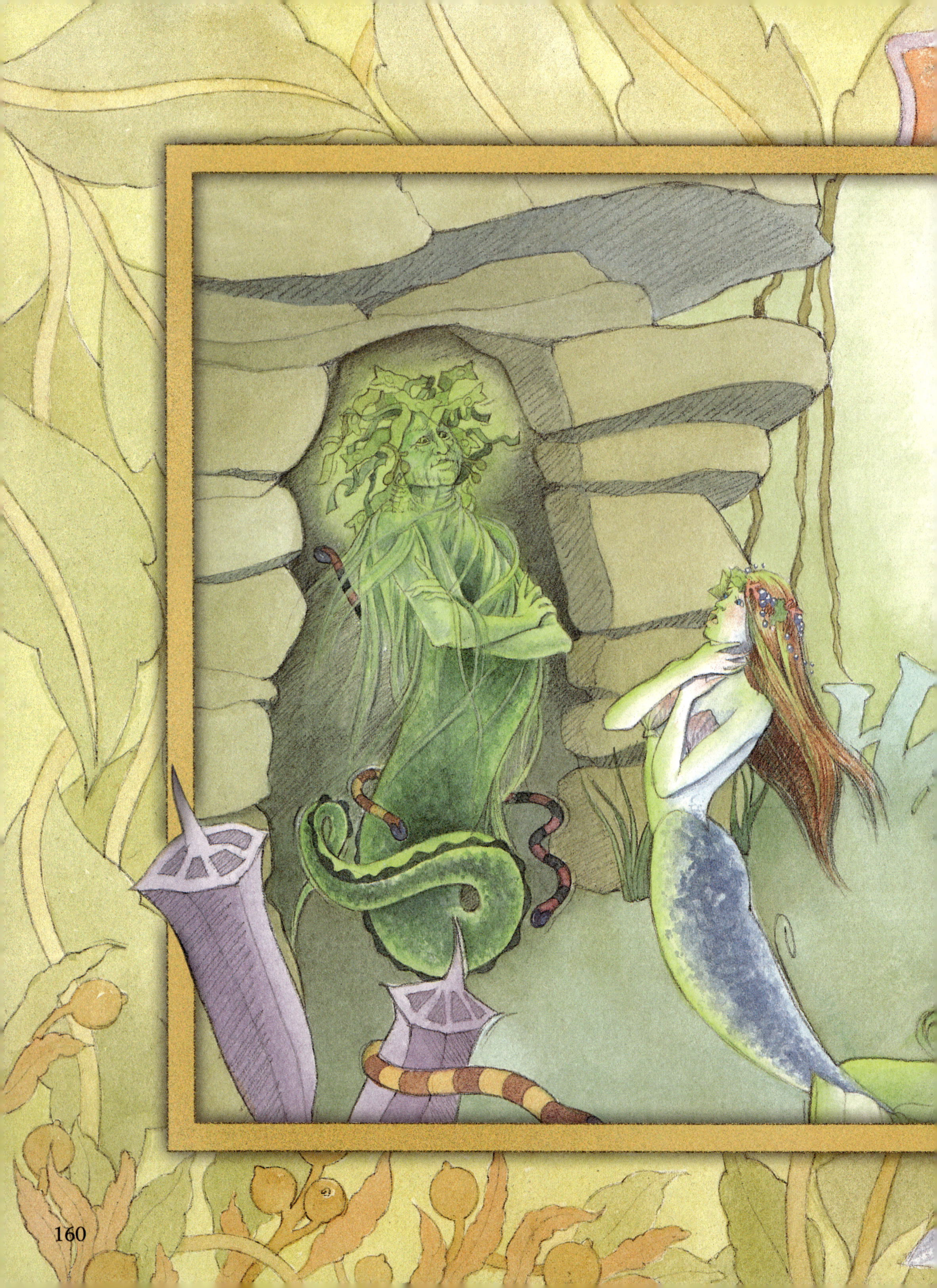

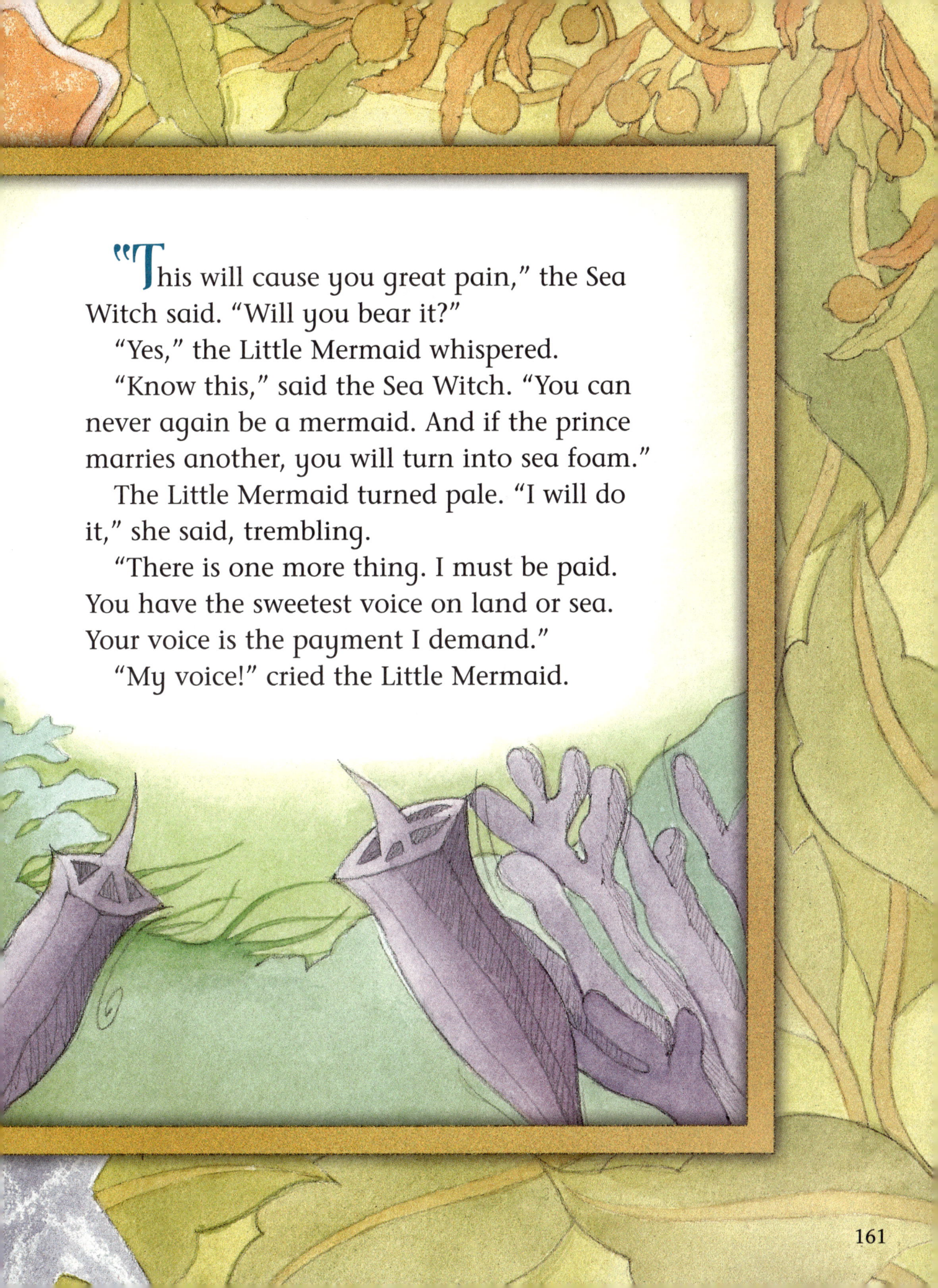

"This will cause you great pain," the Sea Witch said. "Will you bear it?"

"Yes," the Little Mermaid whispered.

"Know this," said the Sea Witch. "You can never again be a mermaid. And if the prince marries another, you will turn into sea foam."

The Little Mermaid turned pale. "I will do it," she said, trembling.

"There is one more thing. I must be paid. You have the sweetest voice on land or sea. Your voice is the payment I demand."

"My voice!" cried the Little Mermaid.

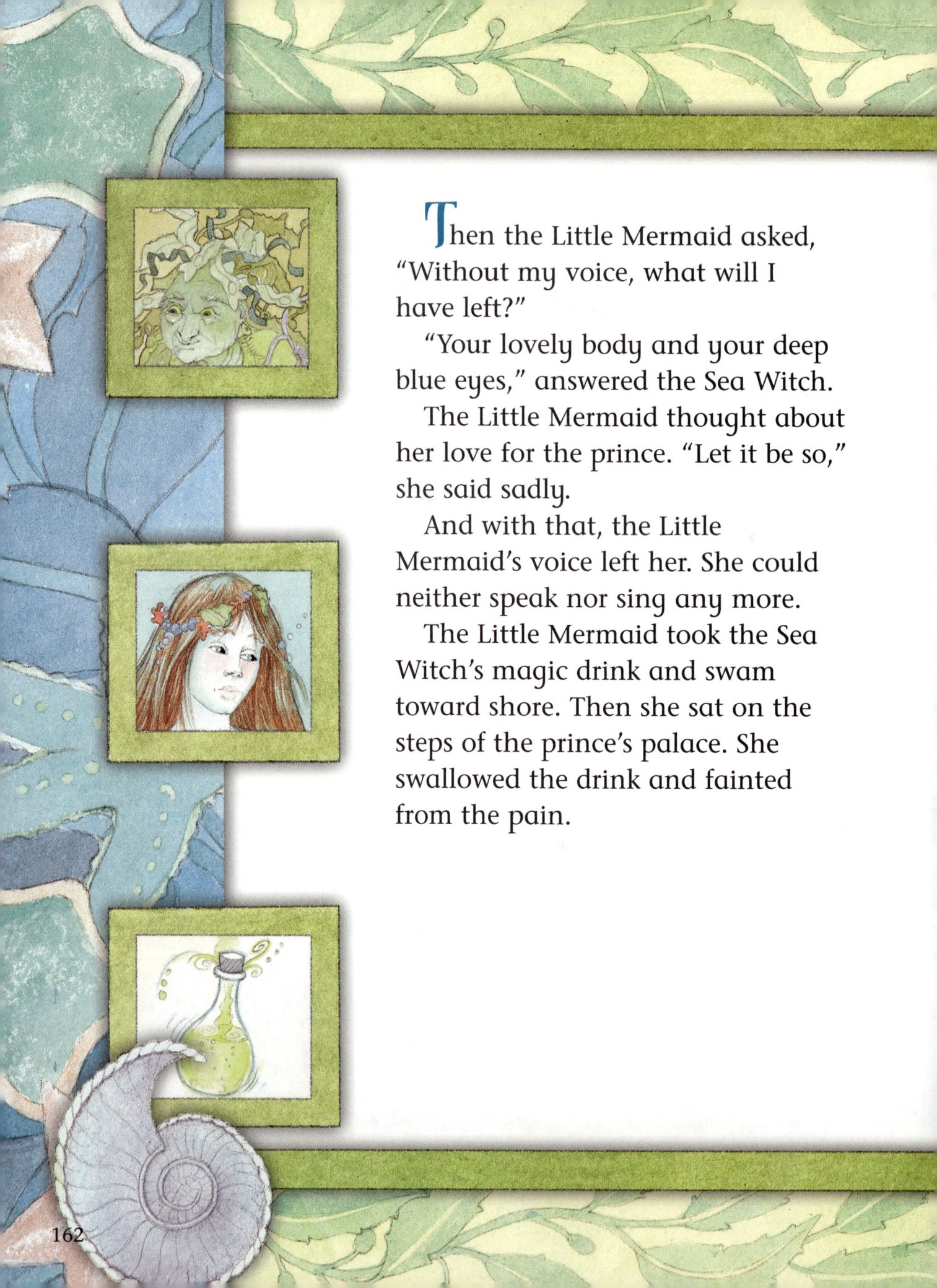

Then the Little Mermaid asked, "Without my voice, what will I have left?"

"Your lovely body and your deep blue eyes," answered the Sea Witch.

The Little Mermaid thought about her love for the prince. "Let it be so," she said sadly.

And with that, the Little Mermaid's voice left her. She could neither speak nor sing any more.

The Little Mermaid took the Sea Witch's magic drink and swam toward shore. Then she sat on the steps of the prince's palace. She swallowed the drink and fainted from the pain.

163

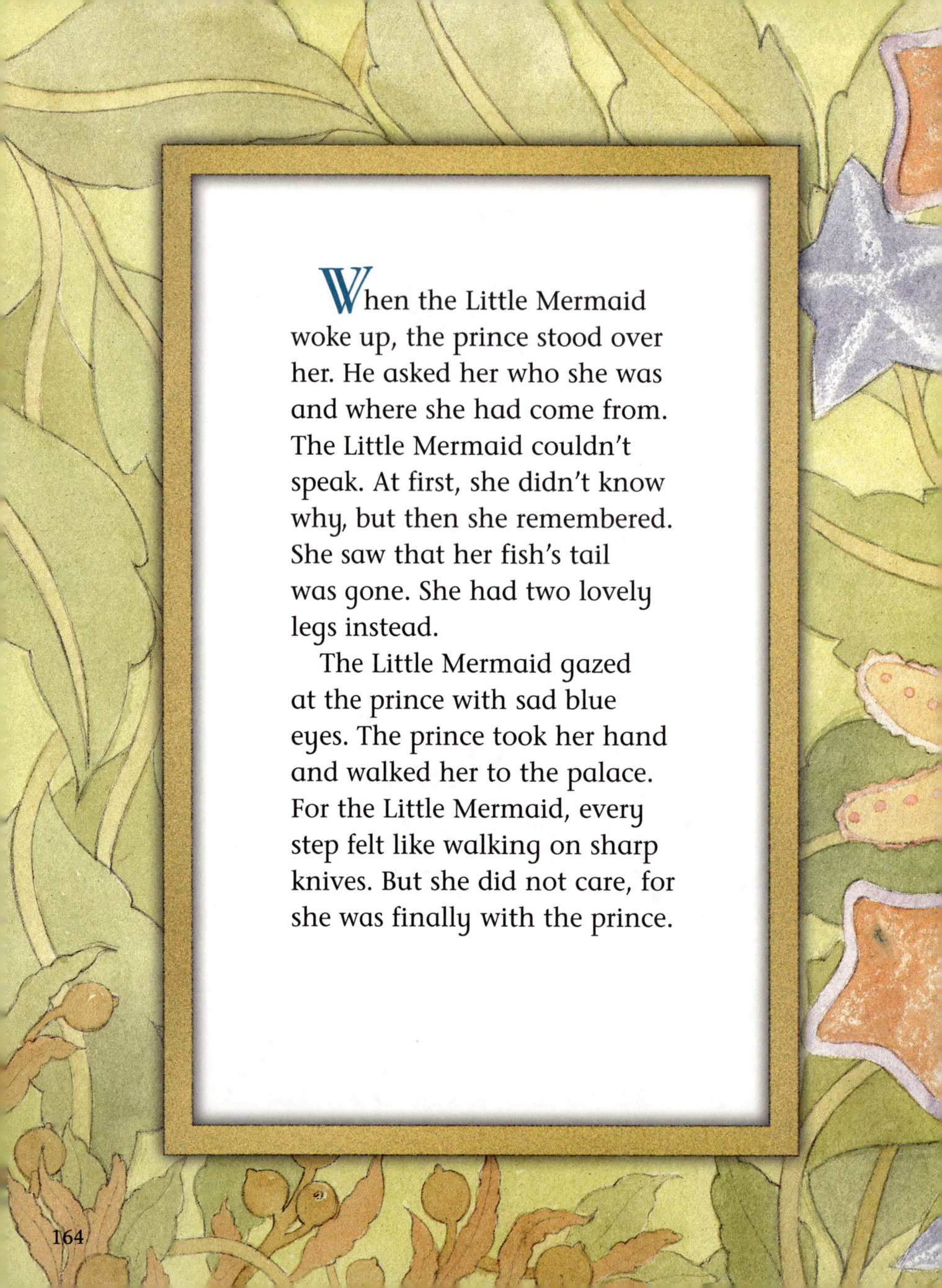

When the Little Mermaid woke up, the prince stood over her. He asked her who she was and where she had come from. The Little Mermaid couldn't speak. At first, she didn't know why, but then she remembered. She saw that her fish's tail was gone. She had two lovely legs instead.

The Little Mermaid gazed at the prince with sad blue eyes. The prince took her hand and walked her to the palace. For the Little Mermaid, every step felt like walking on sharp knives. But she did not care, for she was finally with the prince.

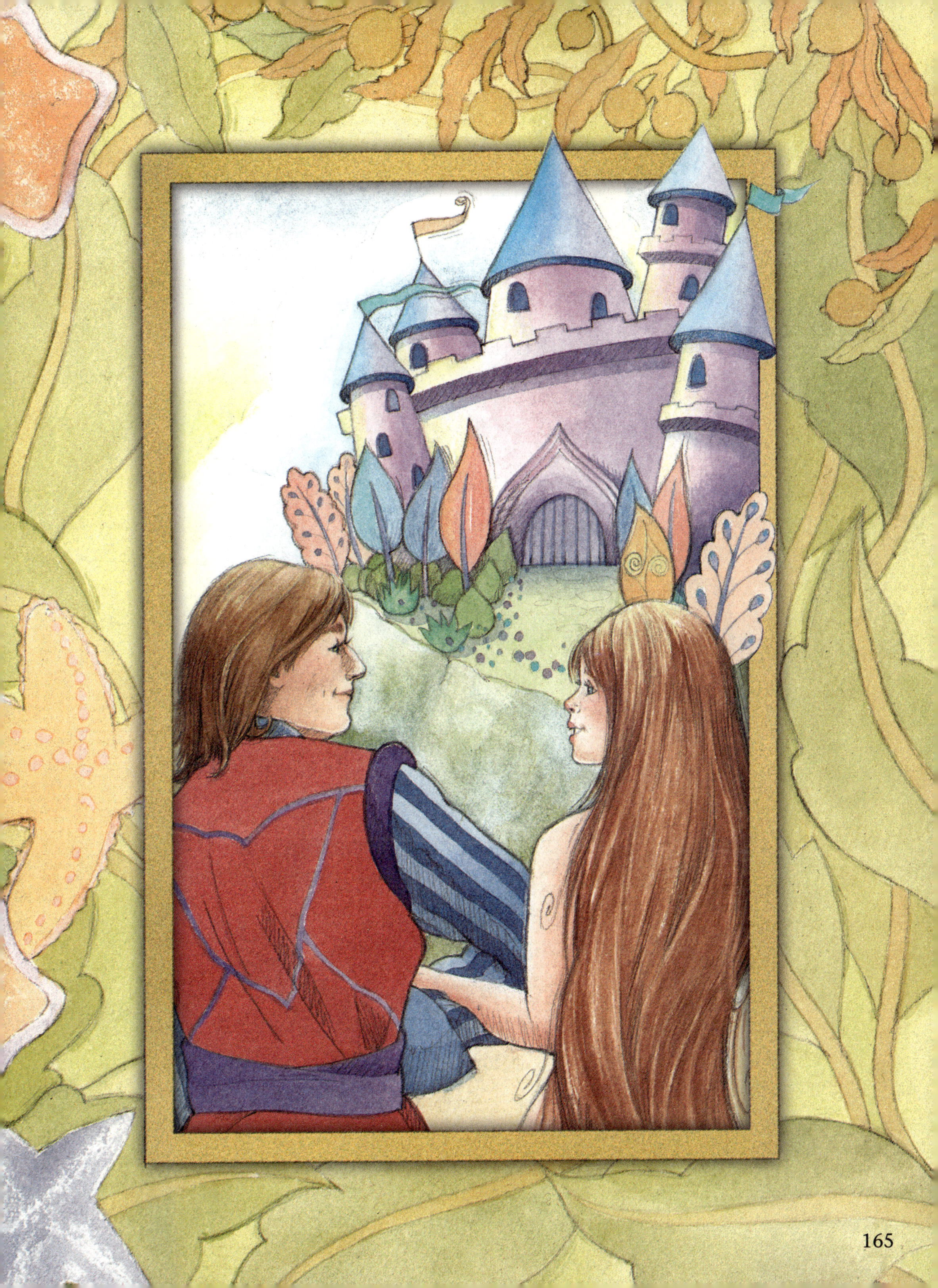

As time passed, the mermaid and the prince spent every day together. They rode horses. They climbed mountains to look down at the clouds. Each and every step caused the mermaid great pain. Yet the prince knew nothing of this.

The prince grew very fond of the Little Mermaid. "You are like the woman who saved me," he said. "She is the only one in the world I can ever love."

The mermaid wished the prince knew who had really saved him. She sighed.

Very soon, the royal family wanted the prince to marry. They chose a princess from the next kingdom for him.

The prince sailed to the neighboring kingdom. He took the Little Mermaid on board the ship with him.

When the prince met the princess, he was amazed. "It is you!" he cried. "The one who saved me! Oh, I am too happy."

He turned to the Little Mermaid. "I know you will be happy for me."

The Little Mermaid felt her heart break.

169

The royal wedding was grand. But, the Little Mermaid did not hear the joyful music. She did not see the beauty around her. The Little Mermaid could think only of all she had lost. She knew that very soon she would turn into sea foam.

That night, everyone went on the royal ship. The Little Mermaid stared out at the sea. Just then, her sisters rose up out of the water.

"We bring a message from the Sea Witch," they said. "If you kill the prince, you may return to us. Please, do it! Hurry!"

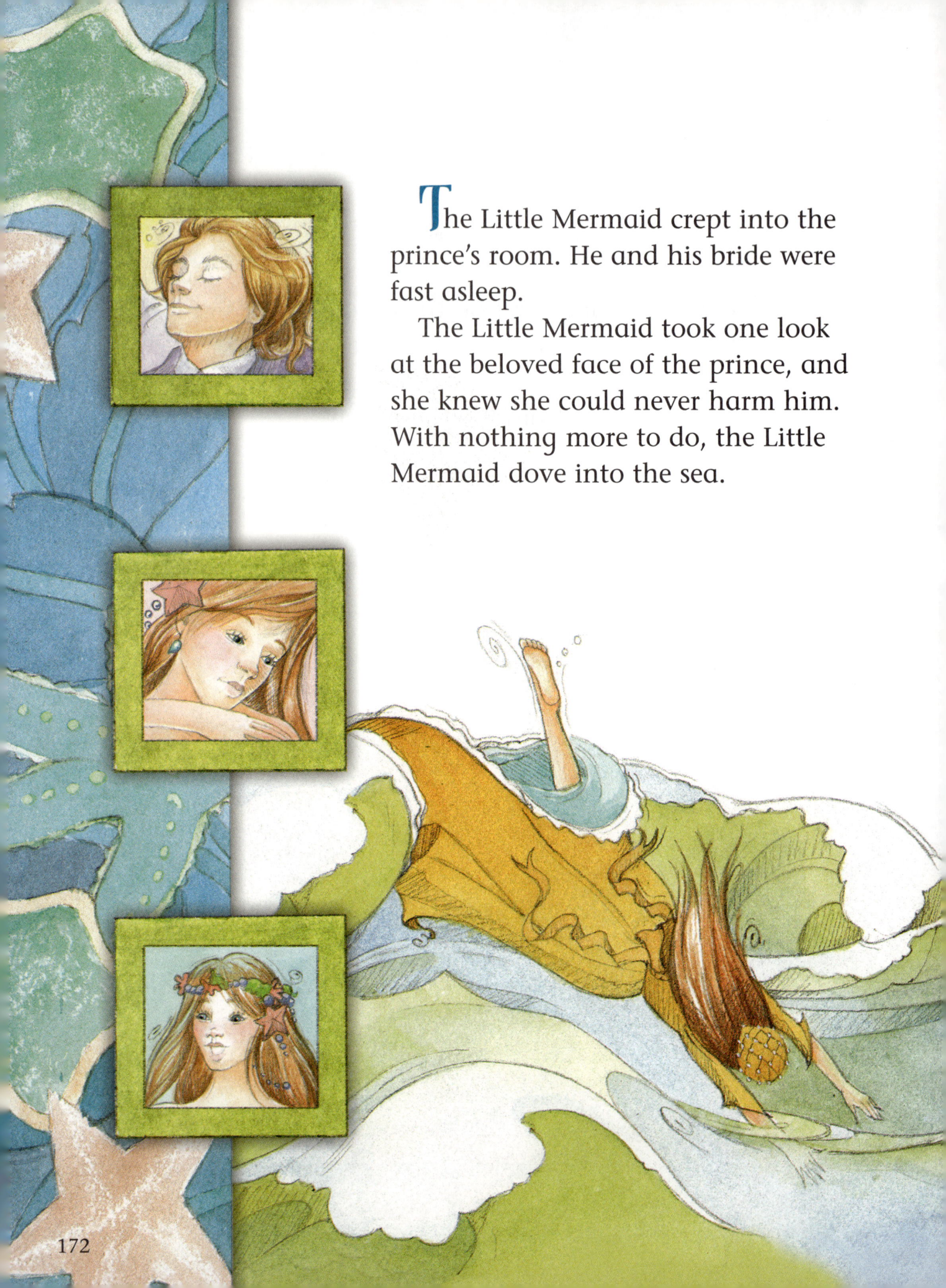

The Little Mermaid crept into the prince's room. He and his bride were fast asleep.

The Little Mermaid took one look at the beloved face of the prince, and she knew she could never harm him. With nothing more to do, the Little Mermaid dove into the sea.

Instead of turning into foam, the Little Mermaid rose up into the air. Angel children lifted her.

"Where am I?" she asked. She had a beautiful new voice.

"You are among the children of the air," they said. "You will be with us forever."

The children explained. "You loved the prince so much, you gave your life for him. This deed won you a soul."

The Little Mermaid blew the prince a kiss and floated toward a cloud. Looking down on Earth, she was filled with great peace, as never before.

Bibliography
"The Little Mermaid"

Andersen, Hans Christian. *The Little Mermaid: The Original Story*. New York: Random House, 1997. The delectable watercolors used by illustrator Charles Santore are perfectly suited to this authentic presentation of Andersen's text. Parents should be aware, though, of the tragic nature of the original story.

Braybrooks, Ann. *Disney's The Little Mermaid*. New York: Disney Press, 1997. Disney's retelling presents a lighter, and very different, interpretation of the classic story of the little mermaid who longs to become human. For the thoughtful seven-year-old, comparing this version with the original can prompt penetrating discussions of the writer's purpose and craft.

Andersen, Hans Christian. *The Princess and the Pea*. Illustrated by Dorothée Duntze. New York: North-South Books, 1995. Hans Christian Andersen is the author of many beloved tales. In this one, a young woman is proved to be a true princess because a lump under her mattress—a pea—keeps her from sleeping.

Andersen, Hans Christian. *The Emperor's New Clothes*. Illustrated by Demi. New York: McElderry Books, 2000. This retelling of the classic tale of a vain emperor tricked into wearing "magical" clothes is set in ancient China and beautifully illustrated. A young boy is the only one honest enough to point out that the emperor is not wearing any clothes (except, in this version, a pair of socks and very imperial-looking undershorts).

Andersen, Hans Christian. *The Swineherd*. Illustrated by Lisbeth Zwerger. New York: North-South Books, 1995. In this tale, a prince disguises himself as a swineherd in order to court the emperor's daughter, a selfish, petty girl who sets great store by appearances.

About "Paul Bunyan"

If you had stood in a forest in the American Northwest in the late 1800s, you would likely have heard the sound of trees crashing to the ground. The logging industry was bustling. During the day, loggers cut down many, many trees. At night, they often sat around campfires and told stories. Many of the tales centered around a larger-than-life lumberjack hero, Paul Bunyan.

Some people believe the tales of this legendary character are based on a French-Canadian folk tale. Others say that the tales were created by a logging company. Still others think that the stories have roots in Europe. Whatever the tales' origins, they have ended up being distinctly American.

While Paul Bunyan was well-known in logging camps, the public did not hear the tales about him until they were printed in a newspaper. James MacGillivray published Paul Bunyan stories in the Detroit News-Tribune in the summer of 1910. Some years later, W. B. Laughead adapted the tales and included them in an advertising pamphlet for the Red River Lumber Company of Minnesota. The stories became quite popular among readers of all ages and began appearing in books and magazines.

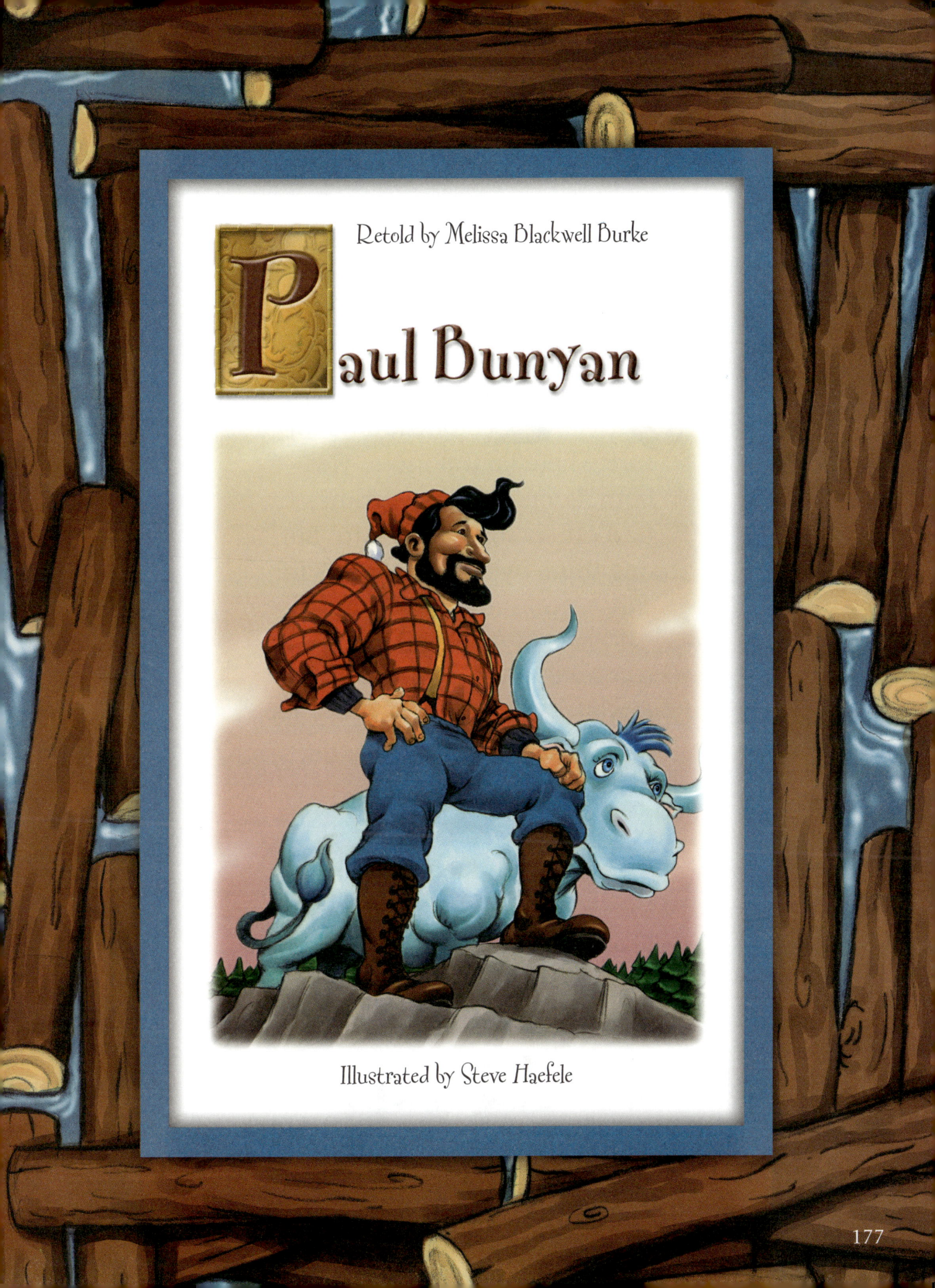

Paul Bunyan

Retold by Melissa Blackwell Burke

Illustrated by Steve Haefele

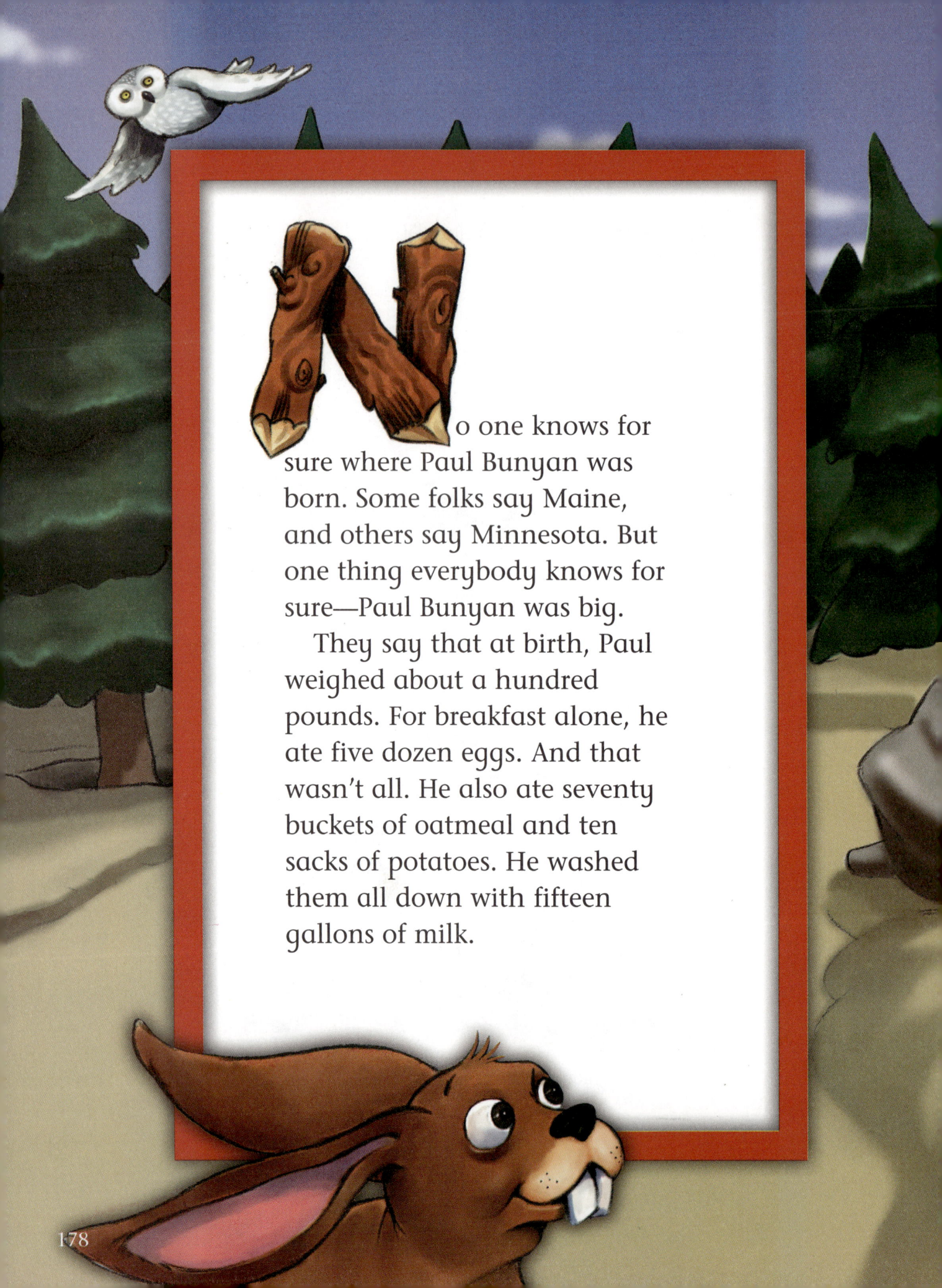

No one knows for sure where Paul Bunyan was born. Some folks say Maine, and others say Minnesota. But one thing everybody knows for sure—Paul Bunyan was big.

They say that at birth, Paul weighed about a hundred pounds. For breakfast alone, he ate five dozen eggs. And that wasn't all. He also ate seventy buckets of oatmeal and ten sacks of potatoes. He washed them all down with fifteen gallons of milk.

179

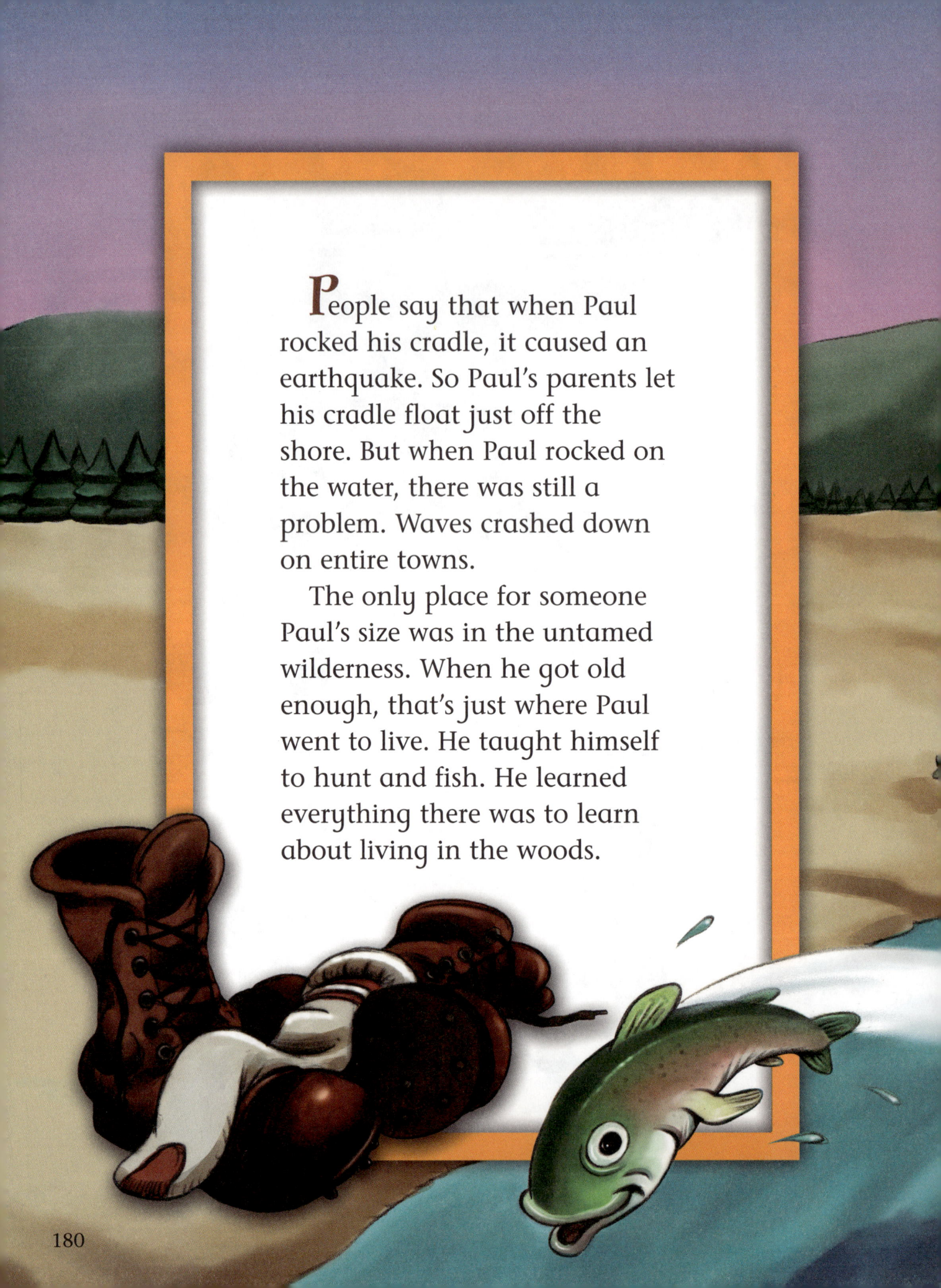

People say that when Paul rocked his cradle, it caused an earthquake. So Paul's parents let his cradle float just off the shore. But when Paul rocked on the water, there was still a problem. Waves crashed down on entire towns.

The only place for someone Paul's size was in the untamed wilderness. When he got old enough, that's just where Paul went to live. He taught himself to hunt and fish. He learned everything there was to learn about living in the woods.

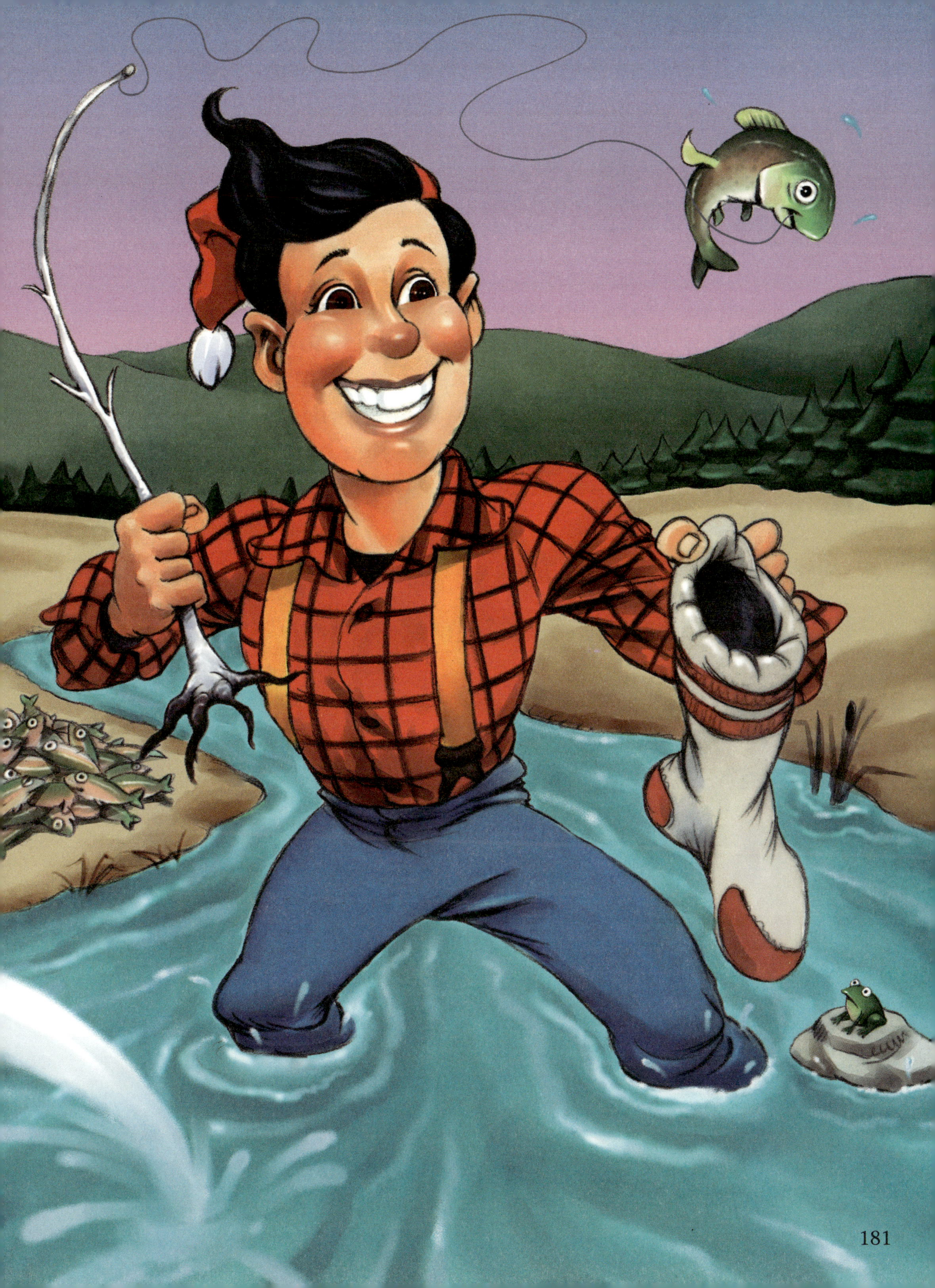

Even so, one frightful winter caught Paul by surprise. One day blue snowflakes began to fall. Soon the ground as far as Paul could see was covered with a blanket of blue snow. The trees looked as if they had been dipped in blue powder.

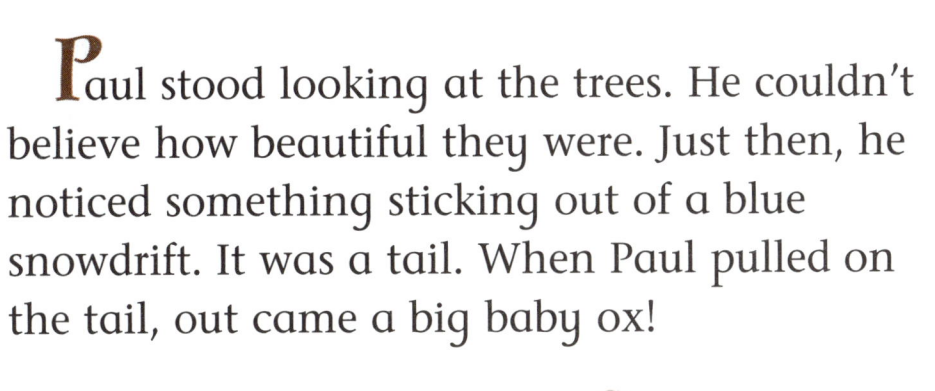

Paul stood looking at the trees. He couldn't believe how beautiful they were. Just then, he noticed something sticking out of a blue snowdrift. It was a tail. When Paul pulled on the tail, out came a big baby ox!

That poor baby ox was just about frozen. He had turned blue, just like the snow. Paul scooped up the ox and carried him home. He set him down gently in front of the fire. Finally, they both fell asleep.

When the morning sun began to shine, the ox nuzzled Paul awake. Paul laughed so hard that it shook the Earth.

"Babe," he said, "you and I are going to be fine friends."

And so they were. From that day on, Paul and Babe went everywhere together.

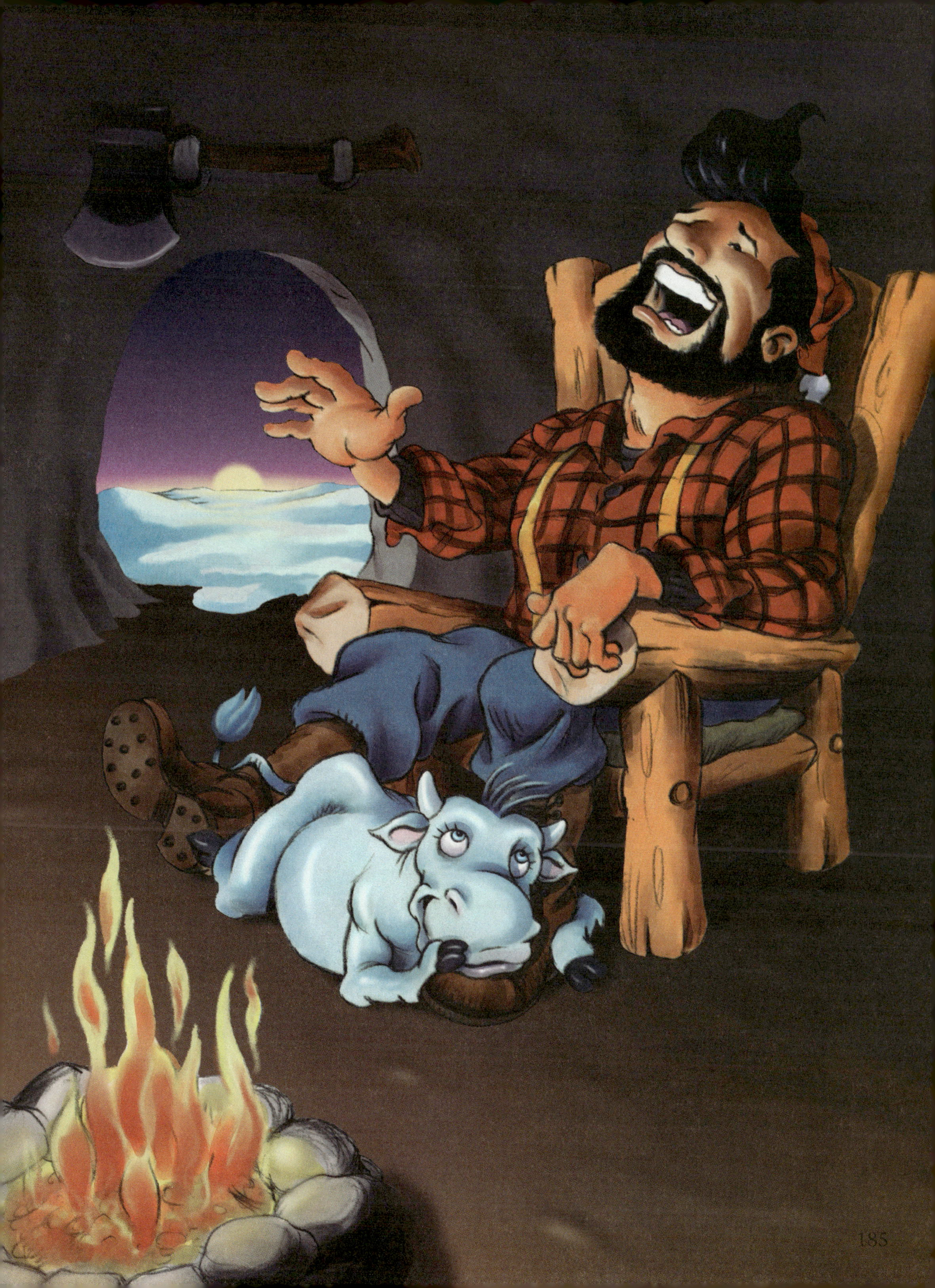

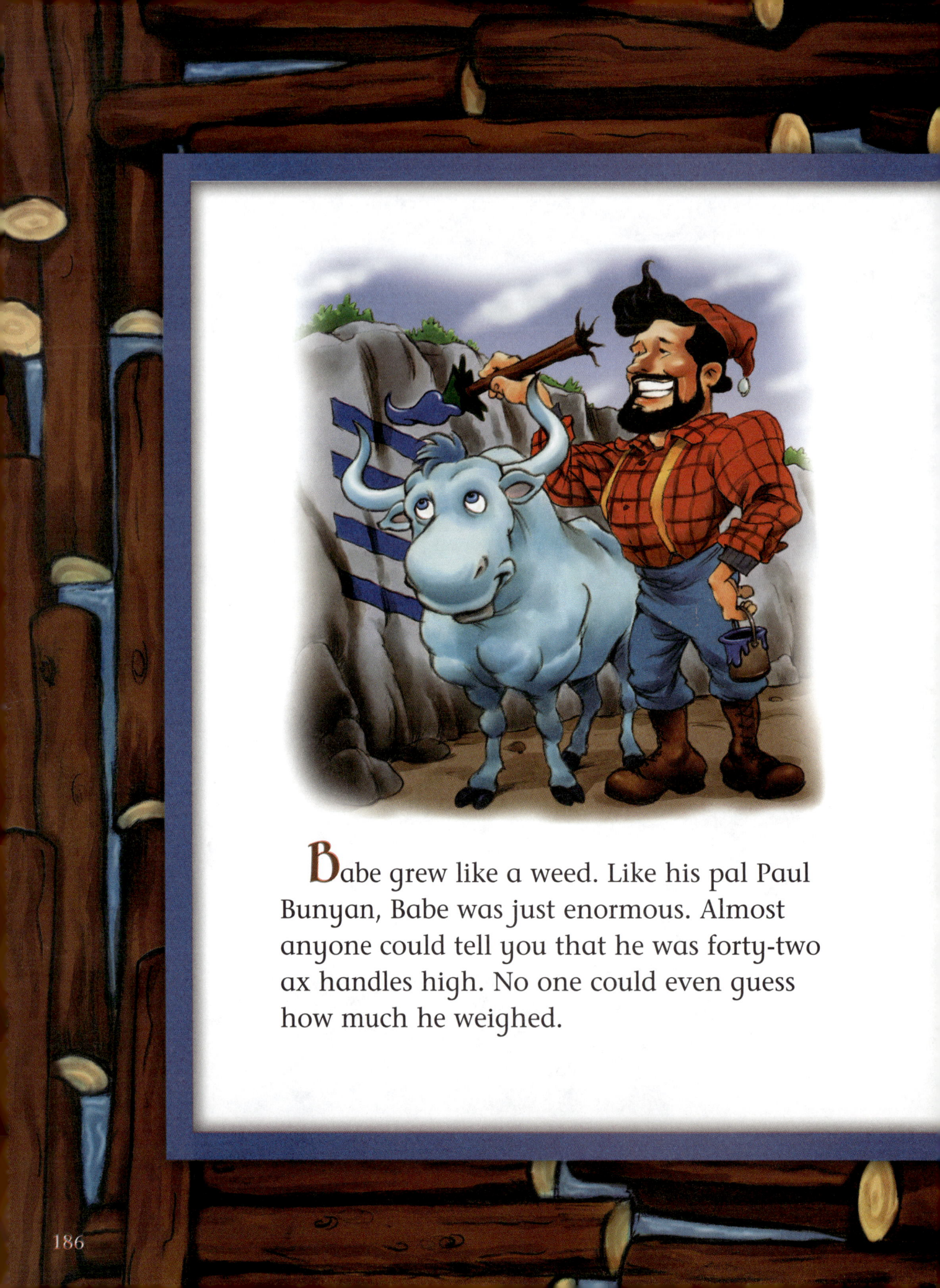

Babe grew like a weed. Like his pal Paul Bunyan, Babe was just enormous. Almost anyone could tell you that he was forty-two ax handles high. No one could even guess how much he weighed.

So Paul and Babe tramped through the woods together. Back then, the forests were as thick as the bristles on a toothbrush. Everywhere you looked stood big, tall trees. Why, you could tip your head all the way back and still not see any sky.

Of course, it would have been nice to let the forests stand forever. But America was as busy as bees in the springtime. Pioneers were building houses and barns and churches and wagons. They needed wood to build all that and no telling what else.

So Paul Bunyan invented logging. He asked Babe to stand back. He gave his ax a mighty swing.

"TIM-BER!" Paul called.

Ten pines fell to the ground, just from that one swing. Paul swung a few more times. He loaded all the trees on Babe's back.

"Let's haul these over to the river," Paul said. "Then we'll send them down to the sawmill."

When they got to the river, Paul could see that it was too crooked.

"Our logs will get jammed on the curves," Paul told Babe. "We need to fix that."

So Paul tied one end of a rope to Babe's harness. He tied the other end around the river.

"Now pull, Babe!" Paul shouted. "Pull with all your might."

In no time at all, Babe had that river straightened out.

191

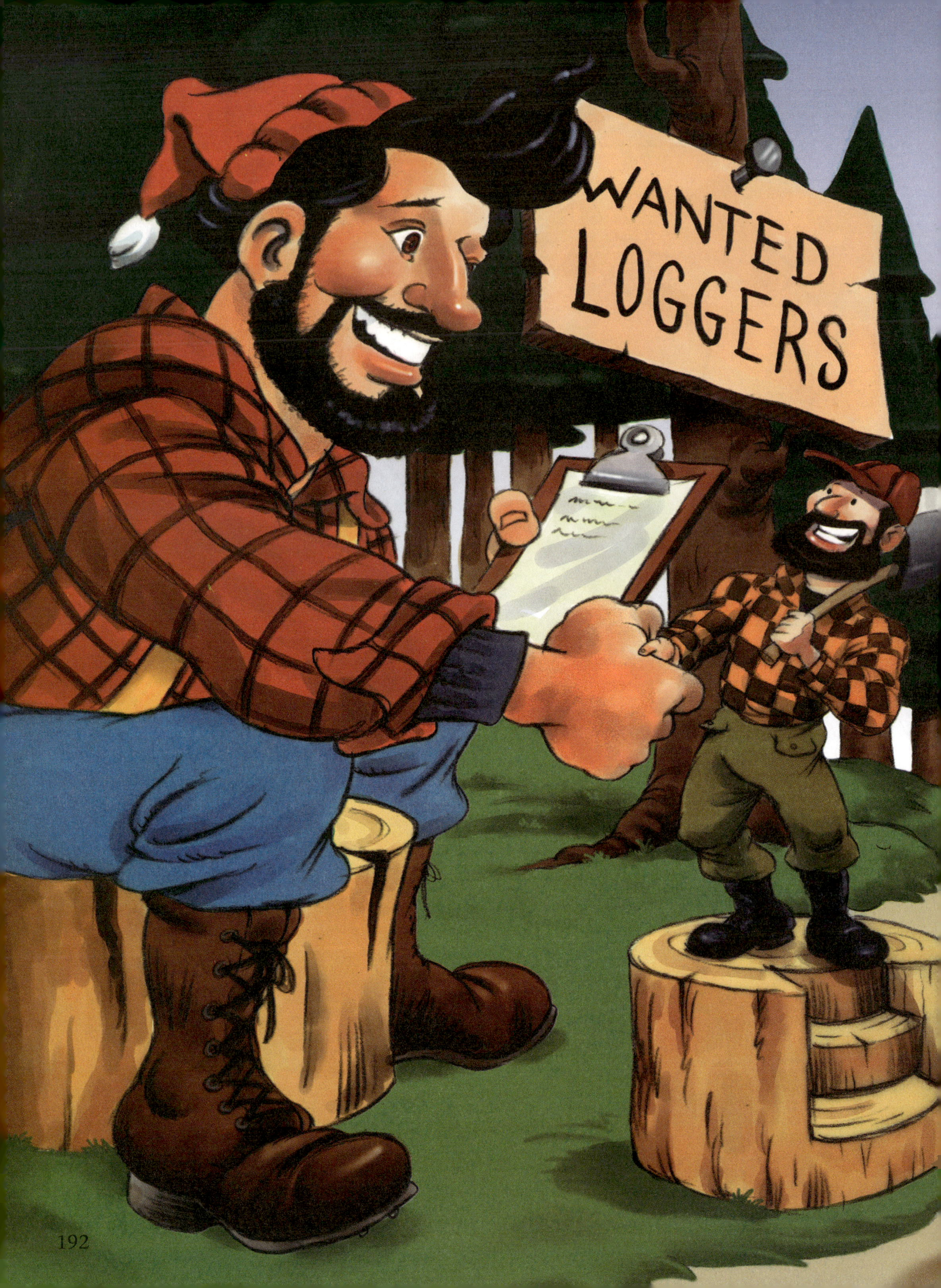
WANTED
LOGGERS

For a while, Paul and Babe worked on their own. Then Paul decided to start a logging camp. He said his loggers all had to be more than ten feet tall. With that kind of rule, he could find only about a thousand men.

The old-time loggers who worked for Paul Bunyan will tell you all about it. They say the camp was big. In fact, they claim it was so big that they needed maps to find their way around.

Paul and Babe dug a few ponds for drinking water for the camp. Nowadays, we call those ponds the Great Lakes.

Of course, the camp had a cookhouse and a great cook, Sourdough Sam. To feed all those hungry loggers, he'd whip up big batches of stew. You might hear tell that he made a mean fried chicken, too. But without a doubt, Sam's sourdough pancakes were the best of all.

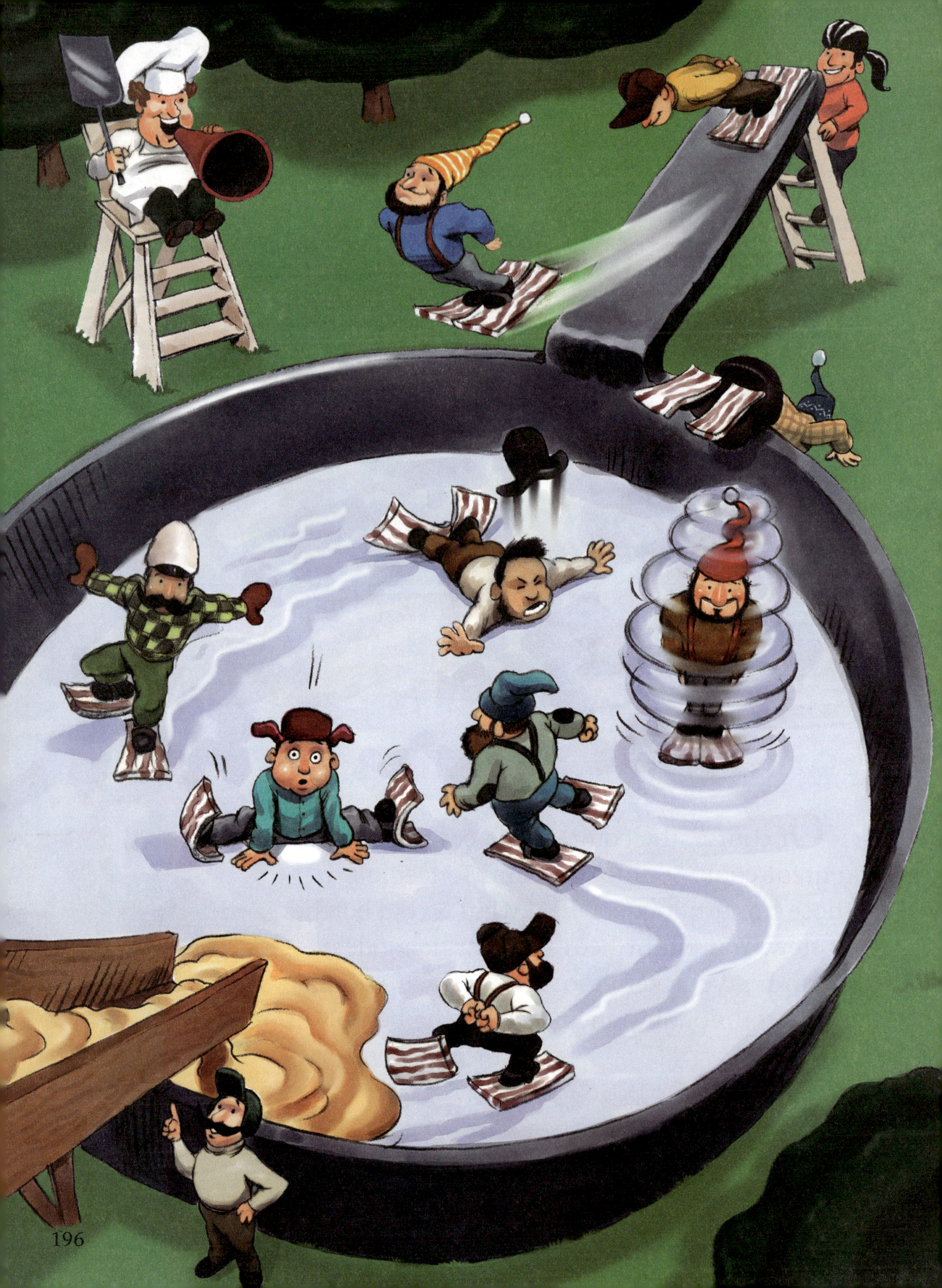

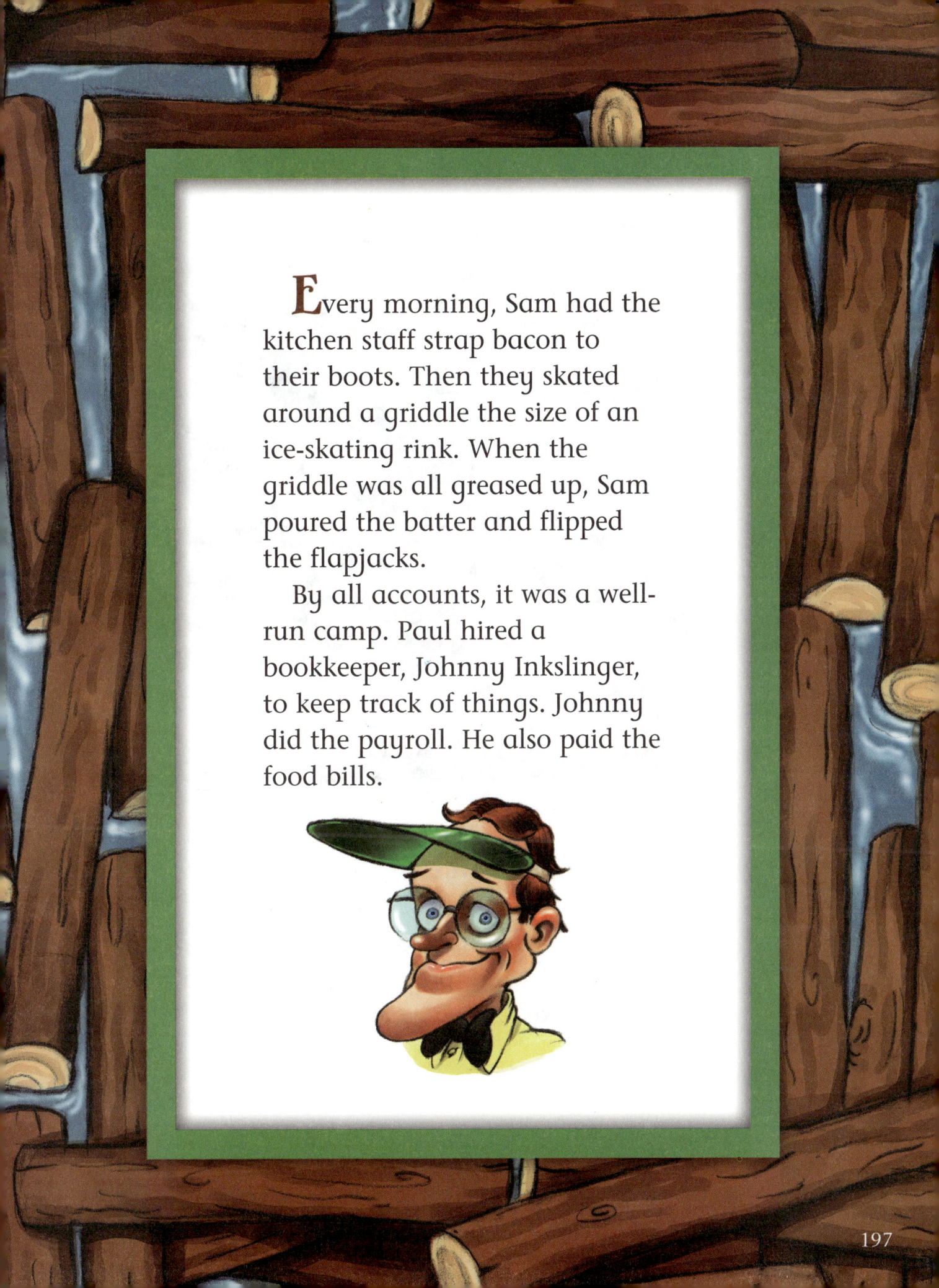

Every morning, Sam had the kitchen staff strap bacon to their boots. Then they skated around a griddle the size of an ice-skating rink. When the griddle was all greased up, Sam poured the batter and flipped the flapjacks.

By all accounts, it was a well-run camp. Paul hired a bookkeeper, Johnny Inkslinger, to keep track of things. Johnny did the payroll. He also paid the food bills.

Think of all the writing Johnny had to do! He felt that he was using too much ink. He tried not dotting his *i*'s or crossing his *t*'s. That saved about five hundred barrels of ink. Even so, he had to use a pen connected to an ink lake.

So things went along pretty smoothly for a while. Then came the Year of Two Winters. People called it that because it was so cold.

Shot Gunderson, the camp foreman, had all kinds of problems. He rode in to talk things over with Paul.

"Boss," Shot said to Paul, "it's so cold that the men's feet are about to freeze right off. What can we do about that?"

Paul was pretty handy with tricky problems.

"Just tell the men to let their whiskers grow," he said. "When their beards get long enough, they can stuff them into their boots. That'll keep their feet warm."

And so it did.

201

Then Shot said, "Boss, when I give orders to the loggers, all my words freeze. They just hang in the air like icicles."

Paul thought on that one for a minute.

"I'll ask Babe to help you haul your words to one place. They'll thaw in the spring and everybody can hear them then."

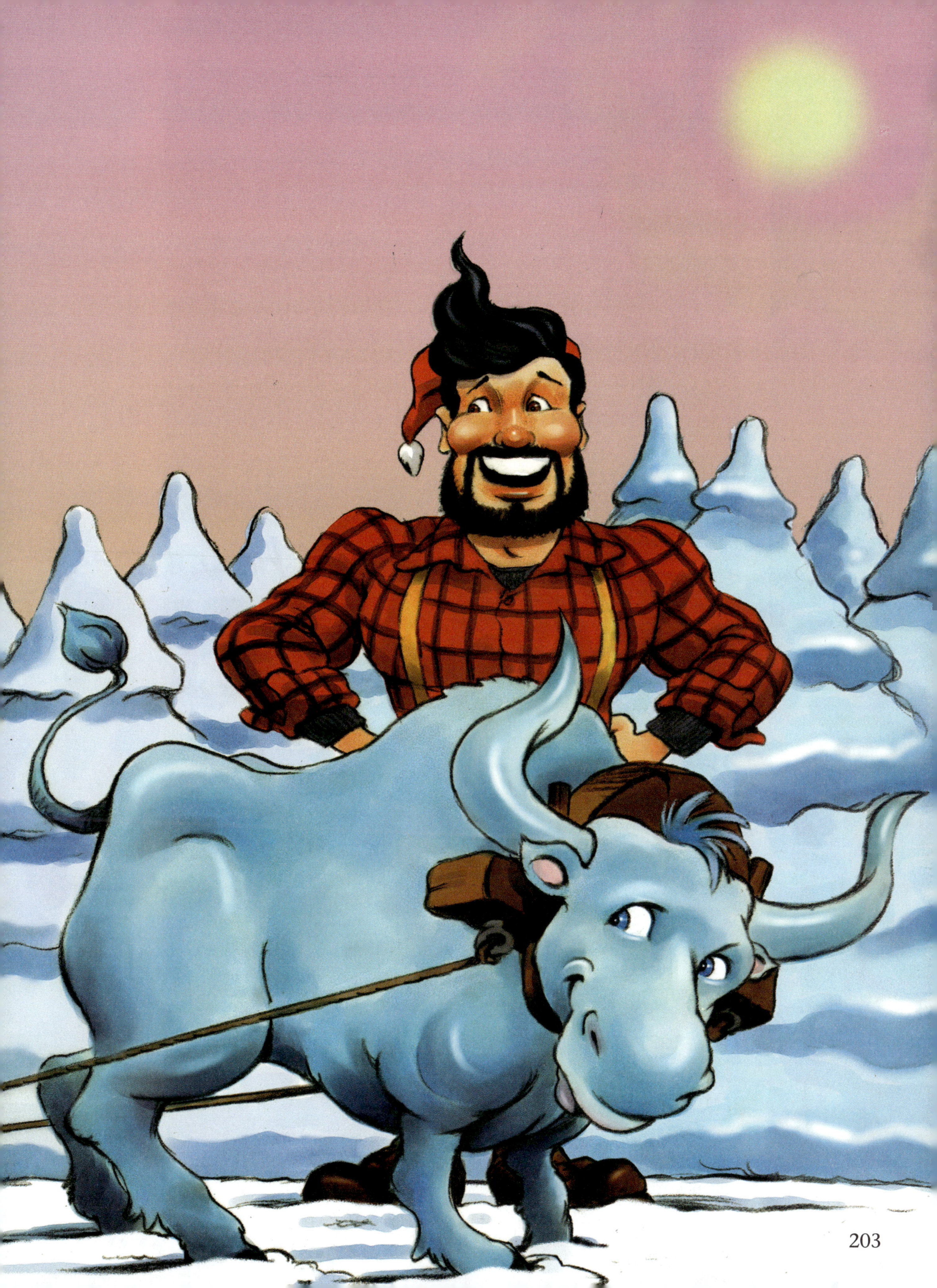

That worked, too. It did cause a little bit of confusion, though. Sometimes words would thaw at the same time. It seemed as if Shot was yelling "Timber!" and "Chow time!" all at once.

After all the trouble that hard winter, Paul was ready for a change. He decided to take the logging camp out on the road. Babe was ready to pull everything along. But Paul wanted to check some things first.

Paul knew that the forests were precious. So he made sure there were a few trees left standing. Also, he replaced each tree the loggers cut with a new seedling.

Paul's crew logged North Dakota, South Dakota, Washington, Oregon, and all points in between. Paul even started out for Arizona. At one point, he began dragging his ax and didn't notice. You'll notice, though. That area is now called the Grand Canyon.

207

You may be wondering what became of Paul Bunyan and Babe. Some say that they are in Alaska. Some say the Arctic Circle. You never know. Keep your eyes open, and some day you just might run into that great lumberjack and his big blue ox.

Bibliography
"Paul Bunyan"

Kellogg, Steven. *Paul Bunyan*. New York: Morrow, 1985. This is a rollicking, dynamically illustrated retelling of the story about America's favorite lumberjack and his incredible deeds.

Wood, Audrey. *The Bunyans*. New York: Scholastic, 1996. This tale introduces us to Paul Bunyan's family. We meet Carrie, Paul's giant wife, and their king-sized children, Little Jean and Teeny. If you were amazed by Paul's creation of the Great Lakes and the Grand Canyon, wait until you hear what the rest of the family were up to!

Kellogg, Steven. *Sally Ann Thunder Ann Whirlwind Crockett: A Tall Tale*. New York: Morrow, 1995. This amazing tale follows the adventures of the toughest living creature in all the frontier—Sally Ann Thunder Ann Whirlwind. This strong, clever woman wins the heart of Davy Crockett by rescuing him from danger.

Kellogg, Steven. *Mike Fink: A Tall Tale*. New York: Morrow, 1992. Like Paul Bunyan, this hero has amazing strength and much wit. Mike Fink can wrestle grizzlies and alligators, and we learn how he becomes king of the keelboatmen.

Ketterman, Helen. *Heat Wave*. New York: Walker & Co., 2000. In this humorous tall tale, a heat wave hits a family farm and weird things begin to happen. After the corn pops right on the stalk, the flowers pluck themselves up and move into the shade, and the cows jump around so much on the hot ground that their milk is churned into butter, a clever young girl finds a way to save the day.

Reading Activities

Order, Please!

Cut out the pictures below. Put them in order to show what happened in "The Three Wishes." Then, number each box from 1 to 6. Use the pictures to retell the story. Use words like *first*, *next*, *then*, and *last*.

The Three Wishes

Detail Mix-Up

Read each sentence below. Find one word that is wrong, and underline it. Then replace the wrong word with a word from the tree to make the sentence tell about the story. Write the correct word on the line.

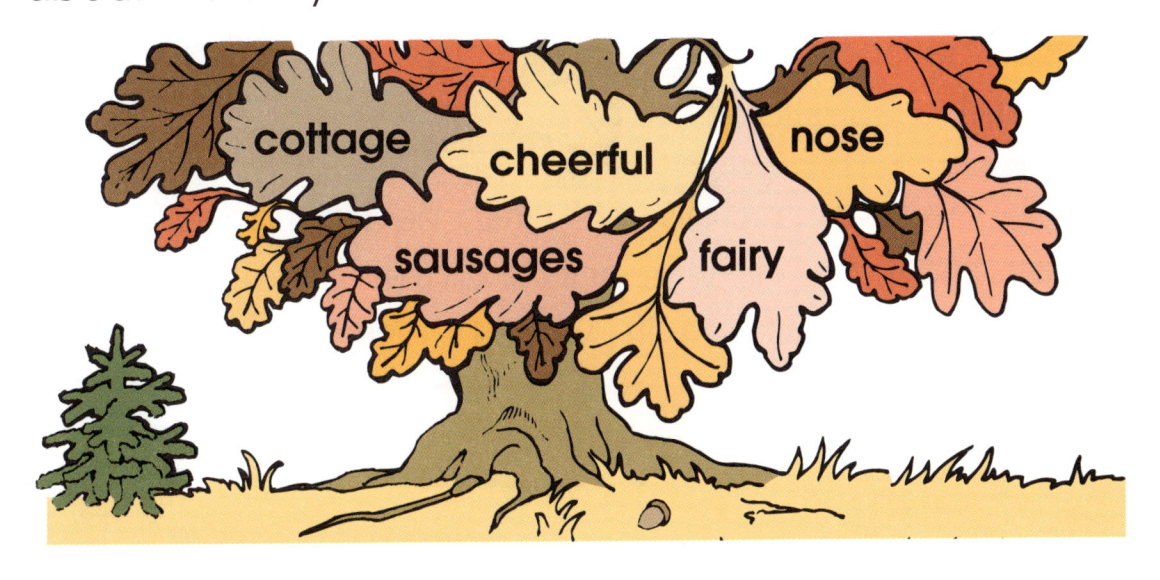

Tree with leaves: cottage, cheerful, nose, sausages, fairy

1. A toad gave the man and wife three wishes.

   _____

2. The man and wife went home to their nest.

   _____

3. The man said he wished he had pancakes for dinner.

   _____

4. The man ended up with sausages on his toes.

   _____

5. In the end, the man and wife were scared about their dinner. _____

Learn to Read With Classic Stories—Grade 2   Comprehension/Story Details

Things Change and Stay the Same

Fill in the chart with the sentences below. Write one sentence in each part of the chart. Then, answer the question.

> The man and his wife dreamed of riches.
> The man and his wife had a dinner of sausages.
> The man and his wife were hungry and poor.

Beginning _____

_____

Middle _____

_____

End _____

_____

How did things change for the man and his wife from the beginning of the story to the end?

_____

_____

_____

Comprehension/Plot

How It Happened

Read each sentence. Fill in the circle to finish each sentence correctly.

1. The fairy gave the man and wife three wishes because

   ○ they were poor.

   ○ they didn't cut down her tree.

2. The man built a fire because

   ○ it was cold in the cottage.

   ○ they wanted to burn some old things.

3. The man got sausages on his nose because

   ○ he said he wanted to know what it would be like.

   ○ his wife said she wished that would happen.

4. The two had to use their last wish to get the sausages off because

   ○ that was the only way to get them off.

   ○ they couldn't think of anything else to wish for.

5. At the end, the two were cheerful because

   ○ their wishes came true about a house and coach.

   ○ at least they had a fine dinner of sausages.

Learn to Read With Classic Stories—Grade 2   Comprehension/Cause and Effect

Real or Not?

Read each sentence. Draw a sausage around things from the story that could really happen.

A man and wife fuss about something.

A man decides not to cut down a tree.

A fairy grants a man and his wife three wishes.

A man and his wife walk through the forest.

Sausages grow from a man's nose.

A man and wife eat sausages for dinner.

The man and wife wish that the sausages would disappear, and they do.

Comprehension/Reality and Fantasy

Learn to Read With Classic Stories—Grade 2

Picture Clues

Look at the pictures on the following pages and answer the questions.

Pages 8 and 9
What clue tells you that the man and wife are quite

poor?_____

Page 12
How do the man and wife feel about seeing the fairy?

_____

Pages 16 and 17
The man and his wife are still working, even though they have three wishes. What does that tell you about them?

_____

Pages 30 and 31
What does the way that the man is sitting tell you

about how he is feeling?_____

Pages 36 and 37
How does the art show you the way the man and wife

are feeling?_____

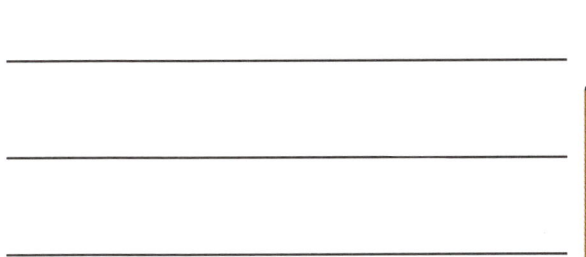

_____

_____

Learn to Read With Classic Stories—Grade 2   Comprehension/Using Illustrations

Wise or Foolish?

Look at each thing the man and woman could have wished for. Would each wish be wise or foolish? Check the box. Then tell why you think so.

☐ wise   ☐ foolish

It is _____, because _____

_____.

☐ wise   ☐ foolish

It is _____, because _____

_____.

☐ wise   ☐ foolish

It is _____, because _____

_____.

☐ wise   ☐ foolish

It is _____, because _____

_____.

Comprehension/Making Judgments   Learn to Read With Classic Stories—Grade 2

What About Next Time?

Think about what the man and wife might do next time. Answer the questions.

1. What do you think the man might do if another fairy asked him not to cut down a tree?

   _____

   _____

2. Say that the man and wife got three more wishes. What do you think they might say to each other before they make any wishes? Why?

   _____

   _____

3. What do you think the man and wife might wish for if they got three more wishes?

   _____

   _____

   _____

Learn to Read With Classic Stories—Grade 2   Comprehension/Making Predictions

The Three Wishes

Thinking About the Story

The paragraphs below tell what two people thought about "The Three Wishes." Read each review. Circle the letter that answers each question.

○   "The Three Wishes" is a great story. It teaches an important lesson—be careful what you wish for! In the story, a man and his wife are careless with three wishes. The story made me think about being happy with what you have.

1. What does this writer think about the story?
    a. The writer likes another story better.
    b. The writer thinks it is a great story.
    c. The writer thinks the author of the story should have changed it.

○   "The Three Wishes" is an old story. It reminds me of "The Fisherman and His Wife." I like that story better. "The Three Wishes" tries to teach readers to think before they do something.

2. What does this writer think about the story?
    a. The writer likes another story better.
    b. The writer thinks it is the best story ever.
    c. The writer thinks the author of the story should have changed it.

The Meaning of This

Complete each sentence with a word from the pan.

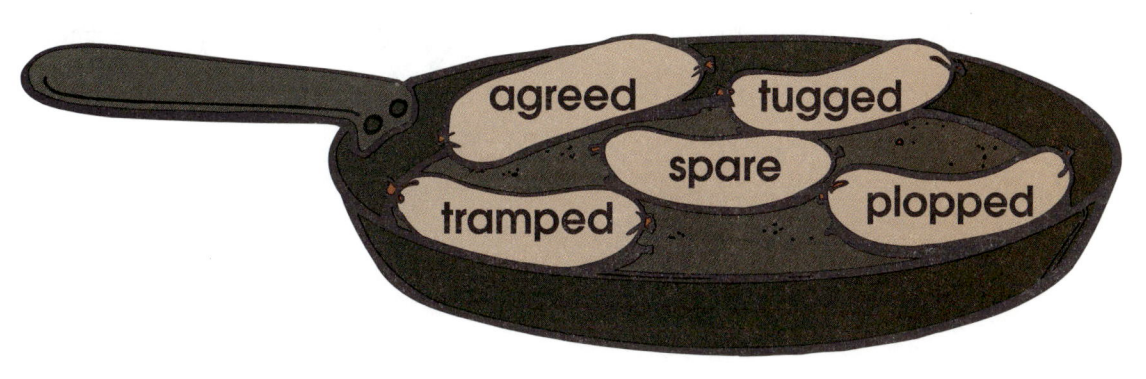

Words in pan: agreed, tugged, spare, tramped, plopped

1. The man and his wife _____ through the forest.

2. The wife _____ with the man that they had found a huge tree.

3. The man told the fairy they would _____ her tree.

4. Back at the cottage, the man and wife _____ down in front of the fire.

5. The man and wife _____ at the sausages on his nose, but it was no use.

The Three Wishes

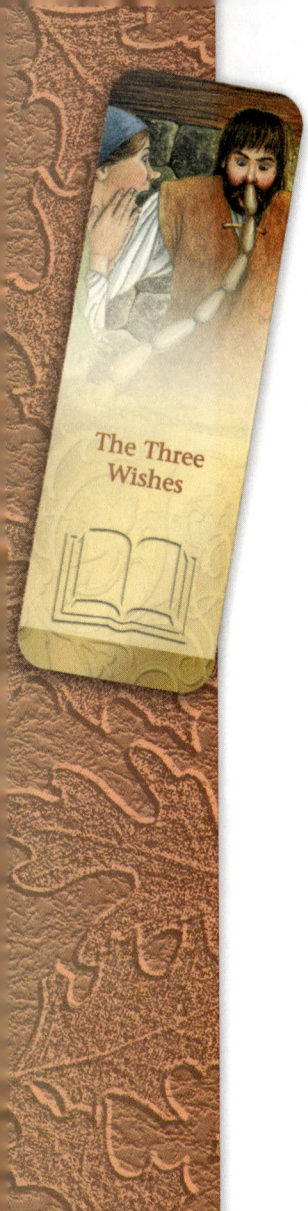

Sentence Scramble

Put each group of words in order to make a sentence that tells something. Write each sentence on the line below the words.

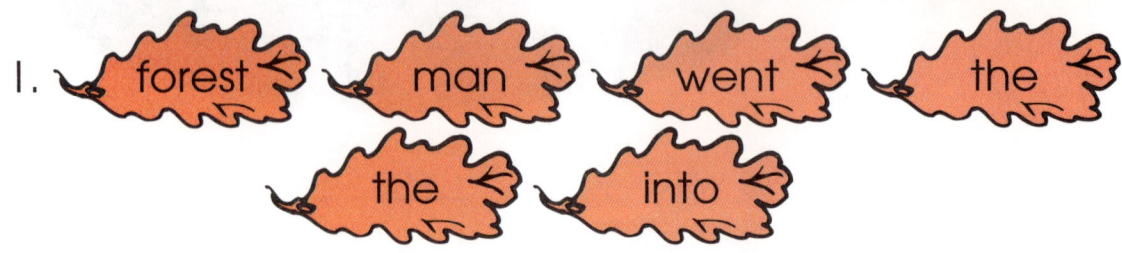

1. forest   man   went   the   the   into

_____

2. cut   the   wood   man

_____

3. of   dreamed   wishes   they

_____

4. sausages   nose   the   hung   his   from

_____

5. dinner   ate   they

_____

Grammar/Sentence Word Order   Learn to Read With Classic Stories—Grade 2

Help the Fairy

Read this sign the fairy has written. Find and correct two capitalization mistakes, two punctuation mistakes, and two spelling mistakes. Make your corrections above each mistake.

please do note

cut down this tree.

It makes a

lovely home for me?

Thank you for being soo kind.

When I grant wishes,

i'll keep you in mind

What the Man Might Say

Think about how the man in the story felt. Help him complete the letter below by filling in the missing words.

Dear Friend,

I had a _____ thing happen to me. A fairy gave me three wishes. When she said it, I felt so _____. My wife and I talked and talked about what we would wish for. By mistake, I wished for sausages. I felt so _____. My wife was angry. She wished that they would hang from my nose.

They did. We had to fix this. It was _____. So, we wished the sausages off. We ate them for dinner that night.

In the end, everything was _____.

But, I do wish _____
_____.

Yours truly,
The Woodcutter

224 Writing/A Letter Learn to Read With Classic Stories—Grade 2

Meet the Ants and the Grasshopper

Read each phrase below. Write **ants** or **grasshopper** to show who the phrase tells about.

1. worked hard _____

2. wanted only to play _____

3. got ready for winter _____

4. tried to help someone by suggesting a work plan

   _____

5. didn't worry about what was coming up

   _____

6. was sorry not to have planned ahead

   _____

Learn to Read With Classic Stories—Grade 2

Compare and Contrast

All About the Ants and the Grasshopper

Think about "The Ants and the Grasshopper." Complete the chart to sum up the story.

When and where does the story take place?

_____

_____

_____

Who is the story about? _____

_____

_____

What happens in the story? _____

_____

_____

_____

Comprehension/Summarizing

Learn to Read With Classic Stories—Grade 2

True to the Story

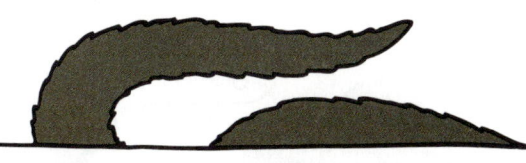

Think about the story "Belling the Cat." Read each sentence. Circle **True** if it was a part of the story. Circle **False** if it was not a part of the story.

1. The mice were happy until the owner got a bird. True **False** ⭕

2. The mice were afraid of the cat. **True** ⭕ False

3. The mice decided to have a party to trick the cat. True **False** ⭕

4. The cat sent the mice a letter. True False

5. One mouse wanted to put a bell around the cat's neck. True False

6. Some other mice agreed the bell was a good plan. True False

7. The old mouse asked who would put the bell on the cat. True False

8. The young mouse put the bell on the cat himself. True **False** ⭕

Learn to Read With Classic Stories—Grade 2

Comprehension/Story Details

How to Bell the Cat

How would you put the bell on the cat? Draw a picture of your idea below. Then write about it.

Give the cat a bowl of milk.

Sing a song to the cat to put her to sleep.

I would stand on a cats back and put it on.

Critical Thinking/Problem Solving

This Is the Reason

Think about the story "The Boy Who Cried Wolf." Draw lines to match the things that happened to why they happened.

1. The boy cried wolf because

2. The village people first ran to help the boy because

3. The boy laughed because

4. The last time, the village people didn't help because

5. The boy lost a great many sheep because

they wanted to help him keep the wolf away.

he wanted some excitement.

the boy had tricked them too many times.

no one came to help since they didn't believe him.

he thought he had played a funny trick.

Aesop's Fables

Learn to Read With Classic Stories—Grade 2   Comprehension/Cause and Effect

About the Illustrations

Look at the illustrations on the following pages. Write a caption from the box that tells what is happening in each picture.

- The boy is pleased with his trick, but the villagers are not.
- The shepherd boy tends his sheep.
- The boy decides to play his trick again.
- The boy cries wolf and the villagers run to help.

Pages 58 and 59 _____

_____

Pages 60 and 61 _____

_____

Page 62 _____

_____

Page 63 _____

_____

Write your own caption for page 67. _____

_____

First, Next, Last

Think about "The Fox and the Grapes." Write **First**, **Next**, and **Last** to show the order in which the events happened. Then draw a picture for each event.

_____, the fox said the grapes were sour and walked away.

_____, the fox tried to get the grapes and missed.

_____, the fox spied some grapes he wanted.

Sweet Grape Snack

Complete the following rhyme with words from the box. Then follow the steps below for a delicious grape snack.

fun   please   treat   dry

Use some grapes that you pick or buy.

Wash them clean, then pat them _____.

Put them in the freezer to freeze.

For an hour, if you _____.

When the grapes are hard, they're done.

Now it's time to have some _____.

Are the grapes sour? No, they're sweet.

Fox would love to have this _____.

Lessons Learned

Think about what each of the stories was mostly about. Write the title of the story to match it with the main idea.

"The Ants and the Grasshopper"   "Belling the Cat"
"The Boy Who Cried Wolf"   "The Fox and the Grapes"

Those who often don't tell the truth are not believed when they finally do.

Title: _____

It is one thing to say what should be done. It is quite another matter to do it.

Title: _____

Some people will talk badly about things they cannot have.

Title: _____

There is a time for work and a time for play.

Title: _____

All Kinds of Characters

Think about each character. Complete the sentence to describe the character. Use the words below.
- not careful to think things through
- not honest because he said things that weren't true
- lazy because he would rather play than work
- unhappy because he couldn't have something he wanted

I think Grasshopper was _____

_____

_____

I think the young mouse was _____

_____

_____

I think the boy who cried wolf was

_____

_____

I think the fox was _____

_____

_____

Comprehension/Characterization   Learn to Read With Classic Stories—Grade 2

Word Parts

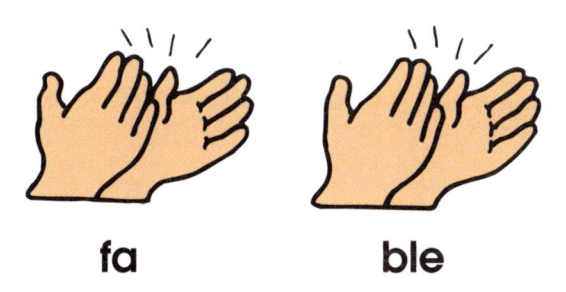

fa ble

Word parts are called **syllables** (SIH luh buhlz). You hear two syllables in the word **fable**. Read each word in the list. Think about how many syllables you hear in each word. Write the word in the correct place on the chart. Try clapping each syllable to help you count.

music   grasshopper   winter

bell   exactly   shepherd

grapes   another   wolf

One Syllable

_____

_____

_____

Two Syllables

_____

_____

_____

Three Syllables

_____

_____

_____

Using Exact Action Words

Action words tell what is happening. Some action words are more exact that others.

Example: The fox **moved**.   The fox **jumped**.

Read each sentence below. Replace each action word with one that tells more about the action. Choose words from the box. There is no one correct answer. You will use only five of the words.

discussed	marched	sat	shouted
watched	stared	chatted	jogged
whispered	waited	turned	gazed
ran	tramped	lay	stomped

1. The grasshopper looked at the ants.

   _____

2. The mice talked. _____

3. The people went up the hill. _____

4. The boy stayed on the hill. _____

5. The fox walked away. _____

Beginnings and Endings

Use a **period** at the end of **telling sentences**.

Use a **question mark** at the end of **asking sentences**.

Use an **exclamation point** at the end of **sentences that show excitement**.

Rewrite each sentence. Begin each with a capital letter. Add the correct end mark.

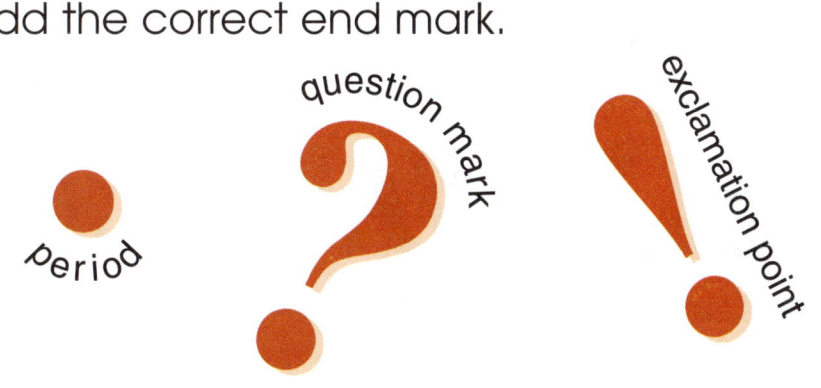

1. i see a wolf _____

2. where is your food for winter _____
   _____

3. the grapes are not tasty anyway _____
   _____

4. who will put the bell on the cat _____
   _____

5. i will play my fiddle _____
   _____

6. watch out _____

Job Hunt

Think about the fables you have read. Write a help-wanted newspaper ad that a character from one of the fables might write. For example, the villagers in "The Boy Who Cried Wolf" might want a new shepherd boy, or the mice in "Belling the Cat" might want someone to put the bell on the cat. Maybe the ants in "The Ants and the Grasshopper" want help collecting food.

HELP WANTED

Job: _____

Wanted! A person who will _____
_____
_____
_____.

The reward for doing this job is _____
_____
_____
_____.

Writing/A Newspaper Ad

Summary Chart

Complete the chart about the story "Rumpelstiltskin."

Who is the story about?	Where and when does the story take place?
_____ _____ _____	_____ _____

What happens at the beginning? _____
_____
_____
_____

What happens in the middle? _____
_____
_____
_____

What happens at the end? _____
_____
_____
_____

Path to Happily Ever After

Think about the order of events in the story. Take the miller's daughter from her home to happily ever after. Draw a line from one event to the next to show the order things happened in the story.

Start

- The miller brags about his daughter.
- The king tells the miller's daughter to spin straw into gold.
- A little man comes three times to help the girl spin straw into gold.
- The little man comes back for the baby.
- The queen guesses the little man's name.
- The king takes the miller's daughter to the palace.
- The miller's daughter promises the little man her first child.
- The little man says the queen can keep the baby if she can guess his name.
- The queen sends servants to find out the little man's name.

Rumpelstiltskin

Comprehension/Sequencing

Learn to Read With Classic Stories—Grade 2

Golden Details

Read each sentence. If it tells something that happens in the story, color the straw **gold** (or **yellow**). If it tells something that did not happen in the story, color the straw **brown**.

Rumpelstiltskin

- The little man becomes the king.
- A miller says something that is not true about his daughter.
- The little man falls into a pot of water.
- The miller's daughter marries the king.
- A little man spins straw into gold.
- The king says the girl must make many pairs of shoes by morning.
- The miller's daughter gives the little man her hat and her gloves.
- The queen guesses the little man's name.

Learn to Read With Classic Stories—Grade 2

Comprehension/Story Details

What a Problem!

In the story, the miller's daughter has problems. She has to find ways to solve them. Answer the following questions about the story.

1. The first night at the palace, how does the miller's daughter solve her problem about not being able to spin straw into gold? _____

   _____

2. The second night at the palace, how does the miller's daughter solve her problem about not being able to spin straw into gold? _____

   _____

3. Why does the miller's daughter promise the little man her first child? _____

   _____

4. How is the queen able to keep her baby in the end?

   _____

Comprehension/Problems and Solutions

Who Said It?

Write a character's name to complete each sentence. You will use some characters' names more than once.

the miller | the miller's daughter | Rumpelstiltskin | the king

1. "Spin all this straw into gold by morning," said _____.

2. "I will give you my ring," said _____.

3. "Well, my daughter can spin straw into gold!" _____ said.

4. "I am here about your promise. Give me the baby," said _____.

5. "Do you know my name?" said _____.

6. "Then, could it be, perhaps, Rumpelstiltskin?" asked _____.

Learn to Read With Classic Stories—Grade 2   Comprehension/Dialogue/Characterization

Well Illustrated

Look at the illustrations on the following pages. Then, answer each question.

Page 77

How did the illustrator show that the miller is very proud of his daughter? _____

_____

Page 79

The author describes the character Rumpelstiltskin as a "strange little man." Does the way the illustrator drew the character match the description? Why or why not?

_____

_____

Page 102

What can you tell about Rumpelstiltskin from this illustration? _____

_____

Page 106

Why do you think the illustrator shows a bit of Rumpelstiltskin's hat in the illustration?

_____

_____

Comprehension/Using Illustrations   Learn to Read With Classic Stories—Grade 2

By Any Other Name

Think about the story "Rumpelstiltskin." Then think about other good titles for this story. Write your ideas.

What is the story mostly about?

_____

_____

_____

_____

_____

_____

_____

_____

What might be another good title? _____

_____

Why is this a good title? _____

_____

_____

_____

Learn to Read With Classic Stories—Grade 2   Comprehension/Main Idea

Once Upon a Time

"Rumpelstiltskin" is a fairy tale. Answer these questions to see how "Rumpelstiltskin" is like other fairy tales.

1. Many fairy tales begin with the same words. How does "Rumpelstiltskin" begin? _____
_____

2. Many fairy tales have characters who can do unusual things. Which character can do impossible things in "Rumpelstiltskin"? What does the character do?
_____
_____

3. Many fairy tales have events that happen in groups of three. What happens three times in "Rumpelstiltskin"?
_____
_____

4. Most fairy tales have a happy ending. What happens at the end of "Rumpelstiltskin"? _____
_____
_____
_____

Genre/Fairy Tales   Learn to Read With Classic Stories—Grade 2

To the Letter

Imagine that you are one of the queen's messengers. To help her keep up with the names she has guessed, she has asked you to put the list in ABC order. Read the list of names. Rewrite it in ABC order.

Pumpernickel

Wilberforce

Sheepshanks

Rumpelstiltskin

George

Harry

1. _____
2. _____
3. _____
4. _____
5. _____
6. _____

Rumpelstiltskin

Learn to Read With Classic Stories—Grade 2   Study Skills/Alphabetical Order

Belonging to the Miller

An important character in "Rumpelstiltskin" is the miller's daughter. Notice the **apostrophe s** in the word **miller's**. It shows that something belongs to the miller. To show ownership, add **'s** to words.

Read each phrase. Write the person's name and the object. Be sure to add **'s** to the person's name to show ownership. The first one has been done for you.

1. the house that belongs to the miller

   the miller's house

2. the hat that belongs to Rumpelstiltskin

   _____

3. the baby that belongs to the queen

   _____

4. the blanket that belongs to the baby

   _____

5. the palace that belongs to the king

   _____

6. the story the servant told

   _____

Word Structure/Possessives

Spinning Word Meanings

Read the words on the wheel. Read the meanings in the list. Match the words and their meanings. Beside each word, write the letter for the meaning.

A. begged
B. girls
C. helpers
D. early part of night
E. strange
F. very worried

- evening ☐
- servants ☐
- maidens ☐
- desperate ☐
- odd ☐
- pleaded ☐

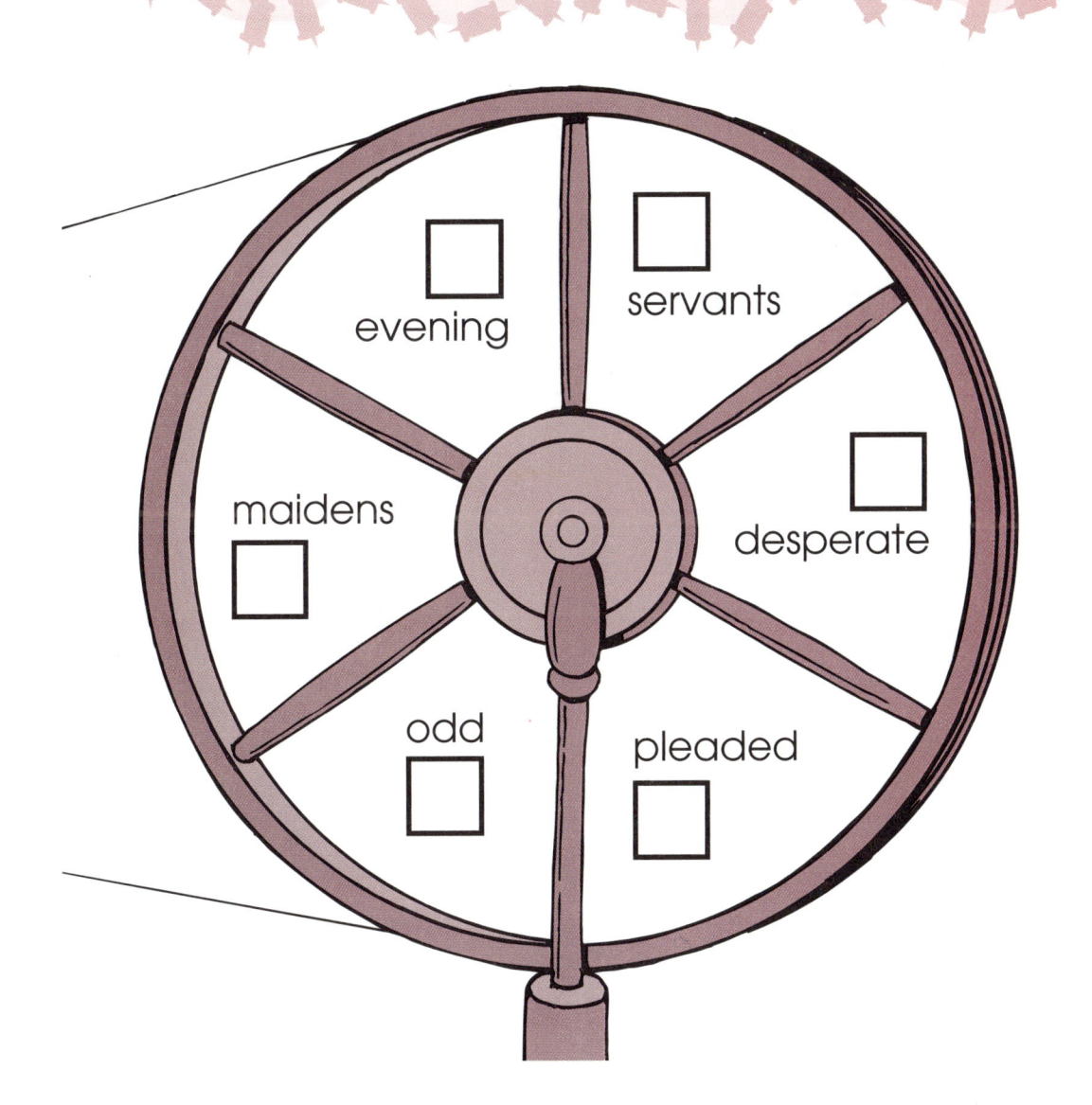

Replacing Rumpelstiltskin

Pronouns are words that can be used in place of nouns. Instead of saying a name several times, we use pronouns.

Example: Rumpelstiltskin can spin straw into gold.
He can spin straw into gold

> Use **he** for a male person and **she** for a female person.
> Use **they** for more than one person.
> Use **it** for something that is not a person.
> Use **I** for yourself and **we** for yourself and others.

Read each sentence. Circle the pronoun that could be used to replace the underlined words.

1. The miller's daughter was very beautiful.

   He   She   We   It

2. The miller liked to brag about her.   **She   They   I   He**

3. The miller's daughter and the king were married.

   They   He   She   It

4. The wedding was lovely.   **We   I   It   They**

5. Write a sentence using **I**. _____

   _____

6. Write a sentence using **we**. _____

   _____

Grammar/Pronouns   Learn to Read With Classic Stories—Grade 2

Sign Up List

One of the queen's messengers posted this sign. Find and correct two capitalization mistakes, two punctuation mistakes, and two spelling mistakes. Make your corrections above each mistake.

Notice

The queen is looking for odd names?

Please write yor name on this list.

If you know other odd names, write them

as well

the queen thanks You for your help.

If you haf any questions, contact the

queen's messengers.

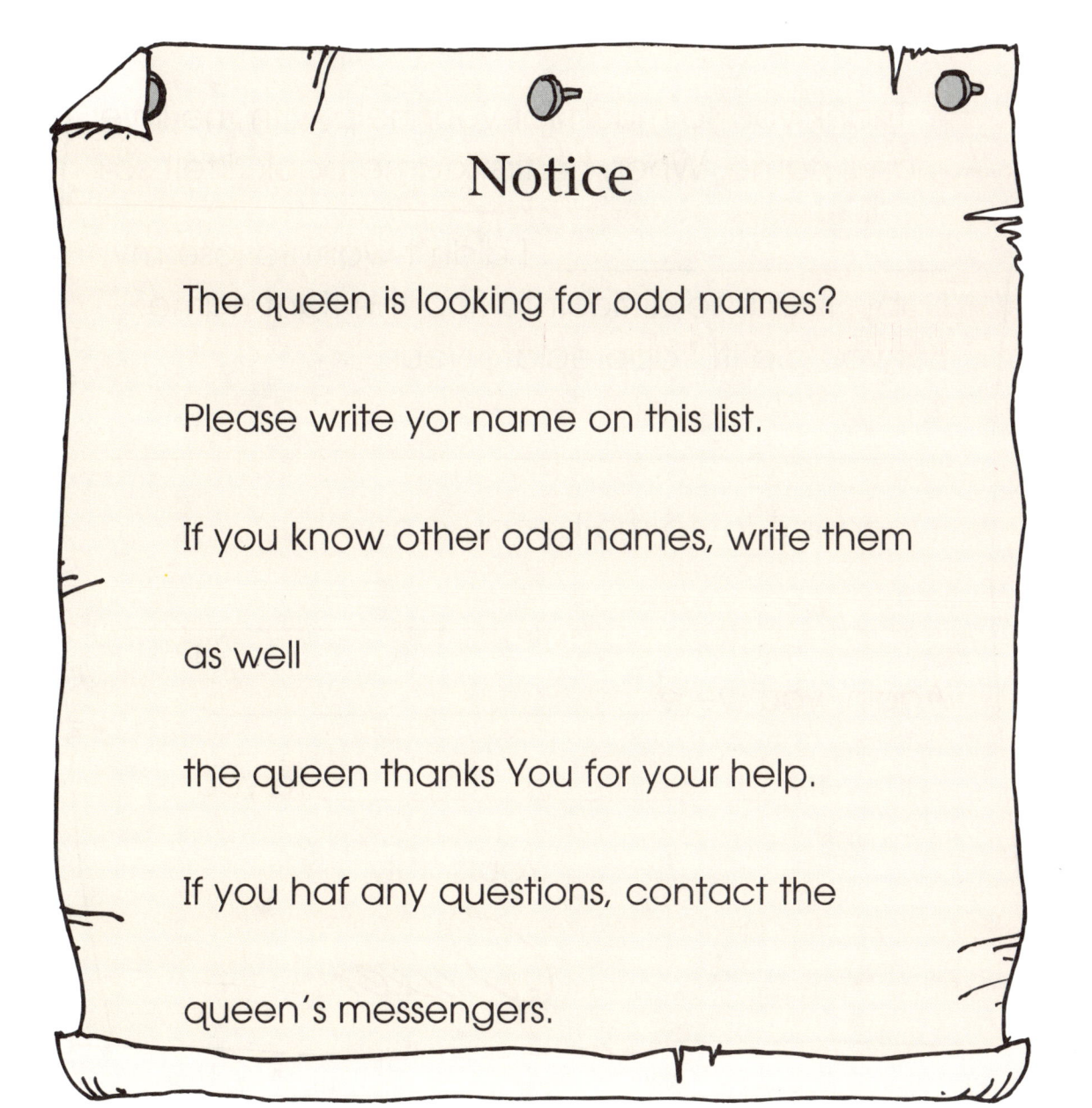

A Word of Thanks

Imagine that you are the queen writing a letter of thanks to the messenger who found out Rumpelstiltskin's name. Complete the letter below.

Dear Messenger,

   Thank you so much for your help with the little man's name. When he first came back, I felt so _____. I didn't want to lose my baby. It was so difficult to find the right name. But you did it! I appreciate your

_____.

It means a lot to me because now

_____.

Again, you were _____.

I am very _____ to you.

Yours truly,

Queen

Writing/A Letter

Action Match

Write a name from the box to match the character and the action. Draw details to finish each character's picture.

Characters
Rapunzel
The witch
Rapunzel's father
Rapunzel's mother
The prince

1. _____ had a strong wish to eat an herb.

2. _____ fell in love with a beautiful singer.

3. _____ promised to give the family's baby away.

4. _____ lived alone in a tower.

5. _____ locked a young girl up in the tower.

Learn to Read With Classic Stories—Grade 2   Comprehension/Characters

Sum It Up

Read each question about the story "Rapunzel" on this page and on page 255. Fill in the circle next to the correct answer to each question.

Who is this story mostly about?

○ Rapunzel's parents

● Rapunzel

○ the prince

When and where does this story take place?

○ yesterday in a city

○ many years from now in outer space

● long ago in a royal kingdom

Sum It Up (page 2)

What happens at the beginning of the story?

○ Rapunzel marries the prince.

● Rapunzel's mother longs for herbs from a witch's garden.

✗ Rapunzel goes to live in a tower all by herself.

What happens in the middle of the story?

○ The witch takes Rapunzel to live in a tower.

○ The witch catches Rapunzel's father taking herbs.

○ Rapunzel and the prince find each other in the wilderness.

What happens at the end of the story?

○ The witch takes the baby from the family.

○ Rapunzel, the prince, and the twins return to the kingdom.

○ The prince climbs up Rapunzel's hair.

Guide to the Kingdom

Look at the places on this map. Then follow the directions on page 257.

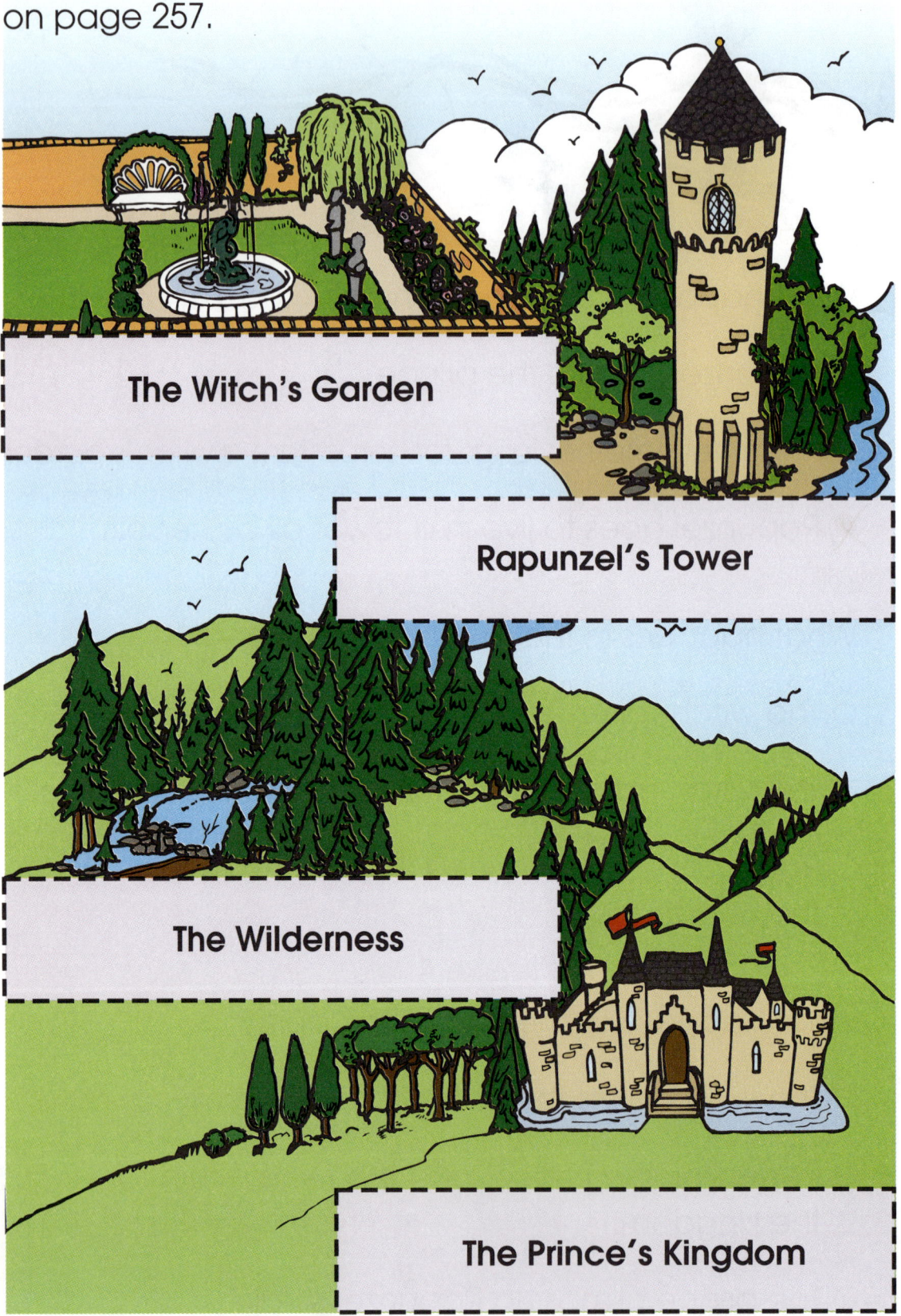

The Witch's Garden

Rapunzel's Tower

The Wilderness

The Prince's Kingdom

Comprehension/Setting

Guide to the Kingdom (page 2)

The action in the story "Rapunzel" happens in several different places. Read the descriptions below. Then cut them out and glue them to the places they describe on the map on page 256.

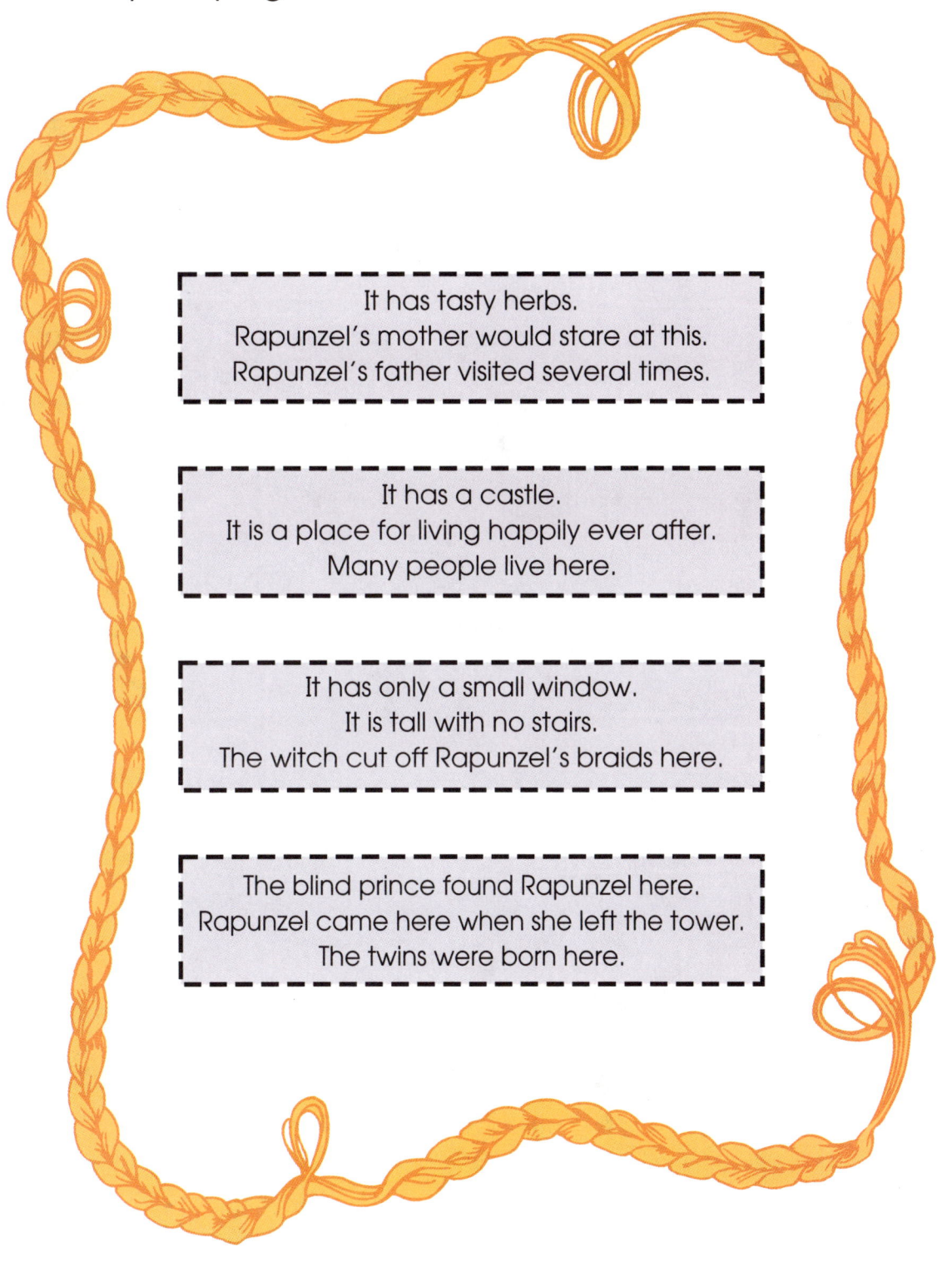

It has tasty herbs.
Rapunzel's mother would stare at this.
Rapunzel's father visited several times.

It has a castle.
It is a place for living happily ever after.
Many people live here.

It has only a small window.
It is tall with no stairs.
The witch cut off Rapunzel's braids here.

The blind prince found Rapunzel here.
Rapunzel came here when she left the tower.
The twins were born here.

Learn to Read With Classic Stories—Grade 2

Comprehension/Setting

Colorful Details

Read each sentence. Color the plant **green** if the sentence tells something that happened in the story. Color the plant **brown** if the sentence tells something that did not happen in the story.

The witch grows to love Rapunzel very much.

The prince hurts his eyes on the thorny brambles.

The witch climbs up Rapunzel's hair to get to the tower.

The prince finds Rapunzel in a nearby city.

The prince asks the witch if Rapunzel could marry him.

Rapunzel's tears help the prince see again.

Rapunzel

Learn to Read With Classic Stories—Grade 2

Comprehension/Story Details

Why, Oh Why?

A **cause** tells **why something happens**. An **effect** is **what happens**. Draw a line to match each cause to an effect.

1. Because his wife wants to eat some herbs,
  • the witch chops off Rapunzel's braids.

2. Because the witch agrees to let the husband have the herbs,
  • the husband goes into the witch's garden.

3. Because rapunzel is the reason the witch gets the baby,
  • the prince, Rapunzel, and their children return to the kingdom.

4. Because the witch is angry at the girl,
  • the husband promises to give the witch the baby.

5. Because Rapunzel's tears drop into his eyes,
  • the witch names the baby Rapunzel.

6. Because the prince finds Rapunzel,
  • the prince can see again.

All in the Name

The **main idea** is what a story or part of a story is mostly about. Read the following paragraphs. Then answer the questions. Write the main idea for each paragraph in one sentence.

The witch's garden was the most beautiful in the land. Tall trees grew in one corner. They made a shady spot to sit. Bright flowers lined the stone paths. Vines crawled along the wall. But the herbs looked so tasty and smelled so wonderful that they stood out among all the beauty.

1. What is the main idea of this paragraph?

   _____

   Rapunzel's hair was so very lovely. It was the golden color of sunlight at the end of the day. It was as thick as a warm blanket on a cold winter night. And how long it was! Rapunzel's hair reached from the very top of the tower to the ground below.

2. What is the main idea of this paragraph?

   _____

3. The title of a story often tells what the story is mainly about. What would be another good title for "Rapunzel"?

   _____

   _____

Learn to Read With Classic Stories—Grade 2   Comprehension/Main Idea

Word Wall

Create a "word wall" with the words from the story "Rapunzel." Read the words in the box. Write each word above its meaning on the wall.

| stared | glow | surround |
| stumble | brambles | frightened |

_____
trip

_____
scared

_____
prickly shrubs

_____
enclose

_____
shine

_____
looked

Tower Sounds

Draw lines to connect words that have the same vowel sound in each set of towers. Underline the letters that stand for the sound. The first one has been done for you.

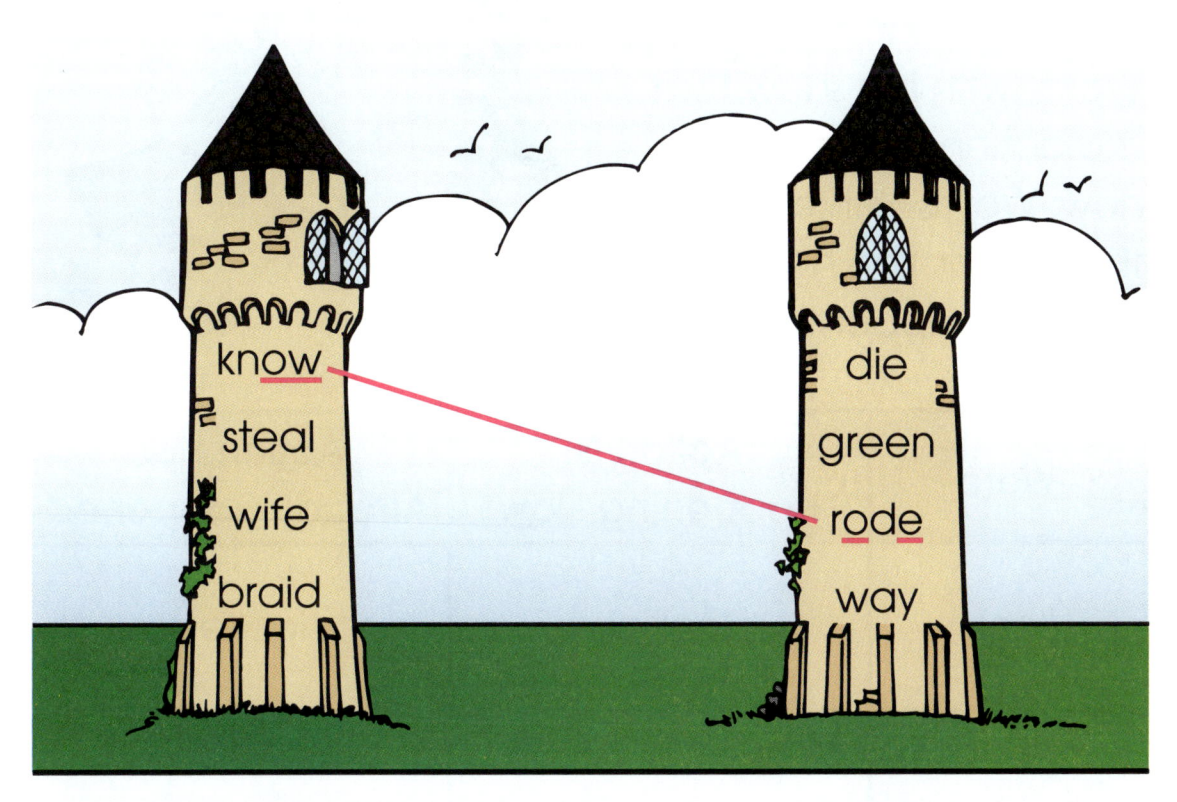

Tower 1 (left):
- kn<u>ow</u>
- steal
- wife
- braid

Tower 2 (right):
- die
- green
- r<u>o</u>d<u>e</u>
- way

Tower 3 (left):
- place
- deep
- rode
- high

Tower 4 (right):
- know
- day
- time
- each

Rapunzel

Learn to Read With Classic Stories—Grade 2   Phonics/Long Vowels   263

A Way With Words

The endings **ing** and **ed** can be added to a word. These endings tell when an action happened. Words with **ing** show that the action is happening now. Words with **ed** show that the action has already happened.

Word	Action Is Happening Now	Action Has Already Happened
look	looking	looked
wish	_____	_____
ask	_____	_____
climb	_____	_____
reach	_____	_____
appear	_____	_____

The Party Is On!

Pretend that the prince and Rapunzel are having a big party to help them celebrate their return to the kingdom. Read the invitation. Find and correct two capitalization mistakes, two punctuation mistakes, and two spelling mistakes. Make your corrections above each mistake.

Dear Friends,

My husband and I are celebrating our return to the kingdom? Please join us for dinner on the ferst day of november. It is a saturday. There will be music and dancing, We cannot wate to see you.

Sincerely,

Rapunzel

Rapunzel Rhyme

Complete the poem. To complete each line, use a word from the list that rhymes with the last word in the line above it.

| day | bound | life | ~~stair~~ |

"Rapunzel, Rapunzel, let down your hair!
The tower is tall and there is no
___stair___."

So Rapunzel's hair would tumble
to the ground.
The witch would climb up with a
leap and a _____.

And on and on things went this way,
Until the prince heard Rapunzel
one _____.

Rapunzel soon became the prince's wife.
She loved him dearly for the rest of
her _____.

Writing/A Poem — Learn to Read With Classic Stories—Grade 2

Story Flow

Read the story events from "The Little Mermaid." Cut them out and glue them in order on page 269.

The Little Mermaid rescues the prince and falls in love.

The prince marries the princess.

The Little Mermaid swims to the top of the sea on her birthday.

The Little Mermaid lives in the prince's castle.

The Little Mermaid joins the children of the air.

The Little Mermaid trades her voice for a life on land.

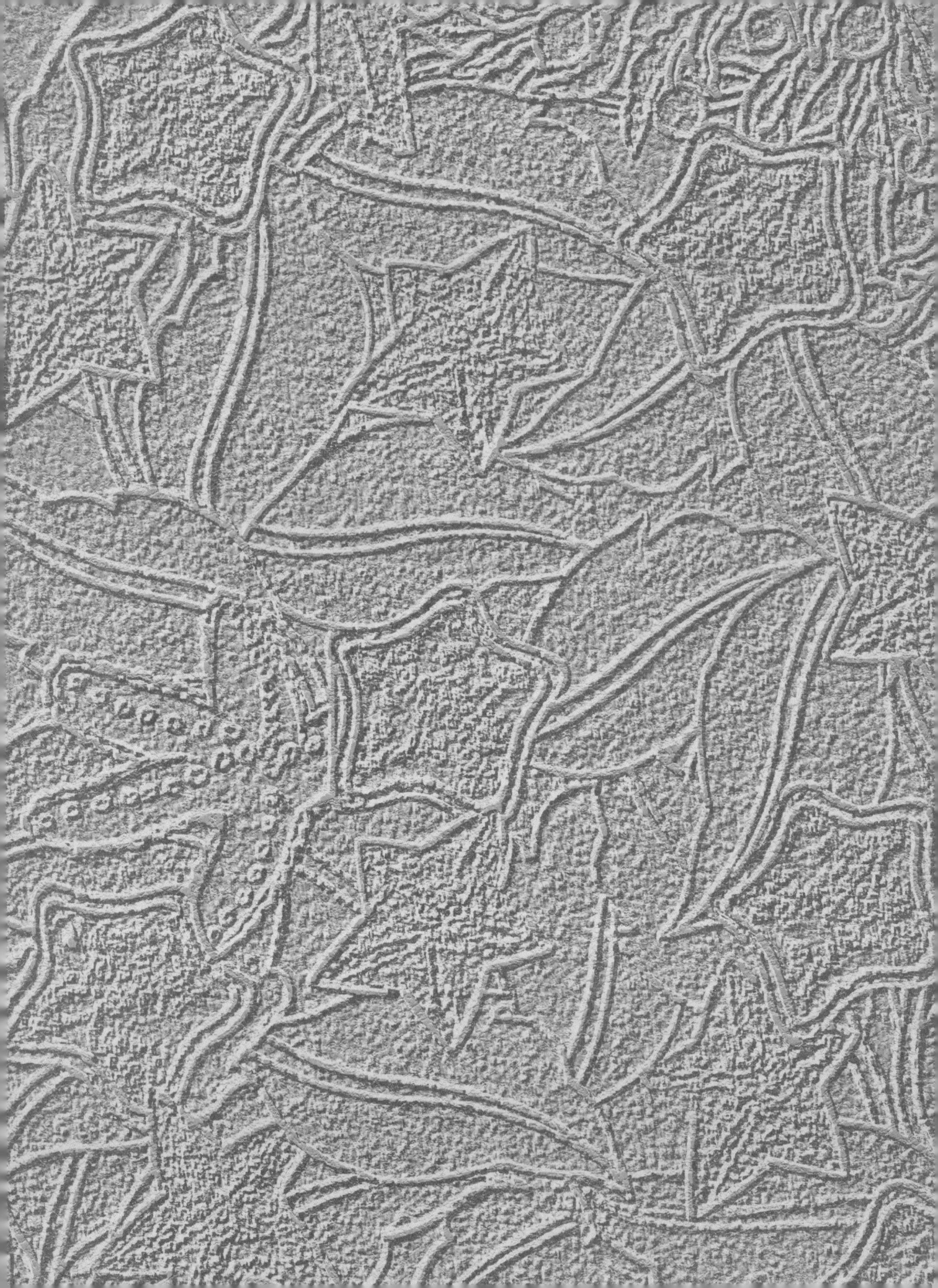

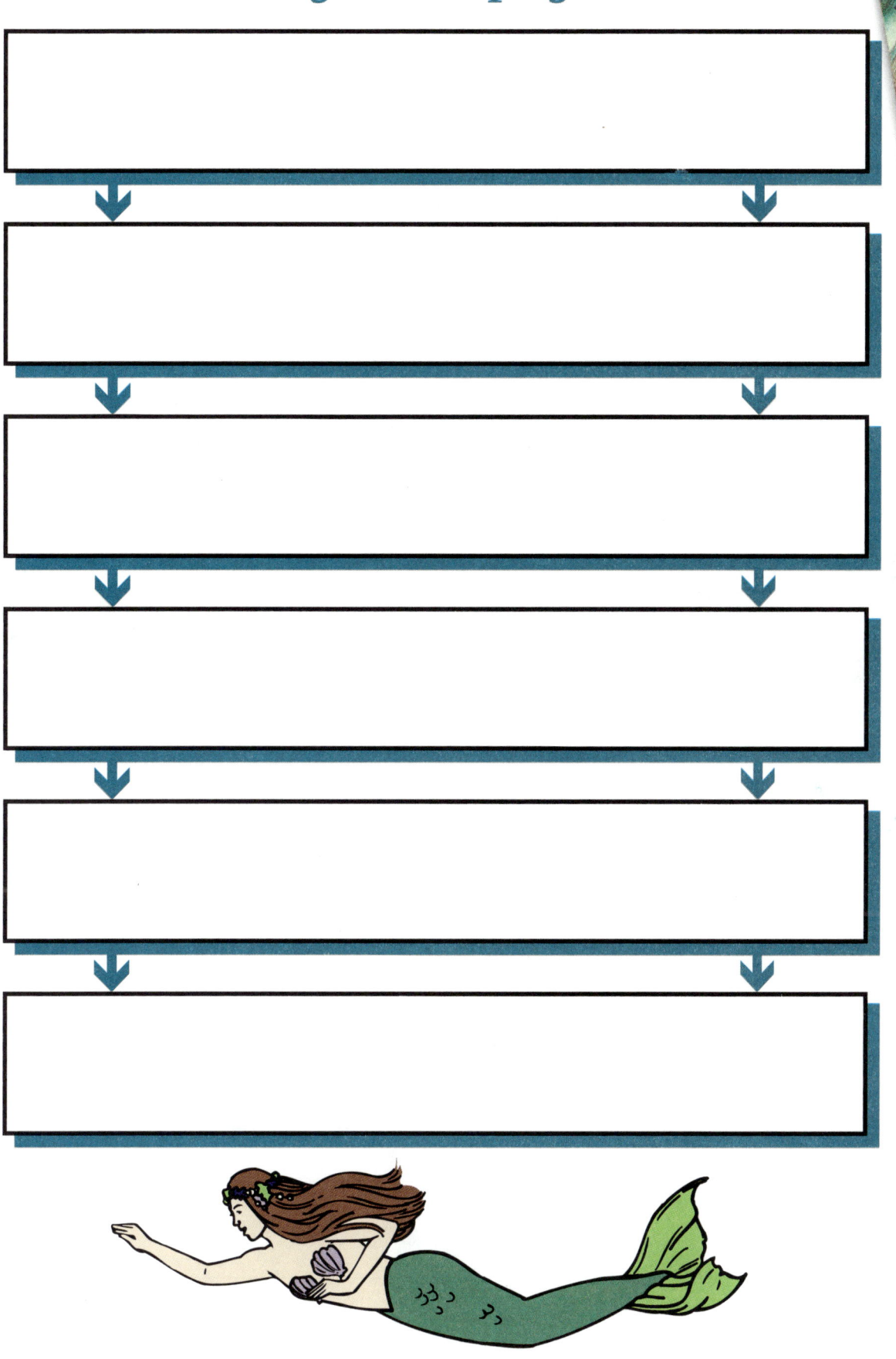

Story Flow (page 2)

The Little Mermaid

Sea Story Map

Fill in the story map to tell about "The Little Mermaid."

The Little Mermaid

Setting:

Where did the story take place?

sea

Characters:

Who is the story about?

girl

What Happens:

What is the story mostly about?

Waves of Details

Read each sentence. If the sentence tells about something that happens in the story, color the wave light **blue**. If the sentence tells about something that does not happen in the story, color the wave **yellow**.

The Little Mermaid loves to sing.

The Little Mermaid saves the prince from drowning.

The Little Mermaid has a pet sea snake.

The Little Mermaid gives her voice to the Sea Witch.

The prince learns that the Little Mermaid was the one who saved him.

After drinking the special drink, the Little Mermaid grows legs.

The Little Mermaid marries the prince.

The Little Mermaid turns into sea foam.

Learn to Read With Classic Stories—Grade 2   Comprehension/Story Details

Ask Little Mermaid

Write the answers Little Mermaid might give to these questions.

1. How did you feel when your grandmother said you could go to the surface when you turned 15?

   _____

2. How did you feel when you first saw the prince?

   _____

3. How did you feel when you gave the Sea Witch your voice?

   _____

4. How did you feel at the prince's wedding?

   _____

5. How did you feel when you joined the children of the air?

   _____

Comprehension/Drawing Conclusions   Learn to Read With Classic Stories—Grade 2

Land or Sea?

In the story, the Little Mermaid lived both in the sea and on land. Read the words in the list. Think about where the Little Mermaid would usually see each one. Then write each word under the correct heading.

Sea Witch   stars   sea snakes   trees
whales   moon   flowers   sunken ship

In the Sea

_____

_____

_____

_____

On Land

_____

_____

_____

_____

Learn to Read With Classic Stories—Grade 2   Comprehension/Categorizing

The Big Idea

Reread these pages of "The Little Mermaid." Then circle the sentence that tells what the page is mainly about.

Page 150

○ The sea had been calm.

○ A great storm broke apart the ship.

○ The ship has a mast.

Page 151

○ The Little Mermaid saw the prince fall into the sea.

○ The Little Mermaid dove into the water.

○ The Little Mermaid saved the prince.

Page 164

○ The Little Mermaid woke up.

○ The Little Mermaid couldn't speak.

○ The Little Mermaid now had legs and was with the prince.

Page 168

○ The prince had plans to marry a princess from the next kingdom.

○ The prince sailed to the neighboring kingdom.

○ The Little Mermaid sailed with the prince.

Characters of the Deep

The Little Mermaid   The prince   The Sea Witch

Write the character's name to complete the sentence. Choose from the list above.

1. _____ wanted to have legs.

2. _____ asked for a voice as payment.

3. _____ fell off a ship and had to be saved.

4. _____ warned someone that a certain wish would not bring happiness.

5. _____ got married in a royal wedding.

Learn to Read With Classic Stories—Grade 2   Comprehension/Characters

Seaworthy Words

On each line, write a word from the list that matches its meaning.

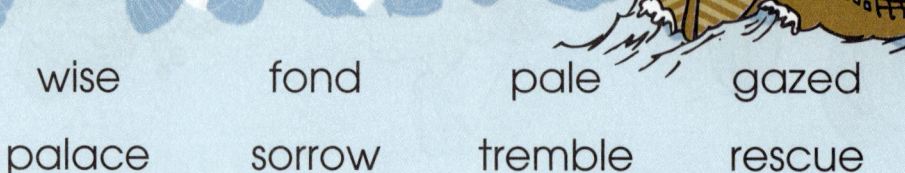

wise　　fond　　pale　　gazed
palace　　sorrow　　tremble　　rescue

1. _____ — looked at for a while

2. _____ — sadness

3. _____ — shake

4. _____ — save

5. _____ — castle

6. _____ — without much color

7. _____ — smart

8. _____ — attached to in a loving way

A Mermaid on Land

The word **land** has a **short a** sound. The word **mermaid** has a **long a** sound in the second part. It is spelled **ai**. The **long a** sound can also be spelled with **ay** as in **say** or **a_e** as in **cave**. Sort the story words in the list by writing them under the correct heading.

way	pain	swam	pay
pale	sad	laid	wave
mast	snake	play	sail

ai as in **tail**

_____
_____
_____

ay as in **day**

pay
_____
_____

a_e as in **save**

_____
_____
_____

a as in **sand**

_____
_____
_____

Learn to Read With Classic Stories—Grade 2   Phonics/Long and Short Vowel a

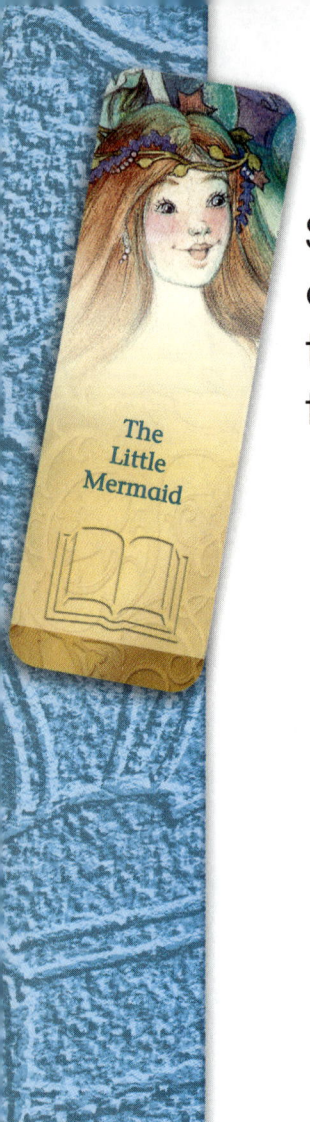

Sounds the Same

Some words sound the same but are spelled differently and have different meanings. Read the pairs of words in the list and their meanings. Choose a word from the list to complete each sentence.

blue — a color
blew — pushed with air

sea — a body of water
see — to look at

tail — a part of an animal's body
tale — a story

to — where something goes
too — also
two — a number more than one

1. The Little Mermaid lived in the _____.

2. The Little Mermaid's eyes were

   the deepest _____.

3. The Little Mermaid walked _____ the prince's palace.

4. The story of the Little Mermaid

   is a wonderful _____.

5. The wind _____ the ship's sails.

The Prince's Journal

Read this entry in the prince's journal. Find and correct two capitalization mistakes, two punctuation mistakes, and two spelling mistakes. Make your corrections above each mistake.

Today there wuz a bad storm. The chip sank. i fell into the sea. Someone saved me? It was a girl I wish I knew who she was. maybe I will know someday.

Describe the Underwater World

Finish this description of the Little Mermaid's home under the sea. Write your words on the lines.

Where the Little Mermaid lived, the water was the color of _____. Some of the plants looked like _____
_____.

Some of the animals looked like _____
_____.

There were lots of _____
_____.

Everywhere you looked, you could see _____
_____.

Writing/A Description

A Giant Retelling

Read and cut out each story event below. Glue them in order to the chart on page 283.

---

(2) Paul left his family to live in the wilderness.

(5) Paul took the logging camp out on the road.

(1) Paul Bunyan was born weighing 100 pounds.

(4) Paul started a logging camp.

(3) Paul discovered Babe the Blue Ox.

Learn to Read With Classic Stories—Grade 2 Comprehension/Sequencing

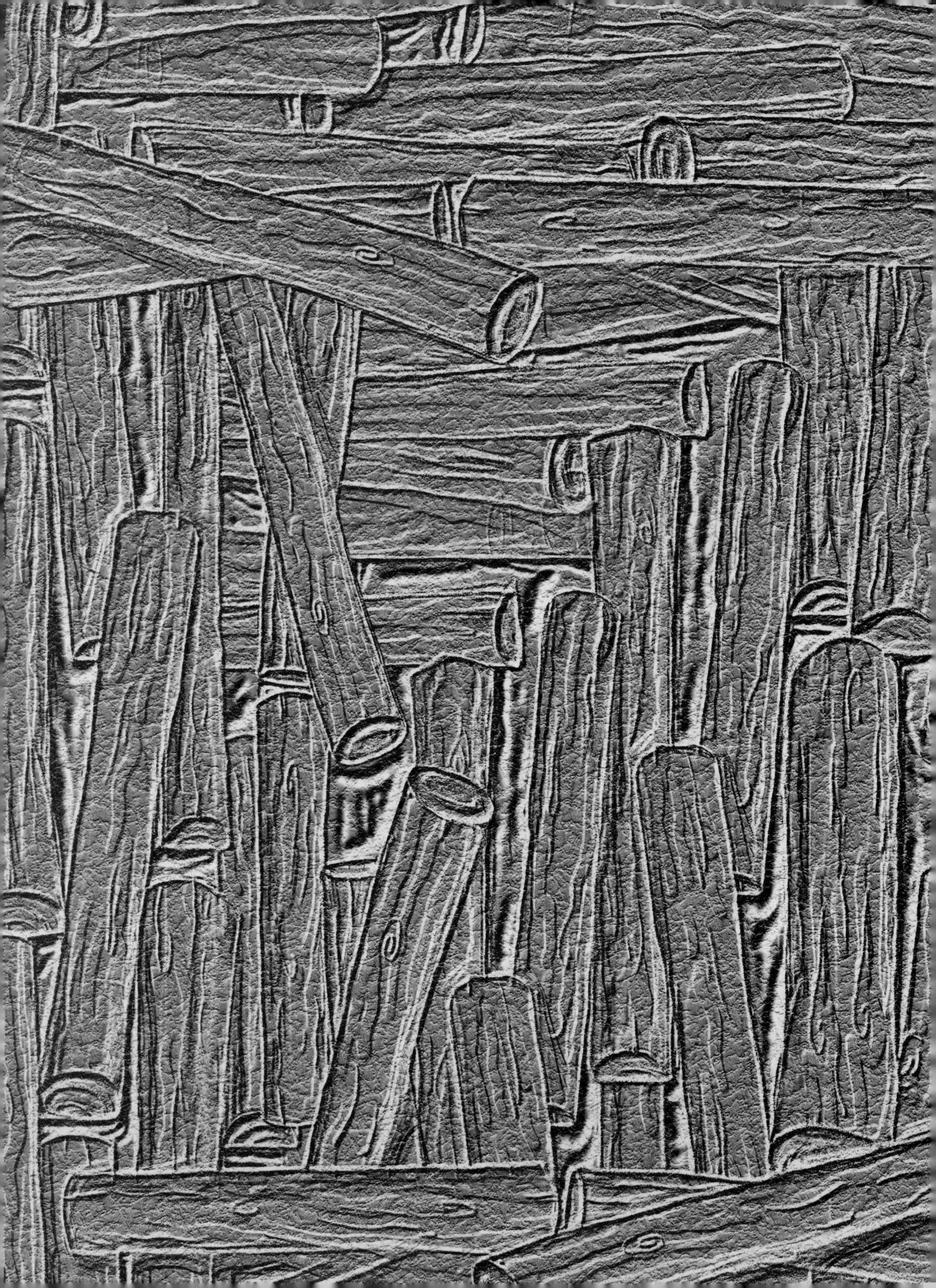

A Giant Retelling (page 2)

Paul Bunyan

The Mighty Logger

Think about the character Paul Bunyan. Circle the words and phrases that describe him.

- hard worker
- foolish
- unkind
- likes to try new things
- cares about Earth
- angry
- strong
- just like other loggers
- shy
- gentle with animals
- sad
- smart

Paul Bunyan

Comprehension/Characterization

Learn to Read With Classic Stories—Grade 2

The Mighty Logger (page 2)

Read the events below. Think about which character trait from page 284 matches each event. Write a word or a phrase on the line after each sentence.

1. Paul Bunyan saves Babe the Blue Ox from freezing.

   very Gentle with animal

2. Paul Bunyan thinks of ways to solve problems at the logging camp.

   _____

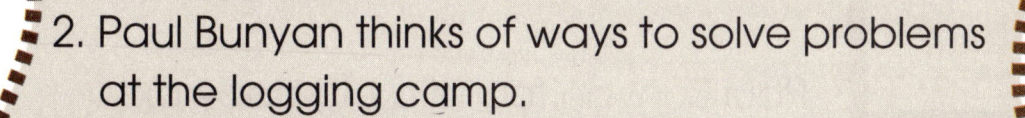

3. Paul Bunyan plants a new seedling for every tree the loggers cut.

   _____

4. Paul Bunyan thinks he and Babe need a change after the hard winter. He decides to take the logging camp out on the road.

   _____

Remembering Details

Read each sentence. Cut out the small pictures at the bottom of the page. Glue a picture next to a sentence if it tells about something that happened in the story. If the detail did not happen in the story, do not glue a picture next to it.

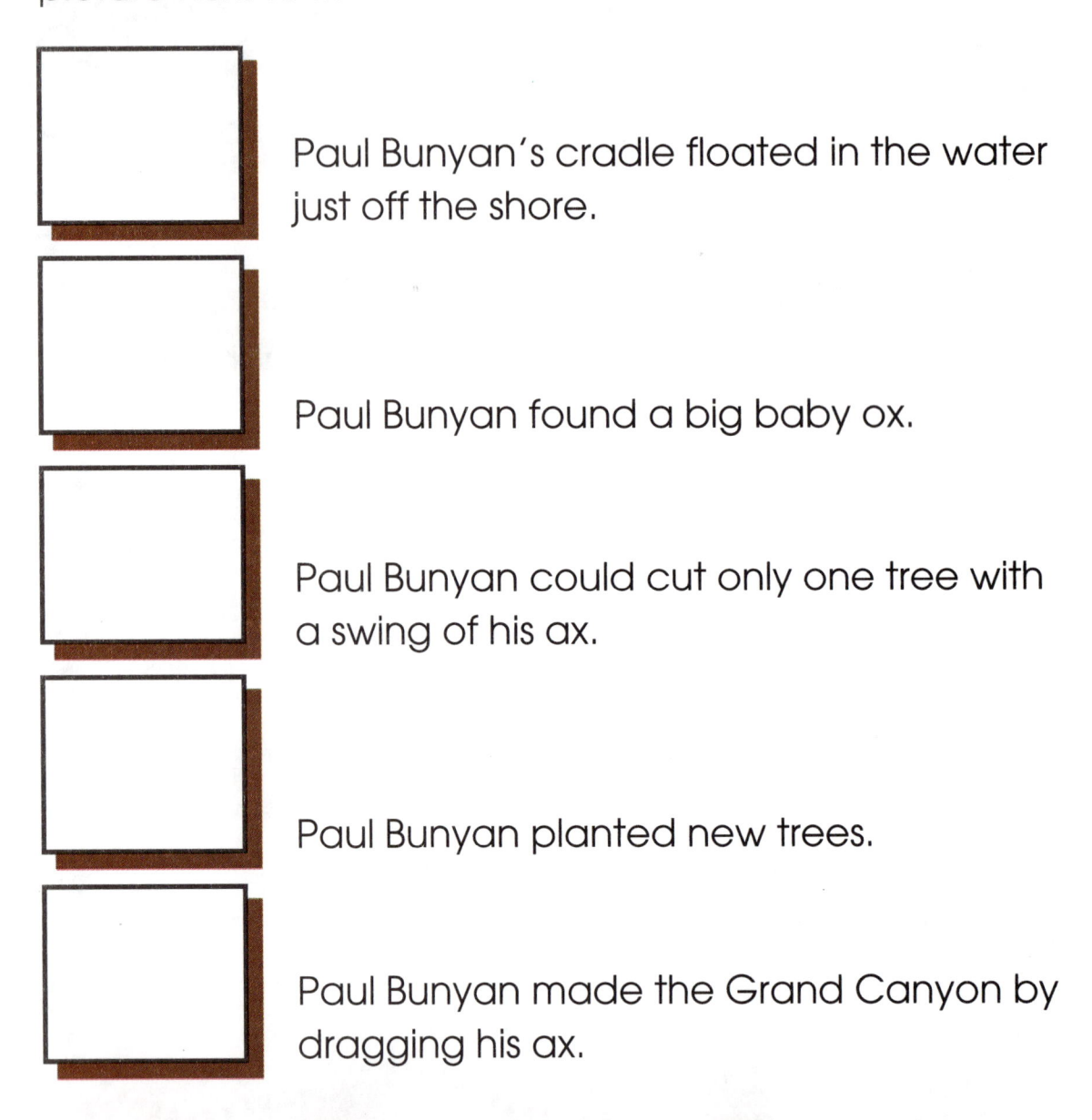

Paul Bunyan's cradle floated in the water just off the shore.

Paul Bunyan found a big baby ox.

Paul Bunyan could cut only one tree with a swing of his ax.

Paul Bunyan planted new trees.

Paul Bunyan made the Grand Canyon by dragging his ax.

Comprehension/Story Details

Learn to Read With Classic Stories—Grade 2

Big Words From a Big Story

Write the words from the list on the lines below to match them with their meanings.

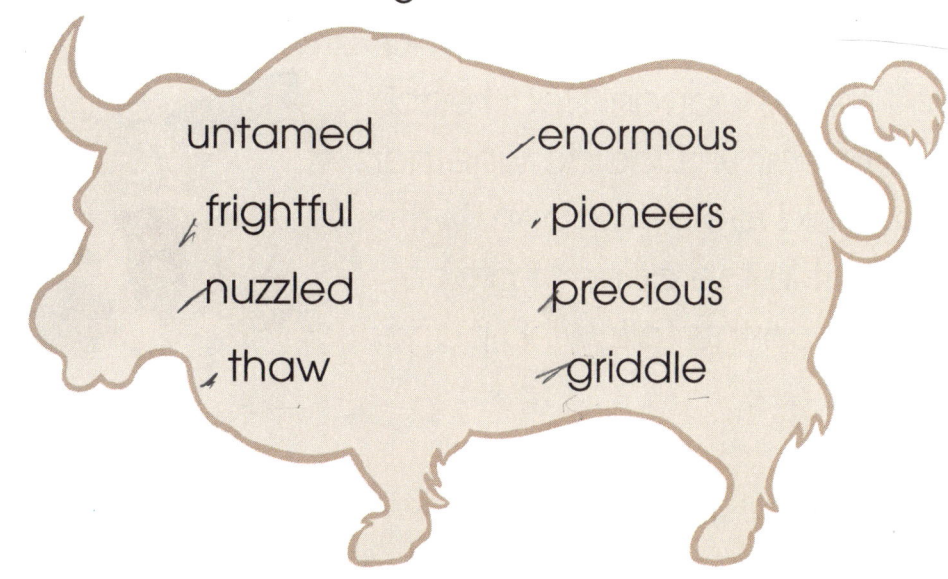

untamed   enormous
frightful   pioneers
nuzzled   precious
thaw   griddle

1. _____ special

2. _____ melt

3. _____ wild

4. _____ very big

5. _____ the first people in a place

6. _____ snuggled

7. _____ flat cooking pan

8. _____ terrible

Paul Bunyan

What Could Really Happen?

"Paul Bunyan" is a tall tale. **Tall tales** are stores about larger-than-life characters. They include things that couldn't really happen. Read each story event below. Decide whether or not it could really happen. Write each event in the correct place in the chart on the following page.

A baby is born.

A baby weighs 100 pounds when he is born.

A man cuts down ten trees with one swing of his ax.

A man cuts down ten trees in one week.

An ox straightens out a river.

A man floats logs down the river.

A man cooks pancakes.

A man skates on a giant griddle with bacon on his boots.

Icicles thaw in the spring.

Frozen words thaw in the spring for people to hear.

Comprehension/Fantasy or Reality

Could Really Happen

_____
_____
_____
_____
_____
_____

Could NOT Really Happen

_____
_____
_____
_____
_____
_____

Paul Bunyan

Learn to Read With Classic Stories—Grade 2   Comprehension/Fantasy or Reality

The Main Event

Reread each part of the story listed below. Then circle the sentence that tells what that part of the story is mainly about.

1. **Page 178—second paragraph**
   - Paul Bunyan weighed about a hundred pounds at birth.
   - Paul Bunyan ate five dozen eggs.
   - Paul Bunyan ate huge breakfasts.

2. **Page 182**
   - One winter, blue snow was everywhere.
   - Paul was surprised.
   - Snowflakes began to fall.

3. **Page 197—first paragraph**
   - The men wore bacon on their boots.
   - The griddle was the size of an ice rink.
   - Sam cooked flapjacks on a giant griddle.

4. **Page 198**
   - Johnny used a lot of ink.
   - Johnny didn't dot his **i**'s or cross his **t**'s.
   - Johnny saved 500 barrels of ink.

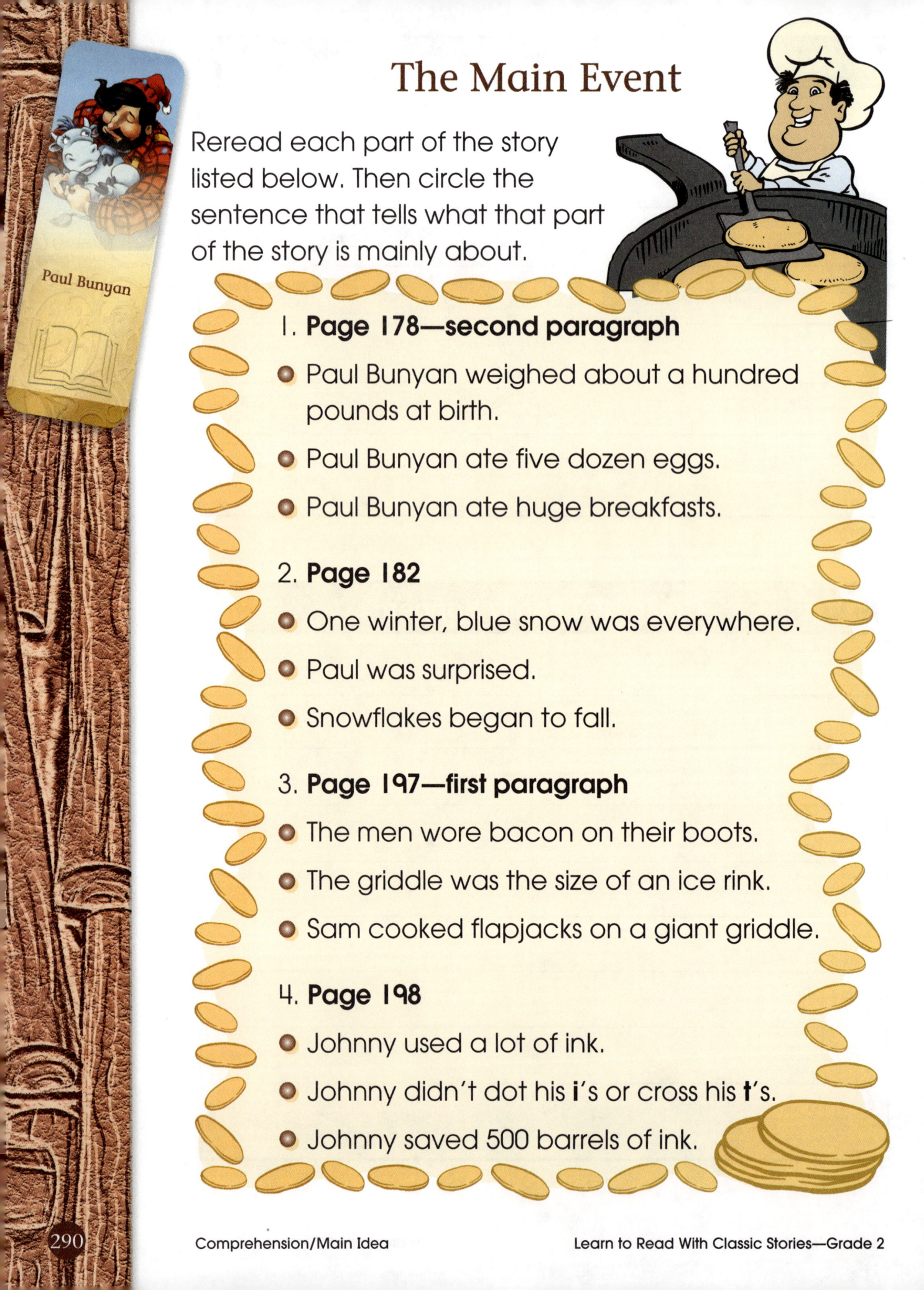

Two for One

Compound words are two words put together to make a new word with a new meaning. Draw lines to put two words together to make compound words. Then write the compound words you made.

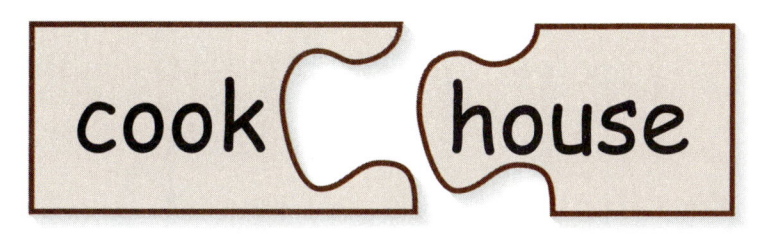

cook — house

Paul Bunyan

oat	keeper	1. _____
earth	roll	2. _____
snow	drift	3. _____
book	quake	4. _____
pay	meal	5. _____
lumber	time	6. _____
pan	cakes	7. _____
sour	mill	8. _____
saw	dough	9. _____
spring	jack	10. _____

Learn to Read With Classic Stories—Grade 2   Word Structure/Compound Words

Blue Blizzard Spelling

Some words are tricky to spell. Use a blue crayon to fill in the missing letter for each word. You will find the missing letters in the snow. Next, write a sentence using each word.

e o l u h o

1. enoug_h_

_____

2. ta____ght

_____

3. th____ugh

_____

4. bui____d

_____

5. w____igh

_____

6. tr____uble

_____

Phonics/Spelling

Sign of the Times

Help Paul Bunyan fix a sign he has written. Begin each sentence with a capital letter. End each sentence with a period or question mark.

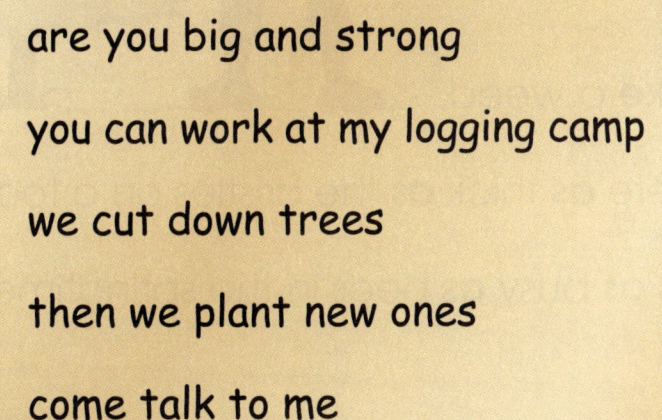

are you big and strong

you can work at my logging camp

we cut down trees

then we plant new ones

come talk to me

_____

_____

_____

_____

_____

As Big as Paul Bunyan?

A **simile** (SIHM uh lee) is a group of words that uses **like** or **as** to compare one thing to another. Read these examples of similes.

- Babe grew **like** a weed.

- The forests were **as** thick **as** the bristles on a toothbrush.

- America was **as** busy **as** bees in the springtime.

Write similes to describe the character Paul Bunyan.

Paul was as big as _____

_____.

Paul was as strong as _____

_____.

Paul ate like _____

_____.

Reading Skills Checklist

Learning certain skills and strategies will help your child become a good reader. The following list shows the goals your child should reach in applying some basic skills during the second grade. Use the checklist after reading each story to assess your child's reading progress. Choose only a handful of skills to check at any one time. Sample questions have been given for each skill.

Skill	The Three Wishes	Aesop's Fables	Rumpelstiltskin	Rapunzel	The Little Mermaid	Paul Bunyan
Cause and Effect Child recognizes that some actions or events can cause other events or results to happen. *What happened to the woodcutter's nose? Why did it happen?*						
Classify/Categorize Child can sort into groups related words or objects. *Which words name places? Which words do not?*						
Compare and Contrast Child can compare and contrast people, places, things, and events. *Who does this character remind you of? How is this character like someone you admire? How is he/she different?*						
Draw Conclusions Child can use information from a story and from real life to draw conclusions that are not stated in the story. *Why did the witch lock Rapunzel away in a tower?*						
Making Judgments Child can decide what he or she thinks about the ideas in a story. *Do you think the miller was right to tell the king his daughter could spin straw into gold? Why?*						
Main Idea and Details Child can tell what a story or paragraph is about and identify details that explain it. *What is this paragraph about? Which sentences tell more about the main idea?*						
Phonics Child can sound out unfamiliar words using phonetic skills. *What sound do you hear at the beginning of the word? at the end? in the middle?*						
Picture/Context Clues Child can use illustrations, sentence clues, and phonetic clues to help identify words they do not know in a story. *What do you do when you come to a word you do not know? What other words in the sentence help you figure out this word?*						

Skill	The Three Wishes	Aesop's Fables	Rumpelstiltskin	Rapunzel	The Little Mermaid	Paul Bunyan
Predict Outcomes Child can make and modify predictions as he or she reads. The prediction need not be accurate, as long as it is generally consistent with what has happened so far in the story. (during reading:) *What do you think will happen next in the story? Why do you think it will happen?* (after reading on:) *Did your prediction match what really happened?*						
Reality/Fantasy Child can tell the difference between a realistic story and a fantasy. *Is this a realistic story? Why?* *Is this story a fantasy? Why?*						
Retell a Story Child can retell major events in a story in the order they occur. *What happened in this story?*						
Sequence Child can tell about a sequence of events in a story. *What happened first? after that? last?*						
Character Child can identify character traits. *How would you describe the prince?*						
Plot Child can tell what happens in the beginning, middle, and end of the story. *How does this story begin? What happens next? How does this story end?*						
Setting Child can tell where and when a story is set. *Where does this story take place? When?*						
Summarize Child can describe the story in one or two sentences. *What is this story mostly about?*						
Visualize Child can form a mental picture of what happens in a story. *What did you see happening in the story? Which words help you make pictures in your mind about the story?*						

Answer Key

211 — Order, Please!

Cut out the pictures below. Put them in order to show what happened in "The Three Wishes." Then number each box from 1 to 6. Use the pictures to retell the story. Use words like *first*, *next*, *then*, and *last*.

213 — Detail Mix-Up

Read each sentence below. Find one word that is wrong, and underline it. Then replace the wrong word with a word from the tree to make the sentence tell about the story. Write the correct word on the line.

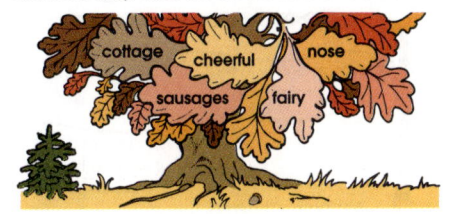

1. A <u>toad</u> gave the man and wife three wishes. **fairy**
2. The man and wife went home to their <u>nest</u>. **cottage**
3. The man said he wished he had <u>pancakes</u> for dinner. **sausages**
4. The man ended up with sausages on his <u>toes</u>. **nose**
5. In the end, the man and wife were <u>scared</u> about their dinner. **cheerful**

214 — Things Change and Stay the Same

Fill in the chart with the sentences below. Write one sentence in each part of the chart. Then, answer the question.

> The man and his wife dreamed of riches.
> The man and his wife had a dinner of sausages.
> The man and his wife were hungry and poor.

Beginning	The man and his wife were hungry and poor.
Middle	The man and his wife dreamed of riches.
End	The man and his wife had a dinner of sausages.

How did things change for the man and his wife from the beginning of the story to the end?

Things changed only a little for the man and his wife. At the beginning they were hungry and poor. At the end, they had a nice dinner. But, they didn't turn out to be as rich as they had hoped.

215 — How It Happened

Read each sentence. Fill in the circle to finish each sentence correctly.

1. The fairy gave the man and wife three wishes because
   - ○ they were poor.
   - ● they didn't cut down her tree.
2. The man built a fire because
   - ● it was cold in the cottage.
   - ○ they wanted to burn some old things.
3. The man got sausages on his nose because
   - ○ he said he wanted to know what it would be like.
   - ● his wife said she wished that would happen.
4. The two had to use their last wish to get the sausages off because
   - ● that was the only way to get them off.
   - ○ they couldn't think of anything else to wish for.
5. At the end, the two were cheerful because
   - ○ their wishes came true about a house and coach.
   - ● at least they had a fine dinner of sausages.

Learn to Read With Classic Stories—Grade 2

216 — Real or Not?

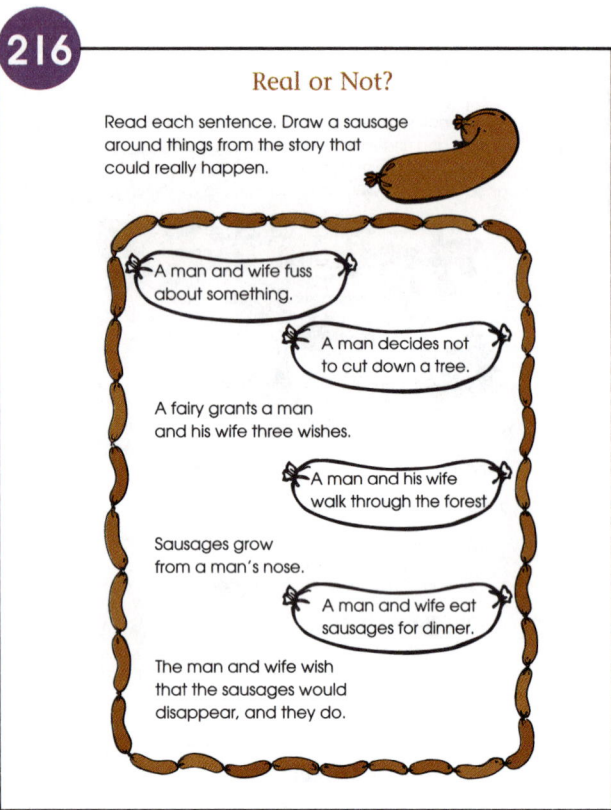

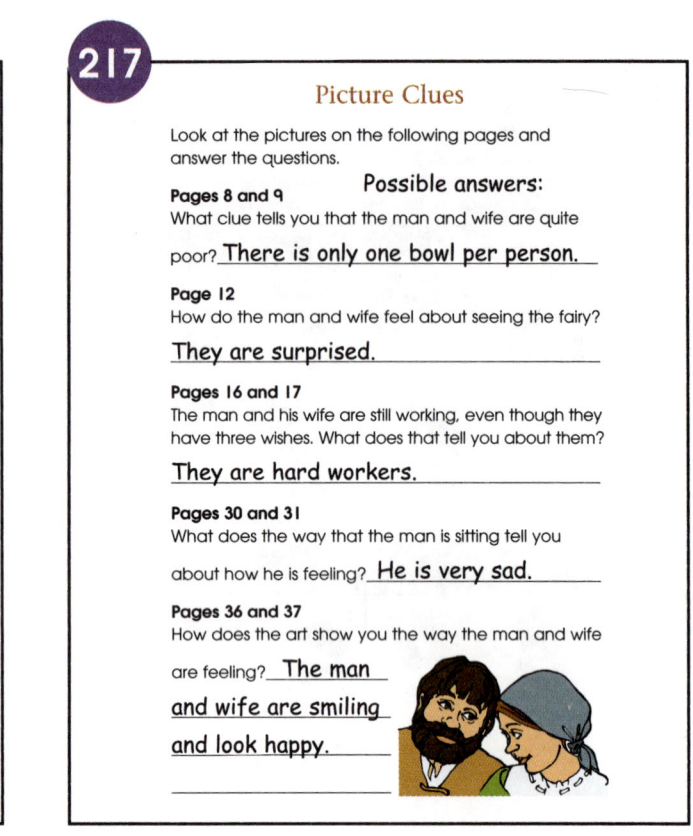

Read each sentence. Draw a sausage around things from the story that could really happen.

- A man and wife fuss about something. *(sausage)*
- A man decides not to cut down a tree. *(sausage)*
- A fairy grants a man and his wife three wishes.
- A man and his wife walk through the forest. *(sausage)*
- Sausages grow from a man's nose.
- A man and wife eat sausages for dinner. *(sausage)*
- The man and wife wish that the sausages would disappear, and they do.

217 — Picture Clues

Look at the pictures on the following pages and answer the questions.

Possible answers:

Pages 8 and 9
What clue tells you that the man and wife are quite poor? __There is only one bowl per person.__

Page 12
How do the man and wife feel about seeing the fairy? __They are surprised.__

Pages 16 and 17
The man and his wife are still working, even though they have three wishes. What does that tell you about them? __They are hard workers.__

Pages 30 and 31
What does the way that the man is sitting tell you about how he is feeling? __He is very sad.__

Pages 36 and 37
How does the art show you the way the man and wife are feeling? __The man and wife are smiling and look happy.__

218 — Wise or Foolish?

Look at each thing the man and woman could have wished for. Would each wish be wise or foolish? Check the box. Then tell why you think so.

Possible answers:

☐ wise ☑ foolish
It is __foolish__, because __when it is eaten, it is gone__.

☐ wise ☑ foolish
It is __foolish__, because __she can't wear such a fancy dress very often__.

☑ wise ☐ foolish
It is __wise__, because __they can use it to buy many things they need__.

☑ wise ☑ foolish
It is __foolish or wise__, because __the jewels cannot be eaten or the jewels could be sold to buy food or other things__.

219 — What About Next Time?

Think about what the man and wife might do next time. Answer the questions.

Possible answers:

1. What do you think the man might do if another fairy asked him not to cut down a tree? Why?

   __The man would not cut down the tree. He would hope that he would get more wishes.__

2. Say that the man and wife got three more wishes. What do you think they might say to each other before they make any wishes?

   __The man and wife would tell each other to be careful with the wishes.__

3. What do you think the man and wife might wish for if they got three more wishes?

   __They would wish for the things they didn't get this time, like the house and coach and clothes and money.__

220 Thinking About the Story

The paragraphs below tell what two people thought about "The Three Wishes." Read each review. Circle the letter that answers each question.

> "The Three Wishes" is a great story. It teaches an important lesson—be careful what you wish for! In the story, a man and his wife are careless with three wishes. The story made me think about being happy with what you have.

1. What does this writer think about the story?
   a. The writer likes another story better.
   b. The writer thinks it is a great story.
   c. The writer thinks the author of the story should have changed it.

> "The Three Wishes" is an old story. It reminds me of "The Fisherman and His Wife." I like that story better. "The Three Wishes" tries to teach readers to think before they do something.

2. What does this writer think about the story?
   a. The writer likes another story better.
   b. The writer thinks it is the best story ever.
   c. The writer thinks the author of the story should have changed it.

221 The Meaning of This

Complete each sentence with a word from the pan.

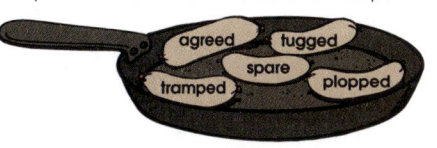

(pan words: agreed, tugged, spare, tramped, plopped)

1. The man and his wife **tramped** through the forest.
2. The wife **agreed** with the man that they had found a huge tree.
3. The man told the fairy they would **spare** her tree.
4. Back at the cottage, the man and wife **plopped** down in front of the fire.
5. The man and wife **tugged** at the sausages on his nose, but it was no use.

222 Sentence Scramble

Put each group of words in order to make a sentence that tells something. Write each sentence on the line below the words.

1. forest / man / went / the / the / into
   The man went into the forest.

2. cut / the / wood / man
   The man cut wood.

3. of / dreamed / wishes / they
   They dreamed of wishes.

4. sausages / nose / the / hung / his / from
   The sausages hung from his nose.

5. dinner / ate / they
   They ate dinner.

223 Help the Fairy

Read this sign the fairy has written. Find and correct two capitalization mistakes, two punctuation mistakes, and two spelling mistakes. Make your corrections above each mistake.

> Please
> ~~p~~lease do not~~é~~
> cut down this tree.
> It makes a
> lovely home for me**.**
> **so**
> Thank you for being so~~o~~ kind.
> When I grant wishes,
> **I'll**
> ~~i~~'ll keep you in mind**.**

Learn to Read With Classic Stories—Grade 2   Answer Key   299

224 — What the Man Might Say

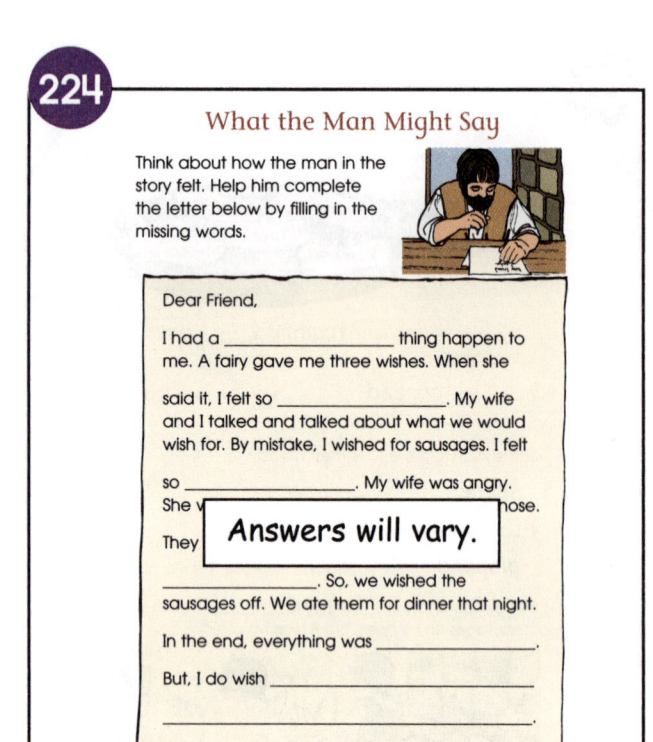

Think about how the man in the story felt. Help him complete the letter below by filling in the missing words.

Dear Friend,

I had a _____ thing happen to me. A fairy gave me three wishes. When she said it, I felt so _____. My wife and I talked and talked about what we would wish for. By mistake, I wished for sausages. I felt so _____. My wife was angry. She w... ...ose. They...

Answers will vary.

_____. So, we wished the sausages off. We ate them for dinner that night.

In the end, everything was _____.

But, I do wish _____
_____

Yours truly,
The Woodcutter

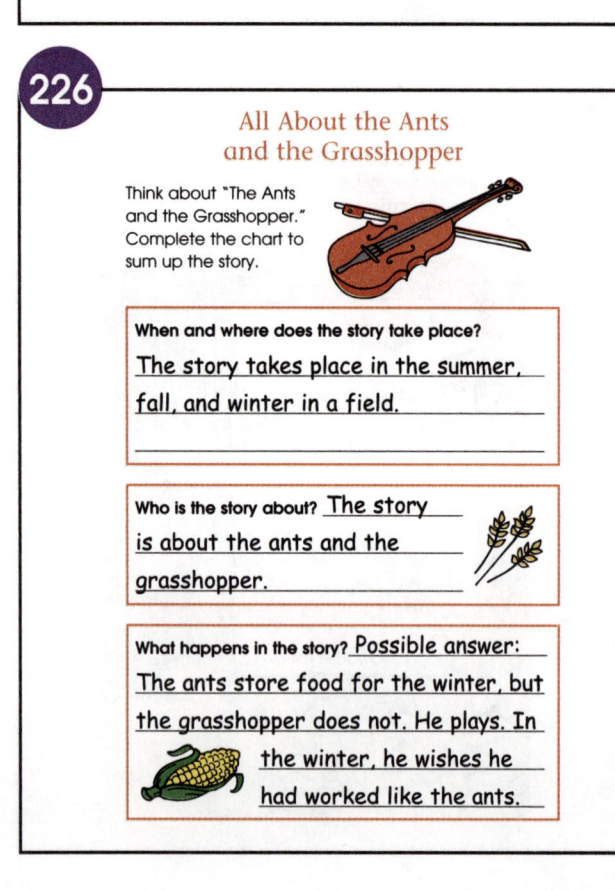

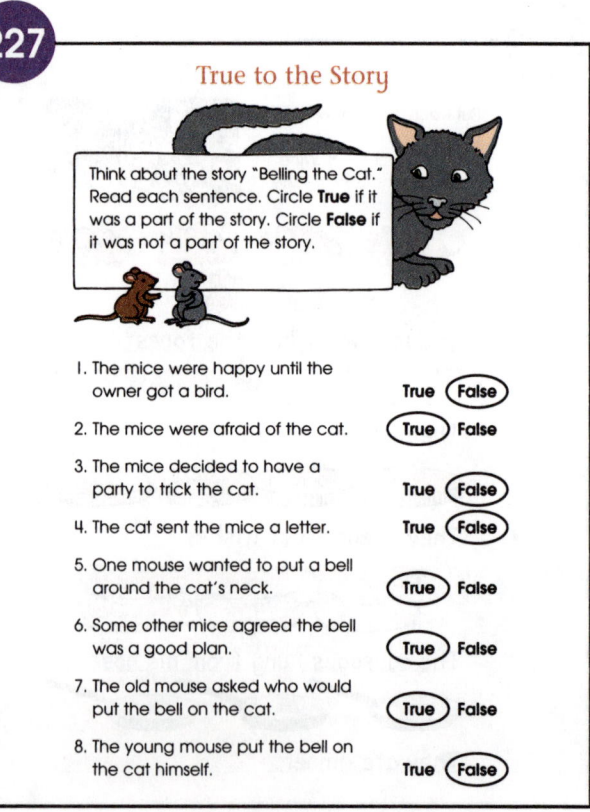

---

225 — Meet the Ants and the Grasshopper

Read each phrase below. Write **ants** or **grasshopper** to show who the phrase tells about.

1. worked hard **ants**
2. wanted only to play **grasshopper**
3. got ready for winter **ants**
4. tried to help someone by suggesting a work plan **ants**
5. didn't worry about what was coming up **grasshopper**
6. was sorry not to have planned ahead **grasshopper**

---

226 — All About the Ants and the Grasshopper

Think about "The Ants and the Grasshopper." Complete the chart to sum up the story.

When and where does the story take place?
The story takes place in the summer, fall, and winter in a field.

Who is the story about? The story is about the ants and the grasshopper.

What happens in the story? Possible answer: The ants store food for the winter, but the grasshopper does not. He plays. In the winter, he wishes he had worked like the ants.

---

227 — True to the Story

Think about the story "Belling the Cat." Read each sentence. Circle **True** if it was a part of the story. Circle **False** if it was not a part of the story.

1. The mice were happy until the owner got a bird. True **(False)**
2. The mice were afraid of the cat. **(True)** False
3. The mice decided to have a party to trick the cat. True **(False)**
4. The cat sent the mice a letter. True **(False)**
5. One mouse wanted to put a bell around the cat's neck. **(True)** False
6. Some other mice agreed the bell was a good plan. **(True)** False
7. The old mouse asked who would put the bell on the cat. **(True)** False
8. The young mouse put the bell on the cat himself. True **(False)**

228 — How to Bell the Cat

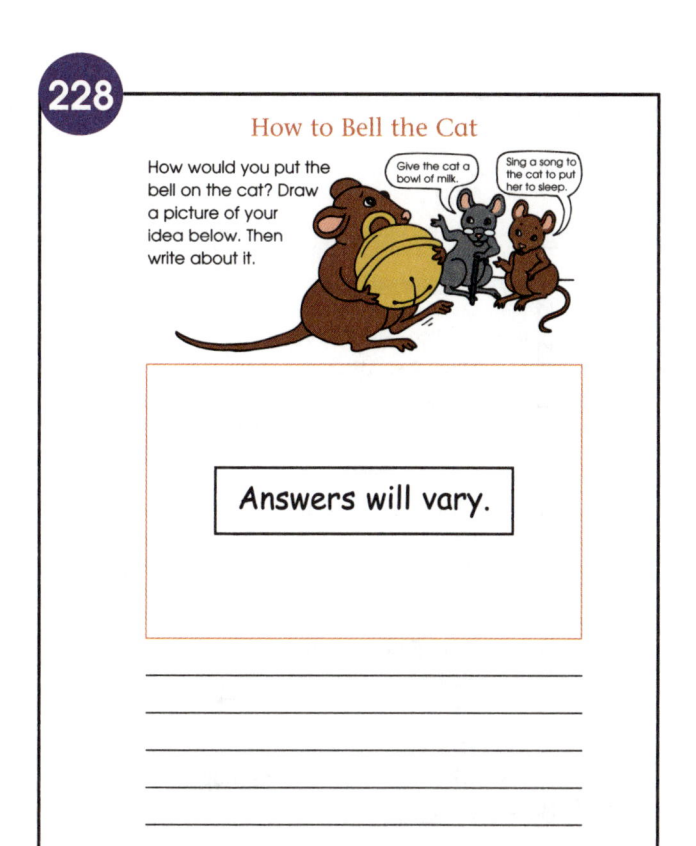

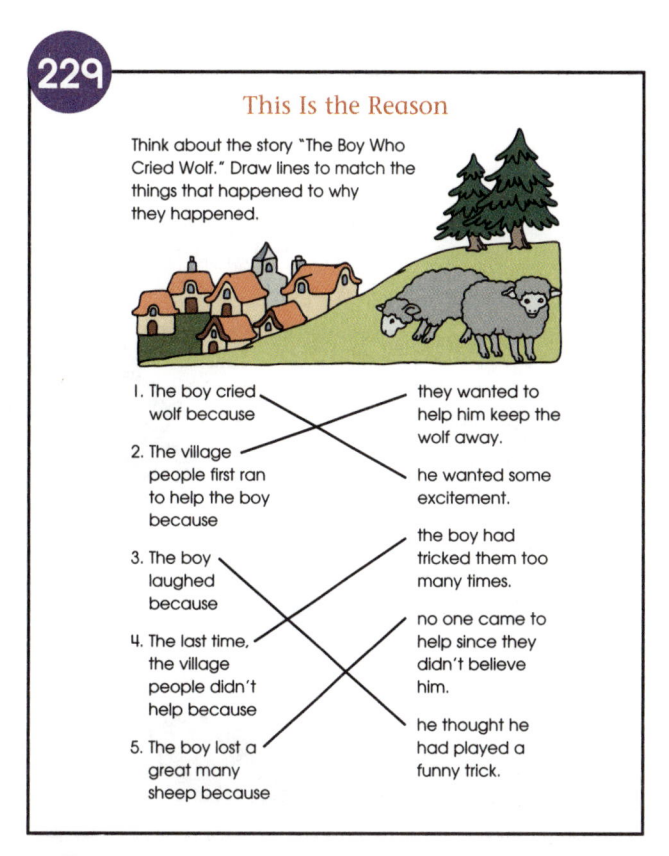

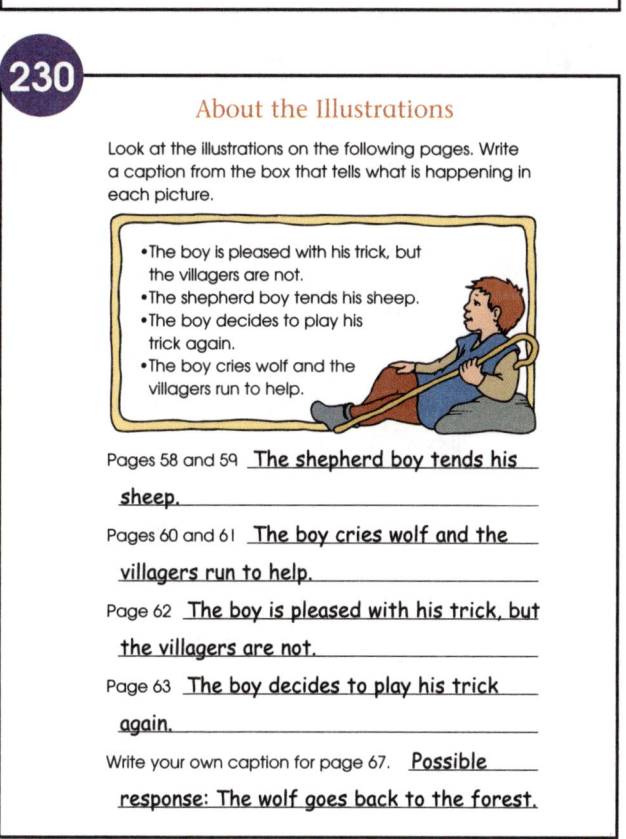

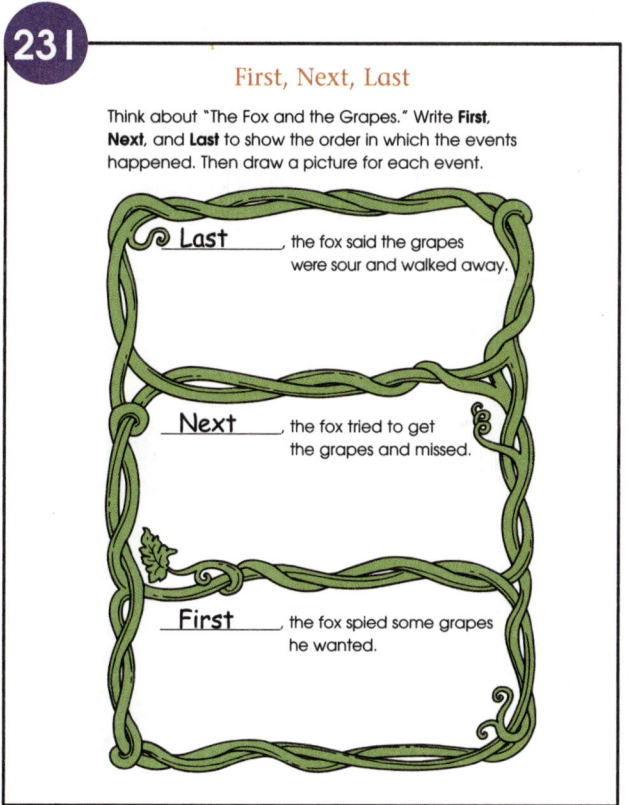

How would you put the bell on the cat? Draw a picture of your idea below. Then write about it.

Answers will vary.

229 — This Is the Reason

Think about the story "The Boy Who Cried Wolf." Draw lines to match the things that happened to why they happened.

1. The boy cried wolf because — he wanted some excitement.
2. The village people first ran to help the boy because — they wanted to help him keep the wolf away.
3. The boy laughed because — he thought he had played a funny trick.
4. The last time, the village people didn't help because — the boy had tricked them too many times.
5. The boy lost a great many sheep because — no one came to help since they didn't believe him.

230 — About the Illustrations

Look at the illustrations on the following pages. Write a caption from the box that tells what is happening in each picture.

- The boy is pleased with his trick, but the villagers are not.
- The shepherd boy tends his sheep.
- The boy decides to play his trick again.
- The boy cries wolf and the villagers run to help.

Pages 58 and 59 **The shepherd boy tends his sheep.**

Pages 60 and 61 **The boy cries wolf and the villagers run to help.**

Page 62 **The boy is pleased with his trick, but the villagers are not.**

Page 63 **The boy decides to play his trick again.**

Write your own caption for page 67. **Possible response: The wolf goes back to the forest.**

231 — First, Next, Last

Think about "The Fox and the Grapes." Write **First**, **Next**, and **Last** to show the order in which the events happened. Then draw a picture for each event.

Last, the fox said the grapes were sour and walked away.

Next, the fox tried to get the grapes and missed.

First, the fox spied some grapes he wanted.

Learn to Read With Classic Stories—Grade 2   Answer Key   301

232 — Sweet Grape Snack

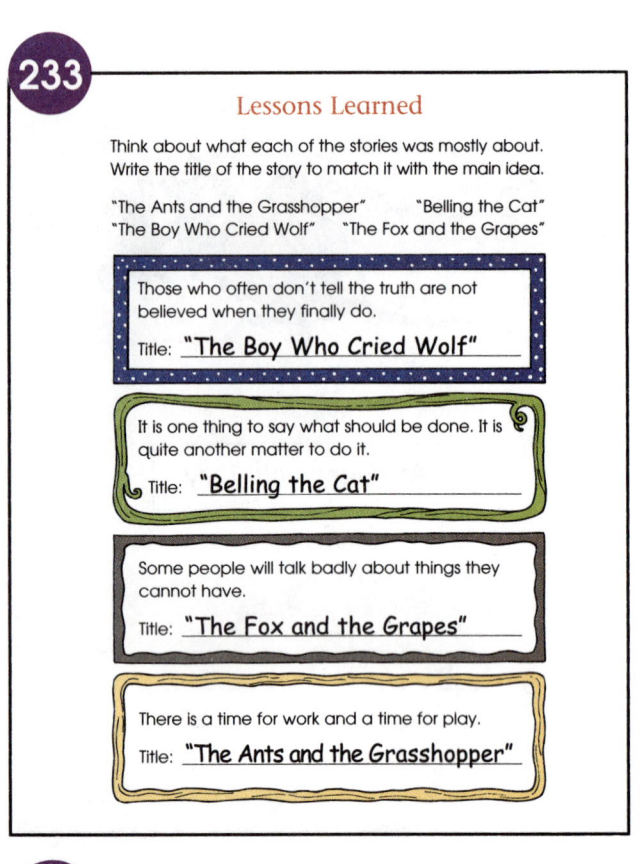

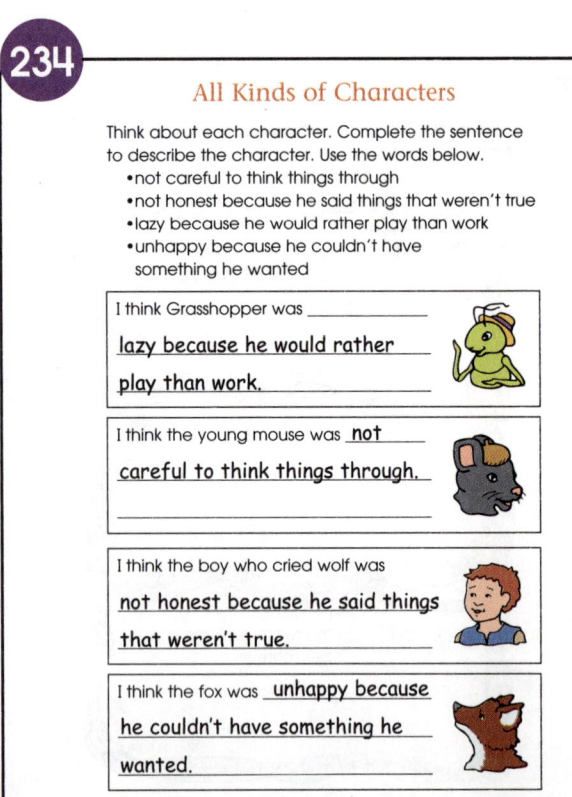

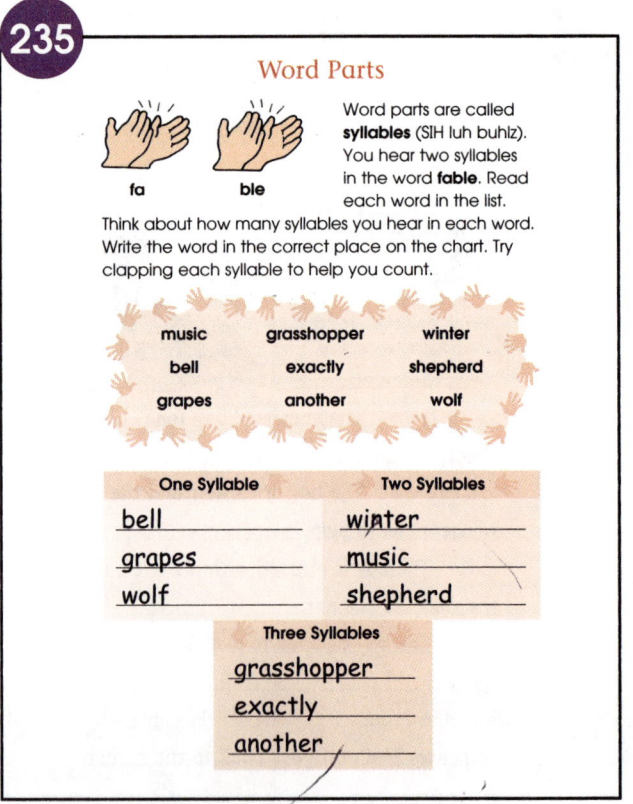

Complete the following rhyme with words from the box. Then follow the steps below for a delicious grape snack.

Box: fun, please, treat, dry

Use some grapes that you pick or buy.
Wash them clean, then pat them **dry**.
Put them in the freezer to freeze.
For an hour, if you **please**.
When the grapes are hard, they're done.
Now it's time to have some **fun**.
Are the grapes sour? No, they're sweet.
Fox would love to have this **treat**.

233 — Lessons Learned

Think about what each of the stories was mostly about. Write the title of the story to match it with the main idea.

"The Ants and the Grasshopper" "Belling the Cat"
"The Boy Who Cried Wolf" "The Fox and the Grapes"

Those who often don't tell the truth are not believed when they finally do.
Title: **"The Boy Who Cried Wolf"**

It is one thing to say what should be done. It is quite another matter to do it.
Title: **"Belling the Cat"**

Some people will talk badly about things they cannot have.
Title: **"The Fox and the Grapes"**

There is a time for work and a time for play.
Title: **"The Ants and the Grasshopper"**

234 — All Kinds of Characters

Think about each character. Complete the sentence to describe the character. Use the words below.
- not careful to think things through
- not honest because he said things that weren't true
- lazy because he would rather play than work
- unhappy because he couldn't have something he wanted

I think Grasshopper was **lazy because he would rather play than work.**

I think the young mouse was **not careful to think things through.**

I think the boy who cried wolf was **not honest because he said things that weren't true.**

I think the fox was **unhappy because he couldn't have something he wanted.**

235 — Word Parts

Word parts are called **syllables** (SIH luh buhlz). You hear two syllables in the word **fable**. Read each word in the list.

fa   ble

Think about how many syllables you hear in each word. Write the word in the correct place on the chart. Try clapping each syllable to help you count.

music   grasshopper   winter
bell   exactly   shepherd
grapes another   wolf

One Syllable	Two Syllables
bell	winter
grapes	music
wolf	shepherd

Three Syllables
grasshopper
exactly
another

302   Answer Key   Learn to Read With Classic Stories—Grade 2

236 — Using Exact Action Words

Action words tell what is happening. Some action words are more exact that others.

Example: The fox **moved**.   The fox **jumped**.

Read each sentence below. Replace each action word with one that tells more about the action. Choose words from the box. There is no one correct answer. You will use only five of the words.

discussed	marched	sat	shouted
watched	stared	chatted	jogged
whispered	waited	turned	gazed
ran	tramped	lay	stomped

1. The grasshopper looked at the ants. **gazed**
2. The mice talked. **chatted**
3. The people went up the hill. **ran**
4. The boy stayed on the hill. **waited**
5. The fox walked away. **tramped**

237 — Beginnings and Endings

Use a **period** at the end of **telling sentences**.

Use a **question mark** at the end of **asking sentences**.

Use an **exclamation point** at the end of **sentences that show excitement**.

Rewrite each sentence. Begin each with a capital letter. Add the correct end mark.

1. i see a wolf **I see a wolf! or .**
2. where is your food for winter **Where is your food for winter?**
3. the grapes are not tasty anyway **The grapes are not tasty anyway.**
4. who will put the bell on the cat **Who will put the bell on the cat?**
5. i will play my fiddle **I will play my fiddle.**
6. watch out **Watch out!**

238 — Job Hunt

Think about the fables you have read. Write a help-wanted newspaper ad that a character from one of the fables might write. For example, the villagers in "The Boy Who Cried Wolf" might want a new shepherd boy, or the mice in "Belling the Cat" might want someone to put the bell on the cat. Maybe the ants in "The Ants and the Grasshopper" want help collecting food.

HELP WANTED

Job _____
Wanted! A person who will _____

Answers will vary.

The reward for doing this job is _____

239 — Summary Chart

Complete the chart about the story "Rumpelstiltskin."

Who is the story about?	Where and when does the story take place?
the miller, the miller's daughter, the king, and Rumpelstiltskin	a long time ago in a kingdom

What happens at the beginning? **Possible answer: The miller brags that his daughter can spin straw into gold. The king takes her to his palace.**

What happens in the middle? **Possible answer: A little man comes and spins all the straw into gold for the miller's daughter. She gives him a ring and necklace. She promises him her first child.**

What happens at the end? **Possible answer: The little man comes back for the baby. The queen doesn't want to give the baby away. The little man says the queen can keep the baby if she can guess his name, and she does.**

Learn to Read With Classic Stories—Grade 2   Answer Key

240 Path to Happily Ever After

Think about the order of the events in the story. Take the miller's daughter from her home to happily ever after. Draw a line to from one event to the next to show the order things happened in the story.

Start → The miller brags about his daughter. → The king tells the miller's daughter to spin straw into gold. → The king takes the miller's daughter to the palace. → A little man comes three times to help the girl spin straw into gold. → The miller's daughter promises the little man her first child. → The little man comes back for the baby. → The little man says the queen can keep the baby if she can guess his name. → The queen guesses the little man's name. → The queen sends servants to find out the little man's name.

241 Golden Details

Read each sentence. If it tells something that happens in the story, color the straw **gold** (or **yellow**). If it tells something that did not happen in the story, color the straw **brown**.

- The little man becomes the king. (brown)
- A miller says something that is not true about his daughter. (gold)
- The little man falls into a pot of water. (brown)
- The miller's daughter marries the king. (gold)
- A little man spins straw into gold. (gold)
- The king says the girl must make many pairs of shoes by morning. (brown)
- The miller's daughter gives the little man her hat and her gloves. (brown)
- The queen guesses the little man's name. (gold)

242 What a Problem!

In the story, the miller's daughter has problems. She has to find ways to solve them. Answer the following questions about the story.

1. The first night at the palace, how does the miller's daughter solve her problem about not being able to spin straw into gold? **A little man comes to spin the straw into gold. She gives him her necklace.**

2. The second night at the palace, how does the miller's daughter solve her problem about not being able to spin straw into gold? **A little man comes again to spin straw into gold. She gives him her ring.**

3. Why does the miller's daughter promise the little man her first child? **She has nothing else to give the little man so she promises him her child.**

4. How is the queen able to keep her baby in the end? **She guesses the little man's name.**

243 Who Said It?

Write a character's name to complete each sentence. You will use some characters' names more than once.

the miller | the miller's daughter | Rumpelstiltskin | the king

1. "Spin all this straw into gold by morning," said **the king**.
2. "I will give you my ring," said **the miller's daughter**.
3. "Well, my daughter can spin straw into gold!" **the miller** said.
4. "I am here about your promise. Give me the baby," said **Rumpelstiltskin**.
5. "Do you know my name?" said **Rumpelstiltskin**.
6. "Then, could it be, perhaps, Rumpelstiltskin?" asked **the miller's daughter**.

304   Answer Key   Learn to Read With Classic Stories—Grade 2

244 — Well Illustrated

Look at the illustrations on the following pages. Then, answer each question.

Page 77
How did the illustrator show that the miller is very proud of his daughter? <u>Possible answer: The miller is smiling and pointing to his daughter.</u>

Page 79
The author describes the character Rumpelstiltskin as a "strange little man." Does the way the illustrator drew the character match the description? Why or why not?

<u>Possible answer: The character matches the description. He is small and looks odd.</u>

Page 102
What can you tell about Rumpelstiltskin from this illustration? <u>Possible answer: He lives in a cottage in the woods. He likes to dance in front of a fire.</u>

Page 106
Why do you think the illustrator shows a bit of Rumpelstiltskin's hat in the illustration?

<u>Possible answer: It shows that Rumpelstiltskin is falling deep into the earth.</u>

245 — By Any Other Name

Think about the story "Rumpelstiltskin." Then think about other good titles for this story. Write your ideas.

What is the story mostly about?

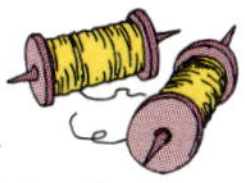

<u>Possible answer: A little man helps a miller's daughter spin straw into gold for the king. In return, she promises to give the little man her first child. She becomes queen and has a child. When the little man comes for the baby, the queen doesn't want to give up the child. The man says she can keep the baby if she guesses his name. She does. It was Rumpelstiltskin.</u>

What might be another good title? Answers will vary.

Why is this a good title? Answers will vary.

246 — Once Upon a Time

"Rumpelstiltskin" is a fairy tale. Answer these questions to see how "Rumpelstiltskin" is like other fairy tales.

1. Many fairy tales begin with the same words. How does "Rumpelstiltskin" begin? **Once upon a time**

2. Many fairy tales have characters who can do unusual things. Which character can do impossible things in "Rumpelstiltskin"? What does the character do?

Rumpelstiltskin. He spins straw into gold.

3. Many fairy tales have events that happen in groups of three. What happens three times in "Rumpelstiltskin"?

The little man spins for three nights. He goes back to the queen for three days.

4. Most fairy tales have a happy ending. What happens at the end of "Rumpelstiltskin"? **The queen keeps her baby, and Rumpelstiltskin is never heard from again.**

247 — To the Letter

Imagine that you are one of the queen's messengers. To help her keep up with the names she has guessed, she has asked you to put the list in ABC order. Read the list of names. Rewrite it in ABC order.

Pumpernickel
Wilberforce
Sheepshanks
Rumpelstiltskin
George
Harry

1. <u>George</u>
2. <u>Harry</u>
3. <u>Pumpernickel</u>
4. <u>Rumpelstiltskin</u>
5. <u>Sheepshanks</u>
6. <u>Wilberforce</u>

Learn to Read With Classic Stories—Grade 2   Answer Key

248 Belonging to the Miller

An important character in "Rumpelstiltskin" is the miller's daughter. Notice the **apostrophe s** in the word **miller's**. It shows that something belongs to the miller. To show ownership, add **'s** to words.

Read each phrase. Write the person's name and the object. Be sure to add **'s** to the person's name to show ownership. The first one has been done for you.

1. the house that belongs to the miller
   <u>the miller's house</u>
2. the hat that belongs to Rumpelstiltskin
   <u>Rumpelstiltskin's hat</u>
3. the baby that belongs to the queen
   <u>the queen's baby</u>
4. the blanket that belongs to the baby
   <u>the baby's blanket</u>
5. the palace that belongs to the king
   <u>the king's palace</u>
6. the story the servant told
   <u>the servant's story</u>

249 Spinning Word Meanings

Read the words on the wheel. Read the meanings in the list. Match the words and their meanings. Beside each word, write the letter for the meaning.

A. begged   C. helpers   E. strange
B. girls   D. early part of night   F. very worried

- evening — D
- servants — C
- maidens — B
- desperate — F
- odd — E
- pleaded — A

250 Replacing Rumpelstiltskin

Pronouns are words that can be used in place of nouns. Instead of saying a name several times, we use pronouns.

Example: **Rumpelstiltskin** can spin straw into gold.
        He can spin straw into gold

> Use **he** for a male person and **she** for a female person.
> Use **they** for more than one person.
> Use **it** for something that is not a person.
> Use **I** for yourself and **we** for yourself and others.

Read each sentence. Circle the pronoun that could be used to replace the underlined words.

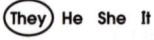

1. <u>The miller's daughter</u> was very beautiful.
   He (She) We It
2. <u>The miller</u> liked to brag about her. She They I (He)
3. <u>The miller's daughter and the king</u> were married.
   (They) He She It
4. <u>The wedding</u> was lovely. We (It) They 
5. Write a sentence using **I**. ____
   Answers will vary.
6. Write a sentence using **we**. ____
   Answers will vary.

251 Sign Up List

One of the queen's messengers posted this sign. Find and correct two capitalization mistakes, two punctuation mistakes, and two spelling mistakes. Make your corrections above each mistake.

Notice

The queen is looking for odd names**.** (~~;~~ → .)

Please write **your** (yor) name on this list.

If you know other odd names, write them as well**.** (added period)

The (the) queen thanks **you** (You) for your help.

If you **have** (haf) any questions, contact the queen's messengers.

306 Answer Key   Learn to Read With Classic Stories—Grade 2

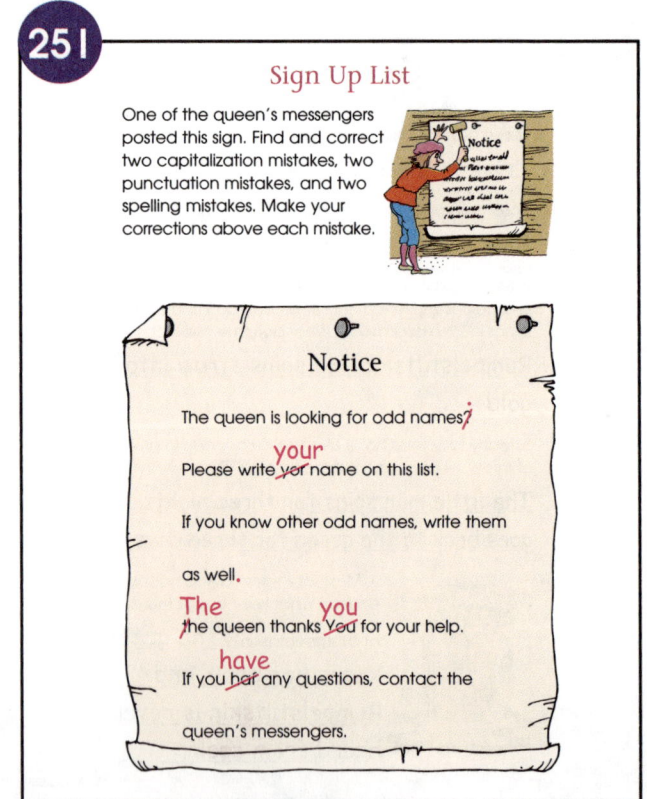

252 — A Word of Thanks

Imagine that you are the queen writing a letter of thanks to the messenger who found out Rumpelstiltskin's name. Complete the letter below.

Dear Messenger,

Thank you so much for your help with the little man's name. When he first came back, I felt so _____. I didn't want to lose my baby. It was so difficult to find the right name. But you did it! I appreciate your

It me _____ **Answers will vary.** _____

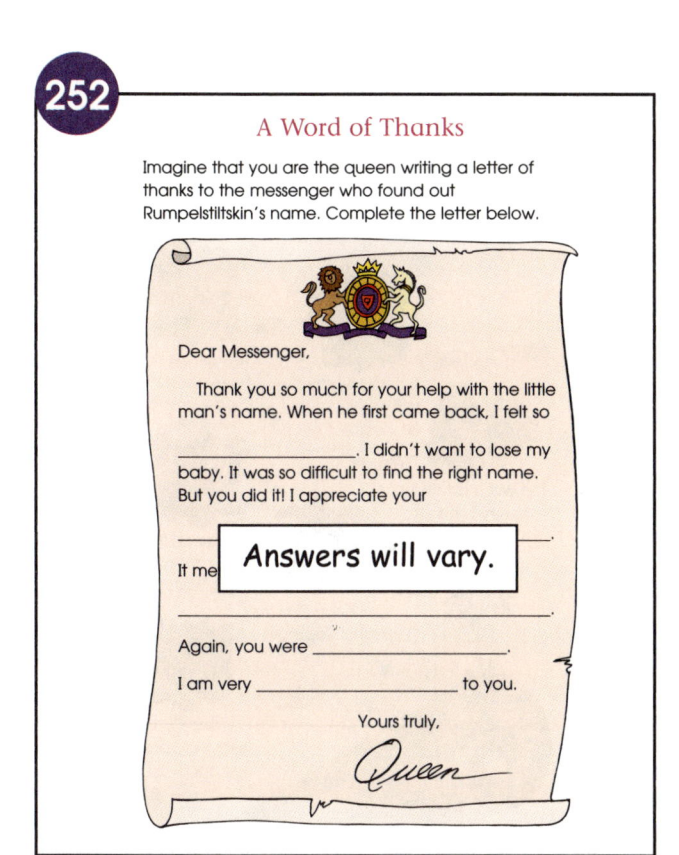

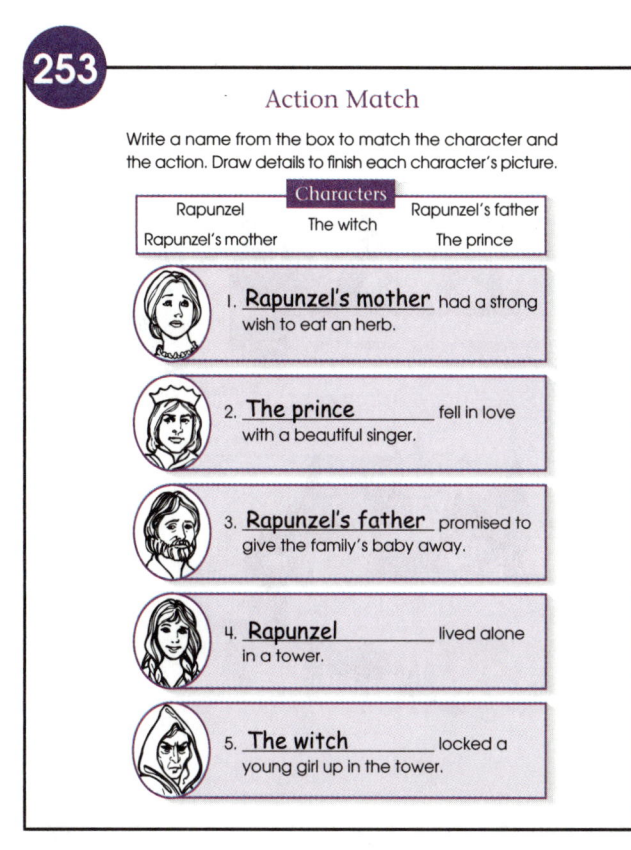

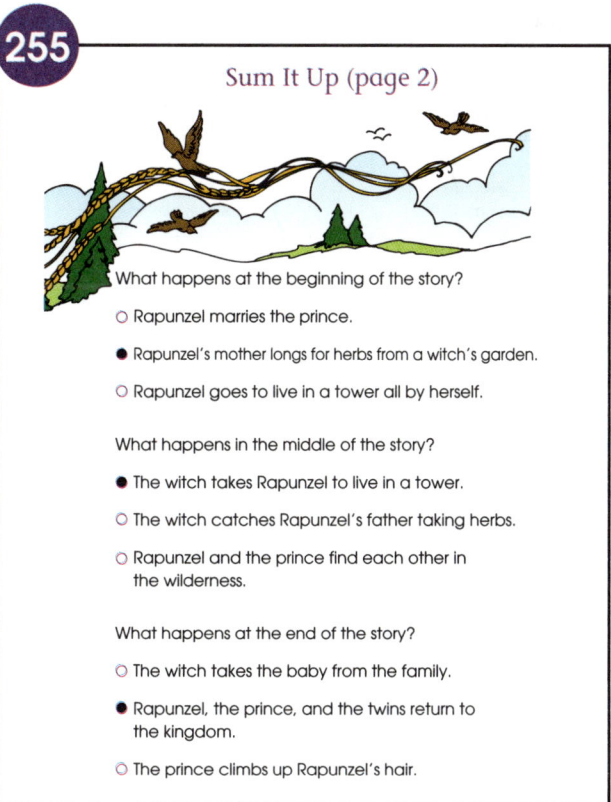

Again, you were _____.
I am very _____ to you.

Yours truly,
Queen

253 — Action Match

Write a name from the box to match the character and the action. Draw details to finish each character's picture.

Characters: Rapunzel, The witch, Rapunzel's father, Rapunzel's mother, The prince

1. **Rapunzel's mother** had a strong wish to eat an herb.
2. **The prince** fell in love with a beautiful singer.
3. **Rapunzel's father** promised to give the family's baby away.
4. **Rapunzel** lived alone in a tower.
5. **The witch** locked a young girl up in the tower.

254 — Sum It Up

Read each question about the story "Rapunzel" on this page and on page 255. Fill in the circle next to the correct answer to each question.

Who is this story mostly about?
○ Rapunzel's parents
● Rapunzel
○ the prince

When and where does this story take place?
○ yesterday in a city
○ many years from now in outer space
● long ago in a royal kingdom

255 — Sum It Up (page 2)

What happens at the beginning of the story?
○ Rapunzel marries the prince.
● Rapunzel's mother longs for herbs from a witch's garden.
○ Rapunzel goes to live in a tower all by herself.

What happens in the middle of the story?
● The witch takes Rapunzel to live in a tower.
○ The witch catches Rapunzel's father taking herbs.
○ Rapunzel and the prince find each other in the wilderness.

What happens at the end of the story?
○ The witch takes the baby from the family.
● Rapunzel, the prince, and the twins return to the kingdom.
○ The prince climbs up Rapunzel's hair.

Learn to Read With Classic Stories—Grade 2   Answer Key   307

256 Guide to the Kingdom

Look at the places on this map. Then follow the directions on page 257.

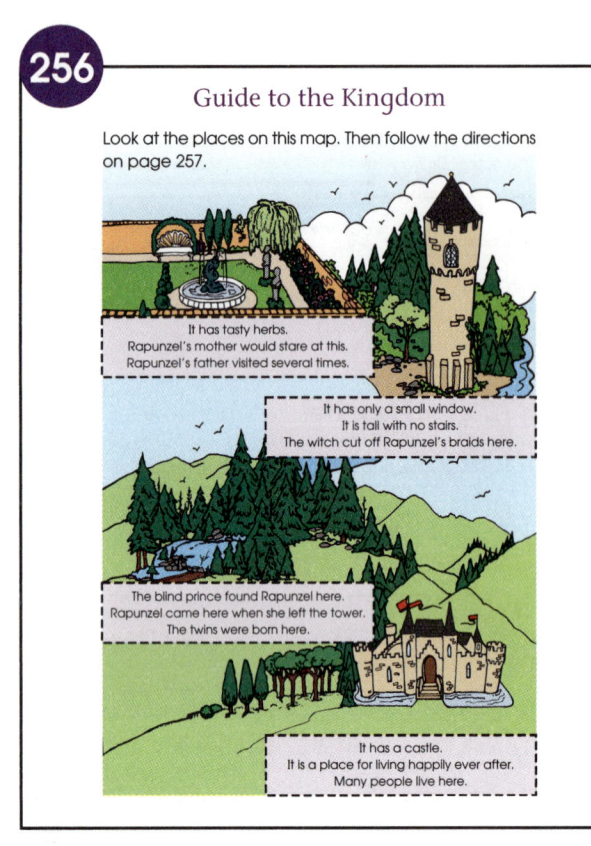

- It has tasty herbs. Rapunzel's mother would stare at this. Rapunzel's father visited several times.
- It has only a small window. It is tall with no stairs. The witch cut off Rapunzel's braids here.
- The blind prince found Rapunzel here. Rapunzel came here when she left the tower. The twins were born here.
- It has a castle. It is a place for living happily ever after. Many people live here.

259 Colorful Details

Read each sentence. Color the plant **green** if the sentence tells something that happened in the story. Color the plant **brown** if the sentence tells something that did not happen in the story.

- The witch grows to love Rapunzel very much. (green)
- The prince hurts his eyes on the thorny brambles. (green)
- The witch climbs up Rapunzel's hair to get to the tower. (green)
- The prince finds Rapunzel in a nearby city. (brown)
- The prince asks the witch if Rapunzel could marry him. (brown)
- Rapunzel's tears help the prince see again. (green)

260 Why, Oh Why?

A **cause** tells **why something happens**. An **effect** is **what happens**. Draw a line to match each cause to an effect.

1. Because his wife wants to eat some herbs, — the husband goes into the witch's garden.
2. Because the witch agrees to let the husband have the herbs, — the husband promises to give the witch the baby.
3. Because rapunzel is the reason the witch gets the baby, — the witch names the baby Rapunzel.
4. Because the witch is angry at the girl, — the witch chops off Rapunzel's braids.
5. Because Rapunzel's tears drop into his eyes, — the prince can see again.
6. Because the prince finds Rapunzel, — the prince, Rapunzel, and their children return to the kingdom.

261 All in the Name

The **main idea** is what a story or part of a story is mostly about. Read the following paragraphs. Then answer the questions. Write the main idea for each paragraph in one sentence.

> The witch's garden was the most beautiful in the land. Tall trees grew in one corner. They made a shady spot to sit. Bright flowers lined the stone paths. Vines crawled along the wall. But the herbs looked so tasty and smelled so wonderful that they stood out among all the beauty.

1. What is the main idea of this paragraph?

   <u>The witch's garden was very beautiful.</u>

> Rapunzel's hair was so very lovely. It was the golden color of sunlight at the end of the day. It was as thick as a warm blanket on a cold winter night. And how long it was! Rapunzel's hair reached from the very top of the tower to the ground below.

2. What is the main idea of this paragraph?

   <u>Rapunzel's hair was so lovely.</u>

3. The title of a story often tells what the story is mainly about. What would be another good title for "Rapunzel"?

   <u>Answers will vary, but should reflect the main idea of the story.</u>

308   Answer Key   Learn to Read With Classic Stories—Grade 2

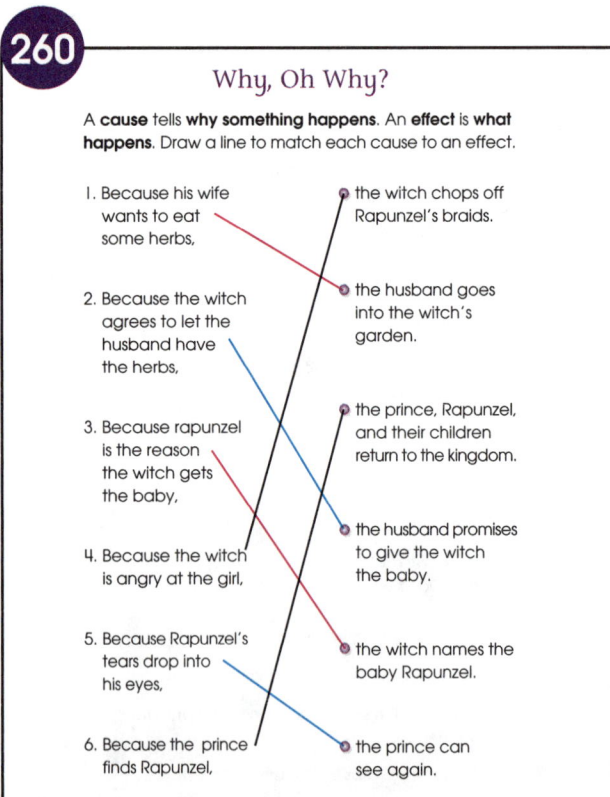

262 Word Wall

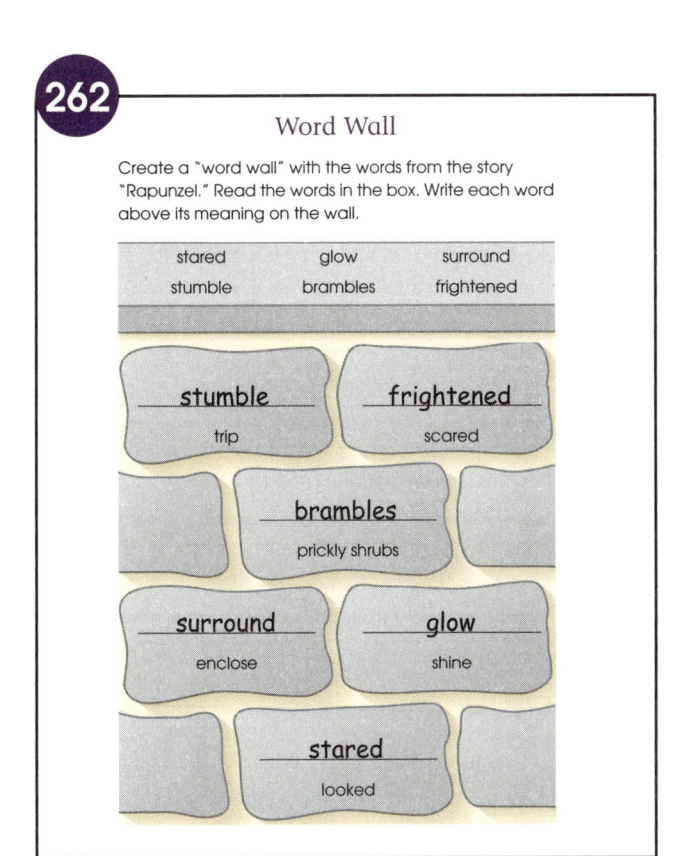

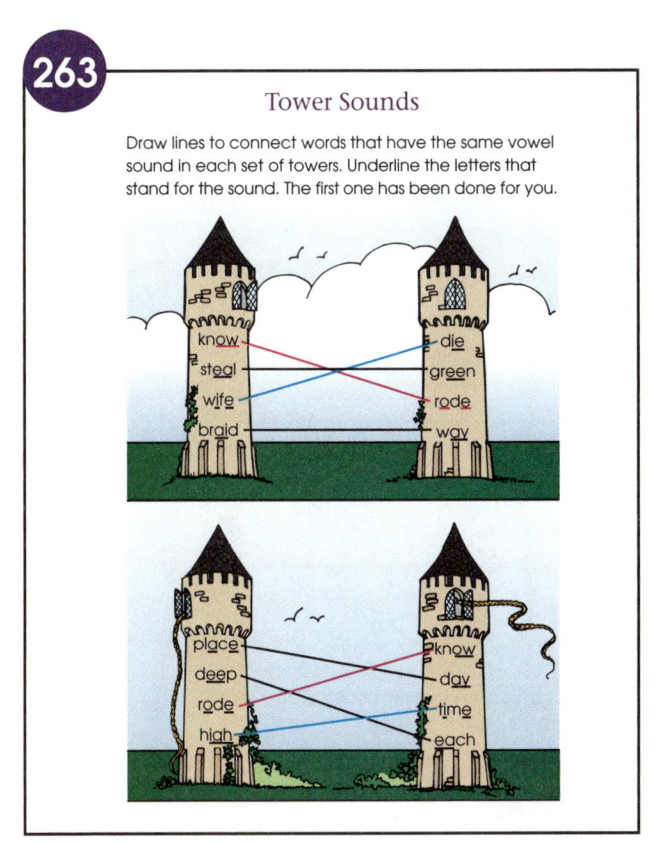

Create a "word wall" with the words from the story "Rapunzel." Read the words in the box. Write each word above its meaning on the wall.

| stared | glow | surround |
| stumble | brambles | frightened |

- **stumble** — trip
- **frightened** — scared
- **brambles** — prickly shrubs
- **surround** — enclose
- **glow** — shine
- **stared** — looked

263 Tower Sounds

Draw lines to connect words that have the same vowel sound in each set of towers. Underline the letters that stand for the sound. The first one has been done for you.

Tower 1 set:
- kn<u>ow</u> — r<u>o</u>de
- st<u>ea</u>l — gr<u>ee</u>n
- w<u>i</u>fe — d<u>ie</u>
- br<u>ai</u>d — w<u>ay</u>

Tower 2 set:
- pl<u>a</u>ce — d<u>ay</u>
- d<u>ee</u>p — <u>ea</u>ch
- r<u>o</u>de — kn<u>ow</u>
- h<u>i</u>gh — t<u>i</u>me

264 A Way With Words

The endings **ing** and **ed** can be added to a word. These endings tell when an action happened. Words with **ing** show that the action is happening now. Words with **ed** show that the action has already happened.

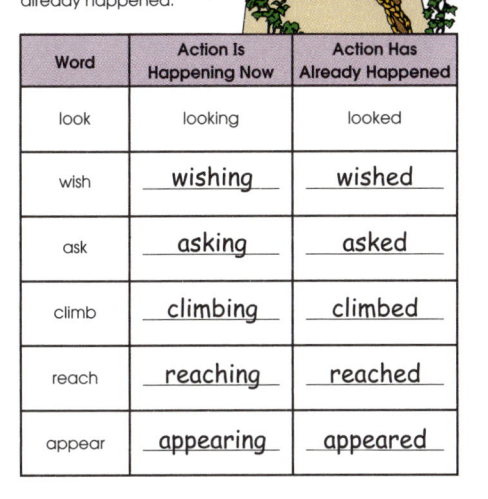

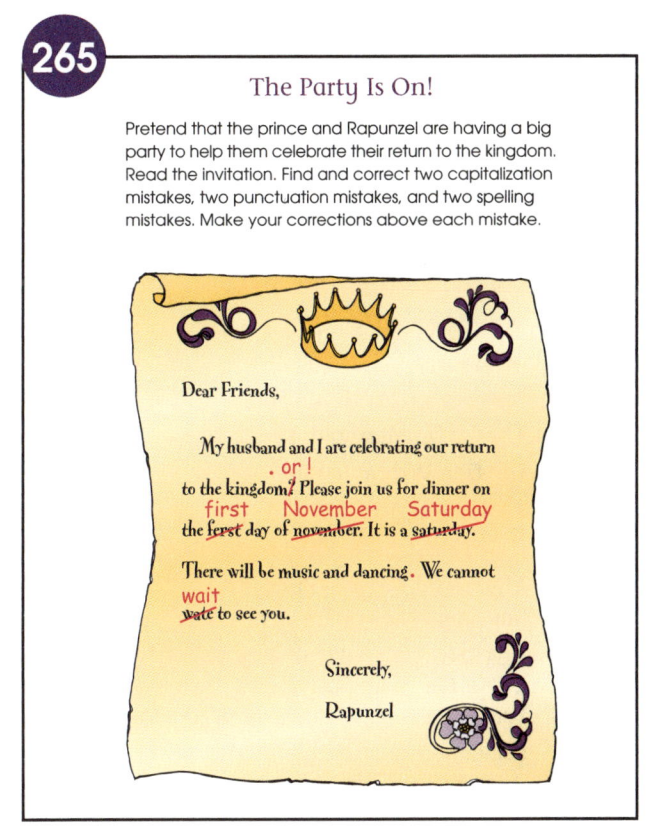

Word	Action Is Happening Now	Action Has Already Happened
look	looking	looked
wish	wishing	wished
ask	asking	asked
climb	climbing	climbed
reach	reaching	reached
appear	appearing	appeared

265 The Party Is On!

Pretend that the prince and Rapunzel are having a big party to help them celebrate their return to the kingdom. Read the invitation. Find and correct two capitalization mistakes, two punctuation mistakes, and two spelling mistakes. Make your corrections above each mistake.

Dear Friends,

My husband and I are celebrating our return to the kingdom~~?~~ **. or !** Please join us for dinner on the **first** ~~ferst~~ day of **November** ~~november~~. It is a **Saturday** ~~saturday~~.

There will be music and dancing~~.~~ We cannot **wait** ~~wate~~ to see you.

Sincerely,
Rapunzel

Learn to Read With Classic Stories—Grade 2   Answer Key   309

266 Rapunzel Rhyme

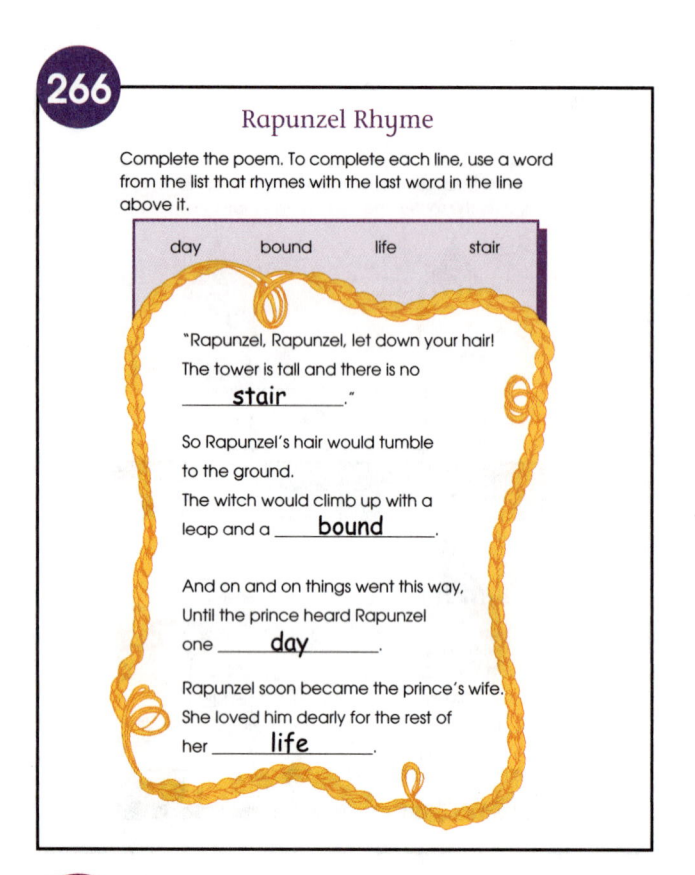

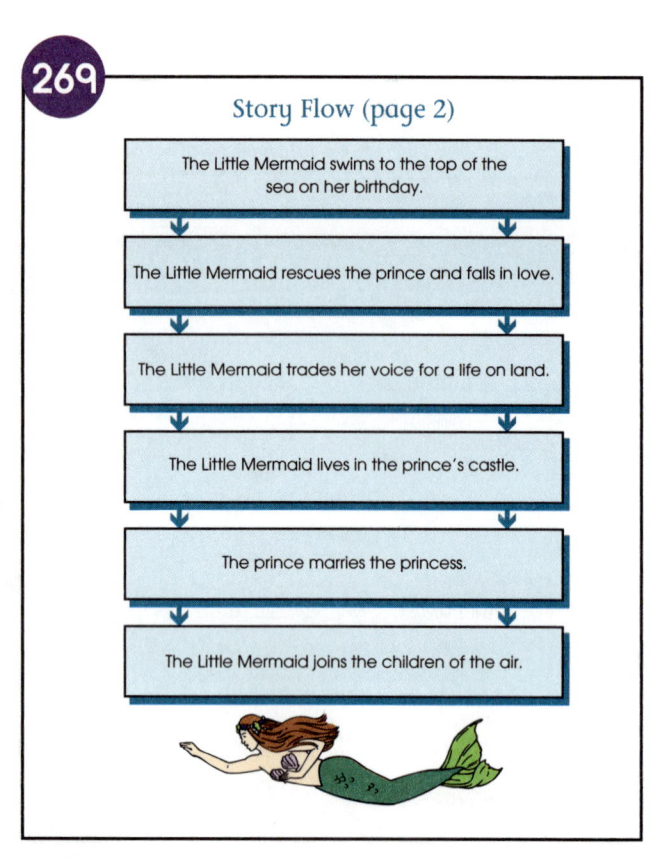

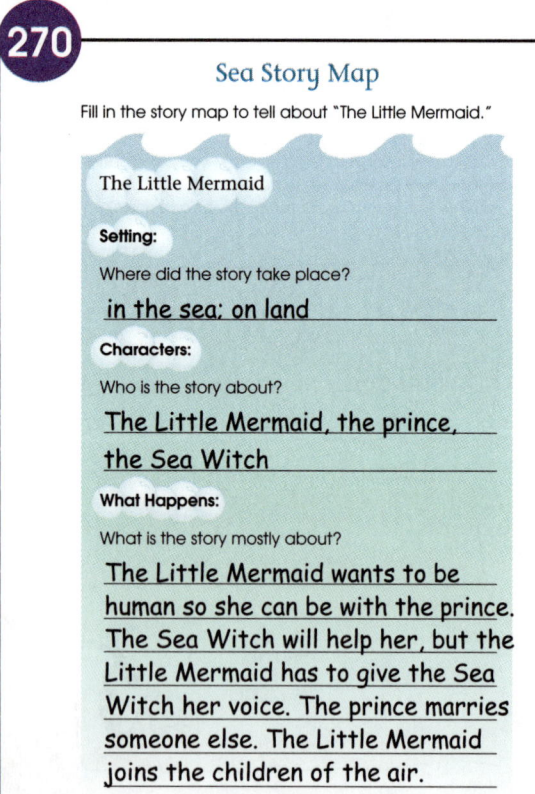

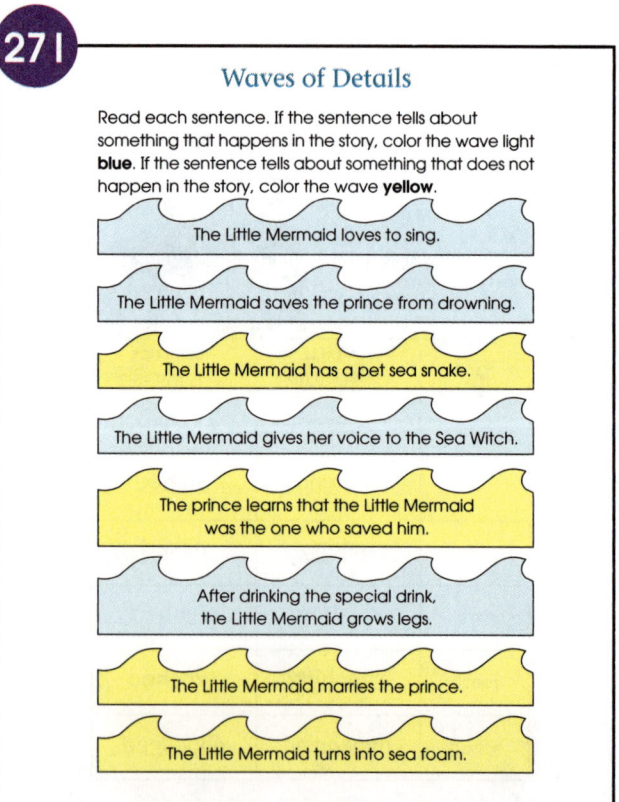

Complete the poem. To complete each line, use a word from the list that rhymes with the last word in the line above it.

day   bound   life   stair

"Rapunzel, Rapunzel, let down your hair!
The tower is tall and there is no __stair__."

So Rapunzel's hair would tumble to the ground.
The witch would climb up with a leap and a __bound__.

And on and on things went this way,
Until the prince heard Rapunzel one __day__.

Rapunzel soon became the prince's wife.
She loved him dearly for the rest of her __life__.

269 Story Flow (page 2)

- The Little Mermaid swims to the top of the sea on her birthday.
- The Little Mermaid rescues the prince and falls in love.
- The Little Mermaid trades her voice for a life on land.
- The Little Mermaid lives in the prince's castle.
- The prince marries the princess.
- The Little Mermaid joins the children of the air.

270 Sea Story Map

Fill in the story map to tell about "The Little Mermaid."

The Little Mermaid

Setting: Where did the story take place?
in the sea; on land

Characters: Who is the story about?
The Little Mermaid, the prince, the Sea Witch

What Happens: What is the story mostly about?
The Little Mermaid wants to be human so she can be with the prince. The Sea Witch will help her, but the Little Mermaid has to give the Sea Witch her voice. The prince marries someone else. The Little Mermaid joins the children of the air.

271 Waves of Details

Read each sentence. If the sentence tells about something that happens in the story, color the wave light **blue**. If the sentence tells about something that does not happen in the story, color the wave **yellow**.

- The Little Mermaid loves to sing. (blue)
- The Little Mermaid saves the prince from drowning. (blue)
- The Little Mermaid has a pet sea snake. (yellow)
- The Little Mermaid gives her voice to the Sea Witch. (blue)
- The prince learns that the Little Mermaid was the one who saved him. (yellow)
- After drinking the special drink, the Little Mermaid grows legs. (blue)
- The Little Mermaid marries the prince. (yellow)
- The Little Mermaid turns into sea foam. (yellow)

272 Ask Little Mermaid

Write the answers Little Mermaid might give to these questions.

1. How did you feel when your grandmother said you could go to the surface when you turned 15?
   happy, excited   Possible answers:

2. How did you feel when you first saw the prince?
   happy, in love

3. How did you feel when you gave the Sea Witch your voice?
   sad, scared

4. How did you feel at the prince's wedding?
   sad

5. How did you feel when you joined the children of the air?
   happy, peaceful

273 Land or Sea?

In the story, the Little Mermaid lived both in the sea and on land. Read the words in the box. Think about where the Little Mermaid would usually see each one. Then write each word in the correct list.

Sea Witch   stars   sea snakes   trees
whales   moon   flowers   sunken ship

In the Sea
- Sea Witch
- sea snakes
- whales
- sunken ship

On Land
- stars
- trees
- moon
- flowers

274 The Big Idea

Reread these pages of "The Little Mermaid." Then circle the sentence that tells what the page is mainly about.

Page 150
- The sea had been calm.
- (A great storm broke apart the ship.)
- The ship has a mast.

Page 151
- The Little Mermaid saw the prince fall into the sea.
- The Little Mermaid dove into the water.
- (The Little Mermaid saved the prince.)

Page 164
- The Little Mermaid woke up.
- The Little Mermaid couldn't speak.
- (The Little Mermaid now had legs and was with the prince.)

Page 168
- (The prince had plans to marry a princess from the next kingdom.)
- The prince sailed to the neighboring kingdom.
- The Little Mermaid sailed with the prince.

275 Characters of the Deep

The Little Mermaid   The prince   The Sea Witch

Write the character's name to complete the sentence. Choose from the list above.

1. **The Little Mermaid** wanted to have legs.

2. **The Sea Witch** asked for a voice as payment.

3. **The prince** fell off a ship and had to be saved.

4. **The Sea Witch** warned someone that a certain wish would not bring happiness.

5. **The prince** got married in a royal wedding.

276 Seaworthy Words

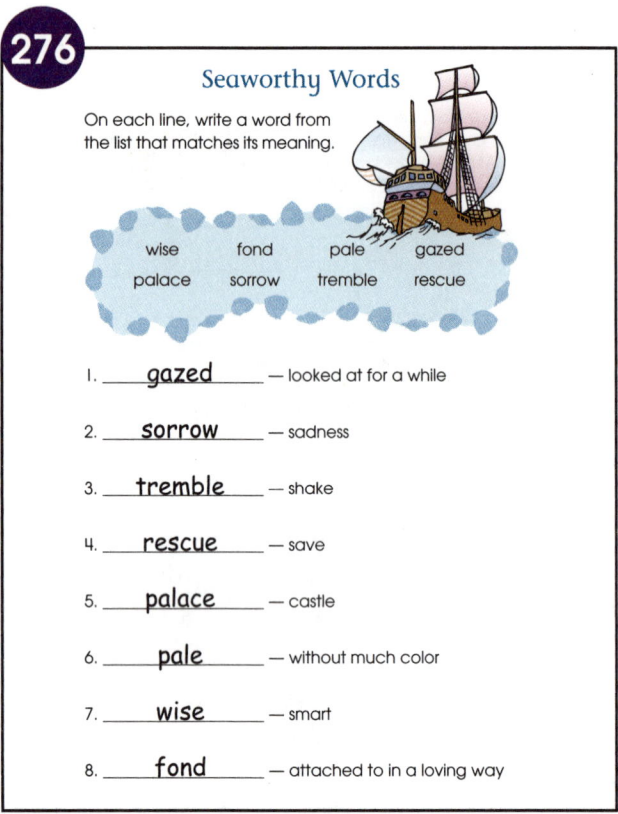

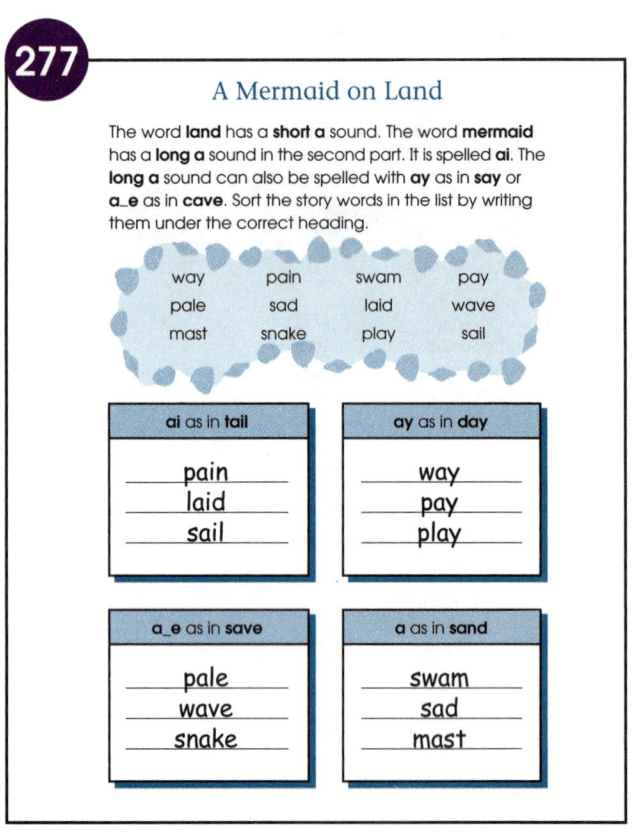

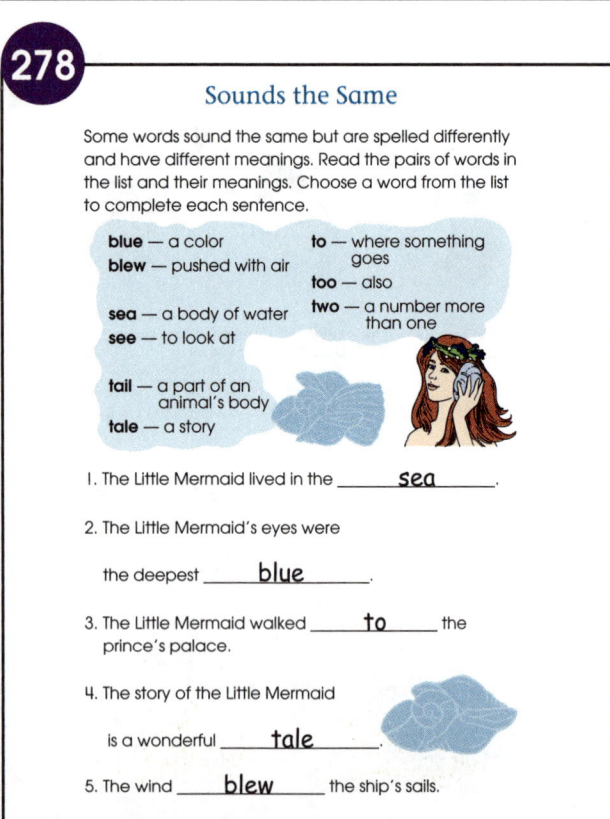

On each line, write a word from the list that matches its meaning.

wise fond pale gazed
palace sorrow tremble rescue

1. __gazed__ — looked at for a while
2. __sorrow__ — sadness
3. __tremble__ — shake
4. __rescue__ — save
5. __palace__ — castle
6. __pale__ — without much color
7. __wise__ — smart
8. __fond__ — attached to in a loving way

277 A Mermaid on Land

The word **land** has a **short a** sound. The word **mermaid** has a **long a** sound in the second part. It is spelled **ai**. The **long a** sound can also be spelled with **ay** as in **say** or **a_e** as in **cave**. Sort the story words in the list by writing them under the correct heading.

way pain swam pay
pale sad laid wave
mast snake play sail

ai as in tail	ay as in day
pain	way
laid	pay
sail	play

a_e as in save	a as in sand
pale	swam
wave	sad
snake	mast

278 Sounds the Same

Some words sound the same but are spelled differently and have different meanings. Read the pairs of words in the list and their meanings. Choose a word from the list to complete each sentence.

blue — a color
blew — pushed with air
to — where something goes
too — also
sea — a body of water
see — to look at
two — a number more than one
tail — a part of an animal's body
tale — a story

1. The Little Mermaid lived in the __sea__.
2. The Little Mermaid's eyes were the deepest __blue__.
3. The Little Mermaid walked __to__ the prince's palace.
4. The story of the Little Mermaid is a wonderful __tale__.
5. The wind __blew__ the ship's sails.

279 The Prince's Journal

Read this entry in the prince's journal. Find and correct two capitalization mistakes, two punctuation mistakes, and two spelling mistakes. Make your corrections above each mistake.

Today there ~~wuz~~ **was** a bad storm. The ~~chip~~ **ship** sank. ~~i~~ **I** fell into the sea. Someone saved me~~.~~**?** It was a girl. I wish I knew who she was. ~~m~~**M**aybe I will know someday.

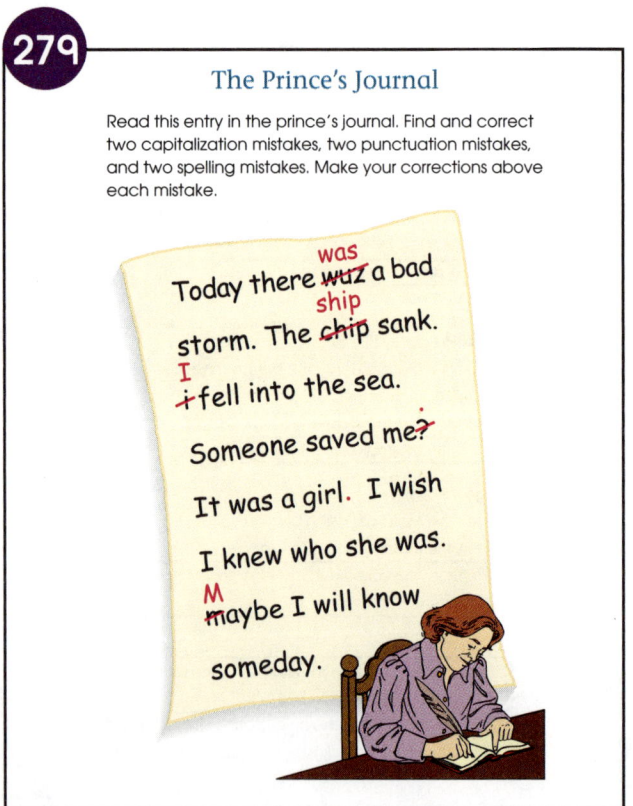

312 Answer Key Learn to Read With Classic Stories—Grade 2

280 — Describe the Underwater World

Finish this description of the Little Mermaid's home under the sea. Write your words on the lines.

Where the Little Mermaid lived, the water was the color of _____. Some of the plants looked like _____.

Some of the animals looked like _____.

The sound of _____.

Everywhere you looked, you could see _____.

Answers will vary.

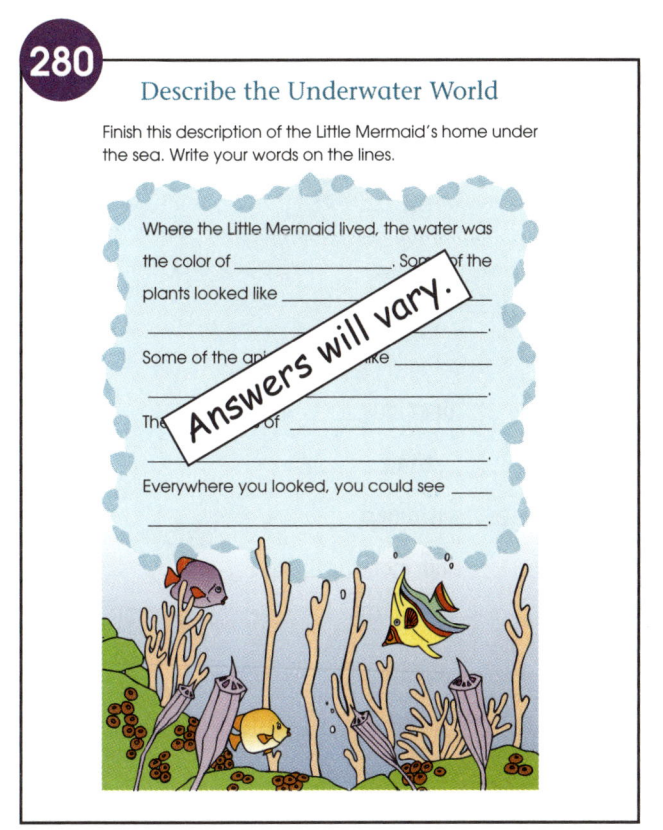

283 — A Giant Retelling (page 2)

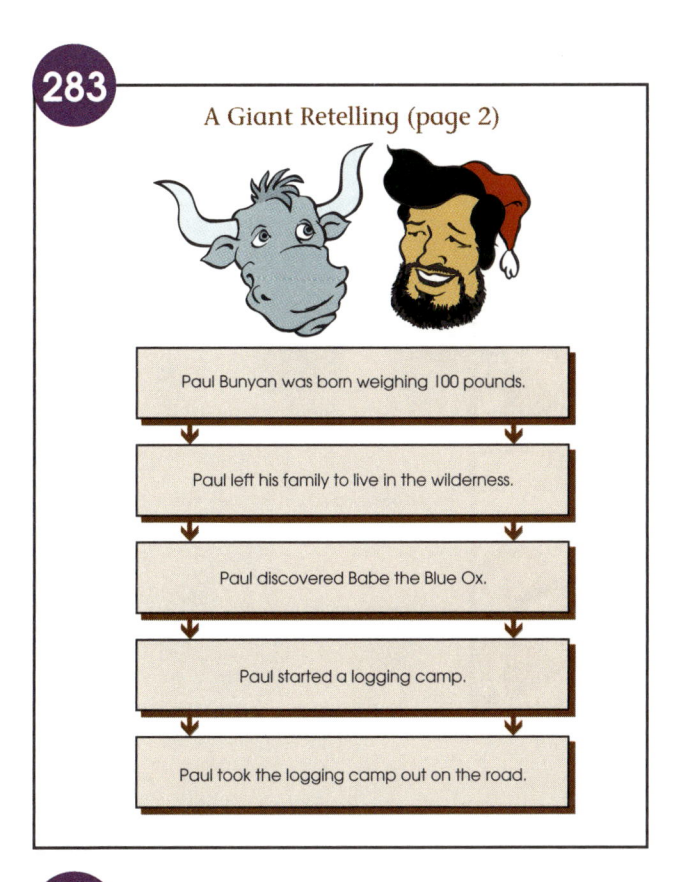

- Paul Bunyan was born weighing 100 pounds.
- Paul left his family to live in the wilderness.
- Paul discovered Babe the Blue Ox.
- Paul started a logging camp.
- Paul took the logging camp out on the road.

284 — The Mighty Logger

Think about the character Paul Bunyan. Circle the words and phrases that describe him.

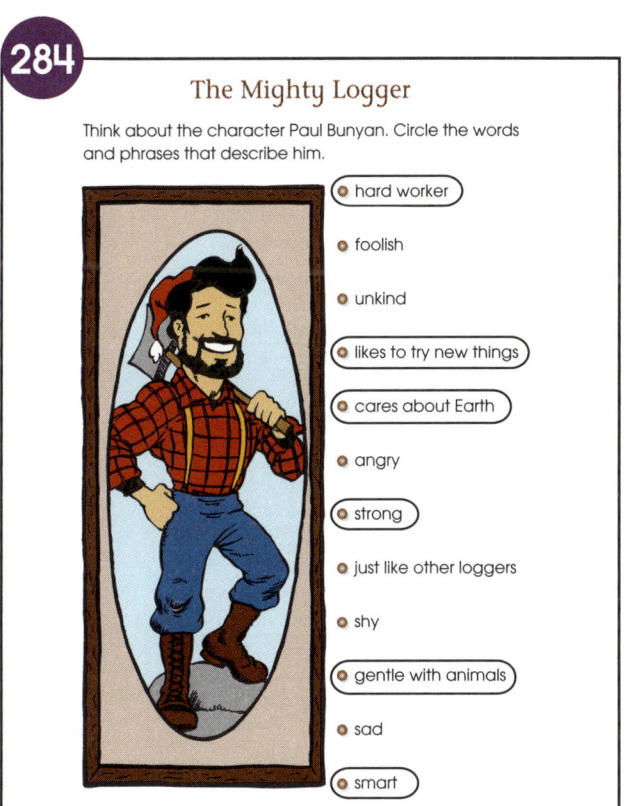

- **hard worker** (circled)
- foolish
- unkind
- **likes to try new things** (circled)
- **cares about Earth** (circled)
- angry
- **strong** (circled)
- just like other loggers
- shy
- **gentle with animals** (circled)
- sad
- **smart** (circled)

285 — The Mighty Logger (page 2)

Read the events below. Think about which character trait from page 284 matches each event. Write a word or a phrase on the line after each sentence.

1. Paul Bunyan saves Babe the Blue Ox from freezing.
   gentle with animals
2. Paul Bunyan thinks of ways to solve problems at the logging camp.
   smart
3. Paul Bunyan plants a new seedling for every tree the loggers cut.
   cares for Earth
4. Paul Bunyan thinks he and Babe need a change after the hard winter. He decides to take the logging camp out on the road.
   likes to try new things

Learn to Read With Classic Stories—Grade 2   Answer Key

286 Remembering Details

Read each sentence. Cut out the small pictures at the bottom of the page. Glue a picture next to a sentence if it tells about something that happened in the story. If the detail did not happen in the story, do not glue a picture next to it.

[picture] Paul Bunyan's cradle floated in the water just off the shore.

[picture] Paul Bunyan found a big baby ox.

Paul Bunyan could cut only one tree with a swing of his ax.

[picture] Paul Bunyan planted new trees.

[picture] Paul Bunyan made the Grand Canyon by dragging his ax.

287 Big Words From a Big Story

Write the words from the list on the lines below to match them with their meanings.

untamed, enormous, frightful, pioneers, nuzzled, precious, thaw, griddle

1. **precious** — special
2. **thaw** — melt
3. **untamed** — wild
4. **enormous** — very big
5. **pioneers** — the first people in a place
6. **nuzzled** — snuggled
7. **griddle** — flat cooking pan
8. **frightful** — terrible

289

Could Really Happen

A baby is born.
A man cuts down ten trees in one week.
A man floats logs down the river.
A man cooks pancakes.
Icicles thaw in the spring.

Could NOT Really Happen

A baby weighs 100 pounds when he is born. A man cuts down ten trees with one swing of his ax. An ox straightens out a river. A man skates on a giant griddle with bacon on his boots. Frozen words thaw in the spring for people to hear.

290 The Main Event

Reread each part of the story listed below. Then circle the sentence that tells what that part of the story is mainly about.

1. **Page 178—second paragraph**
   - Paul Bunyan weighed about a hundred pounds at birth.
   - Paul Bunyan ate five dozen eggs.
   - (Paul Bunyan ate huge breakfasts.)

2. **Page 182**
   - (One winter, blue snow was everywhere.)
   - Paul was surprised.
   - Snowflakes began to fall.

3. **Page 197—first paragraph**
   - The men wore bacon on their boots.
   - The griddle was the size of an ice rink.
   - (Sam cooked flapjacks on a giant griddle.)

4. **Page 198**
   - (Johnny used a lot of ink.)
   - Johnny didn't dot his i's or cross his t's.
   - Johnny saved 500 barrels of ink.

314 Answer Key Learn to Read With Classic Stories—Grade 2

291 Two for One

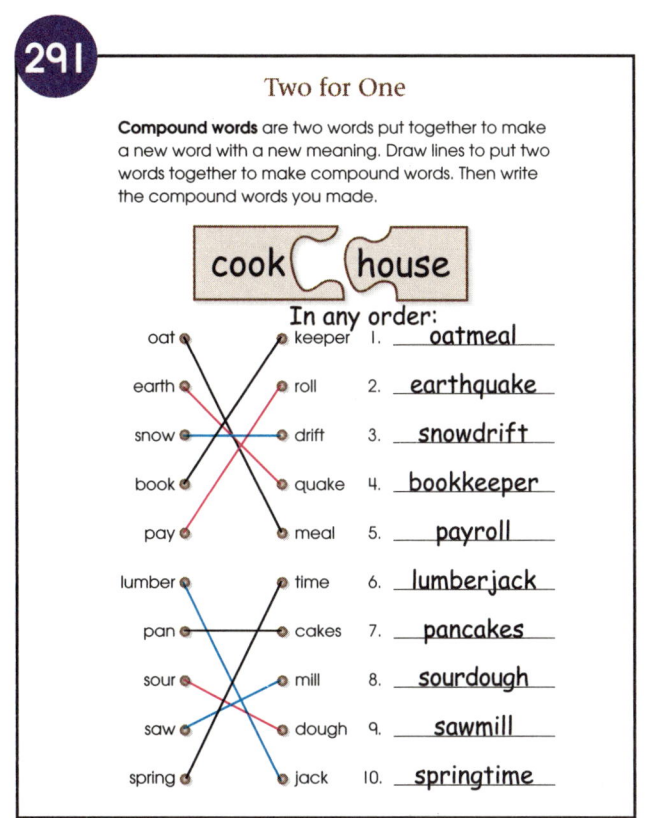

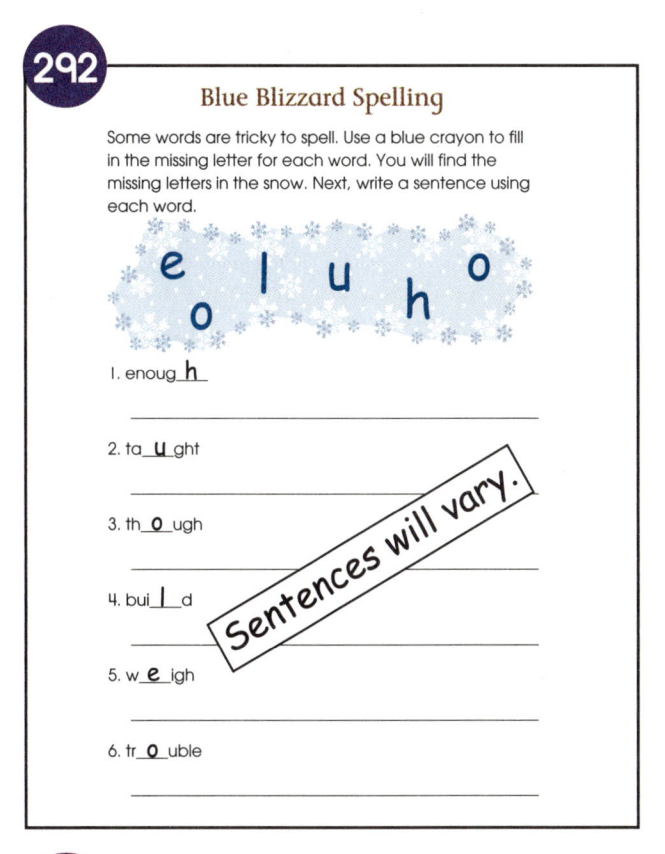

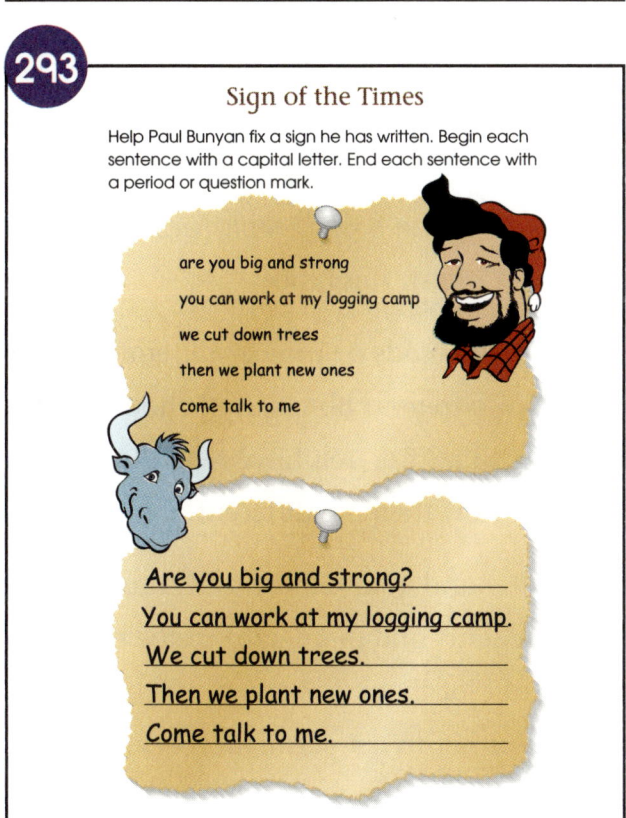

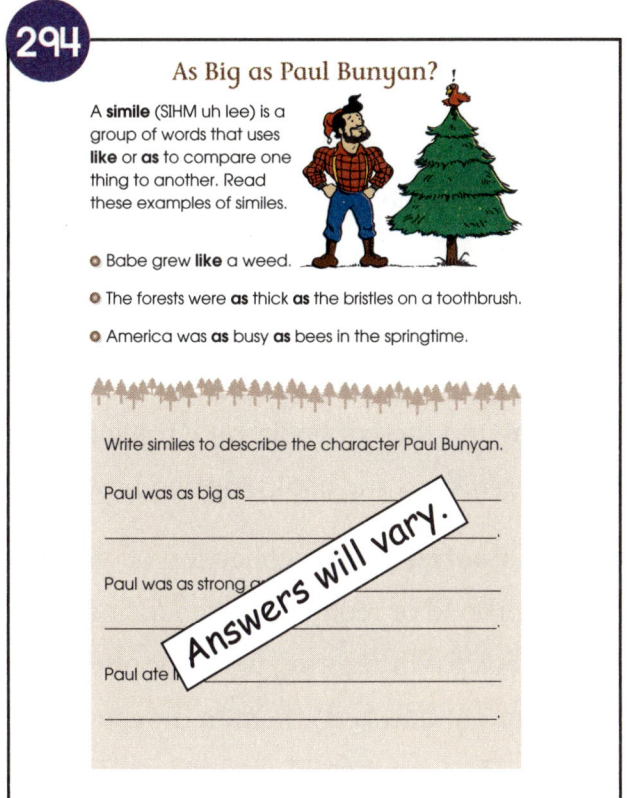

Compound words are two words put together to make a new word with a new meaning. Draw lines to put two words together to make compound words. Then write the compound words you made.

cook — house

In any order:

- oat — keeper
- earth — roll
- snow — drift
- book — quake
- pay — meal
- lumber — time
- pan — cakes
- sour — mill
- saw — dough
- spring — jack

1. oatmeal
2. earthquake
3. snowdrift
4. bookkeeper
5. payroll
6. lumberjack
7. pancakes
8. sourdough
9. sawmill
10. springtime

292 Blue Blizzard Spelling

Some words are tricky to spell. Use a blue crayon to fill in the missing letter for each word. You will find the missing letters in the snow. Next, write a sentence using each word.

e l u h o
   o   o

1. enoug **h**
2. ta **u** ght
3. th **o** ugh
4. bui **l** d
5. w **e** igh
6. tr **o** uble

Sentences will vary.

293 Sign of the Times

Help Paul Bunyan fix a sign he has written. Begin each sentence with a capital letter. End each sentence with a period or question mark.

are you big and strong
you can work at my logging camp
we cut down trees
then we plant new ones
come talk to me

Are you big and strong?
You can work at my logging camp.
We cut down trees.
Then we plant new ones.
Come talk to me.

294 As Big as Paul Bunyan?

A **simile** (SIHM uh lee) is a group of words that uses **like** or **as** to compare one thing to another. Read these examples of similes.

- Babe grew **like** a weed.
- The forests were **as** thick **as** the bristles on a toothbrush.
- America was **as** busy **as** bees in the springtime.

Write similes to describe the character Paul Bunyan.

Paul was as big as ____

Paul was as strong ____

Paul ate ____

Answers will vary.

Learn to Read With Classic Stories—Grade 2

Everyday Learning Activities

Learning can become an everyday experience for your child. The activities on the following pages can act as a springboard for learning. Some of the suggested activities are structured and require readily available materials. Others may be used spontaneously as you are driving, shopping, or engaging in other everyday activities. The activities are arranged according to subject areas.

Reading and Speaking

Word Meanings Play word games with your child. Pick an unfamiliar word that appears in a story or comes up in everyday conversation. Explain the word's meaning to your child. Then ask yes/no questions about the word. For example, after you have told your child the meaning of a word such as *brambles*, ask:

Have you ever touched a bramble?

Would you eat brambles for breakfast?

Encourage your child to ask you questions about the word, too.

Poetry for Life Share poetry with your child to match favorite topics or things that are happening in his or her life. For example, read poems about cats, dogs, trains, losing teeth, or the change of seasons if they are of special interest to your child. Your local library or bookstore will have many collections of poems, some general and some about special topics. Some general collections you might want to look for are *Read-Aloud Rhymes for the Very Young*, selected by Jack Prelutsky and illustrated by Marc Brown; *Sing a Song of Popcorn: Every Child's Book of Poems* selected by Bernice Schenk de Regniers; or *The Golden Books Family Treasury of Poetry* selected by Louis Untermeyer and illustrated by Joan Walsh Anglund.

Comparing Fiction and Nonfiction Make sure your child reads a variety of literature, not only storybooks and poetry, but nonfiction books as well. Go to your library and choose both fictional and factual books on a topic that interests your child. After you have read the books together, discuss the books, noting how they are alike and how they are different.

Found Poetry Start a collection of "found poetry." As you and your child travel through the neighborhood or read books, magazines, letters, advertisements and more, encourage him or her to look for interesting words or phrases. Have your child jot them down in a notebook or cut them out and keep them in an envelope. Remind him or her to get permission before cutting. Have your child read through the collection from time to time.

When he or she has a good assortment, help him or her arrange some of them in a verse to make a "found poem." The poem can be as silly or as serious as your child chooses.

Family Book Club From time to time, hold book discussions about a book everyone in the family has read. Make it a special time, serving simple snacks and beverages. You might want to develop a rating system for books, such as a point or star system. Encourage all members to share things they liked and disliked about the book, any questions they had, a comparison of the book with other books they have read, and whether they would like to read other works by the same author.

Laughing at Language Share the silliness of language with your child. Look for books that contain tongue twisters, jokes, riddles, and jump-rope jingles. You might want to read these: *Anna Banana: 101 Jump-Rope Rhymes* by Joanna Cole, *Bennett Cerf's Book of Riddles* by Bennett Cerf, or *Busy Buzzing Bumblebees and Other Tongue Twisters* by Alvin Schwartz.

Writing

Communicating in Print Encourage your child to write notes, letters, or e-mail to family members rather than making a phone call. Your child might want to share special news or make family plans. If he or she is writing with paper and pencil, suggest adding drawings to go with the writing. Answer any questions your child has about spelling or the best way to say something, but do not correct his or her writing or focus on spelling—just let him or her make the best effort to get the message across.

Keeping Lists Help your child get into the habit of making lists—shopping lists, to-do lists, or instructions for doing household tasks. You might want to provide colored self-stick notes or stickers to brighten the lists.

Homemade Headlines Without showing or reading the headline, read to your child an age-appropriate news article, such as a report about an upcoming community event. Then have your child write a headline that tells about the story.

Theme Journal Invite your child to keep a specific kind of journal, such as a tooth-loss journal or a sports journal. He or she can record memorable events in the notebook and draw pictures to go with the entries.

Example: *Today in soccer we played the Busy Bees. I got to throw the ball in three times. I made one goal, and I almost made another one.*

Writing Captions Encourage your child to join you in keeping scrapbooks and family albums. Have him or her write captions or short paragraphs to go with photos and souvenirs.

We bought this cool kite at a shop near the beach. It was very easy to get up in the air. We had a lot of fun flying it. Everybody who walked by said what a pretty kite it was.

Rebus Messages Invite your child to write a rebus message, substituting drawings for some words. Occasionally write rebus messages for him or her to solve, too.

Example: 👁 will 🐝 home at ||| .

Writer's Walk Go on a writer's walk with your child, on which you both look at objects and think about how you might describe them. When you get back home, each of you writes a description of the object without naming it. Remind your child to use many details. Then read your descriptions aloud to each other and take turns guessing what was being described.

Math

Family Calendar Display a family calendar and refer to it often. Assist your child in recording upcoming family events, such as birthdays or other celebrations, on the calendar. Occasionally ask your child questions that require him or her to use the calendar.

Money Problems Show a collection of coins, including a few pennies, nickels, dimes, and quarters. Make up problems like this: "If you can buy two pencils for a quarter, how much money would you need to buy 4 pencils? 6 pencils?" Have your child show you the coins that would be needed and tell you the amount.

Patterns Help your child look for repeating patterns in everyday objects, such as wrapping paper or wallpaper. Encourage him or her to describe the pattern. Then use simple shape cutouts to create a row of patterns. For example, you might lay out two triangles, a square, two triangles, and a square. Ask your child to describe and then continue the pattern. Your child can create patterns for you to identify and repeat, too.

Address Math Have your child write your house or apartment number. Talk about whether the address is odd or even. Then look at the addresses across the street or across the hall, and identify them as odd or even. Next, have your child write the ZIP code of your mailing address. Take turns using some or all of the numerals in the code to write addition and subtraction problems for each other to solve.

Measuring Hunt Have your child go on a search around your home for measuring devices, such as measuring cups and spoons, yardsticks, tape measures, bathroom scales, and so on. Have him or her make a list of the devices and how they are used. Then let him or her choose one of the devices, estimate the size of some items that can be measured with that device, and measure them to check the estimates.

Science

Explorations Take a "scientific approach" to explorations with your child—encourage him or her to explore, gather clues, tell stories, and see what conclusions he or she can form about the things. Encourage your child to look at common things in new ways. For example, choose a familiar area such as your backyard or a safe park and explore it.

If possible, take a nighttime walk with a flashlight. Talk about differences in how the place looks at night. Listen carefully. The next day, encourage your child to draw and write about your nighttime walk. Share books about the night, such as *Owl Moon* by Jane Yolen, *Night in the Country* by Cynthia Rylant, or *All Night Near the Water* by Jim Arnosky.

Plastic-Bag Garden Help your child fill a twist-tie style bag with potting soil. Plant bean seeds in the soil. Let your child help pack the soil down and water lightly. Fasten the bag and leave it in a sunny spot indoors. When the seeds sprout, help your child take off the twist-tie and roll the top of the plastic bag down.

Social Studies

Personal Time Lines Time lines are often used to trace historical events, but they can be used to record other things, such as family history. They can also help keep track of story events when a story follows a chronological order. Use a strip of paper such as adding machine tape, or tape several sheets of paper together to make a long strip. Help your child choose a topic, such as the story of his or her life. Draw a long line on the paper, and help your child mark it off in equal increments. (If you are tracking a life story, that will probably be in months or years. If you are tracking a piece of literature, such as *Jack and the Beanstalk*, it might be in days or even hours.)

Culture Chart Help your child cut out magazine pictures that represent other places or cultures. He or she can glue the pictures on construction paper or poster board and label them to make a picture chart.

Reading Around the World Help your child choose books about life in other countries or cultures. You might want to share *In My Family/En Mi Familia* by Carmen Lomas Garza, *A Country Far Away* by Nigel Gray, *Happy New Year! Kung-Hsi Fa-Ts'Ai!* by Demi, *My Painted House, My Friendly Chicken, and Me* by Maya Angelou, or *Everybody Cooks Rice* by Norah Dooley. After reading, talk with your child to compare ways the people and places around the world are the same and ways they are different.

Arts and Crafts

Puppet Settings Puppet plays are great ways to dramatize stories. Help your child create interesting stages and backgrounds to use with puppets he or she makes. Try an apron stage. Have your child paint a story background on a cloth butcher's apron, or make an apron for him or her by cutting out a large brown paper bag. Your child then wears the apron and holds the puppets in front of his or her body while performing the puppet play.

Musical Impressions Have your child draw in response to music as you play short bits of various musical selections. Include a wide range of musical styles, such as classical, jazz, pop, folk, and so on. Encourage your child to title, sign, and date each piece of artwork.

Character Puzzles Have your child make a character drawing that completely fills a page to make a puzzle. Then have him or her cut the drawing apart into puzzle pieces. As you work with your child to reassemble the puzzle, talk about the story character.

Art Museum If possible, visit an art museum with your child. Then turn an area of your home into an art display featuring your child's artworks. You might even want to go beyond the refrigerator! Take turns with your child pretending to be a tour guide in your own art museum. Discuss the artwork and the artist.